a caring man

VERTICAL.

a caring man

akira arai

translated by marc adler

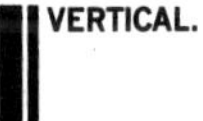

Published by Vertical, Inc., New York

ISBN 978-1-935654-17-9

Manufactured in the United States of America

First Edition

Vertical, Inc.
451 Park Avenue South, 7th Floor
New York, NY 10016
www.vertical-inc.com

...sedulo curavi, actiones Diaboli non ridere, non lugere, neque detestari, sed intelligere.

...I have labored carefully, not to mock, lament, or detest, but to understand the actions of the Devil.

—Spinoza, *Tractatus Politicus,* Chapter 1, Section 4
("human actions" replaced by "the actions of the Devil" in this citation)

PROLOGUE

November 11, 1991, 4:34 a.m.

The alarm rang out.

Assistant nurse Manami Kotegawa, on shift that night and napping in the nurse room, leapt up. "The alarm!" she exclaimed as she opened her eyes. Her mind was filled with contradictory thoughts: *It's happening! It can't be happening!*

Manami rushed to get ready, slipping on her new nurse's shoes—her second pair, recently bought—and dashed out of the room as though launched from a cannon.

She ran down the stairs trying to calm her beating heart, turned the corner around the dispensary room, and shot down the long hallway. The squeaking of her shoes' rubber soles echoed loudly down the dark, empty corridor.

She could hear the same alarm ringing from inside the Neonatal Unit as the room finally came into view. The place she was headed had recently been built next to the unit, a single wall separating the two spaces. More accurately, the small room, about the size of a closet and lacking windows and any kind of decoration, had been created by putting up walls in a corner of the Neonatal Unit.

The little room, dimly illuminated by a night light in the ceiling, was dominated by a new incubator surrounded on all sides by transparent reinforced glass. An arm shined an infrared light down from above, and the legs ended in small wheels. The walls of the room were covered in an off-white fabric, and one wall contained a small door, fifteen to twenty inches on a side, and hinged to allow horizontal opening. The incubator was placed flush up against the door.

Outside the hospital, the odd little door connected the yard behind the OB/GYN ward and the room with the incubator. It worked like a night deposit box in a post office, allowing "packages" to be delivered. The packages moved in the opposite direction of a birth, however—they could enter through the door, but not come out.

A stork had alighted in the yard three minutes before, opened the door from the outside, and "delivered" an infant into the incubator. The weight of the infant was detected by the incubator, causing alarms to start sounding simultaneously in the nurse station and in the Neonatal Unit.

It had taken Manami three minutes to get there. She had no idea whether three minutes was fast, by the book, or slow. She placed her left hand against her chest, which was still heaving, and carefully opened the door to the room with her right hand. A dingy cloth bundle lay inside the incubator, behind the glass. The alarm continued ringing. Manami flipped the switch on the wall near the entrance and the ringing stopped, replaced by silence, but Manami could still hear the ringing in her ears. She approached the incubator and looked inside.

She let out a blood-curdling cry.

Her piercing scream traveled unendingly through the half-open door through which the infant had just been delivered and could be heard clearly in the yard behind the hospital. It was as though she were screaming on behalf of the child, which was lying perfectly still and unable to itself.

Two months earlier, on September 10th, in scenic Nichinan City, Miyazaki Prefecture, a baby hatch euphemistically called the "Stork's Mailbox" had been set up in Jiiku Christian Hospital. It was designed as a rescue system to provide temporary care for unwanted newborns until they could be transferred to orphanages or foster families, the ultimate goal being to protect babies from abortion and murder.

The plans had incited a storm of controversy. More than a thousand people had responded to a prefecture-wide survey. TV shows on national networks dedicated whole shows to the topic, an indicator as to how important the issue was to everyone in Japan. Those in favor of the baby hatch had superiority in terms of votes, but members of the city council who were against the idea made their views clear: the baby hatch would encourage abandonment of babies and was in violation of the Child Welfare Act, the Law Prohibiting the Abandonment of Babies by Parents or Guardians, the Law for Preventing the Abuse of Children, and others.

Conservative city council members used popular sentiment against the baby hatch as a weapon in their campaign of uncompromising opposition to the installation of the Stork's Mailbox.

Kikue Iizuka, director of Jiiku Hospital and the originator of the system, made her case at a public hearing of the city council, describing how similar systems were fully operational and saving many newborns' lives in countries throughout the world. For the benefit of by-the-book centrists whose greatest fear was a lack of precedent, she emphasized that at one time Japan had also had a baby hatch, known as the *sutegodai*.

In existence for only a few years after World War II, the *sutegodai* was used in Tokyo's Saiseikai Chuo Hospital as a way to help war orphans, but in 1948, once the Child Welfare Act was adopted, the system was for all intents and purposes abandoned in part because there simply weren't as many orphans as before.

Kikue was painfully aware of the opinions of residents who vocally opposed the idea. Her heart ached as she read the many letters sent directly to the hospital: *If they know they can't raise them, why do they have them?... If people are given the option to abandon their kids when they get sick of raising them, the number of people who do so is going to go up... We need to ensure our children are getting proper sex education before putting this kind of system in place... People who abuse or abandon their children won't use the system anyway...*

All of you are right. Everything you say is true, she thought to herself. *But once a baby is born, its life belongs to no one. Life belongs only to God.* Kikue's ardent desire was to save as many lives as possible, lives on the point of being extinguished, lives that had been abandoned and that no one was willing to aid.

In the end Kikue's devout Catholic idealism won over the city council. The requisite permits were applied for and received from the Ministry of Health, Labor, and Welfare. The Stork's Mailbox was finally going to be a reality.

Thought had to be given to the location where it would be installed, for the sake of the anonymous visitors who would leave their babies here. From the palm tree-bordered main entrance of Jiiku Hospital, visitors would follow a gravel path along the north side of the hospital to a small, quiet garden where the wide fronds of the palm trees cast deep shadows on the verdant lawn during the day. The Neonatal Unit in the OB/GYN ward gave onto the garden. Kikue decided on this as the place to set up the baby hatch. The construction was a major undertaking, and included work inside the Neonatal Unit as well as tearing down part of the outside wall, but when it was done the Stork's Mailbox was finally complete.

Kikue was very particular about how it would look when finished. An arched canopy was put in above the outer door to provide protection from the rain, with an image below it—of the Virgin Mary cradling the infant Jesus—made to look like a stained-glass window. There were whispers that for an expression of sacredness the plastic used for the stained-glass effect (a compromise due to budgetary constraints) looked too cheap, but Kikue was satisfied. The Virgin Mary's smile, so full of grace and charity, was designed to be a silent appeal to parents at that crucial moment: *Look into your heart and reconsider what you are about to do.*

A sign indicating the location of the garden would be needed for visitors, so a white wooden board was placed before the trees to the side of the main entrance. The words "Stork's Mailbox" were accompanied by an arrow and an illustration of a stork flying with a baby hanging from its beak by one of the male nurses who had a talent for drawing.

A small party celebrating the opening was held in the garden, attended by Kikue and several OB/GYN nurses and doctors. They raised their glasses in a small ceremony.

Among those present in the cheery circle were Manami Kotegawa, a twenty-seven-year-old assistant nurse who had just graduated from nursing school in Miyazaki City, and Yusuke Watanabe, a young but very skilled OB/GYN specialist who was extremely popular with the expecting mothers.

A sense of anticipation could be felt among hospital staff beginning the day the Stork's Mailbox went into operation. The first two months came and went without a "delivery."

"Listen, we ought to be glad that the baby hatch hasn't been used yet," Dr. Watanabe said. "The point isn't to encourage people to abandon their babies, after all."

"But as we speak there are parents out there who might be considering abandoning their newborns," Nurse Kotegawa objected. "If only they would think, 'Hey, I just saw something on TV about that Stork's Mailbox,' we might be able to save a life."

"Well, that is one of the director's goals. Still, you have to wonder how such a basic human instinct like having children and raising them has gotten so warped in people today."

"People have always abandoned babies. Raising a child isn't an easy thing to do."

"I don't remember you mentioning any children," Yusuke teased.

"Hey, you don't have to raise one yourself to know how hard it is. As a matter of fact I'm very close to my aunt, who lives in Shinonome, near my house, and I babysat for her a lot."

"I suppose. I guess that means that you can hook a guy with your amazing childrearing skills," he laughed.

"Ooh, sexist comments, doctor?"

"Sexist com—oh, come on. What's wrong with using your maternal instincts as a selling point in getting a guy?"

"It's not that. It's the implication that women only get married to have kids."

"Oh, so that's the angle you're working, huh? So you're the type who will selflessly sacrifice everything to become director of the hospital."

"Well, not exactly. That would be pretty tough, too."

The pair laughed as they chatted in the hallway outside the Neonatal Unit.

Just two days later, on November 11th, the stork delivered the first baby.

Manami managed to steady her nerves somehow and tried to recall the procedure she had studied in the manual. She checked that the incubator was operational and that the infant was being warmed by the infrared light and maintaining a temperature of 98.6 degrees. She pushed the incubator out of the Stork's Mailbox "delivery room" and hurried to the isolation room.

She wanted to remove the dingy blanket the newborn was wrapped in and replace it with sterile gauze right away, but that was something the on-call doctor had to do. She rushed into the isolation room pushing the incubator and picked up the intercom handset that was connected to the office of the on-call doctor, who happened to be Yusuke that night.

"Doctor Watanabe, come right away! The first child has been dropped off. It's covered in lacerations. I think it's in critical condition. It has male genitalia. Yes, it's a boy."

The newborn infant that had been abandoned in the incubator was covered in what looked like incisions made by a razor blade, and covered in blood. The amateurish way the umbilical cord had been cut indicated to Manami that the mother had delivered the baby at home and done everything herself.

Yusuke listened to Manami on the phone and came running.

What on earth...

Yusuke absently put his hand to his face in shock. The baby had a pulse. It wasn't dead yet. Yusuke could feel a torrent of fury welling up from the pit of his stomach, bringing tears to his eyes. His burning passion turned into iron resolve: *I am not going to let this child die. No matter what it takes, I will save this child!*

CHAPTER 1

1—CONTACT

"I'm sorry, sir, but we're making our final descent now. I'm going to have to ask you to remain seated. Sir!"

A man ran down the aisle, brushing aside the flight attendant's request. Wearing a large, loose-knit wool cap pulled down low over his eyes and a safari jacket with four front pockets, he agilely dashed forward to the first-class section at the front of the plane. Once there, he snapped the shutter in a rapid burst of clicks as though he were firing a machine gun.

The light from the flash lit up the cabin, and several passengers cried out in surprise. His job done, the man tucked the camera under his arm, pulled a pair of sunglasses out of a breast pocket, slipped them on, and ran back to his seat.

The entire operation took less than ten seconds. Once back in the economy-class cabin, the man covered the lens with his hand and snapped several darkened shots in a row, as he always did in order to mark a break between shoots.

The flight attendant, leaning forward in her cabin crew seat located next to the emergency door, had followed his actions with an irate look on her face, but was herself immobilized by her seatbelt and helpless to do anything, caught off-guard by the sudden commotion.

The couple sitting in the seats that had just been lit up by the flash looked at each other in surprise and outrage. The male, who had long hair and wore sunglasses, turned back in the direction the photographer had run and cursed him under his breath but was helpless to do more.

The woman with him had a look of displeasure on her face so evident that it was clearly visible behind her giant sunglasses, which looked like a huge plastic butterfly perched on her nose. She glared at her boyfriend sitting next to her as though it were his carelessness that had exposed her to the paparazzo. Her angelic features were twisted in an expression of anger.

Tuesday, August 16, 2011. Two hours after departing from Miyazaki Airport, JAL flight 1890 touched down at Haneda Airport. The flight attendant gave the photographer a stern talking-to about the incident that had occurred just fifteen minutes before. She was flustered and angry, and her face was flushed crimson.

"I have never seen such behavior on any flight I've ever worked on. What you did was extremely dangerous. You could have caused a lot of trouble."

"I'm sorry," the man apologized insincerely. "I really am." He bowed his head.

"Y-You're sorry? I'm afraid that that's not enough, sir. You really must understand the danger you put everyone in."

"I don't know, I was just overcome by this urge to get up. Listen, I'm sorry. I really am."

"Wait here. The captain is going to have a word with you."

"I'll be right here." The man waited for the flight attendant to step away, then grabbed his camera case and a small Louis Vuitton travel bag and made a dash for the exit, leaving the airplane behind.

The photographer had left his burgundy Cherokee in the Haneda Airport parking lot. The paint job was starting to fade, but he liked this model because the back window was not tilted very much, making it easy to focus from inside the vehicle when surreptitiously shooting subjects. He climbed in and removed his cap.

Suddenly, almost with a swooshing sound, the long hair that had been hidden inside the cap came tumbling out. With a shake of the head to untangle the long black locks and a peek in the mirror for a quick face check, *he* was now a woman: Mariko Amo, thirty-two years old.

She thought of the digital data she had captured with the camera and felt a sense of relief. This week's job had been for a weekly called *In Focus*, and she had finally succeeded in getting a celebrity scoop that would be featured on a decent page. While not a stakeout in the strict sense of the word, she had chased her subject all the way to Miyazaki and tagged them in an airplane, meaning she would get the extra stakeout allowance. Together with the publication fee, her take would be enough to cover about two-thirds of her rent.

Today's job had been a scoop exposing a famous Japanese actress who'd been embroiled in a nasty divorce several months earlier, now on a secret vacation with her new boyfriend. Nobody had known they were in a relationship.

In Focus's editor-in-chief had given her the job after acquiring the flight information in advance; someone inside the airline had leaked the info. Most of the celebrity gossip handled by the celebrity section that Mariko belonged to came through leaks from inside airline companies like this time or from anonymous callers on location: "I saw Yuika Sawajiri and a man driving into a hotel next door to my house last night. I only saw them through the car window, but I'm absolutely sure it was her."

Pictorial weeklies like the one Mariko worked with owed anonymous tips like this to the fact that Japan had become a surveillance society. The tips were given out of idle amusement rather than for monetary gain.

The majority of Mariko's income came from her contract with Koshunsha, a major publisher. She had the paparazzi culture to thank for her living since most of her work involved photographing celebrities at press conferences and other events, as well as one-off jobs involving catching a celebrity in some sort of scandal. She was painfully aware of the fact that she was what was known as a gossip photographer.

Yet, she didn't have time to ruminate on whether that was a good thing or not. She had struggled to carve out a living taking pictures, and before she knew it, this was what she was doing, like it or not. Granted, it wasn't exactly the dream she'd dreamed as a high school graduate aspiring to make it as a photographer. She had vaguely imagined the profession as something more glamorous, more artistic.

She hadn't had any specialized training but would visit photography exhibits now and then. Even though she didn't recognize the names of the photographers or have any kind of expert knowledge, she liked the photographs of people. Whenever she encountered a picture that captured a particular moment in the life of some nameless person, it gave her a warm feeling inside, a feeling that life, that fragile, amorphous thing, had been captured in a worthwhile form. People came in all shapes and sizes but the glorious energy that gave them life was one and the same.

That was the kind of photograph Mariko wanted to make a living taking. It was a simple aspiration.

Mariko's father left when she was in fifth grade, after which she lived alone with her mother, who provided for the household by selling insurance. It would be a lie to say that Mariko didn't hate the father who (she, at least, thought) had abandoned them, but her mother Reiko never gave any hint as to what she felt about the man who had left her. She probably didn't want to contaminate her soon-to-be-adolescent daughter with her own hatred. Mariko was very sensitive in spite of her young age at the time and understood what her mother was going through. She decided never to say a word about her father either.

Then, when Mariko was in her last year of high school, her mother died. Forced to make her way in life from such a young age, Mariko felt no desire to become a run-of-the-mill office worker. After graduating from high school she worked as an assistant to a photographer for a couple of years and then, using that modest connection, landed a contract job as a photographer with a medium-sized publisher. By hook or by crook she'd finally reached a social position today where her business card read "*In Focus* Photographer"—for Koshunsha, a major publishing house.

The job she had jumped into with the photographer when she was nineteen had been a means of learning the trade but remained a bitter experience for Mariko, who had lacked all immunity to the realities of life. The scars her young heart had suffered built up small scabs over time, and when these peeled off, those parts of her were the stronger for it.

Mariko heard from a friend that a particular photographer was in the market for an assistant, and jumped at the chance. The photographer had his own studio and specialized in glamour photography. The pay, unfortunately, was a pittance; she could've made more at McDonald's. But it was a first step on the path to achieving her dream, so she didn't care about the pay.

She eventually got accustomed to the strenuous work but entered into a strange relationship with her boss. One day, Mariko found herself alone in the studio with her boss after finishing a job that had lasted long into the night. He made a pass at her, and she didn't say no. On the contrary, she was elated to discover that any man would find her sexually attractive. Late-blooming Mariko was still a virgin.

She worked for two more years as a low-paid assistant and occasional lover. She got pregnant and went through the ordeal of her first abortion. She was laid off soon thereafter. The photographer told her that the term of her part-time assistant's job had only been two years right from the start. Mariko told him that even if that was the case, she quite wanted to continue their relationship. He gave her a breezy smile and handed her 100,000 yen, calling it her "severance." She never forgot the humiliation she felt at that moment.

When Mariko thought back on the experience, she was struck by how innocent she had been, like a baby sucking on the candy of naivete. She'd had romantic dreams about what it would be like to be a photographer, and while her courageous plunge into the real world had been a good thing, she'd suffered cruelly at the hands of an indifferent world, with no one to protect her. She had been nineteen years old, a thought that evoked a faint uneasiness in what ought by now to have been her heart of steel.

Despite it all, Mariko felt a modicum of pride at the fact that she had made it so far doing what she still loved best, photography. Her private life was in a perpetual state of standby since she never knew when she would get a call for a job, and an actual day off came only once every three weeks. No matter how late at night or early in the morning the call to "Get a move on!" would come in, and she would make it to the location first, lugging her heavy gear on both shoulders. It was a world where the stress was as common as the sexual harassment, and she sometimes wondered how long she would last.

But pennies did rain from heaven on occasion, and there was no luckier scoop for a weekly magazine photographer than to happen upon the scene of a major incident just as it was happening. What to do when you were smack in the middle of it, however, was something she could not have known.

≈

Mariko flew down Metropolitan Expressway 1, making the engine of her second-hand car whine (the odometer was nearing the 200,000 km mark) on her way home to Tennozu Isle. At that very moment, two young men were riding the shuttle to Kasai. They had just returned from Miyazaki on the same flight as Mariko, JAL 1980.

The older of the two was around nineteen and the younger one looked two or three years younger. They were both good-looking—enough so, in fact, that a few of the other passengers had looked back at them as they walked down the aisle to the back row of the bus. The older one had strong eyebrows and lips that gave him an air of resolve which the other lacked altogether.

That aside, they felt *similar.* It must have been a scent of something, of a secret they shared. The scent of having committed a crime likened them to each other.

The younger of the two, who sat by the window, was exhausted and had dark rings under his eyes. He stared absently at the monotonous scenery flowing past the bus window. His pale face was all the paler considering he had just been in Miyazaki in all its midsummer glory. After a while he turned his empty gaze to his companion and said something. His companion didn't look back at him and merely shook his head.

2—Collapse

Mariko sat waiting for the light at the Toranomon intersection on her way home from the *In Focus* office, where she had delivered the photograph data. She turned it over in her mind. Her annual income was down by a million yen compared to two years before. *The damn recession is affecting my pay,* she thought. The magazine would've paid her 250,000 yen a few years before for the pictures of the actress with her secret lover on the plane. What they'd given her today wouldn't even cover her rent for the month. She toyed with taking up the editor-in-chief's offer to switch her contract from "B" to "A Exclusive," which paid a bit better. She didn't want to be tied to one magazine, though, and having the freedom to choose from several takers when you did land a huge scoop was often a big advantage.

The light turned green and she stepped on the accelerator. She moved into the left lane and then turned left at the Iikura intersection below the Noa Building that loomed like a giant round tombstone. She headed for Shinagawa.

She passed Tokyo Tower for the first time in a while. The clear summer afternoon would mean a long line of people waiting to go up to the observation deck. She could hear the attendant saying, "The line is over here if you want to take the stairs up."

She remembered climbing up all six hundred some-odd steps to the observation deck when she was younger. She fell into a momentary reverie. She had been with a boyfriend. They were laughing and out of breath. She couldn't recall the guy's face, though. In retrospect she had gone through a bit of a wild period after breaking up with that photographer. She laughed and shook her head as she drove past the tower.

Just at that moment, there was a tremendous blast, and the earth shook violently. Mariko slammed on the breaks not knowing what was going on, stopping the car by the curb. There was another thundering explosion not two seconds later, followed immediately by a third one, the roaring of the various explosions mixing and causing the entire area to quake. Mariko heard a crashing sound as all the windows in the buildings directly below Tokyo Tower were blown out by the shock waves. The muffled rumbling sounded like a colossal force trying to burst out but being compressed inward. The stereo-like reverberation of the many overlapping sounds engulfed the entire area.

Mariko ducked and covered her ears. She looked in the rearview mirror with trepidation. Nothing. She opened the door and stepped out onto the street, where people were fleeing from the area around the tower. Just at that instant, a woman who was running and screaming was hit by a car and thrown to the pavement. Mariko let out a short cry but before she could figure out what to do, she became aware of an extraordinary change going on.

The panicked crowd continued streaming out, not even glancing at the woman who had been hit and who lay sprawled on the asphalt. Mariko looked at the grounds on which Tokyo Tower stood and saw that the low buildings under the tower were enveloped in white smoke. A sharp smell of gunpowder filled the air. Was a building on fire? Mariko ran towards one of them. Just then, she noticed something that defied belief.

Tokyo Tower was moving.

One of the four outwardly spreading legs of the tower entered her field of vision. A section of the steel frame that was just higher than the buildings was totally demolished. The leg of elegant steel frame that ought to have risen smoothly from the foundation at the surface up towards the sky was hideously blown out and disfigured, and the colossal top of the monument which it was supposed to be supporting was beginning to list. The interconnected web of reddish-orange steel bars stood out against the clear blue sky as it came closer.

Mariko could not believe her eyes. Her brain's attempt to process the events unfolding before her eyes was vigorously rejected by her preconception that what was happening was simply impossible. The reality she was unable to accept soon turned into terror, however, and she had no choice but to accept what she was seeing, in order to save her own life.

Tokyo Tower was falling over, and it was coming straight at Mariko.

At that instant, a terrifying thought went through her head: *How long until it collapses?* It was not a question; it was her desire for a chance. Mariko dashed back to her Cherokee and pulled out her trusty Canon Mark III. She nimbly attached a flexible mid-range 24-105 mm lens. The white lens barrel on the black camera body—this was Mariko's preferred setup of landing scoops when not on stakeouts.

She ran back and peered through the viewfinder. She was too close to the subject. She sprinted away as fast as she could, looking back. She went around onto the grounds of the tower looking for the right angle. Behind her was the concrete wall around Shiba Park with its leafy green trees, preventing her from moving further back. She turned around once more and looked up at the tower. The whole fit in her viewfinder now. She was near the exact spot that the tower was going to fall onto, but the angle was frighteningly exhilarating. Mariko began shooting away.

≈

It lasted a mere minute or two at the most. A solitary young man stood with a slightly bored look on his face near the entrance to the Noa Building at the Iikura intersection. It was the handsome young man who had returned from Miyazaki around ten days ago. He leaned up against the reddish-brown brick-colored wall, looking like he was waiting for his girlfriend to show up.

On closer inspection, however, he was holding a cell phone in each hand. He stared absently for a while and checked the time on the G-Shock watch he wore on his wrist. He then pressed some buttons on the cell phones.

He held the two cell phones pressed against his body, just above his hips, his thumbs flying, like some two-fisted gunslinger in some old western. His face beamed heroically but also with a look of tension. He needed to finish the operation quickly—as if calling someone's cell phone were a sign that the world was about to end.

About five seconds later, a tremendous thundering sound shook the area, followed by two more before the reverberations from the first had even died down. The area trembled.

"Holy shit! Oh my god, yes!" the young man said to himself. "He's a freaking monster!" Overwhelmed by relief at having accomplished his major task, the young man looked up at the sky with pride.

The top half of Tokyo Tower, from the observation deck up, was visible beyond the buildings facing Sakurada Street and swayed visibly. As he stood watching Tokyo Tower begin falling away from him, three policemen who had been on duty guarding the Russian embassy ran up from behind him and across the street, waving their arms to stop the cars since the crosswalk light was still red. The young man smiled happily and took off after them to watch Tokyo Tower's "final event."

When he got to the lot where the tourist buses were parked, the tower's tilting was unmistakable. The collapse was proceeding slowly at first. The two legs pointing towards Tokyo Bay had been shredded by bombs, but the other two legs were still firmly planted in the ground. The sections which had been severed by the bombs were being pushed towards the ground by the tremendous weight from above, but the two legs on the opposite side, which were still rooted, were just barely resisting gravity. The tower resembled a giant boxer hammered by a powerful punch and on his knees trying to decide through the fog in his brain whether to call it quits.

The steel legs which hadn't been exploded and which the young man could see before him were strangely tensed. The next instant, however, a tremendous snapping sound was heard from the back of the parking lot and a fissure appeared in the red legs on the opposite side. The young man had never seen such a large steel structure tear like that.

Once one of the three steel arms that made up a single leg tore through, the other two were sheared off in a matter of seconds. The tower suddenly lurched forward like the losing team in a game of tug-o-war that had been evenly balanced until that moment.

The unfolding chain reaction struck terror into the young man. The base section of the other leg twisted up into the air, together with the asphalt around it, with a loud rumbling, pulling the oxidized dark-brown nerve tissue right out of the earth, flipping two tourist buses which were parked nearby.

"Oh fuck!" The young man jumped back and dashed to the edge of the street for cover. Strands of rusted galvanized steel nerves that had lain underground for more than fifty years were dangling above the ground with pieces of torn concrete still attached. It was an awesome sight to behold.

The outer shell of the elevator that went up and down inside Tokyo Tower was snapped in two by the tilting. The young man thought he actually heard a snapping sound, but it might have just been an auditory illusion caused by the visual overload his brain was experiencing. The outer walls of the elevator tumbled down inside the tower and poured down on the roofs of the buildings below together with shards of broken glass, like a waterfall.

The young man clearly saw people thrown out of the elevators, falling together with the rest of the wreckage. He let out a small cry and put his hand to his cheek: blood. A shard of glass had sliced the pale skin of his cheek.

He became frightened and took off. He ran all the way to the Iikura intersection looking for cover, and looked back one more time. The tower top that had been visible from beyond the buildings facing Sakurada Street disappeared from view as though taking a bow.

≈

Mariko continued snapping the shutter like a madwoman. *Decisive moment*—the words swirled through her mind. The braided steel structure that was toppling over onto her had a majestic beauty. It was as though the world were announcing its end, to her alone.

She inched back as she pressed the shutter release. The giant was 333 meters tall, so it would take even an Olympic athlete capable of running 100 meters in ten seconds half a minute to escape in the direction the steel tower was falling. She would have to dash to the side when the time came to run. Right now she was slightly away from the exact spot the steel structure was going to fall. She still had time to take pictures. She wanted to take a few more. She kept snapping shots as if in a dream.

She initially was confident that the speed of the collapse was not too great. Mariko was in a state of rapture as she captured the sublime beauty of the moment when the steel tower looked like a ballerina, arched up and twirling around on one leg, the final death cry of a valkyrie. For an instant, the tower found a perfect balance and seemed to stop, one leg in the air.

She could hear the tower sing out as if on stage: *Grant me a quick death.*

She held the shutter release down, taking multiple frames in a row. She looked away from the tower for a moment to change the shutter speed to 1/800. Image stabilization was off because it slowed the focus. *Trust your instincts,* Mariko told herself. She looked back up at the tower. It was no longer a tower but a several-thousand-ton mass of steel falling directly at her.

The estimate differed from before she looked away. The angle of the collapse had shifted towards Mariko when the fourth leg had broken off. She continued taking multiple shots in a row. She was no longer looking at the viewfinder but at her own death.

Then she ran. She ran as fast as she could, thinking all the while, *If I die, at least let the camera survive intact.*

3—Press Conference

A press conference on the August 26th Tokyo Tower Bombing Attack was held at 7 p.m. that night in the conference hall on the seventeenth floor of the Tokyo Metropolitan Police Department. The hall, which supposedly had a capacity of two hundred, was packed to overflowing with the media. Menacing rows of photographers stood like a firing squad aiming at the investigation team.

Only the TV crews were running around restlessly. With irritated looks on their faces, a camera operator and a news chief were discussing something while assistants ran in and out of the press conference location talking into their cell phones.

"What does the director want? The goddamn presser's about to start!"

"It's okay. We should go ahead and tape whatever we need, but—wait, hold on..."

"He's saying they're going to switch to a news special on cable."

"On cable? So what the hell am I supposed to call this show during the intro? What news show is this going on? For crying out loud, people!"

It was to be expected. Tokyo Tower had acted as a shared radio tower, emitting terrestrial analog signals to seventeen million households to the greater Tokyo area, and it had been destroyed, plunging every TV station in Tokyo into the biggest panic in Japanese broadcasting history.

Every TV station had emergency transmitters in case transmission from Tokyo Tower ever stopped due to a major earthquake or other natural disaster. Fuji TV and Nichiei TV's backups were located on the roof of one of the buildings in the Shinjuku high-rise complex and were designed to automatically switch over in the event that the analog signal from Tokyo Tower was cut off for any reason. That was the technicians' theory, anyway. Nobody really expected it that to happen.

The results were catastrophic. The emergency transmitters only had around a hundredth the transmitting power of Tokyo Tower. When the disaster occurred, there was a four-second blackout before the broadcasts started up again, but coverage barely extended over the Tokyo Metropolitan area. Reception was worse than for prewar vacuum tube TVs. Who would watch something like that in this day and age?

The TV station engineers were trying to boost the power of the emergency transmitters one way or another to restore reception to a level that would satisfy their advertising clients. Just when the entire industry had been transitioning to terrestrial digital broadcasting, it was suffering a devastating financial blow.

The people of Tokyo were experiencing an inconceivable void of civilization: access to television, as ubiquitous as oxygen and water, had been interrupted.

The Superintendent General of the police force and his deputy sat at the center of the press conference podium, with the Chief of Public Security and the Chief of Criminal Investigation seated to the right and left, respectively. Facing them was a menacing assembly of reporters and photographers, like a group of zombies about to attack.

The Superintendent General, Kenji Kamoshita, read from a text prepared by the head of the Public Relations Department.

"Um, I will now make a report regarding the, uh, current situation as well as casualties arising from the bombing attack by persons unknown of Tokyo Tower, which is under the ownership of Tokyo Analog Signal Transmission Co., Ltd., and is located at 4-2-8 Shiba Park, Minato Ward."

The perfunctory prefatory remark, typical of the police bureaucracy, pushed the already-stressed reporters right to the edge. The hall was asphyxiatingly rank from so many people packed so close together. The newspaper reporters and magazine writers felt beads of sweat running down their backs under their suits even though the A/C was on full blast. Many newspaper reporters made no attempt to hide their annoyance at the fact that the press conference had been scheduled so close to the final proofing deadline of the day.

"TOKYO TOWER COLLAPSES!" worked as a headline for the evening extra edition, but they couldn't very well run with the same thing for the next day's morning edition. On the other hand, it would be unrealistic to expect any substantial announcement regarding the case at the press conference the day it happened. It was going to be tough.

The Chief of Public Security, Junichiro Iwagami, sitting to the left at the table and casting a cool gaze over the press, had an ace up his sleeve.

Naoyoshi Ogata, the Chief of Criminal Investigation, had opposed Iwagami's idea outright during the pre-conference meeting of top brass including the Chief of Public Relations regarding what to say at the press conference.

"We can't know what the perpetrators will do when they hear that. Right now they've pulled off the attack and are like a clam that has relaxed and opened up a bit. We risk shutting it. I'm totally against this. The risk is too great. Not only that, but isn't this rather unlike Public Security and its secretive ways?"

"Superintendent Supervisor Ogata, this is information we're going to have to release sooner or later. At Public Security we know exactly how it'll play out when we toss the press this crumb and they gobble it up. The point is that this will actually give us some breathing room to do what we need, at our pace."

Iwagami's reference to Ogata's rank rather than title was a subtle nudge to use the system wisely and with a bit more savvy.

"The investigation will fail if both Public Security and Criminal Investigation are trying to lead it. Who's going to lead the task force?" Chief Ogata asked Deputy Superintendent General Kokura point-blank.

That was what had been going on backstage before the press conference. In the end, Chief of Public Security Iwagami's view was adopted because, given the scale and modus operandi, the destruction of Tokyo Tower had all the aspects of a terrorist attack—i.e., was a matter of public security.

Chief Ogata gave a businesslike overview of what had happened.

"The explosions occurred at 3:33 p.m. on Friday, August 26th. There were three individual explosions, and the final collapse of the tower occurred at 3:37..."

Someone muttered "a four-minute nightmare," causing several reporters within earshot to think, *Great headline!*

"The cause of the collapse was the explosive fracture of two of the legs and the subsequent toppling under the tower's own weight, approximately 4,200 tons. The fractures were located 36.15 meters above ground. Um, now the casualties... We currently have 382 confirmed deaths, but this figure is expected to rise. There are currently 25 wounded, some in serious condition. Most of the occupants of the buildings immediately under the tower were killed..."

The press corps started shouting questions.

"Are there any indications that foreign terrorists were involved?"

"We don't know at this point."

"Al-Qaeda?"

"We don't know."

"Have the people behind this released any statements?"

"No."

"No one could have rigged such an intricate bomb without being seen. Do you consider the Police Department's inability to stop this act ahead of time a rather significant failure?"

"Um..."

"We've had reports that the Ministry of Health, Labor, and Welfare has set up a task force to look into compensation for victims' families. This incident will undoubtedly be a major blow to Japan in terms of the economic impact, too. TV stations are looking at trillions of yen in damages since Tokyo's broadcasting infrastructure has been destroyed. What is the Police Department's opinion of the lax security which allowed a monument to be destroyed in broad daylight with such ease, when it was capable of causing so much havoc?"

"We are extremely cognizant of the gravity of what has happened," Superintendent General Kamoshita said, wiping his brow.

A young female reporter spoke next. “There has never been a crime in Japan that produced over three hundred deaths. In terms of sheer number, the sarin gas attack in the Tokyo subway pales by comparison. How does the Police Department plan to tackle this crime?”

“I’m leading the investigation, and have every intention of solving this case quickly. I stake the honor of the Police Department on it,” Superintendent General Kamoshita said.

The newspaper reporters were worried about the proofing deadline for the next day’s morning edition and wanted to be more aggressive, but the very scale of the act made it difficult to say anything more. Then, just as they thought the announcement from the Police Department was done for the day, Public Security Chief Iwagami spoke up as though he’d been gauging the right moment.

“Lastly, I would like to make an announcement about the type of explosive used, as analyzed by the Public Security Mobile Investigation Unit.”

A ripple ran through the room. A few of the reporters who had been headed for the door rushed back in.

“These are still preliminary findings, but it appears that the bombs used to destroy the leg sections of Tokyo Tower were homemade and consisted mainly of sodium chlorate.”

Iwagami delivered the statement with no expression on his face, but in his heart he smiled. *All right, you hyenas. Chew on that for a while.*

The papers were filled with giant headlines the next morning, partly because the cautious stories reporters had written in advance of the press conference all had to be rewritten and rushed to meet their filing deadlines.

“WEED-KILLER BOMB USED IN 8/26 TOWER ATTACK”

“PHANTOM OF CORPORATE BOMBERS?”

"RETURN OF SEVENTIES BUSINESS BOMBINGS? POSSIBLE CONNECTION WITH REMNANTS OF EAST ASIA FRONT"

There were still many areas without TV reception, but regional stations and, naturally, Tokyo stations put together news specials with clips from the press conference.

"It was announced right at the end of the press conference that sodium chlorate was the main component of the bombs. This is the same chemical that was used in the corporate bomb attacks against Mitsubishi Heavy Industries and other companies in the mid-seventies by a radical group known as the East Asia Front for the Defeat of Japanese Imperialism. Sodium chlorate is a common ingredient in commercially available herbicides and was known at the time as the 'weed-killer bomb.' In their investigation of the Tokyo Tower attack, the police department are viewing it as a possible link to remnants of the radical Japanese group."

4—Atagoyama Police Station

The headquarters for the 8/26 Tokyo Tower Bombing Attack Special Investigation was set up inside Atagoyama Police Station the day after the bombing.

Atagoyama Police Station was less than two kilometers from Tokyo Tower. The storied station, which dated back to the prewar period, was naturally in a frenzied state since the day before. The officers had worked through the night helping the initial investigation led by the Metropolitan Police, identifying the dead and readying the special investigation headquarters. Dozens of investigators would be showing up at Atagoyama Police Station from the Metropolitan Police HQ as well as from nearby precincts to provide backup, so just setting up the fifth-floor hall as the investigation headquarters required a mountain of hectic preparation.

Many detectives would be staying at the police station during the first period—one month—of the investigation, so cots were brought into the historic judo hall, converted into makeshift sleeping quarters for the detectives.

Iwao Miyamoto, Atagoyama's chief, had been in the hospital for a month due to a liver ailment. He'd received a temporary discharge from the hospital and gone home as soon as he received a report on what had happened. He arrived at the station late that night.

It wasn't to lead his precinct that Chief Miyamoto had left the hospital so hastily. He was an accomplished calligrapher and wanted to write the ceremonial sign stating the name of the investigation headquarters with his own hand for display at the entrance to the hall.

He called his home in Umegaoka from the hospital and had his wife ready his calligraphy ink and ink stone before heading home in his designated vehicle. The resulting sign reading "8/26 Tokyo Tower Bombing Attack Special Investigation Headquarters" evinced a power in the brushstrokes that belied his illness. It was a masterpiece of the calligrapher's art.

The sign written by the "Belletrist Chief" (as he was sometimes called) was displayed at the entrance to the hall. Small dishes containing salt were placed on the floor on either side of the entrance in prayer for a rapid resolution to the case. Chief Miyamoto looked on the completed scene with satisfaction and relegated to his deputy chief the task of organizing the investigation headquarters and handling preparations for the huge logistical operation that would be required starting the next day. He then returned to the hospital in his car.

Contrary to the expectations of the fifty-eight-year-old chief, who hoped for someone at the station to receive the Superintendent General's Award as a prelude to his own honorable retirement, personnel decisions for the investigation headquarters made in the S.G.'s presence were disadvantageous for on-site cops. The Public

Security Bureau had moved in with unprecedented speed soon after the Tokyo Tower bombing.

Specifically, the Public Security authorities got to work right away positioning the Tokyo Tower bombing as a terrorist act equal in scale to the 9/11 attacks in America. As a result, the investigation headquarters would be a joint operation by the Police Department's Criminal Investigation Department and the Public Security Bureau.

The problem was that a few cases handled jointly in the past had left bitter feelings on both sides, feelings etched into each entity's DNA in the form of grudges passed down from generation to generation, creating anti-Public Security bias among detectives and a feeling of disdain for detectives among members of Public Security.

Investigators in the Public Security Bureau always complained how detectives closed an investigation as soon as they caught the culprit without looking deeper into the story behind whatever it was that had happened. They called detective work shallow because of this, and their general attitude was that the nation's stability didn't depend on whether or not some burglar was caught. Let left-wing groups run amok, however, and the country could very well fall apart.

Public Security had an amazingly centralized organizational structure. Each front-line investigator worked by gathering information like pieces in a jigsaw puzzle, while the job of the higher-ups was to arrange those pieces into an overall picture of the case.

In contrast the detectives proceeded like small business owners. In an environment where all detectives were rivals, their job was essentially to compete against each other to find facts and catch culprits—water to Public Security's oil.

Around 9 a.m. the cool professionals of the Metropolitan Police's Criminal Investigation Section One began assembling in the Atagoyama Station hall, their left breast pockets adorned with a red badge that had S1S ("Search 1 - Select") in gold stitching across it.

The station's administrative department and the detectives brought together for the joint investigation team welcomed the members of Section One in the hall. They all sat according to the name cards on the tables, but since so many of them knew each other from the Police Academy or from previous assignments, many a greeting was exchanged in the gruff manner typical of detectives.

"Why's the first meeting of the investigation starting so late, for crying out loud? Tokyo goddamn Tower is knocked over and we're just sitting around. This is outrageous!"

"Word is Public Security and Criminal Investigation were fighting over who'd be in charge at the first general meeting. They couldn't make any assignments until they'd fought that out, apparently."

"I heard the Crisis Management Advisor was telling the task force set up by the Prime Minister's Office that this was a terrorist act."

"Seriously? Then maybe they weren't lying when they said this was going to be a joint investigation."

"The current Crisis Management Advisor is an ex-superintendent general who used to be at Public Security, right?"

"You mean he's the one who got that huge budget approved by the Anti-Terrorism Committee after 9/11 when he was Chief of Public Security?"

"Which is why he'd be dancing in the street if this case turned out to be the same kind of terrorism."

"What do you mean, 'dancing'? I'd watch what I said if I were you. Lots of people died in this attack, idiot," an older detective scolded a younger one in a deadly serious tone.

"Still, what on earth were those newspaper headlines this morning?"

"I haven't heard anything. Making public the results of the

forensics investigation before the special investigation even gets started? What a load of crap."

"Yeah, weren't the forensics results from the Criminal Investigation Department supposed to be reported at the investigation meeting today?"

"Probably just a bunch of guesswork by the Public Security Mobile Investigation Unit anyway."

Detective Tsuyoshi Isogai from the Atagoyama Police Station apologetically entered the discussion the gung-ho Section One investigators were having. "So does that mean that we're going to try to apprehend the perpetrators on the assumption that it was an act of terrorism?"

Isogai was a sergeant detective in the station's Violent Crime Investigation Unit. He spoke with a strong accent that gave away his provincial roots despite having spent the past thirty years in Tokyo. His accent had a warm, welcoming quality that helped sooth the tension at gruesome crime scenes.

"I don't know if it's terrorism or what, but do the geeks over at Public Security seriously think they're going to pull out old data and go, 'Ah, here's the guy that did it'?" bemoaned Munenori Yoshida, a veteran detective from Section One.

He and Isogai knew each other from way back and had worked together on another special investigation two years before. They had successfully solved that case. Yoshida was one of the detectives who was worried about how the joint investigation with the Public Security Bureau was going to work out. As a young detective in Section One, he had worked on a similar joint investigation during the Veda Truth cult case. The two teams just hadn't worked well, and he still remembered the difficulties they had.

"Public Security's investigations are essentially based on information, right? If the guy they want isn't already on their radar, they just go off on a tangent."

"Nice one, Isogai," Yoshida laughed, joined by the other detectives.

A few people started clearing their throats in the hall as this happened. Some plainclothes who were starting to mix in with a crowd that was reaching a hundred people in size had something about them that clearly set them apart from Section One and Atagoyama cops. They were investigators with the Public Security Bureau, and they of the "dank disposition" never liked to stand out.

The first investigation meeting started at exactly 10 a.m., one hour later than was customary.

"Atten-shun!"

The order rang out through the large hall and the nearly one hundred men shot up from their seats. Not a trace of the previous joking remained.

"Salute!"

The men saluted and sat like a receding wave.

The investigators were seated in rows at long folding tables facing the podium at the front of the hall, where Deputy Superintendent General Kokura, who was leading the special investigation taskforce, and Criminal Investigation Department Chief Ogata and Public Security Bureau Chief Iwagami, who were second in command, were seated. The heads of the Guard Department, the Community Safety Department, and the Organized Crime Department also sat in the row as "staff officers" and looked sternly out at the assembled investigators.

Principal investigators had already gotten their summons the previous night. Typically, on-call detectives would get a report about an incident on their radios and then go on standby until the need for an investigation had been confirmed by an initial combing by the Mobile Investigation Unit and any special crime scene units, the special command officer, and the forensics officer.

However, since the incident—the bombing of Tokyo Tower, a major catastrophe—involved the detonation of explosives in two leg structures, it was obvious from the start that there would be an investigation. Naturally, the possibility that it was some kind of terror attack was assumed to be high, so there was no doubt that Public Security's own Mobile Investigation Unit would be deployed to perform an independent investigation of the scene.

Public Security Chief Junichiro Iwagami, deputy commander for the special investigation, began the meeting with a special statement, perhaps with the goal of having his bureau take the initiative in the investigation.

"This ruthless criminal act which has resulted in more deaths than any other in the history of our nation is a direct threat to the very core of our society. We still don't know if a known terrorist group is behind this attack, but we do know this: an act of violence such as this creates a creeping psychological unease among the population that it will happen again, ultimately leading to the breakdown of the entire country.

"Attacking a peaceful society without warning, thereby multiplying the fear caused by such attacks—that's the definition of terrorism. Which is why we can state unequivocally right now that this is an act of terrorism, even without knowing who did it or what their motives were, because they have created fear in the population. We cannot underestimate the significance of choosing Tokyo Tower as a target, either. It is a symbol not only of Tokyo but of the prosperity of our country as a whole. We must confront this depraved act as a challenge to the Japanese nation.

"Today begins our mission. It is our responsibility to find the criminal organizations or masterminds behind this act, expose the entire organization, and bring the full force of the law to bear on it. Do not forget the significance of what I have said here today! I want you to throw yourselves body and soul into your task and catch the perpetrators ASAP!"

"Yessir!" came the thunderous response.

Many of the voices belonged to Public Security personnel. Quite a few of the detectives remained quiet, thinking deep in their hearts that it was their job to nab the culprits in the end. Their powerful resolve and quiet motivation remained inside.

"Those guys from Public Security have a bad habit of never sharing their information, so our joint investigation is 'joint' in name only. It's pointless!" Munenori Yoshida made his opinion known in no uncertain terms as soon as the first investigation meeting was over, his gruff voice rising up out of his large, judo-toughened body. There were still quite a few Public Security officers in the special investigation headquarters, and they heard Yoshida.

A man dressed in a well-tailored suit who had been putting together some documents approached Yoshida.

"Mr. Yoshida, it's been a while."

It was Superintendent Onodera. He had been two years behind Yoshida at Fuchu South High School, and they had followed the same path into the police force. That is to say, they had followed the same path but were walking on different planes on it: Onodera had graduated with honors from the National Police Academy and was now an elite member of the Public Security Bureau, on his way to the top. Being alumni of the same high school, they had naturally run into each other a few times in the past, but to Yoshida, Onodera's cutthroat ambition was irritating. Onodera openly said that the Police Department was "designed around the Public Security Bureau."

Yoshida looked at Onodera and made a whistling sound through his large front teeth.

"Why, if it isn't Superintendent Onodera. I hear you've been shooting off your mouth about Al-Qaeda being behind this attack."

Yoshida was a police inspector. Onodera was a police superintendent. Onodera could have been ten years behind Yoshida in high school, and that would not have changed the fact that Onodera occupied a position above Yoshida in the Police Department's organizational pyramid thanks to his rapid advancement. Even the members of Criminal Investigation Section One, who were not easily shaken, observed the exchange tensely.

"Hey, take it easy, Mr. Yoshida. We're still only eyeballing possibilities here. We've got people looking at this thing from every angle we can think of. We'll know for sure pretty soon, though. We've got people watching every mosque in the country and we're gathering data from CIA and Mossad. We've got Immigration running checks on all foreign nationals who entered the country over the past year, too."

"Yeah, I'm sure looking up bad guys on your computer is real easy. But I seem to remember Shoko Kagehara not turning up in a single one of your databases during the Veda case. You guys took your sweet time after the sarin gas attack, but as soon as Police Commissioner General Kunisada got shot, you started running around arresting everyone in sight for minor offenses to question them. You want to know what I think you are? You're nothing but a bunch of slackers and leeches."

As Yoshida lay into him, Onodera looked at the lower-ranking man through his rimless glasses with that look of condescension unique to the elite.

5—Photographs

Furukawabashi Metropolitan Hospital, third floor, general ward—

The evening sun poured through the emergency exit at the western end of the long hallway, imbuing the linoleum floor with a blazing golden color. A long human shadow that stretched along the floor in front of the light approached, moving irregularly. The face was not visible, backlit and silhouetted as it was, but an outline of long hair glowed like a nimbus, clearly identifying the shadow as a woman.

A male nurse passed the woman from the front and spoke to her. “Well, Ms. Amo. Look who’s back up again.”

The silhouetted woman responded affably. “You’d better believe it. The minute I get this cast off, I’ve got to hit the ground running. There’s no security when you’re a freelance photographer. You’re always one day away from eviction!”

Mariko’s jovial answer made the nurse laugh. “But Ms. Amo, remember that while your ECG came back clear, your head did get a pretty good bang. You’re going to have to take it easy for a while, cast or no cast.” Before Mariko could respond, he continued, “And also keep in mind that what you experienced was no ordinary accident.” He added in a low voice, “Dr. Kumagaya from the psychiatric ward said that there’s a possibility you could have PTSD.”

“Aye-aye, cap’n!” Mariko said in a manly tone, saluting the nurse.

Mariko’s external injuries were diagnosed as an avulsion fracture of the metatarsal bones in her left foot, and it was treated by a minor operation. She did, however, hit her head very hard as she dashed out from under the falling structure of Tokyo Tower, so she was admitted to the surgical ward after undergoing a few tests.

The EMS personnel from a Metropolitan Police mobile unit had found Mariko lying unconscious on the asphalt on Metropolitan Route 301, having just managed to escape the falling metal, rubble, glass, and other debris from the collapsing tower. She had been taken to the designated emergency hospital, which was Furukawabashi Metropolitan, together with other injured people.

The surgical ward hallways were filled with doctors and nurses hectically running around, since so many people who had been seriously injured during the tower collapse had apparently been brought to other wards in the same hospital. Men wearing the dark blue hats and uniforms of the Metropolitan Police had visited

Mariko her second day in the hospital. They asked her how she was. When she told them she was fine, they gave her a single sheet of paper and asked her to fill out her name, address, and contact information. She wondered if she was going to be counted among the victims of the attack.

Her cast was removed the following day and the doctor in charge said she would have to come back for a few more follow-up visits. She arrived home at her Tennozu Isle apartment after an absence of ten days.

Though she lived in "Tennozu Isle," it was in the section to the west of Metropolitan Route 357, which connected with the old Tokyo Bay Expressway heading towards Shibaura Wharf to the north, so her actual address was the very unimpressive Higashi Shinagawa. The only thing visible from the tiny balcony outside her fifth-floor apartment in her "waterfront" neighborhood was the huge warehouses right in front, blocking her view of the ocean. But since the complex was called *Avantic Tennozu,* out of vanity she would tell people she was working with for the first time that she lived in "Tennozu Isle," and not "Higashi Shinagawa."

It was disingenuous. She decided what she'd say from now on: "Why, I live in the Higashi Shinagawa warehouse district. In spring and summer, a rancid stench wafts up from the canal's placid surface. It's magnificent, you must come by and visit sometime..."

Mariko had spent the past five years here engaged in the same soliloquy with herself. She could see the canal through the east-facing windows. It was a stoic, gray landscape, but Mariko didn't completely hate it.

After her father left, she and her mother had to leave the house Mariko grew up in. Her mother got a job selling insurance (just squeaking in under the employee age limit), and they lived in the Kawasaki industrial belt. Mariko remembered the air always being hazy and thick. Still, she found the interplay of light and shadow in a mercilessly concrete landscape had its own kind of beauty.

Late at night after a long day at work, passing the eighteen-wheelers that filled Metropolitan Expressway 1 moving towards Haneda or the Bayside Expressway on the way to her apartment in, yes, Higashi Shinagawa, she'd sometimes be overcome with a strong feeling of affection for Tokyo, this crazy place where she was living as best she could.

I've never tasted the rarefied cream of the very top of society, but then again I've never been one of the cogs and gears squeaking and grinding away terrifyingly at the bottom, she contemplated. *I'm living my life as a free woman in an unequal society.* The small sense of achievement kept her going.

Of course, getting scoop after scoop and moving into one of the skyscrapers she could see on the other side of Rainbow Bridge wouldn't be too shabby, either...

Her sudden hospitalization and absence from the apartment meant that she came home to find her mailbox stuffed with newspapers, and another bundle of them on the ground.

The expiration date of the milk in her fridge was long passed, the Chinese cabbage and green onions she had bought to make *happosai* were withered and dry, and a fine layer of dust covered everything in her three-room apartment. She decided to spend the morning cleaning the place and to dedicate the afternoon to downloading the pictures. Ordinarily she'd dive right into the work first and leave the chores for later; today, she procrastinated for some reason.

The apartment clean, Mariko started closing the windows she had opened when she stopped and looked outside. It was just past two in the afternoon. A small boat was floating past on the murky canal through the shadows cast by the office buildings and warehouses on either bank. The cabin had a black galvanized roof. The cargo it was carrying behind was covered with a blue tarp.

She could not see the captain's face at this distance, but she had a clear image of it in her mind. He was an old man with deep lines in his face and a dark brown scally cap down over his eyes. That was the face of the man guiding the boat along the canal, even if Mariko could not see it. His eyes might have lost their previous gleam, but they still communicated the willpower of a man who had to keep working alone to make a living for a long while yet.

It was, of course, nothing more than a sentimental image that popped reflexively into Mariko's mind. But even if the man transporting that blue-tarp-covered cargo, already out of view beyond a gentle bend in the canal, was not the way Mariko pictured him, there was someone, somewhere in this huge city who fit the picture in her head exactly. Mariko closed her eyes and imagined it. She wanted to photograph that person. She turned toward the phantom of the now-gone boat and snapped the shutter in her mind.

Mariko jumped as though remembering an appointment when she heard the vaguely plaintive sound of the five-o'clock bell from the nearby school. She started the prep work in the windowless north room she used as an office. It contained a simple bookcase she had assembled herself and a wooden worktable painted dark brown. A desktop computer sat on the table.

Mariko pulled the eight-gigabyte flash memory card out of the camera and inserted it into the computer's card reader. Eight gigabytes could hold several thousand photographs' worth of data; the world was witnessing amazing technological advances. The data from her Miyazaki job and from the Tokyo Tower collapse took only a few seconds to download into the computer.

Mariko's heart raced, but not from a feeling of sunny anticipation. There was fear there, too, of opening up a Pandora's box that ought to be left shut, and peering into it. The thought of the scenes that the highly specialized mechanical eye had caught as she instinctively snapped the shutter, which she had not been able to see herself through the viewfinder then, created a sense of foreboding in her.

Small square thumbnails of the photographs began to appear, filling the screen. She clicked on one, enlarging the photograph so that the image filled the entire screen. It was an ordinary photograph, taken immediately after Tokyo Tower had started to collapse. The tower, beneath a clear blue sky, looked like it was falling toward the viewer, but anyone could take a picture like this if they found the right angle. Toward the bottom of the photograph, however, the almost painful-looking shorn legs of the tower after the blast were clearly visible.

She opened the next few pictures—the same shot over and over, as was to be expected, since she'd had the camera in continuous high-speed shooting mode. She scrolled through a lot of frames, moving forward to later data. The tower's tilt grew, and with it the visual impact of something huge suddenly snapping at the root and pitching inexorably over, right onto the viewer. The blue sky was visible through the ruddy orange lattice of the metal frame which seemed to cover the heavens, giving the photographs the look of an abstract painting made up of geometric patterns.

The visual impact would probably be missing had the shots been from the side in a safer position. As she moved through the photographs, the feeling of dread created by a steel structure weighing 4,200 tons falling directly onto the viewer was captured in an angle that heightened the immediacy. Looking at these pictures, anyone unaware of what had happened would assume the photographer had died shortly afterward. And indeed, Mariko's brush with death had been too close.

What kind of guts, what kind of foolhardiness, was needed to take these kinds of photos? Her mind had been blank. Her body had moved instinctively as she snapped the shutter. It was perhaps an instinct that you acquired naturally after years of earning your living as a professional photographer looking for that scandalous shot, that decisive moment in a scene.

She scrolled further now and clicked the mouse to open another picture. She suddenly put her hand to her mouth.

Gasping, she froze.

In the frame was a small child, falling from the observation deck. A girl plunging head first, her eyes wide with fear. She was wading through the air, her arms out feebly like she was in amniotic fluid. No more than five or six years old. She was wearing a denim skirt with a cute frilled hem. A drawing of a white rabbit on her t-shirt, with the letters "NONT..." visible, but cut off. She'd lost her right shoe. She'd also lost her sock on that foot, but the yellow sock on her left foot was still hanging on, just barely, to her toes. The rush of air during the fall must have pulled them off.

The speed of the collapse was very fast so Mariko had shut off the image-stabilizing function in the middle of taking the photographs, relying instead on her own ability. She'd set the shutter speed to 1/800 of a second, giving priority to the focus motor, and kept snapping the shutter. This was all while a massive steel structure was falling directly onto her from a height of around a hundred meters at that point.

And among her pictures was a clear image of a falling child, motionless in mid-air. With perfect clarity, the indifferent mechanical eye of the camera captured the child's expression and even her bellybutton peeking out from under her t-shirt flapping from the wind blast. The Sanskrit word *ksana* had been imported into Japanese to describe a sliver of time; by some reckonings, it defined a span slightly shorter than 1/65th of a second, around 0.015 seconds. If so, then in the following "setsuna," this little girl had smashed into the ground and died.

The dread Mariko had felt had been of these pictures.

She scrolled through them and looked at them all. Her breathing became labored as she vowed not to look away. She looked at the photographs she had taken like a criminal atoning for a crime.

It was not just children floating through the air. There was an old man, a middle-aged woman, a thirtysomething man with his tie flapping in the wind as he floated, his honest face distorted by fear and the rushing air as he stared down his death, fated to come in the next hundredth of a second. There was also a young woman who had already fainted, spared the fear.

Of course it would be untrue to say that Mariko hadn't noticed the people falling from the sky. But it was only during the final thirty seconds of the tower's collapse that the two windows of the observation deck shattered under the groaning of the tilting structure. Mariko kept snapping the shutter as long as her will held out, as she battled her own fear of death. By the time people started falling out of the tower, Mariko's conscious thoughts were edging on a kind of madness, taking picture after picture. She herself had been staring down death.

She got through all the data and then lay face down on her bed in the next room, and wept out loud. The tears flowed without end. She didn't really know who or what the tears were for. She was not crying out of fear of what had happened, but rather out of relief at having survived that moment of fear. She experienced vicariously the fear of the people as they fell, and her sobs were for the horrible end they met in the next instant. They were tears of anger, and of commemoration for the people whom she had captured floating in mid-air.

People young and old, lives of regret, lives of indecision and loss, lives of quiet desperation, people in the prime of their life, people who had perhaps had a date that would have been the best time of their lives, that very night. People who would never have thought that their decision to visit Tokyo Tower that day would turn out to be fatal.

All of these people and lives were captured in the split seconds Mariko had snapped the shutter, freezing them in mid-air, leaving their final signature in each frame, only to be crushed like insects moments later under the impact of a collision that would render them unrecognizable.

These photographs were the "signature of death" left behind by the people who perished in the collapse of Tokyo Tower.

Mariko had never seen such gut-wrenching photographs. And so many in one place. For a while she had trouble believing she was the one who had taken them. Indeed, she didn't want to.

The tragedy was not her fault; she felt the need to reconfirm the obvious. But she had been there and had recorded the split-second personal tragedies as their sole witness.

The fear rose up every time the event came to mind, and when the tears dried she was overcome with nausea. She ran to the bathroom many times to vomit. Amid the acrid stench of her stomach bile, she crouched and thought, *What am I going to do with those pictures?*

6—Not Available

Mariko sat in one of the three reception rooms on the fifth floor of the headquarters of Koshunsha, Japan's largest publishing company. Across from her sat Kohei Sendo, the editor-in-chief of *In Focus,* the weekly magazine. The black leather couches elegantly creased by years of use bespoke the privileged status of the room.

A calligraphy scroll hung on the wall behind the guest seat. The company's founder had been a master calligrapher, and the bold strokes of the inscription showed this. They formed an abstract shape which could be made out as a single meaning if you squinted your eyes: the character *tan,* meaning "liver" and, by extension, "courage."

It struck Mariko as an unusual thing to make into a scroll for display. Perhaps the founder had been a courageous man who found inspiration in the word as he made a name (and a fortune) for himself in the world. Mariko had never met him, of course.

She knew full well that the meeting was going to be important when she was ushered to this particular room. She had felt it the day before when she'd called the editor-in-chief in the early afternoon and succeeded in making an appointment for the very next day.

"I have pictures of Tokyo Tower getting blown up and falling over."

She wondered how many more times she would use this trump card, with other publishers. It all depended on the reaction of the gruff-looking man sitting in front of her. She had sat there in silence for about half an hour contemplating Sendo as he clicked on thumbnail after thumbnail of the photographs in the laptop Mariko had brought. He was totally absorbed by the continuous stills of the tower collapse as by a flipbook cartoon.

In Focus's only serious rival these days was *Japan Weekly*. The latter lacked the ability to strike fear into the hearts of celebrities and politicians the way *In Focus* did, but it could still pack a punch. That was why Sendo had been brought in to man the helm at *In Focus*. His uncanny ability to know exactly what the reading public wanted succeeded in pulling the magazine's circulation out of its previous slump and up to the current 300,000 a week.

It was still Sendo's job to bring together and finalize all the stories the various editors brought in to the Tuesday editors' meetings: what was going on the cover, who would be the nude model, what would be the first special report opposite the nude pictorial, and so on. The other members of the editorial staff had unspoken confidence in his near-supernatural abilities. The publishing business was seeing nearly perfect alignment in dropping circulations, but *In Focus*'s ability to post consistently high numbers was proof of Sendo's skill. The magazine might get bashed in the court of public opinion for running scoops that were in staggeringly bad taste, but survival was everything, and *In Focus* did more than survive.

Sendo broke the silence. "Hmm. This is stunning work, Mariko. But, honestly, it might not be a good fit for us."

Mariko smelled a lie. Or was this guy impervious to her trump card?

She spoke in no uncertain terms. "Why? I've seen all the pictures of the Tokyo Tower bombing that have been published in the past two weeks, and none of them even come close to these. Your rival has stooped to running amateurs' blurry, distant cell-phone photos opposite their nude spreads. You're looking at the only pictures you'll find on our planet that are this clear and this close!"

"All right, all right. Don't get so excited, Mariko."

"Don't tell me not to get excited. Do you have any idea what I went through to get these pictures? One false move and I'd be among the victims being memorialized right now. This was one of my nine lives, Mr. Sendo, so take another look at the pictures. These aren't just scandal shots of the latest starlet like the last job."

Sendo sat back in the deep sofa and listened to Mariko. Mariko was the only one of Koshunsha's forty-five photographers who could argue with Sendo this way, as an equal. Perhaps because of the eight years since she had signed on—a surprisingly long time considering how young she was—she'd never called him "editor-in-chief," but only by name, and it had stuck. She would never have shown it, but she actually had quite a soft spot for him.

"Those pictures of that actress were first-rate. We just got the first run."

Sendo opened up the latest issue to the page with Mariko's shots of the scandal and laid it on the black wood table.

The shots Mariko had taken on JAL flight 1890 were there, opposite the sealed pages containing the nude pictorial of the latest top-heavy bikini model.

A man with long hair and sunglasses and a woman also hiding half her face with huge sunglasses were sitting in the first-class cabin with looks of horror on their faces after some random person had sprung up out of nowhere right as they were about to land. They probably thought the plane was being hijacked. It was a natural reaction, considering the fact that a man wielding some kind of weapon had practically attacked them right before landing, after everyone on the plane, including the flight attendants, had put their seatbelts on. Of course the "weapon" in this case had been a high-performance digital SLR camera.

The issue would hit the bookstores and convenience stores the next day, and people throughout Japan would have their lurid imaginations prodded by the headline ("THIS IS WHY SHE CAN'T KICK HER DIVORCE HABIT: SUMMER FLINGS THAT ONLY *IN FOCUS* KNOWS ABOUT!"). Mariko thought to herself, *Must be rough being a celebrity,* as though she'd had nothing to do with it.

But Sendo, a genius at manipulating the general public's curiosity, just shrugged at Mariko's photographs of the Tokyo Tower attack.

"People are going to be talking about the Tokyo Tower attack for months. The police seemed to have no idea who did it at the last presser."

"I was there, too. Iwagami, the head of Public Security, he acts like he's all business, but he's about as sly as they come. He announces that they don't know who did it or why but that the explosive used in the attack was 'sodium chlorate.' Just that one little tidbit of information, right? And to a man the media's like, 'Sodium chlorate? What's that?' And they start researching it."

Mariko felt a hook in the words "sodium chlorate" and was drawn into Sendo's explanation.

"Well what is sodium...whatever?"

"See? Everyone has the exact same reaction. I looked it up right away. Sodium chlorate is a herbicide and also happens to be an important ingredient if you're making a homemade bomb. It's one of the materials you find in one of those manuals for terrorists when you're making a bomb using only commercially available materials. Mariko, have you ever heard of *The Ticking Time Bomb*?"

"Sure, a bomb that has some kind of timer."

"Yeah, but in this case *The Ticking Time Bomb* is a bomb-making manual for terrorists that was distributed by the organization behind the corporate bombings of the mid-seventies. We've looked all over the Internet and even put our crack team of researchers on it, but we've come up cold so far."

"Why would you even *want* a copy of it? Are you planning on building your own bomb to negotiate a higher salary or something?"

"Mariko, I like your sense of humor, but no. I don't need anything like that. I already make quite a bit."

"Oh, well, excuse me. It must be nice, but I wouldn't know, since I'm a contract photographer and barely manage to scrape by."

Sendo was a quick thinker and ignored Mariko's wise-cracking.

"So anyway, everyone's looking for this thing, and they all wind up at the same place: might not the same people behind those corporate bombings in the seventies—one East Asia Front for the Defeat of Japanese Imperialism—be responsible for the Tokyo Tower attack?"

Mariko hadn't given any real thought as to who could be behind the attack. To her, it had been more like the devastating earthquake and tsunami, or some kind of natural disaster, because what she had witnessed and experienced was the "natural"—i.e., physical—collapse of the tower.

Since the bombing, Sendo had been on the hunt for a more intellectual approach to the event, possibly because there had been such a dearth of high-impact visuals, and collected a stack of documents researching every possible angle.

"I looked into the past of Iwagami, the head of Public Security and deputy commander of the special investigation, and it turns out that he graduated from Tokyo University and worked his way up through the ranks on a career path in the Bureau. In other words, a real dyed-in-the-wool Public Security man. So I've spent the past two weeks wondering why on earth a guy from Public Security which was put through the ringer in a big way during the corporate bombings would want to pull out a card that hints at those bombings."

"What do you mean by a card that hints at those bombings?"

"Well, he didn't come right out and say 'the corporate bombing attacks of 1974 to 1975,' but the first thing you're going to find if you research sodium chlorate on the web is the East Asia Front for the Defeat of Japanese Imperialism, and I'm wondering, is this a trap Iwagami laid for the media? Is it a sign that they're pursuing this as a serious possibility? Or maybe they have no idea so they're just buying time?"

"Wow. I guess if anyone was going to get that much out of that press conference, it would be you." She wasn't kidding. She was impressed.

"Flattery will get you nowhere. I'm not interested in figuring out what Iwagami's real intentions are, though. I don't care if we fall for his trap and run a headline like 'TOKYO TOWER BOMBING—PHANTOM OF 70S CORPORATE ATTACKS?' As long as we move product, I'm happy. But just as I expected, the media narrative is now all about that, which makes sense, because there's only one answer to the riddle Iwagami posed. And that's why I want another angle on this thing."

Mariko's enthusiasm and excitement over the pictures she'd taken of the Tokyo Tower bombing, which had waxed since the previous day, began to wane. "Uh, it's up to you what direction you want to approach the report from, but this is a weekly pictorial magazine, so you're going to need powerful images of the bombing, right? Are you saying you don't need these pictures—which I risked my life to take, I might add—even though all you've got are cell-phone pictures or aerial shots taken after the fact? I mean look, it's no skin off my nose. I don't only work for you. You just happen to be the first place I brought the pictures, but if you say you don't want them, then I've got plenty of other places I can take them."

"Mariko." Sendo leaned forward and turned towards her. Mariko felt pushed back. She leaned back into the sofa. Sendo gave her a crafty look, like he was scrutinizing her. She had to watch out when Sendo had that look in his eyes. They were the eyes of a hyena. Maybe the eyes she had, too. But the years had given Sendo a canny sixth sense.

He peered into her eyes for a few seconds, then finally said, "There's more pictures."

Mariko felt the blood rush away from her head. He had seen right through her.

Two days before, Mariko had gone through all the pictures and discovered the "signature of death" photographs of the victims she'd taken when she'd switched to high-speed mode right before she was about to be crushed by the falling structure. The shock had caused her to pace her apartment the entire previous day like a bear in a cage. She couldn't sell those pictures for money. She couldn't do that to the families of the victims. But she also had a feeling she wouldn't be allowed to just bury all the pictures in a corner of her mind and forget them. She spent the day going back and forth on it and in the end chose a compromise: she would take all the pictures except the "signature of death" ones to Sendo.

"These are amazing pictures, Mariko. But they're Pulitzer-type material. Our publication is interested in more, how shall I put it, something a bit more..."

Sendo's eyes glowed with an inhuman light. *Like the Devil.* The thought came to Mariko in a flash. She knew exactly what he was trying to say. Her heart raced. *Don't finish that sentence,* she prayed. *I'll go now, just don't say anything else.*

As she wished that, Sendo whispered, "Didn't you take any pictures of people? You know, like falling out of the windows?"

Her knees started to shake, and she covered her face with her hands and wept.

7—Parking Citation

"Pulitzer"? Does he think he can treat a grown woman like a child? Mariko shivered as she recalled Sendo's last words and the expression on his face.

Ignoring Mariko crying like a little girl on the sofa, Sendo had said, "Mariko, if you have any pictures of people falling through the air, I'll buy them for this."

Mariko had looked up through the fingers covering her face and seen Sendo opening his left hand with a sly smile. Five extended fingers. Five hundred thousand yen.

How on earth did he expect to publish pictures of people falling to their death in this day and age, what with all the voluntary restrictions publishers placed on themselves because of victims' rights and the possibility of getting sued for defamation?

On the other hand, sitting in the office of a publisher she had visited to sell her pictures and bawling like a kid seemed, well, pretty childish. She had to be stronger. She had to survive.

Just then the phone rang. Her body went into fight mode. Where was she off to now? If she had to crash a celebrity bash, she was in a fix. The revealing party dress she had was at the cleaners. But it wasn't her cell phone that was ringing, so it couldn't be from the editorial department.

She went to the back room she used as an office and answered the phone.

"Um, hello. Is this the residence of Mariko Amo?"

"It is. This is Mariko Amo. With whom am I speaking?"

"Ah, good. I called a whole heap of times, but you were out, apparently."

The person on the line was speaking with a heavy provincial accent that had a warm, affable quality. But Mariko didn't let herself be taken in by the tone of the voice, not in this big city, where people seemed to get murdered on a daily basis. She kept her guard up as she listened to the stranger.

"I'm Detective Isogai, and I'm with the Atagoyama Precinct. I'm calling because I'd like to see if we could meet for a little chat sometime soon... Hello? Ms. Amo?"

What could the police want with me? Mariko thought. *Oh, maybe it's because my Cherokee got towed the day of the bombing. I had parked it on the street.* She was silent as she turned the various possibilities over in her mind.

She didn't think it was a particularly unfair outcome. Her car had gotten towed because she'd parked it in the street illegally the day of the Tokyo Tower attack. She had gone down to the Atagoyama parking lot to pick it up the previous day; naturally, she'd had to pay the astronomical charge for leaving the car in the lot for ten days.

The old guy manning the gate had been kind to her and told her, "You'll get the notification of parking violation and a complaint form in the mail from the Traffic Department. If there's anything you want to tell 'em, you just write it in there."

Apparently he wanted her to leave her complaints to the complaint form. When she got home and looked it up on the internet, it turned out that there were two cases in which explanations were accepted.

1. Vehicle in question is stolen and then abandoned.

2. Vehicle is abandoned due to natural disaster.

Mariko read this and wondered if her situation fell under the second case.

"Ms. Amo? You still there?"

The man's voice snapped her out of her reverie.

"Yes, sorry. I'm listening."

"Oh good. I thought I'd lost you there for a second. To get back to what I was saying, I'm on the investigation of the Tokyo Tower bombing attack. If it isn't too much trouble, I sure would like to have you come down to the station."

Ah, okay, Mariko thought. Now she got what was going on. This man calling himself Isogai had such a gentle manner and such a strong northeastern accent that she automatically assumed he was just the neighborhood patrol officer. But no, he was a detective.

"Yeah, I was there when it happened, and took a lot of pictures. When the tower collapsed I suffered a minor fracture. I was in the hospital until three days ago."

"Yes, I am aware of that. That's why I'm calling."

Oh, right, Mariko thought. The police had done their homework. "Right. So, when and where do you want me to come?"

Detective Isogai gave her detailed directions to Atagoyama Station and asked her to be there at 2 p.m. He added that as a witness her appearance was of course voluntary. But there was a firmness in his affable manner of speaking that let her know that she couldn't refuse.

Just before hanging up Isogai said, "Those pictures you took right before the tower fell over—I wonder if I couldn't get you to let me take a look at a couple of them when you come."

He said "if," but she knew from the force in his voice that, again, he wouldn't take no for an answer.

The next day was Saturday. Mariko applied light makeup and left the house with plenty of time to meet Detective Isogai at the appointed time. With the photographs in a felt designer portfolio, she departed for Atagoyama Police Station by train from the Kita-Shinagawa subway station.

She passed through the entrance to the station building, which had an oddly bucolic ambience, and waited at the first-floor reception desk for around five minutes before a man came up to her. He was short, around Mariko's height, and wore black-framed glasses. His graying hair was held firmly in place with hair gel. He was wearing a plain gray suit, but if he'd been wearing a uniform, he would've looked exactly the way Mariko had imagined him on the phone: the honest neighborhood cop on duty in some police box somewhere. Mariko felt some nerves at her first-ever visit to a police station but relaxed on seeing Detective Isogai.

"Mariko Amo, right? I'm Detective Isogai. We talked on the phone."

"Yes, I'm Mariko Amo. Nice to meet you."

"I'm really sorry to drag you out here on a Saturday like this. I reckoned you'd be working on a regular weekday."

"Oh, don't worry about it. Photographers work irregular schedules, so the day of the week doesn't really matter, like it would for normal people. First, though, will an hour be enough for our meeting today? Since I was going to be out this way anyway, I made arrangements to meet with someone after this."

"Oh, that won't be a problem. This shouldn't take all that much time. By the way, you live at 1-chome Higashi Shinagawa?"

The detective sure talked a lot. And he didn't call it Tennozu Isle, either, Mariko noted. But more than that, she got the sense that he was feeling her out through the casual conversation. Mariko felt that it would be a mistake to underestimate this Detective Isogai character. She reached this conclusion looking at the man standing before her with her photographer's eye.

Isogai took Mariko up to the fourth floor on the elevator and led her into a small, plain meeting room.

"Please, have a seat. Okay, let's get right down to business, shall we? Let me start by asking, why were you there that day? At 3:30 p.m. on the twenty-sixth of August."

No small talk. Mariko wondered if cutting right to the chase was Detective Isogai's style. Or maybe all detectives were that way?

"As you already know, I'm a photographer, and I was on my way home from a meeting at Koshunsha, the publishing company, that day. I drove there, and just as I was turning left at the Iikura intersection on Sakurada Street, I heard this huge explosion."

"But if you live in Higashi Shinagawa, wouldn't it be quicker to keep going straight on Sakurada Street and turn left at Fudanotsuji? No point turning onto a much smaller street at Tokyo Tower, is there?"

Mariko wondered why she had turned there. She couldn't think of any particular reason. "That's true. There's no reason, really. I just like driving the backstreets of Tokyo, I guess, seeing new places, discovering new things. I think I had planned on cutting across to Daimon Street that day. Maybe it's because I'm a photographer."

"I suppose that makes you a bit of an artist. So what did you do when Tokyo Tower blew up?"

"I started taking pictures."

"Wasn't that kind of risky? Didn't you worry about the danger? You did get hurt, after all."

"Are you telling me I shouldn't have been taking pictures?"

"Not at all, not at all. I'm sorry if it sounded that way. I'm just saying that out of concern."

Mariko giggled. It was hard to pin Detective Isogai down, but there was something likable about him. *If he's got a family, he's definitely got a daughter,* Mariko thought. She hadn't brought her camera today, but she wanted to photograph Detective Isogai sometime if she ever got the chance.

"My main object today, though, is to take a look at the pictures you took, if it's not a problem."

"I have them right here." Mariko had brought all the photographs for the police. Whether to show them the photographs or not was up to her—she was under no obligation. But she felt that she should. There was also a part of her that wanted to show all the pictures, including the ones she hadn't shown Sendo, to a neutral observer, and hear an objective opinion about them. She had gotten a full set of high-quality prints done at Epson in Shinjuku, which she always used.

"Thanks," Isogai said as Mariko pulled out a thick sheaf of prints from the portfolio she had placed on the table and began showing them to him one at a time. She watched his expression. She wondered how it would change when she got to the "signature of death" pictures, but contrary to her expectations his expression stayed the same. It took about ten minutes to show him all the photographs.

"Those are some mighty powerful images, all right," Isogai muttered, looking up at the ceiling. His right hand moved as if to grab a cigarette and rose in the air for a moment. Perhaps he'd quit smoking just recently. Government buildings had become no smoking several years before when the Health Promotion Law was enacted.

Old movies always showed detectives and reporters enveloped in a cloud of smoke at their workplaces. *The world sure has changed,* Mariko thought. Even Sendo, who used to smoke like a chimney, never smoked anymore.

"Would it be possible for me to keep these for a while?"

"Actually, those are the only prints I've got. I have to shop them around to publishers and TV stations. It's how I make my living."

"Your living?" Isogai looked at her like she had just arrived from another planet.

"They'll be published in magazines."

"Even the ones of...people falling?"

Yep, just like she thought. Everyone thought the same thing. She thought it herself. This was probably going to cast a shadow on her life for a while yet.

"I don't think Criminal Identification will have any need of these photographs, from what I can tell, so don't worry about it for now. But since there are people in some of them, Forensics Investigation may want to see them. Do you think I could trouble you to come back if the need arises?"

"What's Forensics Investigation?"

"They investigate the human side of these things, the people involved."

"I see. Detective Isogai, can I ask you a question?"

"Be my guest."

"Where are you from?"

"Where am I from? Oh, you mean because of my accent?"

"I'm sorry, I don't mean it in a bad way. It's a very warm accent."

"Well, it's been more than thirty years since I left Aomori for the Police Academy in Tokyo, but I just can't seem to shake this accent. Folks ask me about it all the time."

"Is it because you like your hometown?"

"No, that wouldn't be enough to stop someone's accent from changing."

"So why is it?"

"Well, when you're a detective and part of your job is seeing things like dismembered corpses every day, you sometimes feel like you're getting worn down by it all. So I decided a long time back that I wouldn't lose my accent. That I'd keep it."

"That's a nice story."

Mariko got a fuzzy feeling from getting to know Detective Isogai better. It was hard to believe that this gray-haired man, with his thick Tsugaru accent and his little eyes blinking behind his glasses, worked in a section that specialized in homicides.

"Have you always done this job?"

"I've been here at Atagoyama Police Station for twelve years, working on homicide cases the whole time."

"It seems like someone's always getting murdered in the world today, so it must keep you busy."

"Busy ain't the word. Sometimes I feel like I just can't keep up. Murders these days aren't just some yakuza killing someone, or organized crime battles, or things like that. It's regular people who are doing all the killing. And dying. In one case I was on five years ago, which hasn't been solved yet, a fifteen-year-old kid just minding his own business got stabbed in the back. Talk about senseless."

"When was that?"

"Well, it was five years ago, on November 11, 2006, late at night. Mr. and Mrs. Sakamoto were his parents. Kid's name was Atsushi. He was in the ninth grade."

Atsushi Sakamoto—Mariko searched her memory. She'd had nothing to do with it, but she remembered a small piece in *In Focus*. "The Sakamotos were pretty well-off. They lived in a luxury apartment in Atagoyama. I remember reading about it in a magazine. The boy was murdered on the grounds of a shrine next to his high-rise, right?"

"Exactly. That's an upscale area, and I doubt your ordinary family could live there, without having quite a large income. The kid was found dead on the grounds of the shrine, which was in what you could call a blind-spot, just below the building."

"Did the investigation turn up any likely suspects?" As she said this, Mariko felt silly. She sounded like something out of a corny detective show.

"It's an old case, and it's unsolved, so I can't really talk a lot about it. Plus, I count that case as one of my failures."

"A failure?"

"Yep. There ain't nothing more frustrating for a detective than to *not* catch the bad guy and then have to fill out the forms every year, waiting for the case to be closed."

He was an honest man. Mariko wondered if she would have been happier if this guy had been her father. Detective Isogai had given her a glimpse of a past regret and indeed spoken to her about his painful failure at their first meeting. In a corner of her mind she felt that coming here to help with the investigation had been good for her, too.

"I'm sorry I took so much of your time today."

"Yeah, I've got somewhere I've got to be next, so I'll be going."

After her meeting with Sendo, Mariko had given a lot of thought to the "signature of death" photos and decided not to show them to the media. She would only shop around the other photos of the disaster.

All she had to say on the phone was "on-location photographs of the tower collapsing" and everyone jumped at the chance. "I'll come into the office on Saturday, even Sunday, just let me see them before you show them to anyone else!" they all said. Which was why Mariko was so busy today.

Before getting up, Isogai handed Mariko an envelope containing a five-thousand-yen note. He called it "witness compensation" and had her sign something. Mariko was enjoying her first time being a witness, and as she was about to get up from the metal folding chair and leave the room, Detective Isogai called to her from behind. When he'd phoned her and asked her to bring the pictures, he'd only gotten to the heart of the matter at the end of the conversation as though it were an afterthought. The way he was calling to her now, too, made her think, *This guy's like Columbo from the old TV series.*

"Ms. Amo, if I may. About your car, I'll put a word in with the Traffic Department to cancel your ticket. Go down to the Traffic Department here in the station and they'll pay you back the parking fee you were charged. You've got the receipt?"

Mariko jumped for joy inside. Were all detectives so nice, or was it just this Isogai, who was hard to pin down, who was so affable? She vowed again to get him to let her photograph him. More than the money, she was glad that at least one nuisance in her life had gotten taken care of. She bade Detective Isogai a polite farewell and left Atagoyama Police Station.

8—Legwork

The large hall on the fifth floor of Atagoyama Police Station had been converted into a special investigation headquarters. The hall was hot and stuffy from the large number of investigators in it, which was fitting for the striking sign hanging next to the door.

All the main operations of the criminal investigation were located at Atagoyama Station. These included the most important activities of collecting information from anyone who might have seen someone placing the bombs or checking the area out beforehand, as well as reviewing all security camera footage on the street, in train stations, and in convenience stores in the area—efforts to bring to light the crime using evidence collected through good old-fashioned legwork.

For Yoshida, the lead investigator in the canvassing work, losing to Onodera, a Public Security officer, was not an option.

"I couldn't give a rat's ass what Public Security's thinking, but don't you guys get suckered by all this talk of radicals on the news. We don't need any cluckers! Got it?"

Isogai saw the younger detectives' quizzical looks, and explained, "'Cluckers' is what we used to call it when detectives would jump at the first thing they saw when canvassing an area, kicking up a dust cloud like a bunch of chickens in a coop. You'll wind up on a spit if you do that!"

Isogai made a gesture as if grilling a chicken, and a few of the younger detectives laughed.

"By the way, Inspector Yoshida, we've been going through the Princess Hotel, right near the site, and there are a few foreign guests who have already left the country, so it might take some time to follow up on them."

"Got it, Isogai. How many rooms are there in the hotel with a possible line of sight?"

"Two-hundred and forty of the hotel's four-hundred and twenty rooms are on the side facing Tokyo Tower. The view is blocked up to the sixth floor, making it impossible to see the detonation point from those rooms. Of the foreign nationals staying in the hotel on the day of the attack, fifty-two have left the country. We're getting some help from the Foreign Ministry on this one."

"It wasn't the Invisible Man who did this, so there's got to be someone who saw whoever did it. Find them!" Yoshida raised his fat, burly fingers in the air in front of Isogai, as though in prayer. "And quit calling me 'inspector.' We're beyond that."

Isogai gave Yoshida a kind look from behind his thick, black-framed glasses and bowed his head. Yoshida knew that behind the provincial's kindly demeanor there lay a detective's talent for sharp-eyed observation. Isogai's face was as forgiving as his character was tenacious, and it was his kindly appearance that got witnesses talking.

That evening, Yoshida stopped by Zojoji Temple where the bodies of the deceased were laid out under dozens of tents set up on the temple grounds for families to confirm their identities. The work of identifying the mangled and disfigured corpses just next to the colossal red steel structure which had knocked over part of the cemetery and cast its shadow over the main temple hall reminded Yoshida of the scene on Mount Osutaka after the Japan Air Lines crash there.

The number of victims in the attack was less than the 520 who died in that plane crash, but 402 innocent people, who just happened to pick Tokyo Tower for their last outing of the summer, had lost their lives. Atagoyama Station was straining to deal with finding a place for the bodies and getting enough coffins. All the wholesalers in Tokyo couldn't provide enough coffins, so they got stupa and coffin makers in Hinodemachi in Nishi Tama County to sell them unfinished wood planks which were then delivered to the temple where they were assembled.

Something in the rows and rows of simple, unpainted wooden boxes the length of a man lined up beneath the tents, the white mist produced by the dry ice inside spilling out through cracks in the lids, sent a shiver up Yoshida's spine, in spite of the muggy heat of the last days of summer. The peculiar stench that filled the temple grounds mixed with the sobbing here and there of the bereaved caused a lump to form in Yoshida's throat.

Late that night, Yoshida began getting reports from the Community Safety Department, which had begun interviewing the families of the deceased. He felt his eyes well again on thinking of the sheer number of victims who had lost their lives in the collapse of Tokyo Tower, and their families. There was no way he could lift his head again or call himself a detective if they didn't catch the people who had caused such an enormous loss of life.

They lacked even a single clue, though. *But isn't that the way it always is?* Yoshida thought to himself. *In the end, we've always smoked out that invisible adversary and brought him to justice.*

Yoshida managed to hold back the tears and opened his eyes a crack, seeking an image of the culprits in the void. Could it be a terrorist organization acting out of an ideological hatred of society, like Public Security insisted rather desperately? No, that couldn't be it. The intuition he'd gained from his long years as a detective was nudging him away, however foggily, from the direction the investigation was currently taking.

"Isogai, I'm really counting on you in this investigation," Yoshida, who'd changed into a sweatshirt, said to Isogai, who was getting ready to turn in, too.

Isogai had just placed his thick glasses next to his pillow. He turned towards Yoshida with his kindly face, which was so un-detective-like. "I don't intend to let you down," Isogai said gently, blinking his small eyes.

"We may have a lot of people working on this case, but only a handful of them are worth anything. How many of these snoring louts do you think have the old-school stubbornness to catch whoever's behind this?"

"You're right. Even here at Atagoyama Station, I've seen people make detective from police box duty. It's not like it used to be."

"They call themselves detectives, but inside they're just pencil-pushing bureaucrats. The only detective I know in this station who's a real veteran is you, Isogai."

"Well, it's an honor to hear that from you, sir, since you've taught me so much, but..."

"But what?"

"Inspector Yoshida?"

"What? Why so formal?"

"Inspector Yoshida, the Public Security Bureau is making a fuss about right-wing radicals, left-wing radicals, even foreign elements, but what's your sixth sense telling you on this one?"

"You know, my sixth sense has been kind of quiet on this one. This old bloodhound can't seem to pick up a scent. What do you think?"

"Me? Well, I lack your sixth sense, because you can't have preconceived ideas when you're out doing the legwork, but what I'd really like is to talk to the crew reviewing security camera footage and to get some image, no matter how blurry, of what this guy, or guys, look like, as soon as possible."

"I hope we get off to a good start. This hall's still fresh, but before too long it's going to start smelling so bad from all the guys in here that it'll be impossible to sleep."

"But by that time we'll be so exhausted that we probably won't care about the smell."

"Good point," Yoshida said, chuckling.

Yoshida and Isogai lay down on their adjacent cots and pulled up the covers. Yoshida closed his eyes and fell asleep right away. As he was drifting off, he was chasing the bad guy in his subconscious. He was looking back at Yoshida, laughing confidently.

9—Forensics Lab

November 12th, 8:30 a.m. Sixteenth-floor meeting room at the Metropolitan Police Headquarters—

It was the scheduled time for Kazushige Kusanagi, a lab technician in the Metropolitan Police's forensics lab, to report to the officers in charge—everyone ranked special investigation squad leader and higher—on the results of the analysis of the explosions in the leg structures of Tokyo Tower.

A minor forensics technician didn't ordinarily report analysis results directly to the detectives. Early that morning Kusanagi had reported the results to the head of Criminal Identification, who had ordered his next-in-command to present the report to the higher-ups in Criminal Investigation, which he tried to do but had to give up on because the content of the report was too abstruse. This particular analysis was so important for profiling the perpetrators that an exception was made, and Kusanagi was asked to present the report himself.

The Metropolitan Police Forensics Research Laboratory—known simply as the "forensics lab"—provided backup for investigations together with the Criminal Identification Unit. In addition to conventional methodologies, the forensics lab had sent technicians to the FBI's Behavioral Science Unit and to Scotland Yard to get hands-on training in the fundamentals of profiling, with the goal of improving the level of Japan's forensic science.

Forensics was divided narrowly into the First and Second Forensic Medicine Units, a Physical Evidence Unit, a Document Analysis Unit, and the First and Second Chemical Analysis Units. The unit Kusanagi belonged to specialized in explosives within the Second Chemical Analysis Unit. He had previously worked as a researcher in a private security firm. He was qualified to be a policeman on paper only, as it were, which made him slightly unusual. He had entered the force from the private sector after 2009 as the need for ever greater levels of expertise in criminal analysis grew in Japan, which was becoming a much more diverse society.

Kusanagi poured water from a bottle into his glass and took a sip. Arriving at the conference room with his white lab coat and water bottle, he looked more like a young college professor about to give a lecture. The investigators, who would be the students in today's lecture on the science of explosives, felt irritation at Kusanagi's stately pace, which was so unlike their own perpetual rushing. But they kept it inside and waited for the presentation to start.

"The explosive that was used is a mixture of sodium chlorate, as was announced at the press conference. I was only three years old at the time, but I believe the phrase used for this back then was 'the weed-killer bomb.' It was the main ingredient in the bombs used in the corporate bombings of 1974, as well as in the terror attack on the Hokkaido Prefectural Capitol Building, in which fire extinguishers were used as bombs.

"However, due to the high incidence of cases in which commercially available herbicides were being used in homemade bombs, hydrated carbonates and similar substances now have to make up more than half of any given mixture in order to minimize any potential risks, which makes it pretty difficult to use sodium chlorate as the main ingredient in bombs that had the explosive yield seen in this attack. The other ingredients in the mixture, charcoal and sulfur, on the other hand, are very easy to obtain."

"So the attackers either got a hold of commercially available, Japanese-made weed killer and purified it themselves, or they obtained high-purity sodium chlorate from China or somewhere," Onodera said softly.

"That's the way it looks. Of course in China you can buy even more powerful explosives like potassium chlorate. But that would leave a paper trail. If the perpetrators did make the bomb using materials available in Japan, then they either used sodium chlorate or blasting powder. Blasting powder is a kind of gunpowder that can be mixed relatively easily using commercially available potassium nitrate, sodium chloride, and charcoal, but the resulting explosive yield would be minimal. Plastique can be made from vinyl in which potassium chloride and a softener have been mixed, but the only case of that ever being used was one small bomb that was set off in front of the El Al Building a long time ago. We've only just started collecting and analyzing the remains around Tokyo Tower, but there are already many very interesting things about this bombing."

"The power needed to knock down a structure that big must've been phenomenal, though," Isogai said, licking his pencil and waiting for the response, a little notebook in his hand like a punter calling odds at the track.

"As a matter of fact, judging from my examination of the range of variation in the impact layers caused by heat emission, I don't think that much explosive would have been needed to destroy a single steel pipe. All they needed to achieve their goal was less than one kilo for each detonation. These guys undoubtedly have a lot of expertise in the properties and handling of explosives. Just look at the method of detonation. These guys didn't merely set off bombs. A more accurate description would be that they turned the tower legs themselves into bombs."

"Mr. Kusanagi, we've got a joint investigation meeting at nine, so could you get to the point?" Kunugida, the head of Criminal Investigation Section One, asked impatiently.

"There were a total of six frame structures in the legs to which the explosive devices had to be attached. The four legs, which supported the 4,200-ton weight of the tower, were made up of three square steel pipes each, so to blow up one leg, the perpetrators had to set three devices. They filled each with their homemade bombs, which they then detonated either with a timer or with some kind of remote detonator.

"The hollow construction used for the tower's steel frame was probably ideal for the perpetrators. The principle used in this explosion is the same as sticking firecrackers inside a piece of bamboo and blowing it up. In other words, they carefully filled joints in the hollow square pipes with the explosive material, set the detonators, and placed a lid on the whole thing, thereby turning the leg structures themselves into bombs.

"So what happens after that? Well, we've all seen cartoons where one of the characters pulls the trigger on a gun and the barrel explodes, turning it into something that looks like a flower. *That's* what happens. There's an effect called 'confinement' in explosive dynamics: if you take an explosive force which would otherwise expand out in all directions and put it inside a sealed container, you can do things like propel a bullet in the infinite-diameter direction of the barrel with a very small amount of gunpowder. In this case, the terrorists essentially sealed the barrel of the gun out of which that bullet would be shot. And it was because they understood this principle so well that they were able to demolish the legs holding up the tower with so little explosive material. Not only that, but..."

Isogai swallowed. "But?"

Kusanagi calmly poured water into his glass and took a sip, keeping everyone in suspense. He appeared so amazed at the ingenuity of the method used in the explosion that he sounded like he was boasting about it to the detectives.

Onodera glowered at Kusanagi. *These damn scientists have a tendency to get so excited when announcing their inventions and test results that they forget whose side they're on. Why the hell is this guy praising the brilliance of enemies of the state? I'm going to have to tell the head of the forensics lab to make sure even outside hires undergo proper Public Security Bureau training...*

"So, not only that, but the terrorists also understand the principle of 'dead pressure.' Briefly stated, dead pressure is a phenomenon whereby an excessively tight seal causes outside pressure to cancel out the first motion of an explosion at the instant of ignition. That's why they placed the explosives in parts of the tower's leg structures that were like joints and then put the lids on, making sure to leave plenty of room inside."

"Is that all?" Kunugida asked testily, looking at his watch.

"No. Now we get to the main point. The framework where the bombs were placed was blasted to smithereens, but luckily for us it was hollow, because we were able to collect material from inside the upper part of the pipes, above the blast points. Basically we made a special large collection brush and scrubbed the inside of the pipes like chimney sweeps. And what we found was tiny pieces of the detonators, which had been blown apart."

Kusanagi felt all eyes focused on him. Even Yoshida, who had been slumped over in a heap, raised his face and turned his penetrating gaze towards Kusanagi.

"Pieces of cell phones."

"What?" Everyone had the same reaction, but only Isogai voiced his aloud, in his unmistakable Tohoku accent, with its rising tone at the end.

"Cell phones. There were cell phones inside the detonator devices. We're still trying to figure out what they were used for, but it's hard to believe the terrorists accidentally left their cell phones inside the bombs. We believe there is a high likelihood that they were somehow related to activating the blasting fuses, which ignite the explosive material."

"You mean the blasting caps?" Isogai interrupted, trying to be helpful.

"No, blasting caps are different from blasting fuses. Blasting fuses have four main functions: setting initiation time, ensuring safety in terms of preventing ignition other than at the selected initiation time, making it possible to deactivate the safety mechanism, and acting as the initiation system for the explosive material.

"The fuse is the head of the bomb, so we might to a certain extent be able to profile the technical level of the community to which the perpetrators belonged by looking at what kind of fuses they used. We look at the precision and complexity of the fuses, and whether they were expensive or not. If they use some kind of complex, advanced system, we're probably dealing with a large criminal organization that has serious financial resources. We also look at any similarities with systems used by international terrorist organizations in the past.

"In this case, the terrorists chose the time when the tower would have the most visitors, so we can be sure that they either used a timer or a remote detonator. What's important, though, is how they ignited the explosive material. Theoretically, there exist four possibilities: some kind of impact, hydraulic pressure, electricity, or some kind of chemical. Hydraulic pressure and impact are unlikely. That leaves us with some kind of electrical system or a chemical reaction. We're still not sure. Typical electrical ignition systems ignite the material by using a battery to create a current and amplifying the current with a capacitor. In that case, they would attach a timer to the fuse and set the time for it to go off." Kusanagi sped through this explanation and then nervously clasped his hands before his chest and looked up at the ceiling.

Kunugida looked at his watch irritably. "What's the matter? We don't have time to waste analyzing just the bombs. Get to the point."

"We don't have any clues that would allow us to identify what kind of timer devices were used. We haven't even found any battery remains, which are usually relatively easy to find after a bomb explodes. The terrorist bombings in the seventies that I mentioned before used travel alarms for timers. That's not the case here, though. The problem with an analog watch is that you can't set it to a time later than twelve hours in the future. Of course, a digital timer or similar precision electronic device is a possibility, but that's not something a bunch of amateurs could just read a few books about and then build themselves. If we could prove that that's what they used, then we could be pretty sure that we're dealing with a well-funded, professional operation. Either way, I'm going to work on finding and analyzing any remains that will allow us to identify the fuses as fast as possible."

"What do we know about how they got a hold of the sodium chlorate that was used in the bombs?" Yoshida asked, changing the direction of the discussion.

"We're still looking into that," said one of the leaders of the team that was investigating the provenance of the bombs and related devices. "We've been hitting all firearms dealers, chemical retailers, online chemical vendors, and so on, from every angle. We've submitted official information requests to Yahoo and

Amazon for online customer data and are getting help from the Community Safety Department's High-Tech Crime Prevention Center. It's a huge amount of data, though."

"A huge amount? Well, no shit. As detectives, our job is like looking for a lost grain of rice in the sand dunes of Tottori."

CHAPTER 2

10—The Nichinan Coast

5:05 a.m., August 15th, anniversary of the end of World War Two. Eleven days before the bombing of Tokyo Tower. A small bay fed by the fresh water of the Azusa River on Miyazaki Prefecture's Nichinan Coast, which extends north and south along the Pacific. Small waves lap the shore from the deep blue of the pre-dawn sea. A gentle breeze blows out from shore onto the water.

Yusuke Watanabe, director of Jiiku Christian Hospital, sat peacefully on the breakwater. He picked up a fat worm, its body twisting erratically.

"You're a live one, aren't you?" the doctor said to himself. "No wonder they say, 'tiny worm, big soul.' Sorry, buddy, but I'm going to have to send you to Nirvana for the benefit of my base human desires."

He pierced the body of the wriggling bait with a Hosoji Chinu No. 3 hook, raised his rod in a swift motion, and cast the line far out into the still-dark sea.

The sea and sky were both shrouded in a deep indigo darkness. A dark rosaceous red began to seep faintly into the layer of clouds above the Pacific horizon, auguring the inescapable arrival of dawn.

The previous night, Yusuke had found out on the internet that sunrise would be at 5:34 and had come to the beach alone to get in some pre-dawn fishing. At this hour he might still be able to catch one or two sea bass swimming in from Hyuga Bay before heading back out to sea before daybreak. The fish knew that this area was filled with plankton because it was where the water from the Azusa River, filled with nutrients from the mountains, mixed with the seawater.

The color of the sky changed imperceptibly as Yusuke was busy with his fishing. The horizon was blanketed in a layer of thin clouds typical of Miyazaki, but stars still shone above.

Yusuke liked coming to fish here at this hour. No matter how many years passed, his fishing skills never improved. He had made some fishing buddies, who always ribbed him for his meager catches, but he didn't care. He was happy when he felt at one with the sea, fishing at night or in the morning, watching the float bobbing up and down in the water.

Yusuke had worked at Jiiku Hospital for roughly two decades now and taken over as director from Kikue Iizuka when she'd passed away. The passionate sense of fairness he'd had since he was young—which had earned him the nickname Dr. Justice—had not faded even as he entered his fifth decade of life.

He was a first-rate OB/GYN specialist as well as a licensed surgeon. Over the years of his successful career he had gotten offers from other hospitals—a major one in Tokyo had offered him a mouth-watering package—but Yusuke liked Miyazaki. Living in the cramped conditions of a metropolis like Tokyo just didn't fit his character. He had picked up fishing as a hobby only in the past few years, but he found it to be an ideal pastime for relaxing from work, not only physically, but mentally as well.

Therewasalsoanotherreasonhedidn'tleaveMiyazaki.Itperhaps wasn't the most persuasive of reasons, but twenty years earlier, the previous director, Kikue Iizuka, had started a system called the Stork's Mailbox at Jiiku Hospital, where he'd started working at the time. A response to the growing problems of child abuse and child neglect which seemed to be a symptom of modern society, the system was designed to rescue newborns who had been abandoned by their parents. Even today, Yusuke clearly remembered the first child that was delivered to the Stork's Mailbox.

The newborn was found by the on-duty nurse that night, Manami Kotegawa, who at that time was still a junior nurse. The baby boy had been dropped in the Stork's Mailbox after having been severely abused; its body was covered in lacerations. Yusuke didn't know what the child was doing now. The last time he saw the boy was at a small party organized to celebrate his transfer to an orphanage in Tokyo. The boy had been extremely bright for a five year old and been growing into a very independent, mature child with handsome features and an inner strength that wasn't immediately obvious in his manner. To know him was to praise him. The more excitable among the hospital staff almost went into raptures over his intelligence. The phrase "pure genius" was heard.

Yusuke had saved the boy's life. Put that way, it seemed natural; that was his job as a doctor, after all. But he felt a sense of pride, too. Yusuke had not heard even rumors about what had become of the boy after that, and he wondered if the kid had successfully made his way in an unforgiving world, found happiness in life. Whenever he thought about the boy like this, he felt sure that he had not made a mistake in choosing this slower-paced life here, in the place he was from.

The Stork's Mailbox had saved the lives of thirty-six abandoned newborns over the ten years that it had been in operation, starting in 1991. It had been shut down about ten years ago, however, partly because other prefectures on the island of Kyushu had set up similar systems and the initial goal of their system had been fulfilled. The system also encountered a few problems after Kikue Iizuka had died and Yusuke had taken over.

One newborn who had been brought to the hospital after

being abused by its parents had died, unable to recover from its wounds. The hospital had not been at fault, but the fact was that it was impossible to save every infant that was brought in on the verge of death. Yoshio Iizuka, that first child, had been something of a miracle, in fact.

But popular opinion focused on the sensational, which always rose to the surface above facts. One opinion commonly heard was that the growing number of Stork's Mailbox-type systems led to and even encouraged abuse of newborns. Another held that such systems were no more than garbage dumps for parents who had abused their children to within inches of their lives and didn't know what to do with them. The media had turned their cannons on this single aspect, and public opinion was swayed. Yusuke Watanabe, the hospital's young director, had raised his arms in defeat in the face of this onslaught. There was nothing else he could do.

He thought of that first newborn. Yoshio Iizuka: he would never forget the name. The hospital prepared new family registers for the newborns who, as abandoned children, had none. The hospital also had to choose each child's name. Yoshio had been the first child, so they'd chosen that name, borrowing the Chinese character *ji* from the hospital's own for the first character. Yoshi-o: "caring man."

For the last name, the family court was petitioned and the surname of the hospital's director, Kikue Iizuka, was chosen, but only as a temporary measure in order to avoid overlapping family registers in case the child's parents appeared at a later date. It was a stopgap, and if a foster family were to take the child in, then he would get that family's last name and start his life anew from there.

Yoshio had contracted an infection and lingered on the edge of death for three weeks, but the boy's life force was extraordinarily strong. Just recalling it brought tears to Yusuke's eyes. The hundreds of knife-cuts all over the boy's body, seeping with dark-red blood, formed geometrical shapes, some of which had already formed scabs, indicating that the abuse had occurred in multiple sessions. For three weeks, Yoshio had been a plaything at the hands of the mother who had given him life. To Yusuke, it was the embodiment of evil.

The float suddenly disappeared below the surface. The tip of the rod tensed and the transparent line went taut. Yusuke was yanked out of his reverie and gripped his trusty rod forcefully as he started reeling in the line with his right hand. It was a big one, the first in a long time. He had to reel the fish in carefully to avoid pulling the hook out of its mouth. He wound the line tight, let the fish swim it out a bit, and then pulled it in a bit more.

This one's a fighter. This is what makes fishing so great.

Just then, Yusuke felt a blow to his side and a spreading sensation of heat that was less like pain than like someone pressing a hot *manju* bun against him. He turned and caught a glimpse in his peripheral vision of someone jumping away. He looked down and saw blood spurting out of his side.

He had been stabbed! *Here? On this peaceful beach?* was the first thing that passed through his head.

In the next instant his instincts as a doctor kicked in, and he began to act. He had to stop the bleeding but couldn't find anything to stanch the massive hemorrhaging, having come to the shore before dawn dressed only in a Hawaiian shirt.

He stood and walked unsteadily towards the rocky embankment, tossing his fishing rod aside. His car, which he had parked illegally on the road away from the embankment, was a fifteen-minute walk under normal circumstances. These were not normal circumstances. The blood dripping onto the ground formed faint reddish-black splotches which were quickly absorbed by the sand. Only the thick, oxidized hemoglobin remained on the surface like a red gel.

He began to feel lightheaded and had a sense of well-being. He was overcome with a slightly scary but nevertheless bluish feeling of peace, like the dizziness that comes from standing too quickly.

Yusuke fell to his knees in the sand and slumped forward. He heard footsteps in the sand. He could only move his head. He turned and looked up. A pair of white Converse high-tops with their round logo entered his field of vision. *Someone's here. I'm saved.* As soon as he thought that, the person wearing the converse squatted next to Yusuke and looked into his eyes. Yusuke saw the expressionless face of a young man.

"Help," he said weakly. But the young man simply watched Yusuke in silence, his face blank, as though he were watching the life seep out of an ant he had just stepped on. Yusuke felt his consciousness blanking. The moment before it did, Yusuke noticed something familiar about the young man's face. *He looks like... Yoshio...*

Yusuke's eyes closed.

The young man stood, looked around, and turned back. A clump of palm trees was growing a ways back from the shoreline. He walked towards it. He held a large survival knife in his left hand, covered in thick blood. When he reached the leafy shade of the palm trees, he made a gesture as though pushing back his hair, and with a curt nod signaled to another young man who was waiting there.

It was Yoshio Iizuka. He nodded, signaling his approval.

Yoshio and the young man had followed Yusuke Watanabe to the beach from his house in Shinonome, Nichinan City, on a motorcycle they had rented at a place for tourists. Yoshio had been on the lookout for anyone in the area, any other fishermen that might come, while monitoring the young man's stabbing of the doctor. He had a small video camera in his hand.

Day broke. He looked at his watch: it was 5:34, sunrise in Nichinan City, as Yusuke had checked. The sky was changing visibly now from the blue of night to the pink light of dawn. It was going to be a hot, bright day.

Yoshio looked out at the sea. In the distance he could see

Kojima, an island the guy at the rental shop had told him was inhabited by monkeys. Below that, between the rocky embankment and beach, Yusuke was lying on the sand, undoubtedly still breathing faintly. He could see the fishing rod Yusuke had been using, lying where it had fallen, small.

The transparent fishing line extended from the tip of the rod into the water. The sea bass Yusuke had hooked, one of the biggest fish he had caught in his short experience as a fisherman, pulled the line farther and farther out to sea.

11—Suicide Sites

After returning to Tokyo from Miyazaki, Yoshio Iizuka and the young man were having a "study session" at Yoshio's apartment in Minamisuna. Yoshio had been training the young man for the past year. Killing Yusuke Watanabe on the beach in Nichinan had been the final practical exam that Yoshio had ordered him to undergo, as well as being an initiation needed to lock the young man's mind for a particular purpose. The brainwashing of the youth was nearly complete now that he had passed the practical exam with flying colors.

The youth's name was Midori Sonoda. He had grown up in a wealthy family that lived on the outskirts of Denen Chofu, a well-heeled Tokyo neighborhood. He had an older brother. His mother was a homemaker and his father was an executive at a large corporation. Midori had an inferiority complex in regard to his brilliant brother and loathed the father who had planted the complex in him.

Midori was in ninth grade when he met Yoshio. It was spring, and Midori had been thinking about buying a bag of charcoal and committing suicide by carbon monoxide asphyxiation in his father's Mercedes Benz. Their first contact had been on an internet suicide site. Yoshio had been trawling shady websites for young people with suicidal tendencies as part of his preparations for a certain plan.

One day Yoshio noticed a thread started by someone writing under the name "midorin."

1 midorin: anyone know easy ways to kill yrslf? thx.

The thread was flooded with suggestions. Yoshio visited the site often every day to see what developed.

36 >35 ANONYMOUS: easiest way is charcoal. do it in an airtight place, like a car.
38 >35 Suicide Tutorial: cut the veins in your arm, get in a hot bath. heybangpresto, painless death.
46 >35 ANONYMOUS: jump. thats the only sure fire way.
48 >46 ANONYMOUS: yeah except if you jump from anything lower than the 10th floor you probably wont die. pick a tall building. have fun on yr one way trip.
75 >35 Suicide Tutorial: a book called the Complete Suicide Manual still avaiable on amazon.
86 >35 Suicide Maniac: jump in front of a train if you want to make it hell on your family.
88 >35 loser. come up with something yourself.
125 anonymous pink: hey why dont we make a party of it? We cld all go out with a bang. whaddya say gaiz?
126 anonymous green: im down set a date
127 anonymous yellow: this thread's gonna get 404'd by a mod. u can't organize that kind of shit here
135 meaningless: I have just opened my wrists. I'm getting in the bath now. I'll be on the other side in about an hour. Anyone want to meet me there? lol
145 ANONYMOUS: question for everyone: what's the point of dying?
146 anonymous green: stupid noob is stupid. you kill yourself because there is no meaning dumbass

The thread started to reach capacity after some few

hundred posts in this vein. Yoshio posted something to stir things up a bit.

> 325 YOSHIO: Fun fact: the only murder you can't get convicted for is murdering yourself, i.e. suicide. "Suicide" isn't a crime in the criminal code. So instead of sitting around and whining, why don't you losers get the fuck on with it?
> 326 ANONYMOUS: suicide isnt against the law?
> 327 Suicide Tutorial >YOSHIO: what your doing is aiding and abetting, herp derp
> 328 ANONYMOUS: herp, it's not aiding and abetting if you're saying it to a bunch of people you don't know.

Yoshio dropped the pretense and cut right to the chase.

> 329 YOSHIO: WANTED-SUICIDAL PEOPLE WHO WANT TO CONTRIBUTE TO SOCIETY BY DYING

Posts criticizing Yoshio's flooded the thread, but it was at this time that "midorin" became very interested in "YOSHIO." Contribute to society by dying?

> 330 YOSHIO: Listen, anonymous. How serious are you, really? If you're actually serious, just fucking kill yourselves instead of hanging out here bellyaching. But if you are going to do it, then why not take a bunch of people with you when you die, instead of dying alone? Make the world regret your death! I've got something major planned, so if you're interested, give me your names.
> 356 ANONYMOUS: but thats homicide not suicide amirite?
> 357 YOSHIO: You are indeed right. But you're going to die in the process too, so it's not like they're going to press charges. You might be a criminal, but dead men can't be tried! LOL
> 358 ANONYMOUS: your fucking crazy. why arent the mods calling the cops

Yoshio's posts were deleted by the moderators before long, but one of the youths had contacted Yoshio via the free email address he had posted.

For several days, midorin, a.k.a. Midori Sonoda, sat in his room thinking about what YOSHIO had posted. "I've got something major planned" had to be some kind of bad joke, he thought. But what if he were able to turn his feelings of resentment toward his parents and his older brother into something bigger, something more destructive? How awesome would that be? *So what if it's some anonymous person on the internet who lets me dream these dreams,* Midori concluded, and emailed the guy who went by the handle YOSHIO. He was nervous.

"Hi. I'm Midorin. I'm the one that was looking for a way to kill himself. I read the whole thread. What is this 'plan' you're talking about?"

Yoshio responded to Midorin's email.

"A massacre."

"Yeah, whatever."

"Why would I lie?"

"Srsly?"

"I swear to Satan lol"

Midori didn't believe YOSHIO, obviously. But after emailing back and forth a few times, Midori started to get the feeling that there was something very dark about the guy. And the sheer scale of that darkness was what attracted Midori. He first agreed to meet YOSHIO at a cafe in Akabanebashi a few months ago.

He was stunned on meeting Yoshio. His first impression was, *This guy kind of looks like me. Is it his face?* Midori had striking features since childhood, to the delight of the adults around him. He got "handsome young man" a lot, but it was just irritating background noise to him. Looking at Yoshio, however, he was filled with a narcissistic sense of looking into a mirror. He felt his cheeks flush.

At that first meeting Midori thought, *This guy has charisma.*

They began getting together every week. After a few meetings, Yoshio told Midori that he had a favor to ask him. He explained that in order for him to reveal everything to Midori, there were several stages that he would have to pass through, and that some stages would be passed through naturally, while others could be skipped. The mysterious way he put it was equal parts irking and intriguing, but Midori, who had no interest in living and was contemplating suicide, was curious.

More than anything, however, Midori simply liked Yoshio. Three months after they first met, Yoshio announced that they had "reached the next level."

"You and I must now become true companions." With this, Yoshio told Midori the story of his birth, hiding nothing. Midori was moved to tears by the story, which began with the Stork's Mailbox. Yoshio took off his shirt and pants and showed Midori the scars all over his body, and even let him touch them. Running his fingers over the patterns, Midori couldn't believe the cruelty of a mother who would cut such designs into a newborn's body for fun.

Midori wondered, *Is this why there's such darkness in Yoshio's heart? But he's forgiven the evil mother who did this to him! I can't hold a candle to this guy...* Starting that day Midori began feeling intensely drawn to Yoshio.

One day, at the cafe in Akabanebashi they had been to a few times already, Yoshio turned nonchalantly to Midori and said, "I killed someone when I was living in Tsurumaki Garden, an orphanage here in Akabanebashi."

Midori looked at Yoshio, stunned. Yoshio's black eyes, always cold and unsmiling, stared back at him. Midori got the feeling he wasn't lying.

"It was a kid I had seen at the Akabanebashi subway station a few times. He was about my age. I followed him home to find out where he lived and watched him every day for about a month.

I learned that he went jogging late at night every day, and that's when I started scripting a plan.

"I picked my fifteenth birthday to do it. I stabbed the kid to death with a knife. It didn't really mean anything. I just wanted to experience vicariously what it felt like to die."

Midori felt dizzy. He was paralyzed under Yoshio's penetrating gaze, totally immobilized.

There was something impersonal and distant in his confession, like he was describing someone else's actions. The confession had a hypnotizing effect, and as he listened Midori felt himself being overcome by a pleasant, drowsy feeling.

"You and I must become true companions," Yoshio said as Midori was in this lulled state. He had heard the words before, and they had an electric impact on him. He felt deep down inside that he did want to become Yoshio's "companion." He felt himself nodding, and begged, "Please make me your companion."

"To become my companion, you have to become my equal."

Midori was prepared to do anything asked of him. From the profoundest depths of his heart, he was ready to comply—even if Yoshio had said he wanted him sexually. But it was something else that Yoshio wanted.

"Just as I killed a man at fifteen years of age, so too are you to kill a man."

Midori's immediate reaction was to think of someone to kill. Yoshio told him it could be anyone. But who?

"Think of someone specific," Yoshio told him. "Play it out in your mind."

Midori tried thinking of someone in his class, someone he had grown distant from as his school attendance became more sporadic, but no one moved him. He thought of his homeroom teacher and tried to imagine killing him, but it didn't work. He thought some more, and pictured his own father. He imagined strangling him to death. It went better than expected. His father was the one who had planted the feeling of inferiority in him as a child, so he was able to use his anger as a kind of springboard.

"I could probably kill my dad," Midori said brightly.

Yoshio laughed raucously, momentarily attracting the attention of the old guy behind the well-worn counter, who looked up from his newspaper and over at the pair.

Yoshio ignored him and went on. "The cops would be all over you in a second if you did that." He thought for a while, and then looked up suddenly. "All right. I'll choose the victim, and you, Midori, will do the deed."

Because of Midori's already strong suicidal ideation, it was not that difficult to reorient the trajectory of that inward-pointing destructive tendency towards a more outwardly direction. Yoshio had to correct the path of the urge, reinforce it, give Midori a sense of purpose, make it his only desire. Once that was done, all it would take to lock Midori's mind into the new state was to have him actually commit a murder.

It didn't matter who Midori killed. What mattered was making him actually perform the heinous crime, thereby drawing a clear, bright line between him and the world he had inhabited until now. Nobody committed a crime like that and remained fully connected to society. Once he had completed the rite, the only person he could turn to would be Yoshio. The way of thinking that Yoshio had impressed on him would be locked into his mind through the force of reality, which Yoshio would reinforce by showing him the video of the training session as often as possible. There would be no escape then. Manipulating the teenage boy was child's play for Yoshio.

Thus was born the plan to kill a certain doctor.

Kikue Iizuka had been the director of Jiiku Hospital and the woman who had lent her own name and the name of her hospital to christen the first child delivered to the Stork's Mailbox. His family register read "Yoshio Iizuka." Whenever he said it to himself a cynical smile came to his face. An evil flame seemed to be flickering in a dark, damp place deep inside him. Old Iizuka had croaked long ago, though. If they were going to kill anyone, it would have to be the doctor on call that night...

Killing the man you owe your life to—the thought flashed through Yoshio's mind. That voice that controlled him whispered it directly into his brain. There was a Will that was in control of him and kept a close eye on him, making sure there was no room in him for even the slightest human thing to bloom in his soul. The murder of Yusuke Watanabe would have a twofold purpose: it would be hands-on training for Midori Sonoda, and at the same time it would be a rite through which the last trace of humanity in Yoshio would be eliminated.

Find every single sign of human weakness in your soul and root it out! Yoshio's words were seared into Midori through constant repetition, and after a few months were finally beginning to produce a psychological effect in Midori's mind. Midori started to feel like he understood why Yoshio had chosen the doctor for the "rite to become true companions."

Why Yusuke Watanabe? One reason was to select a prey sufficiently unrelated to Midori to prevent a police investigation from connecting the dots, making it possible for him to author the perfect crime. The second, and no less important, reason was that this was the doctor who had been on duty that night and through selfless effort had saved Yoshio when he was abandoned on the verge of death in the Stork's Mailbox.

Indeed, by bloodying his own hands, Midori also came to understand these reasons and took a decisive step away from his own humanity.

Midori would play a major role in Yoshio's plan, and for Midori, being able to help Yoshio was the greatest joy of his life.

"I'm going to knock down Tokyo Tower," Yoshio told him with a straight face. "The time for you to help has come. There's no real reason to blow Tokyo Tower up, though. It's just going to be a demonstration of my ability to massacre human scum."

What he didn't tell Midori was that he also wanted to erase his own memories of the Tokyo Tower observation deck. He had been forced to visit it on an outing by the teachers at the orphanage he had lived in until graduating from middle school.

Midori thought that Yoshio was kidding around when he first spoke about the plan, but there was no hesitation in Yoshio's eyes. *If we actually pull it off,* Midori thought, *that would be amazing. And if he really pulls it off, he'll no longer be a human being. He'll be a genuine monster.* A kind of piety began to color Midori's thoughts about Yoshio as though he were in the presence of a powerful deity. Doubting Yoshio seemed blasphemous and created feelings of guilt in him.

A few days later, on August 26th, Tokyo Tower was toppled in a spectacular explosion right before Midori's eyes. It was at that moment that Midori began to worship Yoshio like a god.

12—The Awakening

Police reports were filed for approximately 300 cases of child abuse in 2008. 315 children were victims of abuse for which no criminal charges were brought, including 37 children who died as a result of the abuse. 224 were cases of physical abuse, 86 were cases of sexual abuse, and 22 were cases of neglect. 30 percent of these cases involved children younger than five years of age. The biological mother was the abuser in 30 percent of cases, the biological father in 20.9, foster parents in 17.5, and the common-law father in 14.6, the rest being classified under "other." While not included in these statistics, ten cases were reported of newborn infants being abandoned immediately after birth, resulting in death.

Separately, 1,914 cases of child prostitution and child pornography were filed last year, involving 304 victims.

The figures described a rising curve in which each new peak was higher than the last. In a Police Department statement commenting on this trend, it was speculated that "the number of previously unreported cases coming to the surface is growing due to greater cooperation between the police, the Ministry of Health, Labor, and Welfare, and local governments, as well as due to proactive investigation of households where child abuse is suspected." (Source: Yomiuri Shimbun et al, February 21, 2008.)

Five years earlier, Saturday, November 11, 2006, early morning—

November 11th held a special meaning for Yoshio: it was the day he had been delivered to the Stork's Mailbox. He had chosen that day as his birthday. He had been cut up and abandoned on that day, so his biological date of birth had to be a few days before that, or maybe even more. Jiiku Hospital had estimated his actual date of birth based on how developed he was at that time. But for Yoshio, that had no meaning. The day he emerged from between some stranger's legs was irrelevant.

The Jiiku Hospital Stork's Mailbox was his beginning, and he had come into the world as Yoshio, the "caring man," named after the hospital. And on the fifteenth iteration of November 11th, that auspicious day, Yoshio killed for the first time in his life.

Yoshio began feeling an "itch" a few months before his birthday. The itching felt like that of a chick just about to hatch. Something or someone was whispering to Yoshio: *Enough is enough.* He began his preparations.

Yoshio Iizuka woke up at 4 a.m. that day to put into motion the plan he had woven together. Keigo Kunugi, his roommate in the two-person room, was conveniently going away to stay with relatives in Chiba Prefecture. Keigo left at 7 a.m., smiling as he said that he was going to visit some "distant relatives" who had had neither the will nor the financial wherewithal to take him in after he had lost his parents in a car accident, but remembered him every once in a while and did things for him by way of atonement. He was going to spend the night and be back at the orphanage on Sunday night.

Yoshio spent the day studying at the library and returned to the orphanage at eight in the evening. He ate dinner and then chatted with one of the teachers in the teachers' room afterwards. "Look what I borrowed from the library," he said, showing the teacher a copy of the compendium of Japanese laws that he had checked out. "It's pretty interesting."

Impressed, the young teacher laughed and told Yoshio he should think of becoming a lawyer when he grew up.

"Keigo's away tonight, so I'm going to read this until I go to bed," Yoshio said and headed up to his room on the second floor.

It was just after midnight that Yoshio left the orphanage again. As the site for the killing, he had picked the grounds of the shrine right next to the apartment building where his prey lived.

Yoshio jumped on the boy out of nowhere and stabbed him. He'd waited in the shadow of a big tree for the kid to walk past to make sure his face wouldn't be seen, just in case his attempt failed. His only regret was that he wouldn't be able to see the kid's face at the decisive moment.

The boy didn't scream. He just let out a low groan. He fell to his knees, so the knife Yoshio had planted in the boy right to the hilt slipped out of his hand. The boy fell in a twisted heap in the darkness of the shrine, the light reflected from various angles off of the apartment building obscured by the thick foliage of the trees.

Yoshio yanked the knife out. Fresh blood spurted out of the boy, creating a growing black stain in the dark-colored gym clothes with a barely discernible design that the boy was wearing. Not knowing whether the unexpected impact from behind him was pain or heat, he lay flat on the ground, his left arm forward, pushing his right hand back toward the wound but not reaching it, looking for all the world like he was swimming the crawl stroke.

The black blood gushing freely from his back passed through his clothes and dripped darkly on the dirt. Yoshio observed it expressionlessly for a bit and then squatted down next to the boy and looked into his face.

He was still breathing.

The faint light of the streetlamps dappled his shadowed face. Yoshio could only see his right eye because his victim was lying with his left cheek pressed into the ground. The boy had long eyelashes and deep-set eyes. *Eyes have a strange shape looked at sideways. They're like an open wound about to spill its contents,* Yoshio mused.

The eyes were vacant. Yoshio thought he could see the soul's light, illuminating the eyes from inside, slowly fading. And then all of a sudden it was gone. Yoshio was taken aback and fell back onto his rear.

It wasn't that he had witnessed the precise extinguishment of the boy's soul. At the edge of death, the boy's eyes had simply gradually shifted, reflecting a tiny bit of light. In the final instant, the pupils had dilated to full size, and the spark of life gone out.

The victim, a boy the same age as Yoshio, lived in a high-end apartment building called Atagoyama Intelligence Tower. He had seen him first in the Akabanebashi subway station and got a certain vibe from him. Ever since, Yoshio had followed the boy, looking for the right chance.

There was no "motive," in the sense of what a police report might describe as a motive. If the impetus had to be described, it was simply a desire to experience death vicariously by killing someone by way of experiment in his place. His own death was not allowed.

Yoshio had killed someone with his own hands. He felt no emotion, but he was overcome with a feeling like dizziness for a fleeting instant, as the soul left flesh.

When I was a child, back in Miyazaki...

One summer's day, thousands of ants swarmed over the sun-bleached ground, transporting a dead moth. The dense mass of tiny creatures worked together to carry their colossal prize. They spared no effort. Yoshio observed them for a minute. Then he massacred them all with his shoe, leaving no survivors.

His conscious mind left his body then, too. Somewhere high above, there was another self looking down on the massacre of the ants. The world surrounding him felt like a void, empty of all meaning.

This is the same feeling, Yoshio thought. *Imagine how much fun it would be to kill not just one person, but a whole swarm of them, crushing them like ants...*

It was at that moment that Yoshio first became consciously aware of his desire to carry out a mass killing.

Yoshio got back to the orphanage at around 2 a.m. after committing his first murder. He had to change out of his clothes, which had become soiled during the operation. He sat cross-legged on the *tatami* mat for a while under the pallid fluorescent light. Then he got up and took off his white open-necked shirt, which was flecked with blood. He opened the curtains and looked at his reflection in the window.

It was already the middle of November, but the weather was still mild and warm. He looked at his scarred body reflected against the black background of night beyond the window. As he regarded his vacant reflection, hanging there spectrally, Yoshio imagined the scene he had contemplated thousands of times before: his mother happily cutting up his body.

The person who loomed over his infant self like a demon, gleefully slitting his skin, lacked eyes or a nose, the blank expanse of the face having instead only a sliced-open gash of a red mouth smiling horrifically.

The woman who had borne Yoshio had probably been young.

As a human, she was completely broken. She undoubtedly

failed to feel any emotion for the living creature that emerged from her body, much less love. She made a casual incision with a razor blade into the soft, pink skin of the baby that she was planning on throwing into a dumpster anyway. A bright red line of blood appeared. *Neat,* she thought. She cut him vertically, she cut him horizontally, she drew red circles of blood. After a few days of fun, the infant's body was covered in patterns.

Thousands of scars covering his body, like an ever-present crucifix of hatred.

The markings were circles with flowers in them, playing-card diamonds, stars, and even overlapping L's and V's. The sutured parts of the scars, now dry, pulled and stretched repulsively, turning paler than the surrounding skin, and standing out in profile. They were unmistakably drawn in imitation of the Louis Vuitton logo.

Yoshio dropped his blood-stained clothes and shoes in a trash bag, ready to toss in the incinerator behind the orphanage, and got into bed at 3 a.m., as though nothing had happened.

"It" came just before dawn.

He woke from sleep, or perhaps he was still sleeping. Yoshio sat up in bed suddenly, assuming he must still be dreaming, because another Yoshio was still sleeping in the bed.

His upright self was watching a moving image of the boy's killing, like a dream seen through a diaphanous veil. His hand was pulling the survival knife out of the boy's back. In the next instant, a black gap in the shape of the knife blade shot out not blood but something like a black fog which rushed at Yoshio.

The black fog was alive. It buzzed like a swarm of insects which enveloped Yoshio's body in the blink of an eye, swallowing him whole.

After a while, the humming broke down into countless distinct voices, each whispering something different.

Each brief snippet oozed with malevolence and loathing.

kill them... tear them limb from limb... bury them... cut them... burn them to death... make them suffer... before they die... make them into mincemeat... strangle them... stab them... dismember them... their entrails... pull off their nails... make them suffer before you... electrocute them... make them taste... the pain... the torment... then boil them alive... bury them in cement... drop them into the river... cut off their heads... in slices... the cut-off ears...

It was a swirling storm made up of the memories of every murderer that ever was.

The other Yoshio lay inert on the bed. The Yoshio whose body was swarmed with flying insects writhed under the racking gale of intense malice. His organs swelled with the murky evil as he was filled head to toe with a feeling of overflowing hatred emerging from his guts.

The buzzing whispering of the black swarm now unified into a low, hoarse voice that was giving Yoshio some kind of order. Engulfed by the insects, he was once again pushed back down onto the bed face-up by an incredible force, fusing him with the dormant Yoshio. That instant, the insects disappeared.

Immediately, a powerful invisible force hit Yoshio and began flaying him. Bolts of intense pain shot through his body as the force peeled from Yoshio the false flesh of the model student, a role he'd played under circumstances that had been his lot for fifteen years until his independence. Next to him, the eyeless, noseless, empty face of his mother laughed out loud though its red gash of a mouth.

Living his life as a model student, beloved by all who knew him, since the day he was abandoned in the Stork's Mailbox and his life was saved at Jiiku Hospital, had not been a difficult thing to do, thanks to his intellect. But now the time had come for the embryonic demon that lay deep within his heart to shuffle off its human residue and hatch at last. It was the power of this evil embryo that had forbidden Yoshio from committing suicide and ensured that he lived to the age of fifteen.

That night, in the midst of the convulsive seizures, the black swarm of insects joined their voices and commanded Yoshio in a voice that he now heard:

Kill! As many as you can! Kill! Kill!

13—Non-Profit Organization

The year after he graduated from his last year of compulsory education at fifteen years of age, Yoshio Iizuka left the Tsurumaki Garden Orphanage which had been his home for so many years, and began his life alone. The orphanage director had developed a parent's true affection for Yoshio and had tried to get the outstanding student to continue his education, but Yoshio's mind was already made up.

All the teachers at the orphanage expressed regret because Yoshio's test scores were a guarantee of acceptance to any high school he liked. They finally gave in, however, and the director set up a fund to collect money for Yoshio as a farewell gift.

With that money, Yoshio rented a small one-room apartment and got a part-time job. Not having gone to high school meant his resume did not open many doors, but once he turned seventeen and started looking more like an adult, he began falsifying his resume according to the work he was applying for and started landing more lucrative jobs. Yoshio had an intellectual appeal, and he could gain the trust of interviewers and employers by simply projecting that air of intelligence.

He worked blue-collar and white-collar jobs. He never felt either kind of work was difficult or taxing. He became a machine capable of a frightening degree of focus when the Will that dominated him ordered him to concentrate on saving money. The voice of the Will was absolute. What had previously felt like someone whispering in his ear had changed and was now received like infallible dispensation from on high. It was as though Yoshio's human ego had either retreated or completely disappeared.

All he needed in his everyday life was the minimum amount of food to maintain vital functions and—due to his abnormal obsession with hygiene—clothing as neat and clean as a freshly-washed uniform. He read many books in order to learn about chemistry, physics, and mathematics. Beyond the basics, he could find almost everything he wanted at the Seiyo Library in Koto Ward.

Even his living accommodations were simple. He had a three-room apartment in Minamisuna. The building was so old it wouldn't be surprising if it were knocked down any day, so the rent was dirt cheap. Yoshio was like a high-mileage robot able to live on a bare minimum of living expenses. If he'd had a friend, he probably would've looked at Yoshio and said, "The guy's tough, cutting corners in his lifestyle and furiously saving money in order to achieve some really big dream."

When he turned nineteen, Yoshio's savings account boasted a nice little sum. Part of it was spent on surveying Tokyo Tower to blow it up, on purchasing technical reference manuals, on acquiring the materials for building the bombs. While moving forward with his plans to bomb the tower, with the rest of the money Yoshio started a website that would act as a basis for his future activities.

He named the site *Society of Victims of Abuse for the Prevention of Abuse*. He wrote a manifesto of his beliefs based on his own experiences and put it on the front page to draw the public's attention:

"My reason for starting this site is very simple. Somewhere right now, at this very moment, an innocent child is being abused. This is the ugly reality of modern society, and I want to stop it, by whatever means it takes. I know that there is a limit to what I can do alone, however. I myself was the victim of horrible abuse very soon after birth, but thanks to the kindness of many people, I have had the chance to grow into the man I am today, without any crippling psychological problems, a fact for which I am very grateful. I started *Society of Victims of Abuse for the Prevention of Abuse* out of a desire to make my experience more widely known, and in the hope that we can all work together to free our society from child abuse."

He put this message on the top page, and next to it he placed a passport photo he'd had taken at a dingy studio next to the Minamisuna subway station entrance called Takayama Photo Studio. The image of the idealistic young man whose earnestness was only rivaled by his passion for contributing to society added a decisive effect to the message. The page made a strong impression on people who found the site through search engines, and the hit count grew day by day.

An even greater surprise awaited anyone clicking through to the next page, which contained pictures taken of the site owner's scar-covered body, with the heading: "The mother who abused me loved Louis Vuitton."

Presented with the site, anyone with an ordinary sensitivity could not but have a gut reaction that defied intellectualizing. It had the dubious aspect of a site run by a good-looking white guy in middle America promising with a smile that "you too can be saved from the ills of modern society" and preaching the tenets of his new faith. The sort who, two years later, is arrested thanks to FBI profilers for having been a monstrous serial killer whose trail of young female victims held the country in a grip of terror.

But the photographs of the scars had the undeniable impact of verisimilitude: a pop monogram cut into an infant's body, today covering the victim's body with stretched suture scars. People were mesmerized by the intensity of the images, suppressing the odd feeling elicited by the first page that rose like an oily substance.

Within six months the *Society of Victims of Abuse for the Prevention of Abuse* website began to get known throughout the country thanks to word of mouth. People of all ages posted comments to the forum every day. Many of the comments were from young men and women who had been abused as children and continued to suffer from the emotional trauma. Not a few were from young mothers suffering from infant-care neurosis. "I abuse my child, but I really want to stop. I'm at a total loss. What can I do?" Yoshio's honest reaction was "Why don't you just beat it to death?" but he replied with the heartfelt and thorough response the asker wanted. And he would receive messages of thanks...

Yoshio's hypocritical echoes thus consoled and soothed the internet avatars, and the site's reputation spread further. Somehow Yoshio knew just what to say to please people who were struggling in the midst of their suffering. Of course, he also knew how to push them into the depths.

Some of the regular site visitors had already made offers of financial support, commending his efforts and ambition. He received offers to speak about his experiences from child-rearing support offices, child welfare centers, and child psychology treatment centers.

The calls for Yoshio Iizuka to move his social betterment campaign from the virtual world of the internet to the real world grew in number. He felt the tide starting to rise at last. Yoshio finally decided to set up a non-profit organization and establish a foundation for his real-world social activities, taking advantage of the wave of recognition he had received. Everything was going according to the schedule he had laid down when he started the website in June 2010.

"Victims of Abuse Saving Society's Many Abused Children"—he was going to use that saccharine slogan, which would no doubt resonate with today's softheaded society, together with pictures from his infancy, to wring money out of people.

Using that money to blow up Tokyo Tower and kill as many people as possible: this was the purpose of Yoshio Iizuka's non-profit, which would act as the Devil's front-line base to bring fear to all of Tokyo and mock all the good that people believed in and created. To spit on all of it.

It would all come to light, sooner or later. The grand finale was not far off, when the demon named Yoshio Iizuka would sacrifice a number of people proportional to his talents. When that time came, how would everyone react to the fact that the person they had believed to be a young activist working to better society was in actuality a demon that had committed mass murder? How big would the shock be when the world learned that the charitable organization that promoted the cause of peace and protection of human rights had been a funding source for massacre and a disguise for a demon?

How many people would he be able to kill before dying?

That was the only rule of the game that was being played out in the limited time "Yoshio" would exist.

Yoshio was feeling something that he had never experienced in his life flowing like a torrent inside. *Is this what it means to have fun?* he wondered. *Is it when you can feel the blood rushing through your body like this? Is this happiness?*

As he thought this, Yoshio's usual poker face broke into an exuberant smile. Faced with the prospect of his major project, Yoshio displayed an *élan* that had been unthinkable for him a few years before.

It was Monday, April 4th when Yoshio got together the statement of purpose, articles of incorporation, business plan, financial statements, and seven other filings needed to set up the non-profit and handed them in to the non-profit desk at the Administrative Corporation Office of the Metropolitan Residents' Life Section in the Bureau for Lifestyle, Culture, and Sports on the twenty-seventh floor on the north side of Building No. 1 at Tokyo Metropolitan City Hall.

Yoshio had visited City Hall a week before for the first time in his life. He was overcome by a strange, kind of ticklish feeling considering the deception he was about to engage in as he was heading up to the twenty-seventh floor in the elevator. He waited his turn and was ushered to the preliminary consultation desk, where a gaunt middle-aged woman described the process to him. "You're going to have to prepare a lot of paperwork, but you can also hire a certified administrative specialist if you want," she recommended thoughtfully.

Yoshio gave her a cheery smile. "Thank you, but I'm the kind of guy that likes to learn by doing, so could you explain the whole process to me?"

When he returned to the same desk to submit all the paperwork, the same woman happened to be the one to help him. Of the seventeen predetermined "purposes of establishment" to be included in the articles of incorporation, Yoshio first picked "Activities to Protect Human Rights or Promote Peace," and then, on the woman's advice, added "Activities to Promote Healthcare, Medical Treatment, or Welfare" and "Activities to Ensure the Healthy Nurturing of Children."

Apparently a stickler for detail, the woman took quite a while going over every form before announcing, "It's perfect!"

Thursday, September 1, 2011. Yoshio had to wait five months after filing all the paperwork, but finally his non-profit, *Society of Victims of Abuse for the Prevention of Abuse*, was officially incorporated. It was five days after the Tokyo Tower bombing.

Yoshio had had to wait an extra month in addition to the two months of "public notice" and the two months of "public inspection" set down by the law before the non-profit could be registered, because all the directors, including Yoshio—who was going to be chairman—were minors.

It wasn't that there were legal problems with their being underage, but Yoshio's lack of relatives meant that the review had been characterized by bureaucratic caution in the face of potential instability in the organization's management.

The representative officer and chairman was Yoshio. The first director was Midori Sonoda. The others were two youths in whom Yoshio had recognized potential. They were all around fifteen years old and would live and work at the Society once they finished ninth grade, which marked the end of compulsory education in Japan.

Midori Sonoda, 16 years of age. Living with family, Ota Ward, Tokyo.

Kazuhiko Yuasa, 15 years of age. Living in Asano Orphanage, Moriya City, Tokyo.

Takeshi Abe, 15 years of age. Living with family, Hodogaya, Kanagawa Prefecture.

Kazuhiko Yuasa and Takeshi Abe had come to Yoshio's site looking for a little help like moths attracted to a bug zapper. They had been abused. The more violent of them was Kazuhiko Yuasa.

He told Yoshio that his mother had almost killed him when he was seven years old. She had once poured boiling water all over him on the balcony of their apartment and left him there all night. His father was gone before he was born, leaving his mother to raise him alone. Until that time his mother had taken care of him normally, but she started to break down psychologically and use Kazuhiko as an outlet for her stress. The local child welfare office stepped in at that point and placed him in a juvenile psychiatric treatment institution.

Kazuhiko had smiled during the interview and told Yoshio, "I was afraid to sleep. I thought my mom would kill me." Scars from the burns he had suffered as a child peeked out from under the collar of the dark-blue jersey he was wearing.

Yoshio kept a straight face but beamed with happiness inside. *This guy has talent,* he thought.

"Are you ever violent now?"

"No. I pretty much learned how to suppress those impulses

at the short-term institution I was in for emotionally disturbed children."

"Huh. Why hold it in, though, when you can use if for my benefit?" Yoshio said, as he smiled for the first time.

Takeshi Abe's home life was similar to that of Midori's. He hated his father.

Takeshi's father worked as a salaryman in a huge precision instrument factory in Hodogaya. His mother was a garden-variety stay-at-home mom. His father had beaten Takeshi sometimes when Takeshi was still in elementary school. Unlike despicable cases where a mother burns her kid with cigarettes, Takeshi's father simply wanted his son to achieve greater success than he had. If Takeshi brought home bad grades from his cram school, his father would scold him, and if his father was having a particularly stressful time at work, he'd hit Takeshi. But that was generally it.

Even relatively mild cases of abuse could have very grave consequences for a sensitive child, however. Takeshi advanced to a fairly prestigious middle school attached to a local university but stopped going to class in the second half of his first year there, preferring to stay at home all day.

Yoshio noted Takeshi's finely honed sensitivity right away. Finding an emotional hook was important with kids who had such a sentimental predisposition. All he would have to do was find something that Takeshi could live for. It would almost be too easy to manipulate Takeshi's very moldable mind as if Yoshio were breathing a soul into a clay figurine.

Since both of these kids, like Midori, had experienced suicidal ideation, Yoshio had deftly manipulated that psychological aspect of their minds in order to guide them through the various stages of brainwashing, the final stage of which they had now reached.

All that was left was to name a victim for their initiation, which Yoshio was busy scripting now and which would cause them to step beyond the bounds of law-abiding society, and their allegiance to him would be absolute. For Yoshio, their ability to sacrifice their lives the instant he ordered them to die was an inviolable bond of blood to be found neither in the articles of incorporation nor in the statement of purpose of the non-profit.

Establishing the non-profit required six volunteer staff members aside from the four officers. Yoshio selected young people from the website he was running for their earnest desire to contribute to society and their pleasant dispositions. He would decide whether to brainwash them and bring them into the behind-the-scenes business of the non-profit or to leave them as is, running the front financial operations of the business, depending on how talented they were. Not everyone had talent. He would add members to the team gradually, and gradually move some from the front room to the back room.

Yoshio had spent about six months searching the internet and hitting real estate offices to find a suitable location for the office. He finally settled on office space on the first floor of an old apartment building facing the street in Akabanebashi where there was a public health office, not too far from Tsurumaki Garden Orphanage where he had lived. He bought the basic supplies—filing cabinets with locks, a fireproof safe, etc.—and the 1,300-sq-ft location started to look like an office.

Everything above the first floor was one-room apartments, two of which he rented for the three other officers: one for Midori and one for Kazuhiko and Takeshi, who would share. It wouldn't be long before they would fulfill their missions anyway.

And thus in a quiet office in Akabanebashi, Tokyo, was born the bud that would bloom into a criminal enterprise of unprecedented proportions.

14—Media Debut

Friday, September 2nd. The day after starting the non-profit Yoshio was to be the subject of his first media story. He had gotten a request to do a story on the activities of *Society of Victims of Abuse for the Prevention of Abuse* for the lifestyle section of *Morning Daily,* one of Japan's largest papers, headquartered in Tokyo.

The female reporter, named Yukiko Hatakeyama, had initially asked to interview Yoshio in his office, but he tried to keep outsiders out of the place as much as possible.

"Whereabout will you be when we meet?" she asked.

"I'm going to go see the aftermath of the Tokyo Tower bombing," he answered honestly.

"It's become quite a sightseeing destination," she said, rather insensitively for a newspaper reporter. She scanned a mental map of the area and suggested the first-floor cafe of the Tokyo Princess Hotel for their meeting.

On the promised day, Yoshio Iizuka got to the cafe lounge at the hotel first and was drinking a glass of water when a woman in her late twenties who appeared to be Yukiko Hatakeyama arrived about twenty minutes late, photographer in tow. She was out of breath, having run from somewhere. He knew it was her right away. He waved his hand to let her know where he was, the better to make a bright and cheerful impression.

"Yoshio Iizuka? Hi, I'm Yukiko Hatakeyama. We spoke on the phone. This is Mr. Suzuki, the newspaper photographer. Sorry I'm so late. The whole Tokyo Tower thing has caused unbelievable traffic. Our taxi wasn't moving! We got out at the Kamiyacho intersection and ran the rest of the way. You don't mind if I take off my jacket, do you?"

Yukiko Hatakeyama slipped off the beige summer jacket she was wearing, folded it, and placed it on the chair next to her. Her white blouse was damp from the sweat, making her skin and undergarments show through. This made Yoshio uncomfortable, but the smile remained rigidly on his face.

"You know, I saw your picture on the internet, but you're even more photogenic in person. Mr. Suzuki is going to be snapping away during the interview to capture your best expression, but don't mind him while we talk, okay?"

"This is my first interview, so I'm not sure I can respond as well as I'd like to, but feel free to ask me anything you want. I want as many people as possible to know what it is that I'm doing. That's why I'm here today."

"Thank you. Let's get started."

She flipped the switch on a little digital recorder and placed it in front of Yoshio.

"The goal of your website is very straightforward. Essentially, people who were abused as children understand best what it is that abused children are going through, so they want to use their own experiences to do something to help stop abuse. Right?"

"That's not all there is to it, though. The Prevention of Abuse Law was revised in 2008 in an effort to make it possible to prevent more abuse before it even starts, but as long as people who have had no contact with child abuse in their lives aren't aware that something very tragic might be happening in the very next apartment, nothing will change, no matter how many times the law is revised.

"Think of it this way. If you saw a very thin little girl in a convenience store with bruises on her legs beneath her skirt, you might wonder, 'What happened to her?' but not give it more thought or even ask the girl if everything is all right. Not to speak of following her or something, which nobody would do. As long as people lack that awareness, the vast majority of children being abused by their parents will remain undetected, and the problem will go on. There's a limit to what a single individual like I can do, which is why I want to appeal to ordinary people to become more involved."

Yukiko listened with rapt attention to Yoshio speaking like some sort of social activist full of youth and passion. *Yoshio Iizuka is going to turn twenty in November,* she thought, impressed. *He's got charisma for his age.* She felt an instant attraction to him.

"Mr. Iizuka, would it be okay if I asked you more personal questions?"

"Sure. I've decided not to hide anything. It would be great if I could simply not have anything in there that I would want to hide, but I'm just human..."

Yoshio gave a little chuckle. Yukiko was still so inexperienced as a reporter and as a woman that Yoshio's cute, bashful smile made her heart skip a beat.

What she didn't know, however, was that his laugh was a perverse conditioned reflex to calling himself a "human." It was the smile of a demon reminded by his own performance that he was approaching something inhuman.

Look at this dumb bitch, eyes all a-glitter for Yoshio, even though she's barely known Yoshio for ten minutes. Maybe Yoshio should just kill her when she leaves.

"I saw the pictures you put up on your site. I can't even begin to imagine how horrible the cruel abuse you suffered was, but how is it that, despite that horrible experience you had a child, you were able to grow into such a cheerful, ambitious young man?"

"That's a good question. I don't know about other people, but it seems like many kids who were abused when they were very small grow up not being able to fully conquer the effects of post-traumatic stress disorder, which makes it hard to live over the years."

"But you did conquer it. I don't really know that much about it, but the abuse you suffered is classified as 'S-rank' abuse."

"S-rank"? This chick has got to be kidding, Yoshio thought to himself. He said, "S-rank or A-rank, or something. I'm not quite sure, to be honest, plus it happened right after I was born, so I don't have any memories of it. I only found out about it based on the

physical evidence, as it were. Maybe that's a good thing."

"They do say that childhood memories stay with us subconsciously, though."

"Could be. I must've experienced some kind of trauma."

"What kind of symptoms did you have, if I might ask?"

"Well, I lived in an orphanage called 'The Nestlings' Home' in Miyazaki Prefecture until I was about five, and I was an incredibly fearful child. Whenever I saw the teachers being mean to the other kids, I would get so scared that I would spend the whole night quaking in my bed.

"The second child that was abandoned in the Stork's Mailbox was called Ikuo. I saw one of the older female teachers pinching his inner thigh really hard. He had a developmental disorder, and whenever she pinched him and caused him pain, he would cry and laugh at the same time, which I think she just found amusing. Whenever I saw that kind of thing, I would make a vow, under the covers, to always be an exemplary student so I wouldn't get murdered."

Saying this, Yoshio hunched up his shoulders and hugged himself, as though he had returned to a childlike state. As planned, Yukiko was shocked by his story, and her face took on an expression of motherly concern at the same time.

Interviews are fun, Yoshio thought. Sometimes he didn't know how much of what he was saying was a lie and how much was a truthful answer.

"I hear that you were always at the top of your class. You've always been intelligent. Amazing."

"Not at all. I can't stand boasting. If my intellect has been useful for anything maybe it was to read a lot, to try to understand my own psychological makeup and keep close watch over my psyche from when I was a little kid, so that those dark feelings of hatred I had for the mother who abused me wouldn't turn into something bigger inside me. I liked the philosophy of transcending antagonism and achieving a higher plane. It's often referred to as 'sublimation.' That's what I'm talking about."

Yoshio was not lying now, because he had in fact sublimated his hatred for his pathetic mother into the lofty concept of genocide.

"Amazing. Here I am, twenty-seven years old, but I feel like a little kid compared to you."

"Oh, come on. You couldn't get a job at a major newspaper if you weren't pretty darn amazing yourself."

He nailed the exact point of pride she loved being flattered for.

"So, moving on, I'd like to ask you about your future course of action."

Yoshio spent the rest of the time describing his plan to collect donations and other contributions from people sympathetic to the message put out by his website. He would use that money to develop his new non-profit into a more realistic, concrete force for social change. He said it because that was the answer the woman wanted.

Yoshio spoke slowly, weighing each word, as though he were making sure that there was no showiness or deceit in his words. He worked hard to give the impression that he could not be more sincere.

When the agreed-upon hour was over, Yukiko held out her hand, blushing ever so slightly. "I really want to thank you for today. The story will be published in the lifestyle column two weeks from now. I'll send you a copy when it's printed. I'm sure it will be a good piece. We also got a lot of photographs. Work aside, this has been an incredibly inspiring experience for me personally."

"Well, this was my first interview. If your article has some effect on society and my non-profit gets on course, I'll have to find some way of thanking you. And please come visit our office once we've had a bit more time to make it fit for visitors."

"Really? I can come visit you?"

"Of course! In fact, we could even have dinner sometime."

"That would be wonderful! Let me know."

Yoshio made sure that the article would include the website's URL as well as the bank account number where people could make donations to the non-profit and the contact info of the office.

Yoshio Iizuka's first interview was a resounding success.

It was the media debut of a demon who wore the mask of a charming and handsome idealist with an unsullied passion for social change.

15—The Day-to-Day

Yoshio Iizuka's monstrous hypocrisy took on a glittering sheen thanks to the cover provided by the non-profit. He traveled around the country dispensing commentary as an observer at conferences organized by welfare institutions and talking to audiences about the truth of abuse.

"I believe there is only one reason we have not been able to rid the world of child abuse. Human society is humane thanks to the protection of civilization, but in the deep, dark recesses of the human soul there remains an as-yet untamed savagery, which lies dormant in the form of a desire for power. We all possess an instinctual desire to bully the weak. If one feels oppressed by society, the desire only grows stronger.

"The weakest members of society include newborn infants. I experienced what it was like to be on the receiving end of absolute violence, without knowing what the abuse meant, without even knowing the word 'pain.' Everyone is stronger than an infant. That violence is therefore unilateral and irreversible, even symbolic in a way. If there is anything positive that came out of that experience, it is the miracle of my survival, allowing me to tell my tale from this side, the side of the strong, the side I was never supposed to reach."

Yoshio didn't know whether he was actually speaking any truths or not, but the audience was mesmerized by his voice and the rhythm of his words.

Society of Victims of Abuse for the Prevention of Abuse was inundated with inquiries from all over the country: child welfare offices, child welfare centers, other non-profits such as foster parent support centers, social welfare corporations for the prevention of abuse, and more. Yoshio personally received tips about ongoing cases of child abuse. He used his personal network to create a list of abuse cases, and he surveyed it like a map. It was soon after the non-profit really got under way that he began occasionally finding cases that fit his "conditions" and he got down to business.

One day in late November, the Himonya Police Station in Meguro Ward began investigating a case of a man who had beaten his son to death and then disappeared. The man's name was Takahiro Marugame, and he had been living with his common-law wife and her son, Hitoshi. After his disappearance, Marugame was placed on the wanted list on suspicion of murder.

Marugame had worked for a trucking company for a while but was unemployed now. His family had lived on the meager income his wife Keiko earned from a part-time job she had waiting tables. Marugame had begun beating three-year-old Hitoshi a few months before. More than once Keiko had come home from work and, not finding Hitoshi, asked her husband where he was, only to find Hitoshi locked out on the balcony, having cried himself to sleep. Keiko was nevertheless unable to stand up to Takahiro. She would tend to her son's wounds and then leave for work the next day without a word.

One day when she got home she found Hitoshi prone on the *tatami* mats, Takahiro nowhere to be seen. Hitoshi was dead; his neck was broken. Keiko called the police right away. For some reason she couldn't cry and was afraid they would suspect her. She desperately practiced describing what had actually happened while she waited for the police to arrive. It felt strange.

Yoshio had talked to the woman before when she had come

to one of the child welfare offices he visited regularly. He had had his eye on her husband Takahiro Marugame ever since. In fact, the night Marugame had thrown Keiko's son Hitoshi against the wall and killed him during an episode of abuse, Yoshio, Midori, Kazuhiko, and Takeshi had been outside the apartment, fathoming the events inside. It was after ten at night, and the lights were out in the apartments to either side. Violent slamming sounds emanated from inside the apartment. Weak screams, like a child crying, were audible at first, then stopped.

Kazuhiko Yuasa turned to Yoshio. "Should we go in and help?"

"No. At this rate, he's probably gonna kill the kid. We'll wait until he does."

The three officers exchanged glances and fell silent.

They waited about fifteen minutes. No more sounds came from the apartment. All of a sudden, the front door flew open and a man came running out. Marugame's face was pale, and he panicked at the sight of the young men standing outside his door.

"W-Who the fuck are you?"

"We're here from the child welfare office," Midori said. "We are concerned about Hitoshi."

"What? This is none of your business! You stay the fuck out of my family's affairs!"

Marugame took a menacing step forward towards Yoshio as if to punch him, but in that split second Takeshi's stun-gun discharged into the man's side. He fell with a short groan as his body absorbed the 500,000-watt current. The three officers lifted Marugame's body and placed it in the Toyota Hi-Ace van and headed to the basement Yoshio had rented, the unlicensed but skilled Kazuhiko behind the wheel.

It was an empty, undecorated space, surrounded on all sides by concrete walls. To the center of the back wall was attached a contraption composed of a square frame made out of steel construction piping joined together and solidly reinforced by diagonal pipes at each corner, from which hung something that looked like a leather belt with buckles. This device, protruding grimly from the wall of the basement storage room, had such a grisly appearance that just looking at it could induce nausea. The wall behind it had become discolored, as though it had been washed down over and over: pale rust-colored splotches spread dimly over its surface despite repeated attempts to get rid of them.

Several sets of footsteps echoed as a group of people descended the steps.

Yoshio appeared first. Next came Takeshi and Kazuhiko, carrying the still-unconscious Marugame. Midori followed.

Midori helped the two others strip Marugame's small frame naked. Takeshi and Kazuhiko dragged the body up against the wall, and Midori secured Marugame's wrists with the leather buckles so that he hung from the steel contraption and did the same to the ankles. Marugame hung crucified in Yoshio's secret execution chamber. The thought came to Midori that Marugame didn't look like Christ on the cross because his legs were splayed open, his flaccid penis and scrotum hanging comically down. He seemed to recall seeing a painting that looked like this in one of his art textbooks.

Yoshio signaled to Midori with a brusque nod, and Midori planted his foot right in the naked man's scrotum. The unconscious man moaned and came to with a start. The three officers laughed raucously. Marugame looked around blankly, listening to the young men's laughter, unable to comprehend what was going on. Finally, he realized that he was splayed out naked, and started yelling.

"What do you think you're doing? Let me go, you motherfuckers!"

The three officers stopped laughing. A dark mood of foreboding filled the basement.

"Mr. Marugame, do you understand the situation you're in?" Yoshio asked coldly.

"Who the fuck are you?"

"Me? Who I am is irrelevant to you, but I'll tell you anyway. My name is Yoshio Iizuka. I run a non-profit organization called *Society of Victims of Abuse for the Prevention of Abuse*. I was recently consulted regarding your son Hitoshi."

Apparently relieved that, despite the ominous nature of his situation, the people who had kidnapped him were child welfare workers, he began berating them loudly.

"You motherfuckers! You think you social workers can get away with doing this to the parent of a brat you were involved with?"

"Your son is dead, isn't he?"

"That was an accident! I didn't do it."

"That, too, is irrelevant. We were waiting outside for you to kill him."

"What?! Aren't you supposed to *prevent* abuse?"

Yoshio laughed at the man's perplexity.

"On the surface, perhaps. The truth is we couldn't give a damn how many kids die. What I hate is people. Give a brat a chance and he'll grow up to be an adult just like you. Young and repulsive or old and repulsive: that's the only difference."

"There's something wrong with you. Let me go and I won't turn you in. Just hurry up and let me go."

"You'd turn yourself in to the police?"

"No, it was an accident... Aaah!"

Midori kicked the man's hanging scrotum right between his widely splayed legs. Marugame desperately contorted his immobilized body. Kazuhiko and Takeshi laughed at this.

"Mr. Marugame, you're about to experience a form of torture so extreme that it defies the imagination," Yoshio said breezily with a smile. Marugame felt a sense of terror at the smile that made the hair all over his body stand on end. He broke into a cold sweat. The sealed underground room was instantly filled with pungent body odor.

"Are you going to kill me?"

"Yes. But not in any…normal way."

Marugame's scrotum visibly contracted as he stared into Yoshio's eyes, which burned cruelly above the charming smile. Takeshi and Kazuhiko also gulped and looked at Yoshio. They had no idea what kind of torture Yoshio had planned for Marugame. Only Midori crossed his arms and stared at Marugame with the same cold stare as Yoshio.

"You will have to forgive me, Mr. Marugame, if I inform you that you do not, unfortunately, have the honor of being the first to experience this historic execution method."

"H-Historic e-execution?" Marugame's voice broke as he said this, making an amusing sound. His voice was so hoarse it was hard to understand what he was saying.

Yoshio addressed Marugame. "Say, does it seem to you like the ceiling is kind of low?"

The man looked down at the uneven cement floor and up the ceiling, as prompted. The two officers also scrutinized the lumpy, amateurish job of leveling on the raw concrete floor.

"The floor is rising. Bit by bit."

"W-Why?" It was barely a whisper. Marugame was by now completely terrified of Yoshio.

"Hey," Yoshio turned to Midori theatrically. "How many bodies are resting peacefully under the floor?"

"Three."

The look of terror on the man's face was comic. He pulled his chin in and looked down at the floor. His splayed legs began to tremble. Takeshi and Kazuhiko also stared down at the floor as though they could see through it.

"All right, let's wrap this talk show up. It's time for the action to start."

At Yoshio's signal, Midori pulled a survival knife out of his knapsack, which was on the floor. Only Midori knew the procedure.

"Midori, put the thing in his mouth."

Midori deftly pulled something out of his bag that looked like a plastic S&M implement, jogged over to the splayed man, and fitted the thing into his mouth.

"It would ruin the whole show if you bit your tongue and died of blood loss in the middle of the rite."

The man's body odor grew stronger.

Oh boy, Yoshio thought. *Once we get into it, this guy will do more than wet himself.*

"Have you ever heard of 'death by a thousand cuts'?"

The man was too weak to even shake his head.

"It's probably the cruelest form of execution practiced in China in ancient times. In and of itself, there's not that much to it. We're just going to slice the flesh off your body a little bit at a time, with a knife, so that death comes as slowly as possible."

The smell of the man's urine filled the room as Yoshio finished speaking. Drops of urine dribbled from the man's flaccid penis and down along his thigh.

Pretty soon Marugame would empty his bowels. *Man, this can be gross,* Yoshio thought.

Yoshio watched Midori carefully, like a doctor who has taught an intern an intricate surgical procedure. "Proceed," he said and nodded solemnly.

Midori walked up to the man, knife in hand. Then, with a deliberate motion, he grabbed a handful of the loose flesh on the man's chest, and quickly sliced into the flesh around the nipple.

Midori's face was splattered with a stream of gushing blood.

"Still bad at it," Yoshio bemoaned, grimacing.

Midori's eyes glowed with a maniacal intensity in the middle of his blood-soaked face.

Yoshio had taught Midori how to slice the flesh without getting splattered like that: from top to bottom, slowly, with your hand covering it. That way the blood would spurt up at the man's chin.

The man let out what would have been a bloodcurdling scream, had his mouth not been blocked. A comic gurgling came out instead, and saliva flowed freely from his mouth. *What could be more pathetic?* Yoshio thought.

As the blade moved in and a round flap of skin fell away, the blood didn't surge out as before, but rather dripped slowly in a thick, black stream down the chest, stomach, and groin.

Takeshi and Kazuhiko swallowed hard as they watched Midori. He glared back at them, as though Yoshio's madness had taken over him as well. They stood there nervously. Midori turned back to the man's body right in front of him and sliced off the flesh around the other nipple.

"Arrh-gh-ghh!" A long gurgling moan emerged from the man's mouth—the best he could do with his mouth open like that.

"It smarts, doesn't it?" a poker-faced Yoshio asked from behind Midori. Marugame, still fully conscious, nodded vigorously. As though he thought they'd stop if he admitted that it hurt.

"Didn't your son say it hurt, too?"

The man nodded again, his eyes turning up in their sockets from the intense pain.

"But you didn't stop beating him, did you?"

There was no response this time, because he didn't know what response to give to make them stop.

Midori cut off the man's right ear next. The unendurable pain caused the man's abdominal muscles to contract, forcing the gas out of the man's bowels. The stench filled the room. Gasping sounds emerged from Marugame's throat like an asthma attack. The floor and the wall behind were sprayed with fresh blood as though from a broken showerhead.

"I was also cut up just after I was born. Newborns don't have memories, so I don't remember anything, of course. It happened before I even knew the word 'pain,' so I doubt I slobbered and screamed the way you're doing now. So...unattractive. Don't get me wrong, though. This isn't some kind of vengeance we're meting out on parents who abuse their kids. No, I'm going to kill everyone, children as well as parents."

Yoshio approached Midori and gently placed his hand on his shoulder. "This is Takeshi and Kazuhiko's first time. Show them how it's done."

The pair looked at Midori and recoiled back a step.

Glaring at the naked man with a terrifying expression on his face, Yoshio said, "This scum and thousands of others like him abuse their kids with big smiles on their faces. You have to pay it back many times over! Understood?"

"Yes, sir!" Takeshi and Kazuhiko cried in unison.

"Don't kill him right away. Another name for 'death by a thousand cuts' is 'scaling,' because the body starts to look like it's covered in scales as bits of flesh are removed. I want you to spend the rest of the day today giving this guy what he deserves, just like I described it."

Midori held the knife by the blood-red blade and offered the handle to the pair with a demonic look on his face. They exchanged a hesitant glance, and Kazuhiko reached out a shaking hand. He tremblingly grasped the knife by the handle and walked over to the man who was strapped to the wall and moaning from the pain.

Kazuhiko grabbed the man's left ear and moved the blade down. He lacked Midori's resolve, so it didn't go smoothly. The ear hung half-cut from the man's head. Kazuhiko finally finished the job and handed the knife to Takeshi, who was standing behind.

Yoshio looked on with a satisfied expression and returned to his apartment to get to some unfinished business.

16—The Offer

Friday, November 22, 2011. On that day, Mariko Amo turned thirty-three.

Mariko knew plenty of other photographers through work, and there were a few editors she had come to know pretty well, but she didn't know anyone intimately enough to celebrate her birthday with them. Instead, she decided to buy herself a present and go out to eat at a nice restaurant.

She had worked hard this past year. Across the board publishers were paying less due to the economic slump, but 2011, which was rapidly coming to its close, had been a year of unexpectedly high earnings for Mariko. The "bonus" she had gotten thanks to her death-defying stunt had contributed quite a bit.

Three months had passed since the Tokyo Tower bombing, and she had managed somehow to pull through a particularly tough psychological stretch that was out of character for no-nonsense, feet-on-the-ground Mariko. Had it really been an indication of PTSD, as the nurse at Furukawahashi Hospital had said? For just a moment, she had felt the shadow of death. But she was fine now. She had returned to her old self.

Mariko was pondering these things during a late breakfast when her cell phone rang. The LCD screen showed that it was Kohei Sendo from Koshunsha. "Figures," she thought.

"Mariko Amo speaking," she answered in a professional voice.

"Hey, hey, hey! How's the birthday girl? Tell me, what's it like to be thirty-three?"

The abrupt energy in the voice caught Mariko off guard. Sendo was a real rascal. Sometimes he scared her like the devil, but he could also be as generous and cheerful as a little kid. It was probably because of this that she couldn't really hate him despite the depths he was willing to plumb just to sell a magazine.

"Oh, you remembered. Thanks. You didn't have to remember my exact age, of course, but still, thirty-three... What can I say? Things are good. I'm happy. I like myself better with every passing year."

"Well, you got me there. I'm like Chaplin in *Modern Times*, a little cog groaning under the pressure of society's gears, literally destroying my humanity just to get by. It's tough to be a guy."

Mariko laughed. "Mr. Sendo, you crack me up today."

"I crack you up today, do I? Are you saying I don't crack you up every day?"

"Uh, no. You're normally really scary. Not too long ago you had me in tears, remember?"

"Which reminds me, I've been keeping an eye on other magazines, but I can't find them anywhere."

"Find what?"

"Don't play innocent. The pictures you refused to sell me even for five fingers."

First he brings an onslaught of energy and cheer with his sudden phone call, and now this, bringing me all the way down. Yep, the guy's a monster, Mariko thought. "I'm going to hang up if you talk about it."

"No, no, not interested anymore. The whole Tokyo Tower thing is yesterday's news. No one gives a damn about that now. Can't use it to sell any magazines anymore."

"So to what do I owe the pleasure then?"

"Your birthday, silly! I'm calling to congratulate you."

"Really? No, there's got to be some ulterior motive. I mean, we're talking about you. Editor-in-chief of the one and only *In Focus,* before which the celebrity world bows in fear. Why would you call little ol' me to ask how I'm doing?"

"Come on, I'm not that evil. And there is one little job I've got for you, so I'd like to take you out to dinner. We'll celebrate your birthday while we're at it."

Yup. Mariko knew it. She knew he was up to no good…

But still, she was happy that Sendo would call her on the morning of her birthday. She was, after all, maybe the only person in the photography section that could talk to him like an equal, and he was a major editor at a major publishing house. She didn't know what kind of offer it was, but she had survived more than ten years in the industry by wit or by wile, so he wasn't going to give her some piddling little offer. She decided to take him up on his invitation.

"All right. I accept. But you'd better take me someplace nice."

"Don't you worry about that. I've got reservations at eight at a cozy little French place in Nishi Azabu. I'll email you directions."

"What? You mean you weren't going to take no for an answer?"

"Not at all, not at all. If you don't want to come, just say so. Life's always a sequence of fateful choices," Sendo intoned solemnly, and hung up.

Mariko left the house at 3 p.m. and took the subway to Shinjuku. She left her beloved Cherokee at home because she wanted to drink during dinner with Sendo.

You splurge on something nice, girl, the other Mariko whispered to the timid Mariko, who directed herself to the upscale Isetan department store. *Yeah, I'll just do a little window shopping,* she thought. *It's not like I've decided to buy something.* She walked around the first-floor leather goods and shoe section that was filled with famous brands while making excuses to herself as though she suffered from a split personality.

Mariko wasn't a very fashion-conscious person, but she did keep a skimpy black party dress and a long black formal dress in her Cherokee, on hangers to avoid wrinkles. They weren't for dressing up, though. They were more like disguises for when she got a call from the *In Focus* editorial department telling her to crash some celebrity's party and get pictures of someone or to get over to someone's funeral. Which meant that she could hardly remember spending anything on clothes for the past few years.

In the shoe section, into which she had wandered without really meaning to, she spotted a pair of deep purple Ferragamo high heels. It was love at first sight. She picked one up and admired its contours. Simple and elegant. Mariko didn't go for ostentatious designs. She preferred something understated that would add just a touch of elegance to her everyday appearance. She took a look at the price on the small tag. It was a bit more than she paid for a month's parking in Higashi Shinagawa.

The restaurant Sendo had chosen was on a narrow alley parallel to Gaien Nishi Avenue, near the Nishi Azabu intersection. It was located on the first floor of an apartment building and was decorated so as to recreate, in Tokyo, the ambience of a Parisian back-street bistro that is always filled with locals, the kind real connoisseurs always like. Mariko had not eaten in French restaurants very often and felt slightly self-conscious. She pulled up her shoulders and gave her outfit a once-over in front of the restaurant.

December was right around the corner. The days were still fairly warm, but the temperature plummeted at night, so Mariko had some trouble picking out what to wear beneath her thin camel-colored wool coat, the only one she owned. In the end she settled on a black velvet dress. The newly purchased Ferragamo heels added an elegant accent to her feet.

She'd bought them before she knew what was happening. "I'll wear them, so you don't need to box or wrap them," she heard herself saying, then felt her face flush. She felt she'd been exposed as an impostor, someone who didn't move in circles befitting the shoes. She hurried out of Isetan, embarrassed. As she walked down Shinjuku Avenue, she suddenly felt sick of carrying the paper bag containing her old loafers. *I can't walk into a fancy restaurant holding this,* she thought, and found a convenience store along Shinjuku Avenue with a trash can next to the door that she dropped the box into.

By the time she reached the dinner with Sendo, Mariko's day had been filled with ups and downs.

She opened the dark brown wooden door, walked down a long narrow hallway, and entered a space that felt round, like a fox's den. The small interior could hold several couples at the most. The walls were decorated elegantly with old oil paintings, photographs, and copper pans, hammered and polished. It was a soothing place.

What a nice restaurant, she thought, and then heard Sendo call her name. Kohei Sendo was already at a table in the back to the right, waiting for Mariko. He had opaque black sunglasses on, which was par for the course since part of his job was chasing down celebrities, but it made him look like a C-list wannabe.

The waiter was in his late fifties and wore a white shirt, vest, and large white apron around his waist. He took Mariko's coat and pulled out the seat courteously for her to sit.

"Mariko, happy birthday."

He filled the champagne flute he had ready on the table for Mariko. He had arrived early and had already opened a bottle of expensive-looking champagne, which he was drinking.

"Here's to thirty-three!" he said in his gravelly voice and raised his glass. Mariko had not been seated thirty seconds, and already Sendo was in control of the situation.

This guy has an amazing ability to turn people to putty in his hands.

"Would you mind not announcing my age to the whole world? What's so great about thirty-three anyway? If we're still working together when I'm sixty, or eighty-eight, then let's celebrate my birthday."

"I'll be eighty when you're sixty. Of course, considering the amount of bad karma I've accumulated, I'll probably be long dead by then. But anyway, cheers."

Mariko gazed at the bubbles in the champagne glass and felt happy. "Thanks for tonight. Cheers!"

The chilled champagne was delicious. It had been a long time since she last had champagne.

"Mariko, you look really nice tonight. Are those Ferragamos?"

"Wow. You've got quite an eye."

"Listen, editors are essentially catalog salesmen," Sendo said. "'The brand is all the rage this season, and that's going to be *the* color this fall.' Except we're not selling clothes. Magazines create desires, and we sniff out what people want and bring it to them. My outfit does the same thing. We take a broad look at everything going on in the world and tell the reader 'this murder is fascinating' one day and 'this actress's messy divorce is juicy' the next. We're just giving the masses the meat they want."

"Aren't you belittling your profession a bit?"

"Belittling? There's a word I haven't heard in a while. But no, I'm not belittling it at all. It's pure capitalism. You sell what sells. Check this out: murder isn't on the rise, but do you know why you think it is?"

"Because cruel, senseless killings are?"

"Nope. Ratings and circulation. The public loves bizarre murder cases full of intrigue, people killing each other over love and hate, random senseless murders that shake society to its core. It's all someone else's problem.

"Have you heard prosecutors' opening statements recently? They say things like, 'This clavicle bone which was found in the sewer awaited us full of the murdered woman's sorrows.' I think another one was 'The killer is a monster in human clothing, lacking even the smallest trace of humanity.' These guys are, like, quoting classics. Who are they, Dostoevsky? I personally think prosecutors shouldn't be able to do that kind of thing.

"What I'm saying, basically, is that the world is starving for riveting drama. And that's why my magazine flies off the shelf, and my salary keeps going up. The world is a well-oiled machine."

The proliferation of pictorial weeklies in the eighties and nineties was a thing of the past, and it was Sendo's acumen that had dragged *In Focus* out of its previous slump to a constant circulation of 300,000 copies once again with a no-holds-barred approach to getting stories. On more than one occasion he had received that medal of honor known in the business as "getting investigated by the prosecutor's office" for overdoing it.

"Mr. Sendo."

"At your service."

"Can we order?" Mariko said in her nicest possible voice.

Since Sendo seemed to be a regular, Mariko took his suggestion and ordered a strained lily root potage that was pure white and very light on the palate, and the *confit de canard*. Sendo ordered the house terrine with navy beans boiled the way he requested, and steak for the entree.

Every restaurant tried to offer a unique dining experience in terms of the food served, but here not only was the food delicious, but everything from the casual yet attentive waiters to the interior decor, and even the soft lighting, had an amazing effect on the diners, filling them with a sense of contentment.

If anything felt out of place in the restaurant, however, it was the figure of Sendo sitting right in front of her.

"Do you come here often?"

"I do. Have been for quite a while. For important negotiations that require a bit of delicacy, for clients who can appreciate this ambience. I don't just bring anyone." Sendo began eating the steak, which he had cut into mouth-sized bites ahead of time. It was the way impatient people ate. The wine he ordered after the champagne was obviously expensive—Mariko could tell just by looking at the understated label design—but Sendo drank it like water.

Because she was full, Mariko turned down the dessert selection the waiter recommended and instead ordered an espresso. Despite eating the large steak, Sendo ordered the homemade custard pudding to go with his coffee, uncharacteristically making an excuse: he'd acquired a sweet tooth from hanging out so much with his five year old.

"Everything was really delicious. Thanks," Mariko said. "By the way, wasn't there something you wanted to talk to me about? One of those 'delicate' matters?"

She had said it jokingly, but Sendo gave her a serious look. "Right," he said quietly. "Mariko, I've got a job offer for you. I want you to handle the installment of the 'People In Focus' feature that'll run in the second December issue, somewhere before the color nude pictorial at the back, probably page 102 or 103."

"That's just a regular job. You were so mysterious about it that I thought it was going to be some risky stakeout."

"This isn't something one of the people under me brought in, it's my own idea. It's a straight interview, so I decided to bring you in, since your forte is capturing expressions. I haven't decided on a writer, yet."

"Your idea? That *is* intriguing. Who are you after this time?"

"Have you heard of Yoshio Iizuka?"

"No. Who is he?"

"He runs a non-profit called *Society of Victims of Abuse for the Prevention of Abuse*, which he started up in September. They've got a website. I saw an interview with him on the internet recently, and he's also been on cable. I first read about him in the lifestyle section of a newspaper, which incidentally is a great source for news stories before they become big.

"Anyway, this guy has a strange charisma, Mariko. Check out his official site when you get home. He wants to help society by making his own story of child abuse known, or something like that. There's something about this guy that's setting off my sixth sense. He's got that charming smile that'll get him a spot on the broadcast channels as some kind of social commentator when high-definition broadcasts start. He's got the looks and he's got the brains. The women who make up the daytime viewership are going to be in his thrall. In a way, he's just the kind of material my, shall we say, unusual tastes incline towards. That's why I'd like to call dibs on him as soon as possible. And that's why I want you to photograph him. But I don't want the face he presents the world. I want you to capture that interior *je ne sais quoi* that you can't hide even if you try. That's what you're good at, right?"

She finally got what he was beating around the bush about. "What exactly is an 'interior *je ne sais quoi* that you can't hide'?

Why do you assume there's something unhealthy going on? He's putting his own experiences of abuse to work in order to help society, no? What could be nobler than that?"

"I just don't buy it. Nothing sells like a story where beauty, complete perfection, appears, and turns out it was actually rotten on the inside. Call me a cynic, but it's what I do as editor-in-chief of *In Focus*. It's not that there's anything wrong with the idea of making a contribution to society, but this guy says he's overcome really horrible child abuse, and I just want to find a blemish on that beautiful face of his. I know very well that you're the best for this kind of project among the forty-eight photographers we use.

"The only problem is the writer. I swear if I get a piece by a good old 'solid' writer who listens to every word this guy has to say about being abused and contributing to society or whatever and then proceeds to rehash nonsense like 'Hey, everyone, let's stop all this child abuse,' I myself will reject my own project. The newspaper interview I read the other day is a case in point. It was practically a love letter from the reporter to the guy. I had trouble under-standing how something written that way got past the editorial desk."

A small spark of ambition flashed in Mariko's heart just then. She wanted to reply to Sendo's unilateral barrage in some small way.

"I'll take the job, but on one condition. I know, I know, it's just lowly me, but still."

"Shoot."

"Let me write it."

"You? I don't know. I've never seen anything you've written. That's a pretty big risk for an editor. No, I'll get one of our young writers to do it."

"Please. Let me try. After all, someone's going to edit it, right? Put someone talented on it, as insurance. Please? In return I'll capture all the hidden interiors your heart desires."

Sendo gave Mariko a sly look like a man gauging the value of something. Mariko herself was slightly taken aback by her own proposal. She had never even considered being a writer, but there was something about this job that excited her.

"All right, I'll give you the job. But if you come back to me with some lightweight fluff piece you won't hear the end of it. This guy grew up in an orphanage. Your parents passed away, too, right? You're 'all alone in the world' like him. Use that. Talk about your childhoods, dark periods in your past, whatever. Just get him to reveal something about himself."

"Isn't that kind of harsh? Using my own past as bait? Am *I* bait for getting this young man to talk about his past?"

"You think you aren't? Using your own life is how it works in this business, Mariko." The look on Sendo's face as he said this was his scarier one. She could sense behind his words the yell, *What the hell are you complaining about?*

Mariko sighed. "I don't know. Trying to keep up with you is exhausting."

"Oh, come on, Mariko. I always give you work when you are in a pinch, don't I?"

"May I ask you something, editor-in-chief?"

"Why so formal all of a sudden?"

"You believe people are born evil, don't you."

"What? Of course I do. If they weren't, I'd be living under some bridge right now."

17—The Meeting

Friday, November 28th, 2:30 p.m., Shibuya Tokyu Inn, room 309. Mariko was setting up her photography equipment in the room reserved for today's interview by an editor named Nakamura, who worked under Sendo. It was thirty minutes before the interview.

It was clear outside and the sunlight pouring into the room

was beautiful, so she wanted to use ISO 400 film, but paused. *It's autumn after all. 800 is probably better for the skin tone. Shutter speed 1/60, 2.8 or maybe 3.5 f-stop. That should do.*

Indoor portraits didn't really need that much preparation. The editor in charge at *In Focus* would be arriving soon. But Mariko had an idea. Outsiders would get in the way of the "meeting of two lonely souls" that Sendo wanted in order to draw out Iizuka's secrets. Mariko had a feeling today's job would require a great deal of delicacy.

The night Sendo offered her the job, she took a look at the *Society of Victims of Abuse for the Prevention of Abuse* official website and was overwhelmed. The second she saw the top page, she was struck by something terrifying about it that she couldn't wrap her head around. A shiver ran up her spine. But as she read Iizuka's account, the feeling of indistinct terror she felt gradually turned into restless anxiety.

She clicked the icon and went to the next page. She covered her mouth with her hands as though something had suddenly gripped her heart. The photographs of the abuse Iizuka had suffered, arranged in a grid on the screen, had the heading: "The mother who abused me loved Louis Vuitton."

No! You can't do that! Mariko immediately thought. She felt instinctively, *This young man Yoshio Iizuka says all these inspiring things with that beautiful face of his, but he's lacking something inside.*

What he was lacking was the ability to care for himself. The ability to love himself. Human dignity. *He's turned himself into a sideshow freak; he's humiliating himself. He's like a child who's been possessed by a demon. He's hurting himself mentally and physically, with a smile on his face.* Mariko's shock was profound. She sat at her desk, stunned, facing the screen.

And that was why she could not have others present at today's interview, during which she would be coming into contact with a damaged soul.

As she was thinking this, she heard a man's voice through the crack in the door. She had flipped the door lock out in order to prop the door open, so the editor, Nakamura, just walked right in.

"Mariko, sorry I'm late."

Nakamura, who worked in the *In Focus* editorial department, was wearing a parka over a tank top with the number 55 on it. He had previously been in the photography department but had been reassigned to editorial.

"Nakamura, we need to talk."

"Tell me what's on your mind. For you, Mariko, darling of the department, I will walk through fire, swim the—"

"Put a plug in it," Mariko said, as she spun him around and pulled him back into the hallway.

"Wait, what's going on?" Nakamura asked lispingly.

"What we need to talk about is you letting me do this interview alone."

"Yeah, the chief already told me that you're going to be handling the photography and the writing. I'm to proof the manuscript and pick the photographs."

"I want everyone else out of the room during the interview and while I'm taking the photographs."

"What? I have to be in there."

"Mr. Sendo wants this to be a 'dialogue between lonely souls,' and for that to happen, it has to be one on one."

"Listen, we're a major publisher, and there are compliance guidelines that make a man and a woman alone in a hotel room a difficult proposition."

"And that's why you're going to help me out."

"What am I supposed to tell the chief?"

"If you don't say anything, he won't find out. Afterwards, I'll tell you exactly what we said and did in the room. I'll even give you a copy of the tape."

"Fine, then I'll scoop you: 'Hotel Room Tryst between Young Non-Profit Idealist and Beautiful Photographer.'"

"Good, Nakamura. That's the spirit. Now go get some coffee, for about an hour. Ciao."

With that, Mariko closed and locked the door. Now she could concentrate. All that was left was to decide how to structure the interview. She was going to be both photographer and interviewer, which meant she wasn't going to be able to capture the interviewee's expressions as he was talking. She decided to split the hour she had into two parts and do the photography either before or after the interview.

In Focus was a pictorial weekly, so the pictures were everything. *Which means maybe the photo session should come first... No, people's expressions are always stiff when they first meet someone. I'll be able to get a better expression if I photograph him after he's let his guard down a bit during the interview.*

As she went over this in her mind, she gauged possible angles, shoved the sofas around, and turned the digital voice recorder on and paused it so that she could start recording right away. Just then, there was a knock on the door.

Her heart thumped loudly in her chest. She was finally going to meet Yoshio Iizuka, the young man she had developed a strong interest in after seeing his website.

Mariko had experience handling photography for interviews with famous actors and politicians, but things were different today. The fact that she was also handling the interview was part of it, but she'd felt a strange sense of unease since the morning, a mixture of anticipation and anxiety that made her very nervous.

She opened the door and found a young man of slight build standing in the hallway. He was about 5'6", about Mariko's height. A well-shaped head sat on a trim body. He was wearing a beige cotton jacket that emanated a feeling of cleanliness, and slacks of the same color. On his feet he wore Converse high-tops.

She had only seen him in a shoulders-up picture in the newspaper and was surprised that the vibe his whole body gave off was totally different from what she'd imagined. The newspaper photograph had communicated something more intense, the image of an energetic activist. But the young man before her was slender, with an almost frail presence. She had heard he was twenty, but he seemed even younger.

"Hi. I'm Yoshio Iizuka," he said, standing in the doorway. The instant he opened his mouth, he seemed charged with a powerful aura, like a limp balloon suddenly filling with air.

It's the face. The powerful aura that destroys the frail feeling his body conveys comes from his face.

"Nice to meet you. I'm Mariko Amo. I'll be doing the interview."

She ushered Yoshio into the room and led him to the sofa that she had arranged so that a blank wall would be behind it.

She was extremely nervous: her heart pounded so hard she wondered if she'd even be able to do the interview. She poured coffee with her left hand, while her right hand was trembling so much that the cup and saucer rattled. She took a deep breath and said to herself, *It's your first interview, but you've been at thousands of shoots, haven't you?* She calmed down a bit thinking about it that way.

"Thanks for finding time in your busy schedule to meet with me today." She placed the coffee on the knee-high glass table.

"Thank you. Could I also get a glass of water?" He had a soft voice. His tone was gentle.

Two sets of thick curtains hung in front of the window facing Meiji Avenue, but Mariko had opened them and left the white lace ones so as to maximize the effect of the beautiful natural light. The soft afternoon sun lit up the young man sitting in a natural and relaxed pose on the sofa. She sat facing Yoshio, feeling the gap between the way she'd imagined him before meeting him and the real thing right before her eyes.

"Besides the interview, I'm also going to be doing the photography. I'd like to do the interview first. Is that all right?"

"No problem."

Mariko moved the recorder switch out of the pause position.

As instructed by Sendo, she handed Yoshio a copy of the latest issue of *In Focus* and showed him what page the piece would appear on, while describing the purpose of the interview.

The featured person for that issue was a man who was barely thirty but had garnered a lot of attention as an online trader. The headline read: "Money-making secrets from a trader who handles ¥13.4 billion a year!" Mariko was already worried what Yoshio would think.

"The concept behind this feature isn't to present people who are already famous and active in the spotlight, but to interview people in various fields who have big dreams, so that we can communicate that ambition to our readers and cheer them on."

Having said that, Mariko heard a little voice by her ear. It was Sendo, objecting, *Not really, Mariko. This feature is for approaching people in the news from an angle different from the competition and getting them to slip up.*

Yoshio looked at the page with no expression on his face and then started flipping through other pages, one by one. Mariko broke into a cold sweat, worried he would decide not to have anything to do with such a vulgar publication. Almost every color page was a nude shot of an actress, and celebrity gossip stories were splashed across other pages in garish type. The sports column lacked stories since it wasn't baseball season; instead the magazine was covering some group date between Giants players and celebrities.

Yoshio flipped the pages without changing his expression. He had the air of a sociologist dispassionately observing phenomena.

"What's this?" he asked, stopping at a murder story under the headline "Temp Worker Slashed!"

"A man got stabbed to death one night week before last under the Seibu Line guard rail in Ikebukuro. It was all over the papers. Of course, our magazine doesn't have the same approach to these stories, which is why the headline is so sensational. 'Temp Worker

Slashed!' really is inappropriate. The many temp workers who're being laid off wouldn't like that."

Yoshio looked up at Mariko. "I find it pretty funny." His mouth relaxed a bit, and the trace of a smile played over his lips. The killing had been the practice exam in Kazuhiko's initiation, scripted by Yoshio.

"Shall we start?" Mariko asked.

Yoshio put the magazine on the side table and nodded.

"This might sound kind of boring, but the first thing I'd like to ask you is: what is your dream?"

"Huh?" Yoshio blinked, caught off guard by the question.

"Oh, I'm sorry. Is that too abstract for a first question? Please forgive me. I thought about all sorts of things on my way here, but that's the one thing I really want to know. You're still only in your twenties, and you have this amazing goal of contributing to society. When I was your age, I was still figuring out how I was going to make my way in the world.

"What kept me going, though, was the dream of becoming a professional photographer one day, someone whose photographs would move people. I'm sorry. I don't mean to compare myself to you, since obviously I don't have the same aspirations that you do. I just thought there might be some kind of personal dream or inner motivation behind your amazing ideals, something that pushed you to start your non-profit.

"I have to be honest with you. I'm not a professional writer. I'm just a photographer, and this is the first time I'm interviewing my photographic subject."

Yoshio's expressionless eyes, displaying a cautiousness bordering on cunning, stared straight at Mariko. "Why didn't your magazine get a professional writer for this piece? Isn't that kind of an insult?"

Oh boy, Mariko thought. She had been naive in thinking that coming clean would help things.

But Yoshio wasn't angry. Mariko shifted in her seat, buying

some time to settle her nerves and think of an answer.

What is this woman raving about? My dream? What a ridiculous question, Yoshio thought to himself. *With the first newspaper reporter, and in all other interviews since, it's been enough simply to spout some beautiful words about contributing to society, inspired by the idea of ridding the world of abuse, yada yada yada, which is the challenge I've officially laid down before society. But this ludicrous woman is asking about my "own" dream?*

Mariko's face flushed and her head was a swirl of confusion. "I apologize if I've offended you. I truly apologize. The only way I know to apologize is to tell you exactly what I was thinking. I came today because the editorial department suggested that there might be something in me that would let me empathize with you since my father is gone and my mother is dead and I have no brothers or sisters. I'm all alone in the world."

Yoshio eyebrows jumped up and his eyes opened wide. His large black eyes regarded Mariko with their penetrating gaze. She was fixed in place by that gaze. Eventually its sharpness seemed to be suppressed by a force of will and grew gentle. A smile appeared on his face, and he relaxed the muscles in the cheeks of his mask, in order to make this interviewer, who was asking him to empathize with her own background, feel more comfortable.

The woman's words had been a shock to him, but now he had to begin speaking in a friendly manner, with a sense of familiarity, as one might meeting someone from one's hometown.

"Ms. Amo, I should be doing the apologizing. Don't worry about it. Your explanation has actually helped me relax a little. Of course, if you knew your parents at all, then our situations are totally different, and I envy you for that. But I get the feeling that I won't have to pick my words so carefully with you or worry that you might misunderstand my feelings or misconstrue something I say like I've had to with other interviewers."

Mariko raised her head and looked up at Yoshio. His previous frightening expression had changed, replaced by an affable smile full of warmth. She was afraid the whole interview had been ruined, but she appeared to have dodged that bullet.

"Thank you for that, and I really do apologize," Mariko said. "All right, then. I'd like to ask you a few questions by way of starting over. You spent your teenage years in an orphanage in Tokyo?"

"That's right. I was in an orphanage called The Nestlings' Home in Miyazaki until I was five. It was connected to Jiiku Hospital, which has the Stork's Mailbox. They take in abandoned kids who can't find foster homes, but only until the age of five. Luckily, there was an opening at the Tsurumaki Garden in Akabanebashi, here in Tokyo, so I was transferred. It was right smack in the middle of the city. The first thing you see from the entrance is Tokyo Tower looming over you. Though I guess the view is a bit different now."

"Yes. As a matter of fact, I was driving right past the tower when it was blown up."

Yoshio observed the woman in front of him, making small adjustments to his mask to prevent the smile from disappearing. *This woman was at the bombing?* he thought. It wasn't as though she had evidence he did it, but there was something unsafe about the coincidence.

"Really? It must've been quite a surprise. Was it a big explosion?"

"Big's not the word. I'm a photographer, so I just started taking pictures. I took as many as I could right until the moment it fell over. I actually hurt my leg a bit. I was in the hospital for ten days."

This woman was almost one of my victims, the thought sprang up in Yoshio's mind. *And she says she has pictures of the tower falling over.* He began to feel a queer connection to this Mariko Amo woman even though he was meeting her for the first time.

"What kind of pictures are they?"

"They were in lots of magazines and on TV starting around September. You didn't see them? They're shots taken from the foot of the huge steel structure, and you can see it falling right onto you. I took those pictures."

"What a coincidence. I've got clippings of your pictures that I found in magazines."

"Really? Why?"

Why? Because they're a beautiful record of what I did, he thought, but said, "Because I thought they were beautiful photographs."

"Beautiful? I suffered from depression after that. People were pretty brutal with me on the internet. They said I was profiting from the horrible crime."

Yoshio laughed. "That kind of chatter is nothing but bubbles in the sewer. Just ignore it. Can I ask you something?"

"Sure."

Yoshio paused a bit and looked at Mariko's eyes, trying to see into her mind. "Did you take any photographs of people falling from the observation deck?"

Mariko was at a loss for words. She felt a pain inside, like a sharp claw scratching open the closed wound in her heart. "Why do you want to know?"

"Whenever I looked at your photographs, I always wondered if you hadn't taken some of people falling off the observation deck, judging by the angle of the shots. But I didn't see anything like that in any of the magazines. I looked all over. I even searched the internet, but couldn't find anything."

"No, I didn't take any pictures like that."

Yoshio directed his sharp gaze at Mariko. He saw that she was lying. "I see."

"Sorry, we seem to have digressed, talking about Tokyo Tower. We don't have that much time so let's get back to the interview. What was it like trying to get your non-profit organization started?" Yoshio's question still resonated inside Mariko and her heart pounded as she tried desperately to get back on track. "I believe it's been almost three months since you opened the office. What kind of system do you have in place to run it?"

"I'm the chairman and I have three officers below me, although I'm thinking of adding maybe one more. The rest of the staff, around seventeen people, are volunteers."

"You've already got quite a large team."

"Yeah, I only have three officers who have gone through the proper training, but there are quite a few registered members of the website, which is over a year old now, so when I announced that I was going to incorporate I got a very positive response from people saying they'd be willing to work without pay. Thanks to those people, I really haven't had any problems."

"The person who arranged this interview is actually our editor-in-chief, and he said that the person he talked to on the phone was extremely professional." The word Sendo had used was "creepy," not "professional."

"I make sure our employee training is done right because, after all, our goal is to make a contribution to society. We don't want to give people any reason to talk badly about us."

"What does that training involve?"

Yoshio recalled the basic techniques of brainwashing. He attempted to tell the truth without letting Mariko catch on:

"Well, all right. It's you, so I'll tell you without fear of being misconstrued. The fact of the matter is that my staff are all people who've dropped out of society. They dropped out of school, they hurt themselves, they hurt their family, that kind of thing. Almost all of them have been suicidal at some point. Kids like that are so profoundly scarred that in a sense they can't go to their parents or teachers for help. They're alone and they hit a dead end, and all they can see in that darkness is their own pain.

"But one thing they haven't lost is that human potential for recovery. All they need is a bit of light, and the change is like night and day. The absolute worst thing you can do is take a condescending attitude or order them around. Ordinary teachers, instructors, trainers, or what have you generally don't understand that, because they tend to think of themselves as looking down on these kids from above.

"The first thing you do is bring a little bit of light—a single matchstick—to their inner darkness. You tell them, 'Look, I'm just as scarred as you are, but I've got more light over here.' They slowly open up to you, and the emotions they had pent up inside them start flowing. When that happens, you're one of them. You're equals, and as long as you don't do anything to betray them, they're in the clear. They become full-fledged members of the unit and will work themselves to the bone for it. That's why they're so much easier to use than regular kids who're just wasting their lives away."

Yoshio regretted that last statement. *Did I get a little carried away there? "Easier to use" was probably a bit much. From now on I'll say "They've got more character."*

"Wow. I can't believe you're still only twenty. I just turned thirty…something, but I feel like a kid listening to you."

"I just turned twenty, so are we both Scorpios?"

"You're a Scorpio, too? My birthday's just on the edge, on the twenty-second, so I've also got some Sagittarius mixed in, according to the astrology books I've read."

"I'm November 11th. I chose that day, actually."

"You chose it?"

"That's right. If you saw my website, you must know that twenty years ago I was the first beneficiary of the Stork's Mailbox, a system for rescuing abandoned babies that was set up at Jiiku Hospital in Miyazaki Prefecture. The hospital determined the date of my birth based on how developed I was and put that in my family register, but I don't recognize that date. I'm the little baby that was brought into the world at the Stork's Mailbox, and that date is my date of birth."

As she listened to him speak, she noticed that his reserved, quiet manner of speech had gradually altered. Something hot was flowing in the underground currents of his mind.

"That's quite a bleak way of looking at it." She tossed it out, like a pebble into a pond.

"Not at all!" Yoshio was taken aback by his own unexpectedly loud response and looked at Mariko. He worried that the mask might be slipping off his face.

The woman before him looked at him innocently. There was no suspicion in her eyes, but nor was there the attitude of brainwashed worship of, say, Midori's eyes, or the vacuity of the orphanage teachers when they praised the straight-A student. Mariko's look was not the look of adoration that promised the easy brainwashing of the other female reporter. Mariko's look was unlike that of any of the interviewers he'd interacted with over the past month.

What was she seeing?

Suddenly, Yoshio understood. It was *he* who was seeing—seeing the woman before him.

Yoshio felt uncharacteristically disconcerted. He regretted having overdone it and taken on too many interviews. When he got back to the office, he'd tell his assistant to decline all interview requests until further notice.

"Ms. Amo, we agreed to one hour exactly, right? Do you think we could end the interview part around here and move on to the photography you're so good at? Let's see what you can draw out of me that way."

Mariko thought back over the interview, worried she might not have enough material to write something that would convince Sendo. "I hate to be insistent, but could we go back real quick to the first question I asked?"

"The first question? Oh, you mean my dream."

Yoshio was ready.

My dream is to kill as many people as possible before I die. I've always wanted to die young. Just being in this world is an unendurable thing, which is why death is the only thing I've ever thought about. But I don't want to die alone—I hate the world as much as I hate myself. That's why my only dream is to bring about an Armageddon limited in scale only by my own talents, pouring all my power into the enterprise and taking as many people as possible with me. I want the final expression of my hatred, an act of genocide that will take place in

Tokyo, to chisel into the tablet of history the fact that a demon by the name of Yoshio Iizuka had been here, had resided in this world.

"My dream is to save as many people as possible before I die. I believe that the moment I was born, I actually died once, and that's why I have lived my life filled with gratitude for the very fact of my existence. Ever since I was small I thought of different ways I could repay my debt of gratitude to society. I realized pretty quickly that I can't do anything alone. My love of the world is equaled only by the depth of my gratitude towards life itself. My only dream is to organize some kind of festive event limited in scale only by my own talents, pouring all of me into it and involving as many people as possible. I want that event to go down in history as proof that a person called Yoshio Iizuka had received life in this world."

Mariko stared at Yoshio's face, stunned into silence. *How can someone so young have such a noble philosophy?* she wondered. *I'm having trouble just looking out for myself, much less helping others, which I've never even considered.*

"Mr. Iizuka," Mariko said, "I'm moved. I feel ashamed at my own selfishness. You're so young, yet you feel like you... I guess it really must have been the abuse you received when you were just born? I read in one of your interviews that had it not been for the dedicated treatment of a passionate doctor you'd never have survived the nearly fatal wounds your body was covered with."

"I've decided to believe that when that happened, I died and was reborn. That's what I've told myself ever since I was a child."

"It's astounding how easily you're able to channel your abuse in such a positive direction."

"Isn't everyone burdened by some kind of worry or trauma? Each of those worries and traumas flows from a particular place in an individual's personal history. Given those sources, there must also be a state of mind that existed before they came into existence—congenital defects aside, of course. That means that if we could somehow return to that original state, we'd be able to reset the effects of traumas we suffer later on. I believe in the essential goodness of people. People are born as angels but are gradually steeped in the evil of the world and become more and more like monsters."

"You believe in the essential goodness of people?"

This lady is a serious trip, Yoshio thought. "Of course I do, Ms. Amo," he said.

Mariko recalled Sendo's comment that he believed in the essential evil of people, thanks to which he earned his daily bread in this world. He could have just been saying that, of course. People could be a lot more naive than they let on.

"I personally don't know. But what's the big festive event you mentioned? It sounds exciting."

"I can't say too much about the general plans, but you know, I've never felt this strong a connection with someone, Ms. Amo, so I'll tell you a bit about it. It wouldn't be going too far to say that I started up my non-profit to organize this event. I want to put together an entertainment show that will bring tens of thousands of people together in rapturous joy." Yoshio had to suppress a laugh. *It's going to be a rapture all right, but not of joy.*

"It sounds great. When will it happen?"

"There are still a lot of details to hammer out, but it won't be too long now."

"I'm really looking forward to it."

"Ms. Amo, I haven't told anyone about this event yet, so if you could leave it out of your piece, I'd really appreciate it. I want you to give me your word."

"Of course. You know, I can be pretty disorganized sometimes, so I was worried about how this would turn out, but it's gone really great. You've been very open with me. I really appreciate it. Shall we move on to the photographs?"

Mariko stood up and moved her sofa over against the wall to make space for her to take pictures. Yoshio relaxed on his sofa, watching Mariko's movements. Mariko took a few shots to start off without giving them much thought.

"Could I get you to not look into the camera? If you could look toward the window... The light coming through the lace curtains is so beautiful."

Yoshio rotated his body as told, and Mariko squatted down in front of him, snapping the shutter.

"Could I get you to stand by the wall now?"

Yoshio did exactly as he was told, with no complaints, like a professional model. He stood in front of the wall in a casual pose. Mariko snapped the shutter as she looked at Yoshio through the viewfinder. She wanted to capture the spiritual energy that was emanating from inside the slender young man—the life essence of Yoshio, who worked his body so hard, his body so filled with life that if felt like it was about to explode.

Mariko could hardly be called sly, but she had a more-than-solid career as a photographer and decided to ask a slightly mischievous question. It would be a kind of trap to capture Yoshio's reaction.

"Mr. Iizuka, isn't there anyone in the world that you hate?"

Yoshio had removed his saint's mask after the interview, assuming photography sessions were all the same anyway, and was standing there defenseless, as it were, when the question came. He stiffened and looked at Mariko though the lens.

There was a glow of hatred in his gaze—just a tiny flicker of turbulence in his heart, but the mechanical eye of Mariko's camera had captured it. Yoshio instantly felt anger at having fallen for Mariko's trap.

This woman is dangerous, Yoshio thought. *I'm going to have to add her to the black list and have her taken care of at some point.* There was no way he was going to forgive someone who'd laid a trap like this for him. Next time it would be he that laid the trap. On the spur he came up with a way to retaliate that would do some psychological damage.

"Ms. Amo, could you hold on for a second?"

This snapped Mariko out of her trance-like state as she snapped away at the shutter. She looked up from the viewfinder.

Yoshio smiled as he took off his jacket and began unbuttoning his white open-collar shirt.

"Um, wait..."

Yoshio tossed his shirt aside and stood in front of the wall, nude from the waist up. "There we go. You know I've never done this for any other photographer. This should give your magazine something it can use."

Yoshio wanted to employ his whole body to express the outrage he felt. As planned, Mariko seemed to be reeling. She stood slack. The scars of abuse she'd only seen in photographs online were flushed and pinkish. Her honed sensitivity fully understood that this was a bodily expression of Yoshio's brimming anger, and she was duly shocked.

"This should give your magazine something it can use"—the words irritatingly hit the mark. No matter how amateurishly written her column on today's interview might turn out, Sendo would forgive her. He would scream with delight when he saw the pictures of Yoshio Iizuka bare-chested. *The lurid venom we sell society,* Mariko thought. She covered the lens with her hand and took a few shots in rapid succession in order to separate what would follow from the previous data.

Mariko peered through the viewfinder and began snapping the shutter. She was nothing more than an eye. If something happened, she would capture it. If someone were to die right in front of her, her body would keep on shooting automatically.

She felt devastated. Her heart wailed as she collected the day's best work 1/60th of a second at a time as the shutter allowed the light to pass. Yoshio Iizuka's very being exuded pain. The beatific words uttered during the interview were part of the pain. It all dealt grave harm to Mariko.

18—The Demon Before You

Almost three months had passed since the special investigation headquarters had been set up, and it continued to lack even a single lead. At 10 p.m. Isogai was listening to the reports of his junior officers for that day in a meeting of the canvassing unit. A young sergeant with the precinct named Yozo Maruyama had concentrated on door-to-door canvassing of Area Six around Akabanebashi with another detective.

That day he had visited Tsurumaki Garden, the orphanage where Yoshio Iizuka had grown up. He reported that he had asked the director of the orphanage, as well as all the children, about the day before and the day of the Tokyo Tower bombing.

Isogai immediately recalled Yoshio Iizuka. *Ah, the orphanage that young man was at. I wonder what he's up to now? He's probably an upstanding member of society now, working hard.* Isogai felt somehow nostalgic.

"The orphanage produced nothing in the way of leads." Sergeant Maruyama passed a copy of the formatted interview report to the desk officer, who immediately entered the data into the computer. "No witnesses, either. But the kids were clearly shocked by it. Some burst into tears during the interviews. It was heartbreaking. It was my first time in an orphanage. Those places are something else..."

"Maruyama, your personal impressions don't contribute a whole helluva lot to these investigations, okay? Considering how Tokyo Tower is the first thing you see when you go out through the front door, you'd think there'd be at least one or two kids or teachers who would've noticed *something*."

"You would, but there weren't. The orphanage has a tradition of going on 'fieldtrips to Tokyo' during which they'd go up to the observation deck of Tokyo Tower, which was right across the street. I don't know about the big kids, but the little kids apparently loved Tokyo Tower. They were all crushed—figuratively, of course—

when it collapsed. The orphanage director was also pretty sad that there was now one fewer place he could take the kids for some fun. Sorry, I'm digressing again."

Today's kids probably aren't interested in Tokyo Tower at all, Isogai thought to himself. *I wonder if that Iizuka kid, who seemed so mature, ever climbed it for fun.* He recalled the Atagoyama murder investigation five years before and allowed himself to simmer in his memories for a moment.

Isogai had visited the Tsurumaki Garden Orphanage doing door-to-door interviews as a detective in a canvassing unit, Atagoyama murder investigation headquarters, Atagoyama police station.

Fifteen orphans lived there, plus two young children who were in a foster care-type situation: under the Garden's care even though they had families because those families had forsaken them. Of the children, only three were old enough to have been involved in the stabbing murder of Atsushi Sakamoto: Keigo Kunugi (14), Masanori Yasukawa (16), and Yoshio Iizuka (15).

Keigo Kunugi had left early that morning to visit relatives in Chiba Prefecture, where he had spent the night. Masanori Yasukawa had been drinking with friends, even though he was a minor, and his friends confirmed this. Finally, Yoshio Iizuka was Keigo Kunugi's roommate and had no confirmable alibi since Kunugi was not there, but in the course of interviewing one of the teachers, the investigators learned that Yoshio Iizuka had finished dinner at the orphanage at 8 p.m. and gone to his room to read. This jibed with Iizuka's own statement, of course.

The Iizuka boy had made a strong impression on Isogai. Neatly trimmed hair, intelligent face, deep-set oval eyes, determined lips: his well-set features were brimming with intellectual acumen.

His reputation among the teachers at the orphanage was impeccable. He apparently had the best grades in his class. About thirty thousand children from orphanages and similar institutions were matriculated in mandatory education, and the director confided to Isogai that having a stellar student like Yoshio Iizuka among them did wonders for the image of orphans, who tended to be viewed in a rather negative light, often as shabby.

Not only that, but he had overcome the handicap of heartless abuse soon after birth and was becoming a fine young man, the director said. Naturally, the director wanted to help Iizuka go onto high school and further, but the boy wanted to start working as soon as he finished the last year of compulsory education and become independent.

Isogai compared this with his own son Yuichi, who was a college senior. Isogai was seldom home when Yuichi was growing up, and when he was, it was only to break promises with his son to dash off to work. That had made Yuichi resent him. As a college student he finally began to show some acceptance of the fact that his father was a police detective.

Still, his son, who was on the verge of becoming a full-fledged member of society, hadn't done any serious job searching. Instead he would continue at his part-time job—at some fly-by-night entertainment company to boot! Yuichi's actions seemed like a rebellion against his father, a kind of retaliation for being the son of a local public servant.

What should he have done to bring his son up to be a reliable young man like Yoshio Iizuka, who gave not the least outward sign of being orphaned and horrifically abused as a child? Such thoughts played on the edge of his consciousness as Isogai continued interviewing Yoshio, whose alibi had not been completely confirmed yet.

Yoshio said he loved to read and often went to the public library to research things. Isogai later confirmed this on a visit to the library. Yoshio had returned to the orphanage at 8 p.m. The murder had taken place at 1:30 a.m. of the following day, so all Yoshio had to prove was that he had been in the orphanage between 1 a.m. and 2 a.m., since the scene of the crime was less than a thirty-minute walk from the orphanage. Yoshio lacked a rock-solid alibi, however.

Isogai got permission from Yoshio to look through his things, telling him that it was voluntary. He had him show him the shoes he always wore: white Converse high-tops, size 7.

No matter how much more time Isogai spent on the kid, he'd be in the "gray." To begin with, there were absolutely no points of contact between Iizuka and the murdered kid. Nothing connected Yoshio, who had lived in orphanages his whole life, and Atsushi Sakamoto, who lived with his well-off family in an upscale apartment building and who was studying for his high school entrance exams. The straight line described by Yoshio's tragic life and the one described by Atsushi's promising future would run parallel, never intersect no matter how much he extrapolated, Isogai concluded.

And those worn-out Converse. As he looked back on that investigation five years ago, the final curtain dropping on his recollections was that pair of white Converse high-tops, so worn out that the soles had lost their tread, treated with such care and apparently washed often. The image of the shoes clouded Detective Isogai's vision.

"Speaking of which, do you know who Yoshio Iizuka is?" Sergeant Maruyama suddenly asked.

"Maruyama, cut out this mind-reading of yours. I was just thinking about that Iizuka kid. Why do you know him?"

"You haven't seen him in the news recently?"

"In the news? What did he do?"

"What did he do? He started a non-profit called *Society of Victims of Abuse for the Prevention of Abuse*. He's really popular, and I think he's still doing it."

Isogai had no idea that the kid he had interviewed five years ago was doing that kind of thing now.

"I didn't ask, but the director of the Tsurumaki Garden was real proud of him and told me all about it. It sounded like he wanted to show what a great place he was running, since Iizuka had grown up there and gone on to become such an exemplary person. I explained to him that these kinds of police canvassing operations interview everyone they can in the vicinity of a crime, but he was real worried that people might get the wrong impression if they saw cops poking around a place that takes care of kids who don't have parents. The guy went on and on, telling me that Iizuka is going to be on some morning talk show tomorrow. I could barely get a word in edgewise."

Isogai couldn't care less about the director, but it was nice to hear a heart-warming story for a change—the Iizuka kid had grown up and was putting his tragic past to work for the benefit of society.

True, he had never gotten a solid alibi for Yoshio Iizuka way back when. But there had been no mistakes in the investigation. He felt like a small ray of new light had lit up a dark, untouched place in a corner of his mind.

"Where's this non-profit of his?"

"It's actually not that far from the orphanage. I think it's in Area Four of the canvassing investigation. The non-profit's office only opened on September 1st, though, six days after the bombing."

"Which means that the guys in charge of that area haven't gone by there yet? I don't remember seeing a report."

"They might've asked a few questions. But the office wasn't there when it happened. What can they report, other than 'Subjects don't know anything'?"

"Listen, Maruyama. Your report tells me that the kids bawled because Tokyo Tower's gone. What on God's green earth does that have to do with the investigation? Nothing, it's just a distraction. Make it tighter, 'cause you're just making it hard on the desk officer. They've got thousands, tens of thousands of pieces of information to compile."

"Right, sorry. I'll be careful."

The next day, Maruyama, who had had the ABC's of canvassing operations drilled into him by Detective Isogai, turned on the TV at 7:30 a.m. at the Atagoyama special investigation headquarters. In order to keep tabs on how the investigation was being reported in the media, a small 20" TV set was placed on top of the short filing cabinets lined up against the north wall of the room.

Maruyama had been up all night and had slept for about two hours before dawn in the kendo dojo. He had been woken by the operatic snoring of the guy in the next cot. His wristwatch began emitting the small electronic beeping of the alarm as he was sitting there groggy-eyed.

What's the alarm for? he wondered for a moment before recalling that he'd set it the previous night to the time a program would be on and that he'd catch if he was able to wake up. He folded the futon and blankets and arranged them the immaculate way he'd been taught at the Police Academy, then put them away on the cot. He headed for the fifth floor investigation room.

Maruyama's desk was on the opposite side from the TV, against the south wall, so he walked all the way across the large hall, grabbed a chair belonging to one of the older detectives who had not come in yet, and watched, slung low in the chair with his legs thrown out in front of him.

It was a popular show called *Morning, Madame!* Every Tuesday they invited to the studio celebrities from different fields to get to know them and what they were up to. A comedian who was popular with housewives hosted the show, sometimes broaching topics that seemed a bit too serious for its viewers, which was actually what kept the ratings solid. Maruyama heard the comedian's high-pitched voice introducing today's guest.

"All right, then. Today's guest on our regular segment 'Who's in the News?' is Yoshio Iizuka! Let's have a big hand!" The host and the three other regular guests clapped as Yoshio came onto the set. His passionate dark eyes, closely cropped hair, broad forehead, and well-shaped eyebrows made quite a strong impression. At a gesture from the host, Yoshio Iizuka sat in a seat in the center.

"Mr. Iizuka, thanks for coming. Welcome, welcome!"

"Good morning."

"Oh my gosh, I've been *so* dying to meet you!" one of the regulars said, twisting in her seat coquettishly.

"Yoshie, you keep yourself under control, woman!" the host scolded, jokingly. "I don't care how long you haven't had a man, we're having a serious discussion today. Let's keep it proper."

"What serious discussion?" another regular asked.

"All right, you two, pipe down," the host said, swatting the two unruly guests on the head with what looked like a script he was holding.

"There might be a lot of viewers who haven't heard of Mr. Iizuka yet, so let me give you a brief introduction. Yoshio Iizuka is the chairman of a non-profit organization called *Society of Victims of Abuse for the Prevention of Abuse,* which is actively trying to rid the world of child abuse."

"Oh, them. I've heard of them."

"Yeah, I read in the newspaper that he has some website that became super famous."

"That's right," the host said. "Today we'll be getting Mr. Iizuka's thoughts as we discuss school bullying, which is a topic of great interest to our viewers. I heard you started your society in order to put your experiences of child abuse to work for society. Were you very badly abused?"

"It's all relative, I suppose, but I did hear that when they found me at the hospital I was on the verge of death."

Maruyama gave out a long yawn in his seat, trying to clear his head. He leaned back in the chair to stretch his back and saw someone behind him.

"Good morning, sir!"

It was Sergeant Isogai. "You sure are taking it easy, watching TV first thing in the morning. I believe your desk is over there."

"I apologize, sir, but this is also part of work…"

"If watching TV in the morning was part of our work, investigations would be the easiest job in the world."

"Detective Isogai, this is Yoshio Iizuka, the guy I was telling you about. I confirmed that he was making a guest appearance in the newspaper TV listings, so I thought I'd watch. His office is in Area Four, but it's not unrelated to Area Six, which is ours."

Isogai blinked his small eyes and watched the TV screen. Iizuka hadn't changed that much, he felt, from when he had interviewed him for the investigation five years ago. He had always had a mature, intelligent look. The kid was now on TV addressing the audience on the topic of bullying. A female comedian was having an exaggerated reaction as he rolled up his sleeve, revealing scars of overlapping L's and V's that had been cut into his arms with a blade.

Isogai felt bad for some reason as he watched Iizuka. He was making his TV debut by "selling" his pitiful tale of child abuse, something people would ordinarily try to conceal. Isogai felt like he was watching a young man with no parents and alone in the world being forced into doing something desperate.

"Okay, Maruyama, digging deep is part of investigating, I'll give you that. But the Area Six team haven't finished by a long shot, and we should be working on expanding our legwork. I'm the one who has to stand up at the joint investigation meetings every day and announce that we haven't found anything. Find a witness who saw the bad guys!"

"Yes, sir! I'll do my darndest today," Maruyama replied, turning off the TV and returning to his desk, crossing the early-morning room where investigators were beginning to assemble.

19—A Spark

"Isogai, I gotta tell you, it's a total disaster. A complete no-hitter. My batters can't even graze the ball, no matter how madly they swing. If this were baseball, I'd be out on my ass as a coach by now. But the police aren't allowed to lose games. We have to keep fighting until we win. It ain't fair, I tell you."

Isogai was meeting with Inspector Yoshida in order to report what they had found out over the past week and to hammer out the direction of the investigation for December.

"Inspector Yoshida, I've never heard you complain like this. I'm sorry my team can't provide any information that could help you put together your strategy. But I'm sure we'll find a useful lead somewhere. I'm convinced of it."

"I hope so. The chief of Section One was screaming at the recent late-night meeting, which was out of character for him, but he just won't listen to excuses. Proof of how desperate Public Security's getting is the fact that they've started picking up communists and right-wingers for minor infractions and throwing everything at them in the hopes that something will stick. Iwamoto didn't put it exactly this way, but they can't use Onodera's international terrorist theory as an excuse anymore. If we think even for a second that the culprits have left the country, then the wind will totally go out of the investigation's sails. I happen to believe that whoever did this is still somewhere in the country. How are we supposed to face the families of the victims otherwise? You know, Isogai? For the past few days I've had the feeling that the guys we're after are very close to us."

"I hope your hunch is right. All right, I'll start with the report for the past week then."

Isogai handed a binder containing the report to Yoshida and began relaying the information the canvassing unit had managed to pick up, adding his own analysis along the way.

"We talked to every single guest in the 240 rooms facing

Tokyo Tower in the Tokyo Princess Hotel. There were quite a few foreigners staying in the hotel, some of whom had already gone home, so we got English-speaking staff from the hotel to call them, but either way we got no reliable witness information. A lot of people were real excited about having seen the tower fall over, though. The explosion was so loud that everybody who was in their room was glued to the window watching 'the event of the decade.'"

"'The event of the decade'?!" Yoshida turned up his head from his squat body with a look of horror on his face.

"Those are not my words. It's what the hotel guests were calling it."

"Do they have any idea that it was 'the massacre of the decade'? Unbelievable!"

"I agree. It's because of that climate in society that families of the victims get so sensitive. Community Safety has been interviewing survivors, even the really badly injured ones, and it looks like there's a lot of traumatized people, so they're biding their time. Those who escaped with a light injury were inside one of the buildings near the tower, so none of them saw it actually falling over, as I reported last month. The terrorists have to have watched the decisive moment from some vantage point."

A faint spark flashed through Yoshida's mind just then. He closed his eyes, following the weak hunch. *The terrorists must also have watched it...* It had to be so. Criminals capable of pulling off a flawless bombing attack would have to have been watching their handiwork go off perfectly, somewhere safe and sound.

If they didn't use a timer, they would have had to be near the site when they detonated the bombs, either inside a building in the vicinity, or in the hotel. The terrorists could be among the hotel guests Isogai had interviewed as witnesses. There needed to be another run-through of the guest list from a different perspective.

Another possibility was that the leader of the group had watched from some high vantage point while an underling pressed the detonator button. But where? What would be the best vantage point for watching the bombing, the Massacre of the Decade?

"Isogai, you said something about 'the event of the decade' just now. Can you think of anywhere that would be box seats with the best view for the terrorists, who knew exactly when the show would start?"

"Well, an observation deck, of course. The other observation deck in the area would be the Roppongi Hills observation deck. You'd have a completely unobstructed view of the tower collapse from there."

Yoshida's face lit up for just a second. He felt like he dimly saw someone standing there with a smile on his face, watching the incident unfold.

"Isogai, let's find everyone who was on the Roppongi Hills observation deck between 3:30 and 3:37 p.m. on August 26th."

"No offense, but how? They don't have a guest list, after all."

Isogai was right. But in order to mobilize the sixth sense he'd cultivated over his many years as a frontline investigator with Section One, Homicide Subsection, he absolutely needed a "vision": *Maybe they were watching.*

As long as he had even that foggy vision, Yoshida felt the confidence to go after the bad guys. Until now he had been unwittingly influenced by the Public Security Bureau clamoring about the involvement of terrorists and organizations and hadn't been able to investigate by following his signature "hunch."

We live in a world where kids who can't distinguish fiction from reality replace reality with the fantasies in their heads and stab random strangers on the street, Yoshida thought. *We can't logically rule out the possibility of some delusional nut thinking it would be "fun" to knock down Tokyo Tower and actually doing it. I can just imagine how amusing it must be for whoever did this to watch the police and the media go on and on about terrorists and organizations.*

He decided to propose to the investigation committee to start considering the perspective of a senseless crime committed simply for the pleasure of committing it, which had been difficult to imagine until now given the sheer scale of the thing.

"Isogai, I want you to put a message on the Police Department's website and the websites of all individual precincts asking anyone who was on the Roppongi Hills observation deck at 3:30 p.m. on August 26th, the time and date of the Tokyo Tower bombing attack, to cooperate with the investigation. Anyone who saw Tokyo Tower fall over was probably riveted by the sight and are unlikely to have forgotten it. We need to find out if there was anyone there who reacted in an unusual way as they were watching it happen."

"That might indeed be a good line to work. All right, I'll do it right away. Inspector Yoshida, the way you're breathing—you seem like you're really charged. All this talk of forensics and profiling… When it comes right down to the line, it's that hunch that matters most for a detective."

"Isogai."

"Yes?"

"Do you remember what I said the first or second day of the investigation?"

"No. You said something?"

"I said I felt like I just couldn't pick up the scent. I just can't see this whole thing being the work of terrorists or extremists or whatever. Nobody even issued a statement claiming responsibility!"

"Which means we have no idea what the attackers' motive was."

"Listen, when we were kids, we'd swipe spoons from the kitchen, line them up on the railroad tracks, and watch the train flatten them."

"You did what? I can't believe it. That's incredibly dangerous. What if you derailed a train that way?"

"I was a bad kid, let me tell you. But for kids these days, that's nothing. And I say 'kids,' but our whole country is turning into a nation of infantilized adults. There's plenty of people in their forties and fifties who aren't fully grown up."

"So you think someone would blow up Tokyo Tower, killing 402 people, just because?"

The day after Yoshida and Isogai went to the last weekly report meeting in November for the canvassing investigation, all officers from team leaders and up met in a small conference room at the Metropolitan Police Headquarters for a report by Kazushige Kusanagi, the forensics technician, on remains found at the scene of the crime.

Dressed in a white lab coat as usual, Kusanagi arrived from the building adjacent to police headquarters, a pitcher of water in hand. Just the sight of him made the overworked and overstressed detectives' blood pressure rise.

"Hello, everyone. Thanks for finding time in your busy schedules to come today."

"So this report's about some cell phone? What's this all about?" Onodera asked with irritation. He was running out of patience because the information collection operation under Chief Iwagami had shown no progress. His tone indicated that if this was another pointless report, heads were going to roll.

He was under tremendous pressure from top brass at the Public Security Bureau under Chief Iwagami, who in turn was under pressure from top government officials. Even Onodera, who occupied an elite management position in the force, was starting to feel mental and physical exhaustion in the face of impossible demands to hand in a report detailing specific changes for future terrorism countermeasures—a request which did not give any thought to the current state of the investigation.

"Uh, yes. I believe I previously reported that part of an *au* cell phone had been found at the scene. At that time, we didn't know what purpose it had served, but we've put together a hypothesis on the basis of other things we have found."

The investigators listened to Kusanagi with rapt attention, their eyes, grimy and sunken from lack of sleep and fatigue, glowing strangely. The atmosphere was almost cutthroat as though starving men were about to fight over a piece of food tossed to them.

"My theory is that the cell phone was used as a detonator by the attackers in order to detonate the bomb remotely. After getting the forensics squad to significantly broaden the scope of their collection activities, we finally found this." Kusanagi held up a plastic bag containing a small object before the detectives.

"What is it?" Isogai asked, voicing everyone's thought.

"It's a spring. We have collected fourteen of them, and they have tested positive for blasting powder, although only in trace amounts. I believe this points to vibration-type blasting caps, designed to use the cell phones' vibration function. When a call is placed to a cell phone that is embedded inside the bomb, the phone vibrates, and the vibration is amplified by these springs. That probably causes the pin to pop out in a device in which ignition fluid is mixed with an ignition inducer, setting off the blasting powder and detonating the sodium chlorate bomb."

Kusanagi was not exhausted like the detectives and gave his report beaming with confidence and energy. Section One Chief Kunugida grimaced as though someone had turned his rack another notch. He spoke as though it were a chore. "Assuming your 'theory' is correct, what's the *point* of a cell phone being used as a detonator?"

"That whoever did this doesn't match any existing profile," Kusanagi replied bluntly.

"So you mean this is a new kind of criminal?" Isogai asked.

"Exactly. You can run checks on criminal files all over the world and probably not turn up a single case of someone detonating a bomb this way. It's unique, and simple. In fact, the way it allows remote detonation is nothing less than genius. I mean, all you have to do is call the bomb."

Onodera was overcome with a desire to lock this harebrained explosives geek in a dark cell and "re-educate" him. *Anyone who uses the word "genius" to describe a method of performing mass murder needs to spend some time with my less scrupulous acquaintances at the Public Security Bureau for some retraining. Just as soon as this case is solved.*

The usually reticent Inspector Yoshida suddenly spoke up. "You know, Kusanagi, I think I'm starting to get a clearer picture of the people behind this thanks to you."

Everyone looked at Yoshida as though expecting the second coming.

"I think we've been looking for something too big," he continued. "I have a hunch that's growing stronger by the minute, and my hunch is telling me that whoever did this thing was just out to show the world what a genius he is. He's young, too, judging from the fact that he used cell phones for this. We've spent so much time chasing after terrorists that we've wound up going in the completely wrong direction."

Onodera looked like an ogre as he contemplated what Yoshida was saying. The other detectives, too, sensed something convincing about his words.

Chief Kunugida asked, "So it was just for fun?"

"Exactly. The most horrific crime in Japanese history, committed simply to do evil and enjoy it."

"Right, then," Kunugida jumped into action. "We can't risk focusing only on that, but for now let's re-profile the attacker or attackers as being members of what I suppose we can call the cell-phone generation, including everyone from teenagers up to people in their thirties, with the motive being 'fun.' I want the investigation directive revised by tomorrow for distribution at the joint morning investigation meeting so that everyone will be on the same page."

Kunugida's orders flew. Zombiefied selves reinvigorated by the new turn of events, the detectives rushed back to their posts.

About one week later, information from a few people began coming in in response to the message placed on the websites of police departments nationwide: "If you were on the Roppongi Hills observation deck around 3:30 p.m. on August 26, 2011, please contact your local police. Your cooperation in solving the Tokyo Tower Bombing is appreciated."

The investigation headquarters, which had been at a standstill for three months, began bustling.

20—Witnesses

The new investigation directive for the special investigation headquarters was implemented thanks to the sharp eye of Inspector Yoshida and would focus on people in their teens, twenties, and thirties. Isogai's most important task at the moment was getting solid witness information in order to establish an accurate profile of the perpetrator on the basis of actual sightings.

Thursday, December 14, 2011, 3:30 p.m. A young man had seen the webpage and sent an email to public relations, and Isogai decided to have him come in for an interview.

Junichi Tsukuda was twenty years old and had dyed red hair. He was nervous about the first-ever encounter he was about to have with a police detective thanks to a connection with the Tokyo Tower bombing case. It was also kind of fun, so he brought his girlfriend along.

"Thanks for coming today. I'm Detective Isogai. I'm in charge of this case. You came all the way out from Hachioji, right?"

"No worries. It's actually kind of exciting, like I'm an extra in a cop movie or something. You don't look much like any actor I know, though. I was wondering what police detectives looked like."

"Son, this ain't no movie. Let's get that straight. This is an *actual* crime, and more than 400 people *actually* died. What I want you to do for me today is tell me exactly what you remember, as accurately as possible."

Junichi's girlfriend, sitting next to him in a miniskirt and leggings, nudged him with her elbow. "Quit goofing around," she whispered.

"So to start, you were present at the Roppongi Hills observation deck around 3:30 p.m. on the 26th of August this past year, is that correct?"

"We were," answered Yumi Ito, the girlfriend, who was itching to talk. "We were going to see a movie, but Jun, this dumbass, didn't know the movie we wanted to see had already stopped showing the week before, so we couldn't see it, and we decided to go to the observation deck since we had nothing better to do. I swear, what do you have that cell phone for, if you can't even look up a movie with it? You are so disorganized."

"Oh, that's rich, coming from the queen of disorganization."

"Hey, how about you two bicker on your own time? So you were both on the observation deck at three thirty, right?"

"It was a long time ago, so I don't remember what time it was, exactly. We saw Tokyo Tower fall, though, so I guess we were there at that time. Man, that was a serious trip, huh, Yumi?" Junichi said, glancing at Yumi for support.

"It was unbelievable. We were standing at the window facing Tokyo Tower right from the start, and I look up, and there's this huge boom, and the windows are, like, shaking. I think, 'What the fuck?' I have no idea what's going on, and then I look and see this like white smoke rising up from the bottom of the tower, and then the tower starts to fall over, you know, away from us. The whole scene is burned into my memory." Yumi became more and more excited as she spoke and leaned over towards Isogai, her hands gripped in her lap.

"And if we had seen that movie, we wouldn't have witnessed it. You should be thanking me, you know." Junichi, proud of his perverse reasoning, nudged Yumi.

"Seriously, Jun? You are such an idiot. How can you say something like that after we saw that documentary on the families of the victims? Don't you remember the story of that seventh grader who lost his entire family?"

"Yeah, I do. I also remember you turning to me and saying, 'That was the coolest thing I've ever seen' afterwards. So quit acting all goody two-shoes just 'cause we're at a police station."

"Listen, could you two answer my questions a bit more seriously? This is really important. Depending on the information you give us, you could help solve this case."

"No way!"

"Yes. One of our theories is that whoever did this was watching, to see if everything went off as planned. That's why we're talking to people who were on the observation deck. We've gotten lots of little tips over the past three months, but no solid leads. You're the last lead we've got right now."

Junichi and Yumi nodded solemnly on hearing this.

"You said just now that you were on the side facing Tokyo Tower right from the start. Was there anyone in the vicinity who had any kind of unusual reaction? This is of utmost importance, so I want you to think back real hard."

The pair tried to recall the scene from nearly half a year before as though they were replaying a scene from a movie in their heads. Yumi thought of something first.

"Jun, do you remember what I said then?"

"No. All I can remember is us saying 'holy shit' and freaking out."

"The guy next to me said, 'Go!' I told you about it afterward. I said, 'Everyone's acting like it's a show, watching other people suffer.'"

"Oh yeah, I remember that. I said the same thing, 'Go,' to myself. Detective, the tower started to fall and then kinda like stopped halfway. I found out later in the newspaper that it was because the leg on the other side hadn't been blown up, right? But anyway I was sitting there thinking, 'Dude, it's not falling over!' so I was sending amazing, like, vibes to the tower, you know, like, with my mind."

"Yumi, you clearly heard someone say the word 'Go'?"

"Yes, clearly. No doubt about it. That doesn't mean that guy did it, though. I mean, this dumbass says he was screaming the same thing inside his head, even if it wasn't out loud."

"Yumi, don't 'dumbass' me, okay?"

"Do you remember what the person who said that looked like?"

"I don't remember his face, but I remember he was really good-looking. I remember thinking, 'Wow, he is my type.'"

"What? Your type? Isn't your type, like, me?"

"Hm. I don't know."

Junichi glared at Yumi with a seriously angry look on his face.

"About how old did he look?" Isogai asked in a serious tone, but felt his palms becoming moist.

"I don't know. He was young, around my age. Maybe a bit younger?"

"How tall was he?"

"Well, all I have is a vague impression, but I'd say he wasn't much taller than me."

"And how tall are you?"

"She's 5'5"," Junichi butted in, upset that his girlfriend was dominating the conversation. "In heels she's as tall as me."

"What about his clothes? Do you remember something about them?"

"No, I don't. Oh wait, he was good-looking, so I looked at his shoes. You know how classy women always say, 'Judge a man by his shoes'? Ever since I heard that, it's like a habit with me, looking at guys' shoes."

Junichi peeked at his feet dangling out under the conference room table. When he left the house he figured he didn't need to dress up to go to a police station, so he was wearing dingy Puma sneakers.

"So what kind of shoes was he wearing?"

"White Converse high tops."

Isogai squinted his small eyes behind his glasses even more and stared into space. He couldn't be sure that this was his man, but he matched the profile.

"Yumi, Junichi. Is there anything else you can recall?"

Yumi crossed her arms and furrowed her brow as she combed through her memories, but Junichi just stared at her from the side with a glum look on his face.

"That's all I can remember."

"If you were shown a picture, Yumi, do you think you could identify the guy you saw?"

"No, I don't think so. All I remember is that he was good-looking, but I see good-looking guys all the time all over town, so I don't think I could identify him. But you never know until you try. I might see him and say, 'That's the guy!'"

"I understand. I might have to ask you two to come back again at some point. I hope that's okay."

"No problem! Anytime. This was fun. And hopefully we can be of use," Yumi said cheerily. Junichi pouted in silence.

Isogai bid farewell to the young couple and saw them out of the room. He sat back in the chair and drew a picture of the perpetrator in his head. Around 5'6" and considered good-looking by at least one young woman. The silhouette in Isogai's mind of the twenty-year-old was wearing white Converse—

His ruminations were suddenly interrupted just then by a commotion outside. It sounded like people were arguing. Isogai opened the conference room door and looked into the hall. Junichi and Yumi were standing, facing each other, Junichi with his arms crossed, his face flushed and looking dissatisfied. He kicked the hall floor with the tip of his dingy sneaker.

"I had no idea you were such a flirt. Looking at other guys' shoes? Give me a fucking break! You're probably batting your eyelashes after every old guy wearing a nice pair of shoes. Huh? What do you have to say to that?"

21—The Mole

The detectives from Public Security in the frontline units participating in the special investigation had started getting desperate in the face of a complete lack of useful leads. They were picking up left-wingers, right-wingers, and yakuza left and right on the tiniest of charges or having them come in for questioning voluntarily, but no matter what they hit them with, nothing would stick. The Public Security Bureau was under tremendous pressure from serious government brass and was on the verge of engaging in information-gathering activities so aggressive that they risked a scandal.

Superintendent Onodera was still operating under the assumption that a sleeper cell of some Japanese extremist organization had joined forces with an international terrorist group and been activated, but information obtained by the Cabinet Intelligence Research Office from CIA, Mossad, and other foreign intelligence sources showed absolutely no activity among overseas cells with regard to the Tokyo Tower bombing attack, nor was there any top-secret intelligence that they had entered Japan.

As regards domestic terrorist organizations, there were reports from the Public Security Intelligence Agency and investigators who had taken part in the dismantling of the Veda Truth cult: "Anore," the organization created by Fumihiro Kayu after splitting from guru Kagehara, was a purely religious organization with 1,251 adherents. According to informants infiltrated into the organization the group focused exclusively on religious activities, and involvement in crime was unthinkable. The re-emergence of the Veda Truth cult was thus dropped as a plausible lead in the investigation.

Public Security Bureau Section One had a report on activities among New Left groups, which started showing renewed signs of life around 1995.

"There has been thorough surveillance of such groups ever since they were caught intercepting police radio transmissions and bugging the house of the Police Commissioner General. There have been no signs pointing to any involvement with the Tokyo Tower bombing."

Chief Iwagami crossed his arms and frowned, as though trying to solve a complex math problem. "If the motive were ideological, then the choice of Tokyo Tower as a target would be obvious: they would be destroying the very symbol of Japan's rapid economic growth in the postwar period. Nothing more, nothing less. If they were aiming to strike a blow to the communications infrastructure, then blowing up the new Tokyo Sky Tower that's going to be the center of terrestrial digital transmissions in a year would be a lot more effective."

"This is 2011. Wouldn't it be kind of silly for a supposedly ideological criminal to attack a symbol of the high-growth period now?" asked Onodera.

"That's exactly my point. Because if that were the case, this could be interpreted as a kind of greeting card, a prelude to some much bigger thing they are planning to pull off."

"But what could they be targeting next?"

Iwagami gestured Onodera over and whispered in his ear so the other investigators couldn't hear. "We have no idea what the attackers' ideological background is. I want you to spread the 'backroom' investigation out into the civilian population."

"Got it."

In the course of monitoring the many different citizens' groups it was sometimes necessary to place moles in them in order to gather intelligence. But the current agents could not find signs of any activities related to the Tokyo Tower bombing.

Some infiltrating agents reported encountering young people bragging that they had bombed Tokyo Tower. A follow-up investigation always revealed such statements to be false, nothing more than idle boasts uttered out of frustration with their daily lives.

Investigators with the Public Security Bureau continued to gather intelligence, day in, day out, but the vast majority of it pointed to a complete absence of masterminds or leaders filled with resentment who wanted to change the world by attacking companies, the way they did in the seventies. The general populace seemed to be enjoying the benefits of an at least superficially tranquil and peaceful society. There were no serious indications of ideological tension these days.

However, from among that vast pool of intelligence, Superintendent Onodera received a certain report from a young investigator named Kunio Dan who was in charge of surveillance over non-profit organizations.

"Superintendent, this non-profit started up a few days after the Tokyo Tower bombing. It might be unrelated to the current investigation, but—"

"Get rid of all your preconceived ideas. Tell me the facts."

"A non-profit called *Society of Victims of Abuse for the Prevention of Abuse* was incorporated on September 1st, on the street in Akabanebashi where that public health center is located. Its chairman is a young man, still only twenty years old, named Yoshio Iizuka. He's gotten quite a lot of coverage in the media. He's becoming a bit of a celebrity."

"What's so suspicious about that?"

"Well, nothing, sir. It's not suspicious. The non-profit's goal is to make a positive contribution to society. I looked up its charter, and it's classified as a corporation established to 'promote peace and protect human rights.'"

"Then it should be beyond the scope of the investigation."

"Well, sir, that's what I thought."

"So why are you talking to me about this?"

"Well, it's just my opinion, but you said that—"

"Just spit it out!" Onodera's nerves were frayed from the intense pressure filtering down onto his shoulders from Chief Iwagami, himself under pressure from above.

"Yes, sir. If you look at Japanese history, including the civil rights protests by the *dowa* 'untouchables,' the farmers' protests in Sanrizuka when Narita Airport was being built, the student riots in the early sixties over the U.S.-Japan security treaty, what you see is that it's always groups that have the greatest ideological purity who clash with the government, because state power wants nothing to do with ideological purity.

"From what I've seen on TV and the internet, this Yoshio Iizuka is a flawless picture of ideological purity in his struggle to save society's abused children, willing even to lay bare his own story of horrific abuse in his desire to contribute to society.

"Now, I've only read about this in books, but the arrested members of the East Asia Front for the Defeat of Japanese Imperialism were all the epitome of ideological purity, passing as upstanding citizens while embracing their unrealistically beautiful dreams of a better world. This is just my opinion, but I think Public Security is going to have to start keeping an eye on such people, people who are serious in their pursuit of their unrealistic ideals and beliefs. I apologize for the subjectivity of my analysis."

About halfway through, Onodera had started listening seriously to the thirtysomething investigator's explanation. *This guy's onto something. Of course, Public Security is an elite outfit. It's not surprising to find a real thinker or two in it.* "That's an interesting point of view. It's worth giving some thought to the idea of monitoring groups when they show signs of that kind of idealism. I want you to infiltrate a collaborator into this society of whatever it's called, and leave him there for a while."

"Yes, sir. I'll arrange it immediately. In accordance with the goals of its founder, this non-profit finds young people who have suffered abuse and rehabilitates them, which means I'll have to find someone from the civilian population that fits. Also, everyone who works there is around fifteen or sixteen years old, so whoever I infiltrate will have to be a minor. This will all have to be done off the record, with your approval."

Onodera waved Dan away in silence. *Just get on with it,* he muttered in his heart.

Assistant Inspector Kunio Dan had graduated from the Police Academy with flying colors. Currently thirty-five years old, he was working in the Administrative Department, Public Security Bureau, Metropolitan Police, mainly tasked with civilian (i.e., non-extremist) affairs. He got to work immediately on organizing the Youth S ("Spy") operation to infiltrate a fifteen- or sixteen-year-old boy into *Society of Victims of Abuse for the Prevention of Abuse.*

He quickly compiled a list of a dozen or so candidates from the Police Guard Department Planning Office, but finding someone who fit the operation was hard. He even combed through lists from various child welfare and foster-care organizations, looking through the profiles provided therein for cases of boys suffering from the after-effects of abuse at the hands of a mother or father. There were no perfect matches, though.

Dan had an idea. On Onodera's authority, he contacted the youth coordinators of the Community Safety departments at the Atagoyama, Shibuya Sakuragaoka, and Kishimojin police stations, which were working together under the special investigation, to obtain data on teenage boys who were troubled, had engaged in delinquent behavior, or had been sent to family court for being violent with their parents.

The final candidate that turned up was Kazuma Hoshino, a fifteen-year-old boy living in Numabukuro, Nakano Ward, Tokyo. He was raised by a single mother and had appeared in family court once for repeated shoplifting, which a psychiatrist had diagnosed as a "manifestation of continued infantile dependence on the mother." In other words, an Oedipus complex expressed as habitual petty theft.

Dan immediately started observing Hoshino and came upon a perfect chance one day. He was tailing Kazuma in Ikebukuro and followed him into a bookstore, where the boy slipped some kind of magazine into his school bag. *Gotcha,* Dan thought, looking around the bookstore as though he were an accomplice, hoping none of the employees had noticed the theft.

Kazuma left the store with an innocent look on his face and headed down Meiji Avenue. "Hey, kid," Dan called from behind. Caught off guard, Kazuma turned back and tried to take off running, but Dan grabbed his arm an instant before.

"What's the idea, bringing me here?"

Dan and Kazuma sat facing each other on sofas in a Renoir cafe outlet.

"I'm not a truant officer, don't worry."

"Then what are you? You just threatened to turn me in for shoplifting. Oh, I get it. You're one of those perverts who likes young boys."

"Listen, kid. Do I look like a child molester to you?"

Kazuma inspected Dan's face and clothes. He was wearing a dark blue pinstripe suit with a sky blue necktie. His neatly combed black hair was wavy and sleek, his bright eyes retained the carefree look of a college student, and his face was what would be called handsome. Only his thin lips imparted a slightly callous look to the lower half of his face.

Dan pulled his badge out of his coat pocket and showed it to Hoshino.

"You *are* a cop!" Kazuma exclaimed. *This is it, I'm going to juvie,* he despaired, imagining a small, dark cell. *But if this guy's a cop, why did he bring me to a posh cafe?* His heart thumped as he grew confused.

"Are you going to arrest me?"

A smile—more like a twitch at the edges of his lips—crossed

Dan's face. "I might have to. Depends."

"On what?" Kazuma was at a total loss. He was confused, and pain shot through his temples.

"There's something I want you to help me with."

"Help a cop?" Kazuma's eyes opened wide at the unexpected words.

The man facing him smiled faintly. His eyes shone with the certainty that he had ensnared his prey.

22—Results

"Aroma of lavender… a touch of bitterness… Insomnia caused by stress and fatigue… Effective in fighting headaches and menstrual pain…"

This pale yellow color might be my favorite color. It's calming just to look at.

Mariko flipped through the pages of the *Encyclopedia of Herbal Teas* as the aroma from the various herbs that filled the jars tickled her nose. Ever since she had read an article in the lifestyle section of her paper that promised "choosing an herbal tea to match each day's mood will enrich your life," Mariko had made a daily habit of pouring herself a cup of herbal tea. It was a small effort on her part to achieve some sort of relief from the incredible stress incurred from working the celebrity section at *In Focus*.

She had trouble picking up regular hobbies because her interests tended to peak and trough in extremes. Even her thoughts jumped around during the day. Having herbal tea as a hobby was different, however, because it didn't require such a heavy commitment. She could simply pick one of the eighteen varieties she had bought that she thought fit the day's mood and make herself a cup whenever she felt like it.

Whenever she felt like something soothing or needed a bit of a boost, she would pick one of the flavors and pour the hot liquid into her body. It felt like she was washing away the grime and greasiness not just out of her body but her mind as well.

By the middle of December all the well-known buildings and structures in Tokyo were aglitter in a festive Christmas mood. She had driven her Cherokee across the Rainbow Bridge the night before on her way home to Tennozu Isle. A large Christmas tree in the courtyard of a shopping mall along the bay had been decorated in orange and bluish purple lights, creating a joyful mood.

And yet, Mariko was feeling down. She knew the reason, but not how to fix it. She felt like she had gone back to being a naive nineteen year old.

She had woken once at 8 a.m. but had pulled the covers up and gone back to sleep. By the time she had resigned herself to waking, gotten up in her pajamas, and started making herself some tea, it was past eleven.

She placed a pinch of lemon balm leaves in her teacup. An indescribable aroma rose up and filled her nostrils when she added the hot water, which she was careful not to allow to become too hot. She'd initially reached for hyssop over lemon balm, but all that was left in the jar were small twigs and no petals. *Have I been drinking that much hyssop lately*? Mariko wondered. According to the encyclopedia, hyssop had a "gentle aroma that helps heal deep psychological wounds."

She knew that lemon balm "helps lift fallen spirits," but she was so wounded that what she wanted was the effect of hyssop. A magazine lay on the dining table Mariko was sitting at. It was the early printing of *In Focus* that would go on sale this Friday. It had been delivered by motorcycle courier and contained the interview and photographs of Yoshio Iizuka that Mariko had done.

Naturally, Sendo, with his genius for sniffing out the foulest stories and boosting sales, had done a little jig of joy. So happy had he been, in fact, that he had tried to hug Mariko, but she had agilely twisted her body and evaded just in time. They might be on close working terms but she had no intention of letting Sendo hug her.

Plus, what was getting her down was the "catch" that she had made and that had Sendo so overjoyed.

The "In Focus: People" column which featured the Yoshio Iizuka interview that week was two columns, 18 characters wide and 39 lines long, with a large photograph drawing readers in with its searing impact. It was Yoshio, bare-chested. Despite the photograph being on a black-and-white page, the faint scars from the abuse seemed to glow red, jumping out at the eye with a livid realism. The title splashed across the top read: "The Scarred Saint."

Sendo had changed Mariko's original title without asking. Her title had been: "Overcoming the Trauma of Abuse, Now on the Road to Helping Others."

Either Nakamura or Sendo had also rewritten a lot of her piece. They hadn't changed the main point, but obviouly the editor-in-chief had wanted to emphasize the gritty details. Surprisingly for Sendo, however, he had not made any significant alterations to the tone of her article, which was conscientious praise of Yoshio.

That was an indicator of how happy he was with the photograph. There was likely a narcissistic self-satisfaction, too, at his own brilliance in sending in Mariko, with her relatively similar background. It had resulted in Yoshio unexpectedly opening himself up this much.

Mariko had opened to the page with a heavy heart the night before and was overwhelmed by the impact of the photograph, which she herself had taken. She had arrived at a plane very far from what she imagined as a nineteen year old dreaming of becoming a photographer. Camerawork shone a light on society's evils, but there were also beautiful things in this world. Some pictures even warmed the spirit of the people who saw them and left a lingering sense of contentment for at least half a day. In fact, there existed miraculous photographs that crystallized the undisputable truth of love.

The photographs Mariko took and sold for money, however,

were of the dark parts of the world: dissipated lives of celebrities, murders, children on the verge of death, and Yoshio Iizuka smiling defiantly as he presented his painful-looking body to the world.

I want love! I want to be head over heels for someone. I want to be loved. I don't care who. Just to love and be loved. To wake up first, crawl out of bed, and take a picture of my lover's sleeping face, brimming with love. To have his child, cherish it, raise it. Will that day ever come?

No. It won't, Mariko told herself, and felt blue again.

Chapter 3

23—Miyazaki Prefectural Police

Isogai had the good fortune to spend New Year's Eve at his house in Edogawa Ward, near the Sumida River, and had New Year's Day off. The break was an unexpected gift and was made possible because a witness at the Roppongi Hills observation deck had seen a person who might just be one of the attackers. The turn of events would steer the investigation in a surprising direction in the new year. The new profile was of a handsome young man who wore Converse high-tops.

"Isogai," Yoshida had said, "it's going to be all uphill from here until we solve this case. At least take New Year's Day off."

Isogai had gladly accepted Yoshida's kind words, which were also a pat on the back. His son Yuichi was out of the house, working as a stage hand on the set of a music program that was Japan' premier broadcast on New Year's Eve, as part of his job at the production company. It was the first New Year's holiday that Isogai spent with just his wife Akiko and his daughter Kazue, who was a college student.

After eating the traditional buckwheat noodles at midnight, Isogai left his wife and daughter sitting at the *kotatsu* watching the TV in silence and went over to the sofa on the other side of the room, where he paged through some materials he had brought home from the special investigation headquarters.

The materials were a compilation of data from the Miyazaki Prefectural Police Headquarters sent via the Investigation Assistance Department at police headquarters, detailing the Jiiku Hospital Director Murder Case that had occurred on August 15th. According to the desk officer at the Investigation Assistance Department, the detective in charge, one Shuji Fukada of the Miyazaki Prefectural Police Headquarters, was requesting a meeting with Isogai after having run into a dead-end in his investigation in Miyazaki Prefecture. The forensic evidence left at the scene of the crime by the person believed to have murdered the victim, a doctor named Yusuke Watanabe, included Converse footprints while the stab wounds were made by a survival knife. This evidence matched that of the Atagoyama murder case that Isogai had been in charge of some years before and which Detective Fukada had come across when searching the police database.

Isogai could not help feeling a bit low as he read the files on New Year's Eve. Like the bells of the Buddhist temples that unceasingly rang out the old year on this night, the evil of humanity seemed to have no end and forever kept echoing out of the past into the present.

Atsushi Sakamoto would be in college now if he hadn't been murdered at the shrine next to Atagoyama Intelligence Tower, Isogai thought, suddenly realizing that Atsushi and his daughter were the same age. Or would have been. Isogai vaguely recalled being very worried around the time of that murder case by his own son Yuichi's troubles at home and the difficulty of the challenges young people in general faced in society.

Isogai felt a sudden pang of guilt. He asked across the room, "Kazue, how's school?"

Kazue turned away from the TV she was watching and looked at her father, surprised. "What?"

"College. The one you didn't get into, and had to study an extra year to finally get in to. How is it?"

"Dad, are you being sarcastic? It's not good or bad, it's just college."

"Really? Okay. As long as you're doing all right."

Kazue seemed uncomfortable conversing with her father, with whom she hadn't spoken in a long time. Her sharp tone signaled her discomfort.

"Dad, you're tired. Why don't you just turn in?"

"Good idea. As soon as I finish reading this."

"Work?"

"No rest for the wicked."

"So is it true that the guy who blew up Tokyo Tower is handsome?"

"What?" The question caught him off-guard. "Who told you that?"

"Everybody's talking about it at school. Don't you ever look at the internet? The guy who saw him has a blog. Everyone's reading it."

Is that what's going on? A confidential police investigation directive is grist for some internet rumor mill? It was a small shock for Isogai, who sat staring at his daughter for a moment.

"Honey, shall I make some tea?" his wife asked.

"That would be great, thanks."

Miyazaki Prefectural Police Detective Shuji Fukada, who was investigating the stabbing murder of the director of Jiiku Hospital, met with Isogai on January 16th.

It was a cold day, and a wet snow fell, but the small meeting room was hot and stuffy because the heat was on too high, making it difficult for Isogai to concentrate. He didn't feel like he was completely prepared to meet with this visitor from a distant prefecture. Fukada was five years younger than Isogai and also a sergeant detective. He greeted Isogai informally and immediately got down to business. Isogai got the impression that Fukada had not outgrown the impulsive style of investigation that characterized inexperienced detectives, perhaps due to the fact that he worked in Miyazaki Prefecture, which was a fairly rural area, compared to Isogai, who had handled many cases involving extreme violence in Tokyo. But more than that, the impression was created by the look of helplessness that Fukada gave him at having come to a dead-end in the case.

"I sent you all the materials we have regarding the murder of the director of Jiiku Hospital in Miyazaki. Have you had a chance to look through them?"

"I have. It wasn't in the files, but I hear that you and the victim were friends. My condolences." Isogai bowed his head.

Fukada bowed his head in response. "Yusuke was an outstanding doctor, and an outstanding person. He was passionate and had a strong sense of justice. We were the same age, but he was actually something of a role model for me. I can't believe that anyone would want to kill a man like him, which is why I think this is a random killing. He just happened to be in the wrong place at the wrong time. I can't see personal animosity being a motive here. We live in an age where that kind of thing happens in Miyazaki, too, not just Tokyo."

"You came to see me because you did a search of the police database for the evidence you have—the survival knife wound and Converse prints—and it matched the Atagoyama murder case I handled. Is that right?"

"That's right."

"But Detective Fukada, that case is more than five years old. It's seems like quite a stretch to think that there's some connection just because the weapon was a survival knife and the killer wore Converse shoes in your case, too. You'd have to think there's been some demon running around out there through the ages, never aging, always looking like a young man. Whoever the killer was in the case I handled is five years older now."

"I understand that, Detective Isogai. But there are no other leads left to follow."

"Investigations were easier when things like money and hate were motives in murder cases. These days there are lots of cases where none of that matters. It's gotten harder for us."

"When you investigated the murder of Atsushi Sakamoto in 2006, did you assume from the start that the killer was young, too?"

"I did. The only things the forensics team managed to get were the Converse footprints and the fact that a survival knife was the murder weapon, based on the wound in the victim's back. That was all we had to go on, so we went with a young killer, although today I can't say for sure that that was the right thing to do."

Isogai had regrets about the case, and as he thought of them he also vaguely recalled ruminating not too long about the case, but he couldn't remember when. He tilted his head slightly. *Who did I talk to about this, and when was it?*

"What was your role in the investigation?"

"Interviewing potential witnesses. We canvassed the whole area including the shrine, everyone living in the apartment building where Atsushi lived, Atagoyama Intelligence Tower, and all the way to Akabanebashi."

Fukada nodded deeply, as though reminded of his current struggle. "And you deduced the Converse from the footprints?"

"That's right. And also a ten-centimeter survival knife from the stab wound."

"No fingerprints?"

"Nope. Not on the victim's clothes, not anywhere. A single stab wound in the victim's back. The killer apparently didn't touch anything else. He had probably scoped the whole thing out ahead of time and waited for the kid."

"Same with the Miyazaki murder. Footprints and a stab wound. The only other thing we have that could be called definitive is hair. We found a few strands where the footprints were, a little ways from the site of the killing, so we think they could be key.

The hairs were dyed a color called 'chocolate brown' using a paraphenylenediamine oxidation dye that's used by salons in a process involving bleaching the hair and then dying it. Which means the hair could belong to any one of the many young people you see these days with light brown hair. We succeeded in getting a DNA sample, too, so if we ever catch the guy, we can link him to the murder pretty solidly."

"The killer did it early in the morning, yes?"

"Yes. Sunrise was at 5:34 that day, and we estimate the time of the murder to have been no more than thirty minutes before that."

"So the killer methodically followed the victim out to his fishing spot and killed him there."

"That's the hypothesis we were working on. But we can't find anyone who would have a motive to kill him. Watanabe was an object of gratitude, not hatred." As soon as he said this, Fukada felt unsure of what he had come all this way for. He felt a sense of foolishness welling up inside him for having rushed to Tokyo just because the footprints and stab wound were the same as those of a five-year-old unsolved mystery in the middle of the metropolis that was Tokyo.

"Were there any other clues whatsoever in Dr. Watanabe's killing?"

"To be honest, I think I have failed."

"Failed?"

"That's right. Failed." The heavy significance of the word weighing on his heart, Fukada felt like he could not bother Isogai any further with the matter. At the same time, however, he had decided that he could not return to Miyazaki without something, some new fact or piece of evidence.

"Detective Isogai, could I ask for any kind of advice that you might have, since you've been in this business longer than I have? About how to go about the investigation in a way that will put Watanabe's spirit to rest?"

"Put his spirit to rest? Listen, I know what you're feeling, but don't you think personal feelings might get in the way of the investigation? I really, truly feel your pain. But emotions only cloud your vision."

As he said this, Isogai was compelled to look inside himself for his own faults.

Then he remembered. *It was when I met Mariko Amo. I thought about the Atagoyama killing for the first time in a long time.*

"Yusuke Watanabe was the director of Jiiku Hospital in Nichinan City, right?"

"Yes. He took over as director at a relatively young age, after the previous director, Kikue Iizuka, passed away. He was a talented doctor and very well-liked."

"You interviewed everyone at the hospital, of course."

"We were there so much I think they started to get sick of us. But we couldn't find anything new. Just last week I went by to talk with a nurse named Manami Kotegawa."

"Detective Fukada, do you know someone named Yoshio Iizuka?"

"As a matter of fact I do. Nurse Kotegawa talked about him. Apparently he's all over the news these days. Everyone at the hospital just loves him. He was the first child saved by the Stork's Mailbox, a system pioneered by Jiiku Hospital to rescue abandoned babies. Nurse Kotegawa told me that it was Yusuke who was the one that saved his life. The baby had been pretty badly abused before being abandoned. She was praising him to the skies, talking about how he was using his own experience of child abuse in order to help stop abuse. I had heard good things about him before, too, when I went to an orphanage called The Nestlings' Home as part of the investigation. Yoshio Iizuka is like a hero to everyone who has ever known him."

"I interviewed him in my case, too."

"You mean the Atsushi Sakamoto case?"

"Yeah. The murder took place in Atagoyama, and the

orphanage he was living in at that time was nearby."

"What were your impressions of him?"

"All I heard too were good things from the people in the orphanage. Iizuka moved from Miyazaki to Tokyo when he was around five, so I doubt he kept in touch with Dr. Watanabe when he did so. He's a responsible kid, though, so it's not impossible that he remembered the debt of gratitude he owed Watanabe and corresponded with him somehow, maybe by email or regular mail."

"That is a possibility. Do you know where the office of his non-profit is located?"

"I do. You know, until recently I had no idea he had gotten so famous he was on TV. The office is actually within the range of the special investigation. One of the detectives downstairs told me where it is."

24—Negative

Detective Fukada, desperate for any clue however small that would help his bogged-down investigation, decided to pay a visit to the office of the *Society of Victims of Abuse for the Prevention of Abuse* non-profit organization run by Yoshio Iizuka.

As soon as his meeting with Isogai ended, he braved the sleet and headed straight for Akabanebashi without making an appointment.

Fukada had luck: Iizuka was out but would be back in about thirty minutes. Fukada told the secretary that he had come all the way from Miyazaki and would like to wait until Iizuka returned. The boy who spoke with Fukada passed the message to one of the officers, who promptly called Yoshio's cell phone to ask for instructions. Yoshio told him to have the visitor wait in the waiting room until he returned.

Midori Sonoda was seized by a terrible panic when

he heard that a detective had come from Miyazaki. He was absolutely sure that this Fukada guy's showing up without an appointment had to do with the killing of the director of Jiiku Hospital. *But nobody could see through Yoshio's perfect scenario so easily!* Midori told himself to calm his nerves. He anxiously awaited Yoshio's return.

Yoshio got back to the office not long after. Midori ran to the entrance and told his mentor what was going on with a pleading look in his eyes. Yoshio had considered every possibility in the taxi on the way back, so he was completely calm. What was the likelihood of Midori being pegged as the murderer of Yusuke Watanabe on a beach in Nichinan? Nobody could solve a murder that fast, especially one that had been designed to eliminate all imaginable risks. No, some kind of coincidence—something Yoshio hated—had to be behind the detective's sudden appearance.

You can do this, Yoshio, he told himself, suppressing any agitation by sheer strength of will. To Midori he said, "'Yoshio' will meet him and find out what's going on. You don't have anything to worry about."

The sleet that had been falling since morning was now full-blown snow, but the wet streets prevented it from accumulating in white drifts. The tires of the cars driving around made noises as they passed through the sherbet-like ice. Yoshio handed his cream-colored coat to an assistant and, rubbing his hands, which were numb with cold, entered the waiting room where Fukada was waiting.

"Hi, I'm Yoshio Iizuka, the chairman," Yoshio greeted Fukada calmly, sizing him up. Just as he thought, there didn't appear to be any deep suspicion of him in the older man's tanned face.

"I'm Detective Fukada with the Miyazaki Prefectural Police. I apologize for coming without an appointment. I'm sure you must be very busy. I won't take up too much of your time. Would you be willing to help us with an investigation?"

"Of course. You must be freezing in this Tokyo weather,

coming from warm Miyazaki. I don't know if you know this, but I lived in Miyazaki until I was five." Noticing just then that the knit cap he'd worn against the cold was still on his head, Yoshio took it off and put it on the sofa next to him.

"I did know that, actually. I'm here today because I'd like to ask you a few questions about the murder of Yusuke Watanabe, who I think you were acquainted with." Fukada kept a close eye on Yoshio's reaction as he said this.

Yoshio intentionally made a small pained expression and said, "I read about the murder last year in August, the day after it happened. I was just...so shocked. I wonder if you can understand."

Fukada scrutinized Yoshio's face.

"I owe my life to that man." Yoshio's face broke into an expression of sadness as though the shock of hearing the news were coming back to him.

"Yes, they told me at the Jiiku Hospital. Mr. Iizuka, do you remember a nurse named Manami Kotegawa?"

"Oh boy, that name brings back a few memories. She must be the one I used to call Mami."

"She's been there twenty years. She's head nurse now."

"Mami is head nurse? Wow! She and Dr. Watanabe were the ones who found me abandoned in the Stork's Mailbox."

"Dr. Watanabe and Nurse Kotegawa had worked together for many years, and he was her closest friend at the hospital. Her grief at his death was really heartbreaking to see."

"So what it is that you'd like to know? I want the murderer caught and the case closed as quickly as possible. I want to help you in whatever way I can. Just let me know."

"I appreciate that. To start with, I'd like to know if you kept in contact with Dr. Watanabe in any way whatsoever after you moved from Miyazaki to Tokyo. Email, postcards, letters, anything. And if so, were there any indications of anything strange going on in his life? Any changes?"

"Unfortunately, I haven't been in contact with Dr. Watanabe even once since coming to Tokyo fifteen years ago."

Fukada didn't hide the expression of disappointment on his face. In the taxi on the way here, he had absently looked at the sleet and the cold Tokyo view and had imagined he would have a breakthrough here—that he would obtain some kind of miraculous lead or find that crucial thread that would lead to solving the case, instant payback for all his hard work until now. Such daydreams were an indication of how desperate he had become, now that he had conclusively expended all of his resources.

"Dr. Watanabe never sent you a postcard or anything like that?"

"No, unfortunately. Detective Fukada, I bet you're thinking what an ingrate I am, for going on just now about how Dr. Watanabe saved my life, and yet never sending him even a single holiday greeting card or anything."

Fukada shook his head and looked down.

"It might be hard for someone from a normal, loving family, someone who didn't grow up in the circumstances I grew up in, to understand this feeling, but I really don't want to remember my time in the orphanages. If possible, I'd like to erase the very knowledge I have of having been born into the cruelest kind of abuse. Dr. Watanabe was the person who saved my life, but he's irrevocably connected in my mind with all that horror. So even though I wanted to repay my gratitude to him, at the same time he was someone I needed to completely forget about. Do you see what I'm saying?"

Fukada knew a lot of kids who had gotten involved in crime from his time in the juvenile department of the Miyazaki Prefectural Police, but he had never known anyone who had grown up in an orphanage, so Yoshio's words had the ring of truth. For Yoshio, Jiiku Hospital was probably part of a past he just wanted to forget.

Fukada had come to Tokyo alone, the low and heavy winter

sky weighing down on the city. Now, the idea of leaving the past behind—which Yoshio had injected directly into the center of Fukada's mind—successfully demolished the last vestige of his will to go on fighting. A honey-voiced demon seemed to be whispering to him, *That's enough, just go to sleep now.*

His subconscious admitted defeat. For a moment Fukada watched Yoshio, who had turned his face towards a corner of the window-less waiting room with a distant look on his face. Then he stood up with resolve.

"Mr. Iizuka, thanks for your time today. I'm going back to Miyazaki on the first flight tomorrow. My house in Shinonome is right near the Watanabe family home. I don't suppose you'll ever be coming back to Miyazaki, but since you apparently travel around the country giving talks, if you're ever in the area, please come by to light an incense stick for him."

"Of course. I'll find a way to see if I can't make it there somehow." Yoshio got up and went to open the door. Fukada followed; his eyes fell on something as he was about to leave the room. Just as the referee was about to count "ten" to the fallen Fukada, his subconscious whispered to him again; he impulsively snatched Yoshio's knit cap, which was lying on one of the sofas, and slipped it quickly into his blazer pocket.

In the airplane on the way back to Miyazaki, Fukada wondered why he had grabbed Iizuka's cap. He harbored absolutely no suspicion that Iizuka had anything to do with Watanabe's killing. He was convinced by what Iizuka had said in Tokyo. No matter how he thought of it, there was not an iota of rationale for the impulsiveness of what he had done. That said, detectives were known to do such things on occasion.

I am at a total loss, obviously, Fukada reproached himself. *I mean, to do something that irrational, just on a hunch?* And yet, deep inside, he still held out a contradictory hope.

When he arrived at Miyazaki Airport, he made straight for the forensics department at police headquarters. He wanted to have them perform DNA tests on the sweat and hairs on the inside of Iizuka's cap and compare the results with the strands of brown hair Yusuke Watanabe's killer had left behind.

The forensics department asked Fukada, as per regulation, how he had gotten a hold of the hat. When he couldn't answer, the forensics chief, who was about ten years Fukada's elder, quickly figured out what was going on and said, "Shuji, listen. You know that the results won't be admissible even if we get a positive match, don't you?"

A few days later, the results came back: an unquestionable negative match. That was when Detective Fukada's mental state started to become imbalanced, having lost that last little bit of unfounded hope it had.

25—The Coming of Death

Mariko heard the phone ringing and picked up her cell phone, which was charging on her desk. She looked at the LCD screen: "Number Not Available." She pressed the talk button and listened.

"Hi, it's Yoshio Iizuka. You interviewed me not too long ago..."

Shocked, Mariko pulled the phone away from her ear and gripped it with both hands. She took a second to collect herself before she could speak. "Wow, you really surprised me. I never expected you to call me. What can I do for you?"

"Oh, I'm sorry to have surprised you like this. You gave me your cell number after the interview, so I got up the courage and called you."

"Mr. Iizuka, I told the editorial department to send your office a carton with a dozen copies of the magazine. Did you get them?"

"Yes, thank you for that. I feel like I was asking a lot, but it's just that your piece was the best I've seen so far, and I wanted copies to show people when I tell them what we're all about, and to give to important visitors."

"It looks like you're even busier this year than you were last year. I saw you on TV the other day."

"Yeah, I'm a bit embarrassed by it all. It's not that I want to be in the media so much, but working to better society doesn't pay for itself, so I go on TV as a way of getting companies and other groups to donate money. That's my real goal with all of that. What with all of our office staff, even if they're volunteers, our overhead is getting pretty high."

"It must be hard to run an organization like that. I've been a freelance contract photographer my whole life, so it's pretty impressive to watch you."

"Ms. Amo?"

"Yes?"

"During that interview, I felt kind of at home, like I was with someone I grew up with. I was wondering if you could call me 'Yoshio.'"

Mariko stiffened. She felt her face flush. *Was this the kind of thing he would say?* She felt a bit self-conscious, but for his sake she said, "Sure. You call me 'Mariko,' then. Deal?"

"Deal. Mariko, I called you because I was wondering if we couldn't get together. There are a few things I'd like to get your opinion on."

"That's fine with me, but I don't know how my opinion on anything could be of any use to you..."

"It's kind of hard to discuss on the phone. Thing is, I present this façade of self-confidence when I'm with people, but the truth is I'm still young. This whole 'making a change' thing is a lot of pressure on me. Of course, that really was the only way forward for me, given my life, but sometimes I'd just like to get things off my chest with someone."

The words touched a nerve deep inside Mariko. *I should've known that's what it was. The poor kid's only twenty.* She said,

"Yoshio, you probably know way more about the way the world works than I do, so I doubt I could be of much use to you in that sense, but I'm pretty sure I can help you vent if that's what you need. I'm older than you, after all. I'm old enough to be your aunt."

"What? No way! I've thought since we met how attractive you looked. So, okay. We're both busy, and if we just leave it at 'let's get together sometime,' we'll never actually do it. How about setting a time and day right now?"

Yoshio's forthrightness caught Mariko off-guard. It made her feel slightly giddy, and also slightly awkward. Was she this way when she was his age?

She asked when would be good for him, and they settled on meeting at his Akabanebashi office at 7 p.m. the following Friday. They would then go somewhere for dinner.

Yoshio's call made Mariko feel like some part of her that had been blocked off since the previous year had opened up and started to glow a bit. She had lived alone in her apartment for five years, but she had rarely felt lonely. Her job as a photographer, chasing after celebrity scandals and scoops, kept her going, but it sometimes felt like she was slowly fraying at the edges.

Whenever that happened, she would take shelter in her nineteen-year-old self. It was only in that fragile place that she became an artist capable of expressing the essence of human existence. It was only then that she truly liked herself.

Next Friday. She was already starting to think about it. *What to wear, what to wear... It's not like it's such a huge deal. It's just hard for a woman in her thirties to express herself in a casual way, without getting too extravagant. Not like I own anything extravagant, but still. I'll wear the deep purple Ferragamo high heels I wore to dinner with Sendo the other day in Nishi Azabu. The only coat I have is the camel one, so it'll have to do. I can wear the black velvet dress I—wait, that'd be the exact same outfit as that evening!*

≈

Yoshio hung up and leaned back in the waiting room sofa. He was pensive. He already knew which mask he would present to Mariko Amo. The mask of "the youthful idealist making a contribution to society," which he had used for the interview in November of the previous year, had slipped, if only for an instant. Meanwhile that reporter for *Morning Daily*, Yukiko Hatakeyama, prey to her own half-baked idealism, had bought right into his hypocritical show as well. She had called him a few times after that, in fact.

But for this Mariko woman, he would have to special-order a different mask, the mask of "the idealist who accidentally revealed his inner turmoil." For her, he would be the flawed young man fighting for justice in the world, but whose soul contained much darkness, the psychological trauma of abuse suffered at his mother's hands, which had never completely healed. A young man who had to use the weapon of his upbringing to get by in the world, without the benefit of higher education, whose only option was to start a non-profit. The "real Yoshio Iizuka" mask.

Since Mariko reeked of feelings of resentment towards her father and a dose of self-pity related to the death of her mother, he was confident that she would be utterly taken in by his performance. People look for themselves in others, was how Yoshio saw it, and a smile crept across his face as he thought about how he was going to serve Mariko up.

February 17, 2012. 7:15 p.m.

Mariko got to Yoshio's Akabanebashi office a bit late. She pressed the button at the reception desk and a pale-skinned young man emerged. He opened the door and guided Mariko to the waiting room. They passed through a large room filled with desks, and a few of the young people there looked over at her. The only people working in the office were young men, all about the same age.

One of them had clean, regular features that Mariko thought made him look a lot like Yoshio. He had previously sported dyed-brown hair but had trimmed his now-black hair short all around, the same height from above the collar to behind the ears, wanting to project the same neat image as Yoshio. This was Mariko's first meeting with Midori Sonoda.

She waited on the sofa in the spotlessly cleaned waiting room. Eventually there was a knock on the door and Midori entered with hot green tea in a paper cup. He had grabbed the tray with the green tea from another young volunteer who was still in the office and come in to keep an eye on Mariko. It didn't sit well with Midori that a woman he didn't know was coming at this hour to see Yoshio and go out with him.

Midori's adoration of Yoshio grew stronger by the day. Yoshio couldn't care one way or the other about it, but there was something abnormal in the way Midori worshipped Yoshio. Midori's face, which gave an impression of fragility compared to Yoshio, had recently taken on a somewhat macho look, and he had been exhibiting the kind of leadership one would expect from a trusted lieutenant over the other officers and volunteers, as though he considered himself Yoshio's heir apparent. Yoshio observed this without much interest but was grateful for Midori's role in passing down his ideology and handling the "study sessions" that maintained the brainwashing.

After a time Yoshio came into the waiting room. "Mariko, I'm so sorry to have kept you waiting. The interview took longer than I expected. That TV station is a disorganized mess."

"Don't worry about it. I was about fifteen minutes late myself."

Mariko was dressed in jeans and a black loose-knit sweater. She had gotten a bit excited after the phone call from Yoshio inviting her to dinner and had spent some time deciding what to wear. In the end she decided to go casual.

"Well, we've got reservations, so let's be off," Yoshio said. He waited for Mariko to get up, and they left the office.

Midori saw them off at the main entrance. Yoshio informed him that Mariko Amo would be the victim for a new officer, so Midori watched them with a peaceful mind. "Come again," he said and bowed politely.

The restaurant where Yoshio had made reservations was a stand-alone vegetarian place about ten minutes by taxi from the Akabanebashi office. Yoshio was not in the habit of meeting people for enjoyable dinners like this, so he took Mariko to a place he'd been taken by a publisher before. That meeting had been for a piece that brought him together for a kind of dialogue with a college professor who was a specialist in child welfare. They'd spoken for about an hour. Yoshio remembered how excruciatingly boring it was. But the private rooms, divided off from the rest of the restaurant by sliding paper doors, had a clean, pleasant feel. For Yoshio, who couldn't eat animal flesh but could somehow stomach vegetables, the food was fine too.

They didn't speak very much in the taxi. Yoshio didn't see the need to engage in ice-breaking banter, and Mariko was too nervous to talk. She had never gotten together privately with anyone she had met through an interview, much less entered into some kind of romantic relationship with one of them. She couldn't imagine this unprecedented reencounter with Yoshio developing into something like that, but the butterflies in her stomach were an indication of her awareness of Yoshio as a member of the opposite sex.

Once together and riding in a taxi to a dinner date with him, Mariko began wondering exactly where this whole thing was headed. She had no idea what the stirring inside her meant. Could it be guilt gnawing at a thirty-three-year-old woman going out for dinner with a man more than a decade her junior? Yoshio was young and—looked at as a member of the opposite sex—

undeniably handsome and charming.

For his part, Yoshio was silently making sure today's mask fit snugly over his face and thinking that he should just play it natural. It was a strange feeling. He'd rid himself completely of so-called "natural" human emotion by force of the Will; acting natural for him meant that the demon within would be acting like a human. It would be a very sophisticated performance, not presenting the bright-eyed idealist he fooled society with, but rather allowing the woman Mariko to catch small glimpses of another Yoshio—abused, pained, dark inside. He recalled the consternation he had caused in her two months earlier, during the interview, and was determined to approach the situation with utmost care that evening.

The entrance to the restaurant had a rustic feel thanks to the sign, which was made of driftwood processed into a simple thick plank, with the characters *Ryozeñan* written on it. Mariko was very surprised that Yoshio had picked this place.

Someone as young as Yoshio appreciates the aesthetic appeal of "wabi"? She discovered a hidden side to him and admired his social intelligence, unexpected, but befitting the chairman of a non-profit.

Yoshio told Mariko that he had ordered a fixed course. Mariko, still nervous, nodded in silence. A soft light filtered through the paper screens and lit up the private room. It was hard to believe they were in the middle of Tokyo; there seemed to be no cars passing or people talking. The quiet was only broken by the intermittent sound of a bamboo tube tapping against the stone fountain in the garden.

Yoshio seemed vacant, having cast aside his customary stance. Mariko received the same impression she had when he entered the hotel room before the interview. *Could this be the real Yoshio?* During the interview, Mariko had witnessed the vulnerable young man transform into an eyes-wide-open, take-on-the-world social reformer brimming with energy.

He looked smaller than before. There was something in his narrow shoulders that made Mariko feel like she should say something to him. "This restaurant is really charming. Thanks for bringing me here today. I had no idea you liked this kind of place."

"What kind of place did you think I would like? Denny's?" Yoshio asked with a wistful smile.

"No, not at all. The interview was actually a very educational experience for me. I learned a lot about the way our society works. But I still didn't get enough of a feel for you as a person."

"I'm very simple in my lifestyle. I'm a minimalist when it comes to food, shelter, and clothing. I can't understand people who stuff themselves, get drunk, go around in glittering jewelry, that kind of thing. What about you?"

"Me? I'm just average. I do occasionally envy people who are living the good life, though. I don't like things that are very ostentatious. I hardly have any clothes. I mean, look at what I'm wearing today, even though you asked me out to dinner."

"The only clothes I have are these slacks, a white shirt, and a jacket. I have several changes, of course. The only shoes I wear are white Converse. They're all pretty dingy and worn down, but I keep them clean."

Converse... Mariko suddenly recalled Detective Isogai. "Where do you think you get that stoicism from?"

"'Stoicism'? I never thought of it that way, but it's not like I'm some self-denying ascetic or anything. I just decided early on that this is the way I would live my life. I can't imagine living it any other way."

"You know, it's weird, but I really have no idea what kind of life you lead. Everyone's got a hobby, something they do to relax, but with you I just..."

"Hobbies? I don't have such luxuries," Yoshio smiled. "I've always been interested in chemistry, though. I buy different chemicals online, do little experiments at home. But that's about it."

"Chemistry? I don't know a single thing about chemistry. Maybe H_2O. That's all the chemistry I know."

"You've got to know what $NaHCO_3$ is."

"Um, let me... No. I have no idea. I give up."

"Sodium bicarbonate."

Mariko gave him a blank look.

"You know, baking soda!" Yoshio giggled like a child. He had a sudden urge to explain to Mariko the involved chemical formulas he had used to remove the hydrated carbonic acid ($H_2CO_3(aq)$) from commercially available sodium chlorate ($NaCLO_3$) and purify the result to where he could use it in a bomb.

One of the screen doors slid open silently just then, and the waitress came in with a few dishes in an elegant presentation, including *konnyaku* with white sesame and new shoots and fried *kuwai* on a light bed of salt. It all looked delicious.

A bit of sake would go well with this, Mariko thought. But when, upon taking their seats, the rustically dressed waitress had asked Yoshio if they would like something to drink, he'd ordered water for the both of them without asking Mariko. She thought it was pretty rude of him to do that, since he had invited her to dinner, but she decided to keep her mind open for today. She really knew nothing about this young man. "You don't drink?" she asked.

Yoshio was mechanically masticating the food, which had been so elegantly prepared in the kitchen, almost as though he were counting the number of chews before swallowing. He instantly suppressed the intense anger he felt at Mariko's question and looked up with a fake smile on her face. "I can't, not even a drop. Just smelling alcohol makes me ill. Oh! I'm sorry, I just assumed... I forgot to ask. Would you like to order something to drink?"

"No, it's okay. I have the occasional drink, but I've been trying to cut back even at home. I've been drinking herbal tea instead."

"Herbal tea?"

"Yeah. There's a whole variety. Some calm you, some revitalize you when you're tired. You pick the one you want depending on your mood that day. I even bought an encyclopedia of herbs. But I don't know how long it'll hold my interest. I go through phases."

A heavy sense of boredom settled on Yoshio's mind as the discussion turned to herbs. He felt guilt at wasting precious time for his project whenever he spent time on meaningless things. "You mentioned that you're a freelance photographer. What's a typical day like for you?"

"My schedule is very irregular, because I don't have a steady level of work all the time. Sometimes I'm out all night on a job. Sometimes I'm home all day. Photographers that work for pictorial weeklies are on twenty-four-hour standby. You can get a call at midnight or early in the morning."

"You live in Higashi Shinagawa, right?"

"I do. How do you know?"

"It's on your business card. Higashi Shinagawa, third street."

"I often tell people I live in 'Tennozu Isle, on the waterfront,' because it sounds classier. But it's just an old apartment building surrounded by warehouses and ugly office buildings."

"And you live alone?"

"Yeah. I've lived by myself for about five years now."

Body of single woman found strangled in apartment—Yoshio scrolled through a few such scenarios in his head. If he could get to know her well enough for her to invite him to her apartment, he could just send in Seiichi Imamura. Or, since he could find out the exact location of her apartment without much trouble, he could find out her schedule with a bit of surveillance, then get Imamura to dress as a package delivery guy and send him in at the right time. Either way, it wouldn't hurt to become closer to this woman and get her to open up to him. "Other than your work as a photographer, is there anything you do on a daily basis, like jogging, or taking walks, or..."

"You know, thinking about it, I really don't. I don't have any hobbies to speak of. One thing I have wanted to do for a while is portraiture, but not work-related. I want to take pictures of total strangers whose whole lives you can see etched into the wrinkles in their faces, in the way they hold themselves, their gestures. Pictures that capture that moment where life itself is embodied in human form."

"I really like the photograph you took of me."

"The one in the magazine?"

"Yeah."

Mariko didn't know what to feel. The photograph of Yoshio shirtless that ran in *In Focus* was gruesome to look at. The photograph captured the pain of being a twenty year old who had thrown himself into the void, having no choice but to reveal his own tragic past and live his life that way. "I'd like to photograph you again, if possible."

"Anytime. I don't believe I make such a great subject. Do you want me to strip and show you my scars again?" Yoshio asked with a breezy smile on his face, and looked at Mariko.

"No! No, that's not what I meant," Mariko rushed to say, afraid that Yoshio had misinterpreted her words. "Sorry. What I want is just a normal, everyday portrait of you, when you're at ease, when you've let your guard down. What I want to capture is the real you, that's buried deep inside your soul."

"The real me?"

"This might be kind of forward, but it's kind of hard to watch you, because you're so young, and yet you're working so hard to make a change in society—too hard, maybe. Which is why I want to capture the Yoshio that isn't working so hard, you when you're in a more natural state."

Yoshio got a distant look in his eyes, as though thinking about his childhood. "You see right through me, don't you? I'm actually very weak. There's a darkness inside me that won't go away."

"A darkness?"

"Yeah. And I know exactly where it came from or when it started."

“The abuse you were subjected to by a parent you never met?” Mariko asked hesitantly. She looked into his eyes to see if the question had hurt him. He didn’t return her gaze, staring absently at the paper screen over her shoulder instead, with a placid look on his face.

“I don’t have any memories of the abuse. I don’t even remember my parents’ faces. Whenever I think about the scars, it’s like there’s something otherworldly about them, like they’re just a dream. I don’t hate whoever did this to me anymore. But when I think that I’ll never be able to escape this disfigured body, that’s when the darkness seeps in. Hiding it is scary, though, because I feel like I’m being sucked into that darkness inside myself. And that’s why the only option I have, really, is to put the ugliness out there for everyone to see, and keep close watch over myself.”

“Ugliness? You’re not ugly at all! In fact you’re quite attractive. I just meant that it’s painful to watch you, but what you’re doing for society is amazing. It’s not like there are very many young people with your ambition out there.”

“I guess I think I’m ugly because it’s been beaten into my head by society. You know, it’s funny, but I actually believed a stork had brought me into this world until I was about two or three years old. I was so gullible. And when I found out that wasn’t true, I remember I was so ashamed I could’ve died.”

Yoshio looked down at the empty plates on the table. An off-white hand-made dish had held a *kuzumochi* cake that he had forced himself to swallow earlier.

Yoshio didn’t know whether being incapable of tasting food was a sign of some kind of psychological disorder or not, but the whole process of ingesting food, converting it into energy, and excreting it was so grotesque to him that if he didn’t have to eat in order to keep his body functioning, he wouldn’t.

His mind was as empty as the dish. He had descended into a dark mood at some point while being with Mariko in this restaurant, which was frequented by publishing types and other intellectuals.

In order to designate Mariko as Seiichi's prey, it would help to become more intimate with her, exposing his own inner shadows as a cover for feeling out her daily schedule. At times he became unsure of where exactly the line dividing the performance from the reality lay, and it was through that crack that feelings of uncertainty emerged.

"Mariko." Yoshio shifted his gaze from the now-empty dessert dish to Mariko. His eyes were filled with the sadness of a child abandoned by its mother. It seemed to penetrate Mariko to the core. "This is the first time I've ever told anyone about the darkness in my soul. I was always on my best behavior at the orphanage so that the teachers would like me. I studied hard and always got the best grades so that I could fend off bullies. But now that I hear you say it, it's like I'm realizing for the first time how hard I've been working."

Mariko was moved by Yoshio's forthright confession. And she realized that what she had been looking for, from having dinner with him like this, was exactly this moment. Her unconscious wish had been to see the real Yoshio Iizuka, the damaged and vulnerable human being behind the mask of the idealistic chairman of a non-profit that he wore for society. She sensed that he had opened up to her for the first time now. She had a strong desire to help this vulnerable young man.

"You know, at your office I noticed that..."

"What?"

"I noticed that all the staff are teenage guys. Is it your policy not to hire women?"

Yoshio considered the question in silence. *Female staff?* He had never given it any thought. *Scary.*

"I just thought maybe you didn't like women. Because of your mother and all."

"That's ancient history. I don't harbor feelings of hatred for women or anything like that. In fact, I probably could've benefited from having an older sister like you around."

"Older sister, huh?" Mariko snickered.

"I remember people coming to visit me in the orphanage in Miyazaki when I was five. They were potential adoptive parents. At first they would like me."

"So there was a system of adoption, then."

"It's a weird feeling for a kid, thinking that you might become a member of these people's family."

It seemed to Mariko like Yoshio's eyes were welling up. He had the look of a child seeking the kindness, which he'd never experienced, of a mother or family. It completely lacked the intensity it had during the interview, that almost intimidating force. He seemed now like a teenager filled with angst. Mariko was feeling affection for Yoshio.

"But they would all see the scars and get scared off."

A feeling of indignation filled Mariko. "To be honest, before coming tonight I had no idea what we could talk about. I was worried that if you were the same person you were during the interview, our conversation would be stiff and impersonal. But I'm really happy that you opened up like this to me. I'm just a photographer, making my living taking pictures of celebrities, and I don't know much about anything, but the one thing I do have is an eye for people. I hope you'll continue to confide in me."

Each dish had been simple but prepared with obvious care. You could feel the spirit of the chef. Mariko was happy that Yoshio would invite her to such an elegant place, but not because the food was good, and good for you. What made her happiest was the discovery that Yoshio, whose private life was a closed book to Mariko, was the kind of person who appreciated these moments. In fact, after feeling so distressed at all the pain in Yoshio's life, it was a relief to Mariko to be able to think, *Ah hah. He's human!*

26—An Offering to Evil

Seiichi Imamura lived with his father Masao and mother Yasue in Science City, Ibaraki Prefecture, where the University of Tsukuba was located. Around October of the previous year Seiichi discovered and started frequenting the official *Society of Victims of Abuse for the Prevention of Abuse* website. He didn't read newspapers and hated television and was unaware of Yoshio's media appearances.

The website, which Yoshio had set up about a year before he started the non-profit, hadn't changed a bit, and he continued to use it as a tool for recruiting "talented" young men to fill the ranks of his organization.

Seiichi registered as a member and started emailing Yoshio directly after about a month spent getting a feel for the site. His initial reaction was that the site administrator had suffered horrific abuse, but the things he talked about were too hard for Seiichi to understand, much less enter into a discussion about.

"I'm violent with my dad every day," he wrote in one email. He was still in eighth grade then but was already a towering 5'9" and built like a tank. He had been just under average height in fifth and sixth grade and thought that he'd inherited the genes of his father, who had a fairly small build, but he underwent a sudden transformation when he moved into seventh grade and joined the basketball team. He was now so tall that he literally looked down on his father. It was around that time that he started getting violent against his father.

"He hit me a lot when I was little, so I'm getting my revenge," he wrote.

Masao Imamura had always been a timid and diligent salaryman. He beat his wife and young son when he drank as a way of relieving the stress he was under at work, and Seiichi was getting payback. In another email he wrote, "The pathetic way he grovels before his bosses at work like some kind of slave makes me want to beat him."

"So why are you considering suicide?" Yoshio replied. "Make your dad *your* slave. Be the king of your house."

"I'm disgusted with myself when I beat my dad," Seiichi responded. "I doubt my life will be any less pathetic than my dad's. He's the one who brought me into this world, after all. I'd rather just die before going out into the world as an adult."

He never mentioned his mother in the emails. It seemed like she didn't exist, or he was ignoring her. Yoshio didn't feel like asking either way. Seiichi was just a sniveling baby in Yoshio's opinion and wouldn't be useful anyway. He decided to remove him from the list of potential recruits and encourage him to commit suicide by pointing him in the direction of a few simple suicide manuals.

But one day he discovered something interesting in one of Seiichi's emails: his father worked at a company called Nippon Chemical Industries, a wholly owned subsidiary of the Yotsui Chemical Group that made, among other things, bleaching agents for paper pulp and safety flares for use after car accidents.

"He's the stupid warehouse manager at a stupid company that makes stupid shit," Seiichi said scornfully of his father, giving Yoshio an idea. He made a detailed online investigation of the company; according to his web search, Nippon Chemical Industries had a large plant near a polytechnic institute in Shiomi, Ibaraki Prefecture. As Seiichi had said, it manufactured a wide variety of industrial materials and chemical components, including bleaching agents, ion-conducting materials, and, in recent years, plastic drink bottles. In 2001 it was absorbed by the Yotsui Chemical Group in a semi-hostile takeover, the main reason for which was a patent that Nippon Chemical Industries had been granted for a chemical component used for making specialized urethane products. Demand was growing for the chemical, needed in applying antibacterial treatment to heat-resistant, flexible products to be sold for their anti-bacterial properties, like the arms on eyeglass frames.

As he made his bombs, Yoshio found time to spend on his "hobby" research and had found a list of chemicals with high toxicity levels online. He had also read academic papers like "Crisis Management: Chemical Attacks and Terrorism," which included a list of the names of toxic chemical substances. Yoshio immediately found one among the products made by Nippon Chemical Industries.

He asked Seiichi, "You said your dad is the warehouse manager?"

"Yeah. At home he's always boasting about how he's in charge of the most dangerous chemicals the company handles. What an idiot."

Yoshio told Seiichi the name of one of the chemicals he had learned about on the internet and had long been interested in and asked him to find out if it was something his dad was in charge of. Sure enough, it was something Nippon Chemical Industries made, and Seiichi's dad was in charge of it.

Yoshio looked up. He felt like bowing to the amorphous Will. He was overjoyed at the fact that a coincidence, those things about which he was always so wary, had worked in his favor this once, in the service of the Demonic Will's plans.

Preparations for the first chapter in his genocidal story were moving apace. Yoshio continued using Midori, Takeshi, and Kazuhiko to make the weed-killer bombs, but he was about to find the missing piece needed for his great final event, which might be soon in coming.

Yoshio arranged a meeting with Seiichi. He was a big, burly kid with the intellectual development of a toddler. *Might actually be better this way,* Yoshio thought. *Mind control will be a cinch with this guy.*

He cajoled Seiichi to stay in school until graduation, then hired him as an officer for his *Society of Victims of Abuse for the Prevention of Abuse.* The boy had in a way been hired thanks to his father's connection so it couldn't be helped if he was a bit soft in the head. It nevertheless took a bit of work at first to train him to the level where he could perform average duties. Once that was done, Yoshio would call him into the study room and spend long hours teaching him how to manipulate his weak-willed warehouse manager father.

Despite having already been tasked with the critical job of stealing large quantities of a chemical from his father's company, Seiichi had not even completed the murder that was the initiation rite for the final stage of brainwashing. Failure was not an option in this mission, however. It was a singular opportunity that God—or rather Satan—had bestowed on Yoshio.

He had used two different methods to brainwash his employees. The first was one that the Moonies had used at one time: sleep deprivation and repeated imprinting of instructions while in a dazed state. The second method was a more intense one used on officers to lock in their thinking. It required dirtying their hands with an actual killing, thereby isolating them from society, and then regularly showing them the video of the killing, burning it into their consciousness.

Yoshio had Midori, Kazuhiko, and Takeshi work in shifts keeping Seiichi awake for three days and three nights, putting him in a state of extreme sleep deprivation, and then imprinting instructions on the screen of his dazed mind.

The first thing Yoshio commanded Seiichi to do was to be nice to his father. "You've miraculously transformed into an upstanding human being because you started working for the betterment of society under me. You're going to get on your knees before your father, who has lost hope in you for joining this suspicious *Society of Victims of Abuse for the Prevention of Abuse* right out of school, and beg his forgiveness for all the physical violence you've subjected him to."

Seiichi had above-average stamina and insolently answered "over my dead fucking body" to this through the fog of sleepiness enveloping his brain. Yoshio stared at him with a terrifying look on his face. Seiichi flinched and cringed; he was new to the organization and had not undergone the baptism of Yoshio's true terror. He curled up his broad-shouldered body and lay still on the office floor, eyes looking down.

They kept him awake another night. Instruction continued the next day.

"All right, Seiichi. Just think of it as a new way of tormenting your old man. You raise him up to the summit of joy and then kick him off the edge. That simple."

Seiichi's curiosity was piqued, and he nodded at Yoshio with groggy eyes.

"Tell your dad exactly what I am about to tell you, okay? 'I've made fun of your job in the past, but now that I'm working for the betterment of society, I feel like I understand how tough it is to be a salaryman. I want a part-time job at your company so I can see your workplace. I can do odd jobs around the warehouse."

With a sly look, Yoshio added dramatically, "Actually, change 'your workplace' to 'a man's workplace.' I'll leave everything else up to you. I want you to use whatever aspects of your personal relationship with your father you have to in order to get the right response. Understood?"

Seiichi accomplished his mission with dumb fidelity. As Yoshio expected, Masao listened to his son with joy and immediately got permission from his boss to give Seiichi a part-time job at Nippon Chemical Industries to assist his father.

Seiichi filed shipping receipts and helped other workers pull products for shipping from the warehouse, where they were piled in tall stacks, all the while studying the way chemicals were organized at the company. Masao got teary-eyed at the thought that his Seiichi, who had become such a troublemaker in eighth grade, was now such an upstanding member of society.

Some nights he even took Seiichi, who still wasn't old enough to drink, to Masadori, a *yakitori* restaurant in front of the Shiomi train station, and drank with him like workplace buddies. Seiichi's task as masterminded by Yoshio had entered the final stage.

The warehouse where the industrial chemicals were kept was unapproachable due to multiple layers of heavy security that were in place. Seiichi nevertheless succeeded in finding out where the many security checkpoints were.

"Wow, this is some serious security," Seiichi said, stroking his father's ego. "And you're in charge of it! That's so cool!"

Elated at the flattery, Masao proudly detailed the security system to Seiichi. The personal security card Seiichi's father always used allowed entry into Zone One. The card could easily be swiped from his father. Zone Two and Zone Three were completely impenetrable thanks to the biometric fingerprint security system the company had in place. The fingerprints of a small number of trusted long-time workers were scanned and stored for authentication for entry. Unless this system could be broken through, it would be impossible to enter the Dangerous Substances Warehouse with the distinctive black and yellow zigzag design painted on its walls.

Seiichi called Yoshio in despair. "I've figured out practically the whole inner system, but the last part is busting my balls."

Yoshio was so angry he would have beaten Seiichi to a pulp if he were there but controlled his anger and said softly, "Seiichi, listen to me. I thought you wanted to become an officer in my organization."

"Of course I do. That's why I swallowed my pride and begged my asshole of a dad to get me a job in this shitty company. Please understand that."

"Funny, but I don't. If you can't produce results, you're of no use to me. Go jump off a bridge with your old man."

"Wait! Let me think of a way..."

"What's the final security system?"

"It's a computer-controlled biometric authentication system that only registered workers can open."

"Biometric authentication?"

"Yeah, only workers who have had their fingerprints scanned and stored in the system can get through." Seiichi heard Yoshio's high-pitched giggle on the other end. "What?"

"Seiichi, you are so fucking stupid."

"Why?"

"You can get into the warehouse with an index finger?"

"Yeah. A card key and a fingerprint scan. Both."

"And you can get the card, right?"

"Of course. My dad's got it on him all the time."

"So then what's the fucking problem? You just get his index finger, too."

Seiichi fell silent. Of course. It was that simple. It also scared him that Yoshio could arrive at the method so quickly.

The next night, Seiichi invited his father to Masadori.

"Listen, I don't care if you're still underage," Masao said in a good mood. "You're an upstanding member of society and I say you can drink even if the law says you can't!"

Seiichi just nodded and smiled but observed his father in a cold-blooded way. They got off the train at their station and walked, both tipsy. When they reached a deserted spot near the university, Seiichi turned to his father.

"Dad, remember when I was a little kid and you used to hit me till my nose bled?"

Masao flinched and looked up at his son, who was still smiling. His son was completely reformed now. *He's just bringing up old memories,* Masao thought, relieved. As he was thinking of a reply, a sudden force exploded into his face, breaking his nose. It began bleeding profusely. He stumbled back and was trying to get his balance when another punch came flying in. The diminutive Masao fell flat on his back onto the asphalt. Seiichi straddled him and beat his father's face with his fists.

Then he got to work.

It wouldn't be difficult. He stuffed a handkerchief in his father's mouth so that no one would hear the screaming. He looked around, but Science City was empty. He pulled out a cleaver he'd brought from home in a shoulder bag and sliced off the top two joints of his father's index finger, leaning his weight into the knife.

Seiichi contacted Yoshio to let him know he'd acquired the "biometric key." He entered the Dangerous Substances Warehouse at 2:30 a.m. with Kazuhiko, Takeshi, and Midori.

Seiichi knew the patrol schedule of the security guards. Chemical plant warehouses were difficult for outsiders to penetrate thanks to periodic government-mandated anti-terrorism directives which included reinforcement of outer walls and installation of security cameras. But they were porous when it came to inside jobs.

Nippon Chemical Industries was proud of the security system that it had spent so much money on, so the number of security guards they hired to patrol the warehouses was never more than one guard in any given zone, and patrols stopped at 2 a.m. After that, the only security in place was mechanical surveillance from the security room using security cameras. Naturally, almost everything was visible to the security cameras, but all they could do was record the undeniable fact that chemicals had been stolen from the premises.

The chemical Yoshio had ordered the young men to acquire was stored in 54-liter drums emblazoned with a United Nations seal indicating that the content had cleared the international inspection standards for transportation of dan-gerous substances. One section of the warehouse was lined with these drums, specially designed with a two-layer interior anti-corrosion coating of epoxy resin and phenolic resin.

On the outside, the drums carried three warning signs. One was a skull and crossbones indicating acute toxicity. Another was a health warning indicating that exposure to the content of the drum could result in respiratory sensitization, mutation of reproductive cells, cancer, and a litany of other ailments. The last sign was an environmental logo warning of potential harm if the content entered a natural waterway.

When Midori saw the labels warning of the extremely poisonous nature of the content of the drums, an image of Yoshio's smile flashed through his brain and filled him contentment. Each drum weighed nearly sixty kilos, so placing them on a cart and then loading them onto a two-ton truck they had parked in back was arduous even with four guys working together. After twenty trips back and forth, the four officers were drenched in sweat.

Day was breaking by the time they reached the border of Ibaraki Prefecture. Seiichi's chest filled with pride at the thought of having completed a difficult task in accordance with Yoshio's orders. Yoshio was waiting to greet them when the truck loaded with the drums arrived. In the meeting room, everybody patted Seiichi on the back by way of congratulation. He'd been the leader of the mission. He stood there with an awkward and embarrassed smile on his face, taller than everyone, looking like a telephone pole.

Even Yoshio, who rarely smiled in front of the other officers, broke into a wide grin, displaying his perfectly aligned white teeth. With this chemical in his possession, he would at last be able to put the finishing touches on the plan for the final event to come. He was ecstatic with joy. "Thanks to Seiichi, this is the most important day since I started the non-profit. What do you say I take you to a really nice restaurant for lunch to celebrate?"

Midori, Kazuhiko, Takeshi, and Seiichi were stunned. They stared at Yoshio. The leader they worshiped had not treated them with such human kindness. Kazuhiko spoke first. "I've never seen you eat at a nice restaurant, Yoshio. What will you eat?"

"Who said I would eat?"

"But you just said you were going to—"

"I know what I said. I'm inviting the four of you. You eat what you want. 'Yoshio' never eats more than the bare minimum needed for survival. I'll watch your magnificent waste from my seat of honor."

Midori was so overcome with emotion that he was almost in tears. Takeshi's pallid cheeks flushed red, and he scratched at the burn scars on his neck, stunned by the unexpected kindness shown by their savior and suddenly realizing how starved of love he was. With a look of resolve on his face, Kazuhiko vowed in his heart to follow Yoshio to the grave if need be. Seiichi's heart welled with even more pride at the realization that all of this was a result of his own expert handling of the mission.

Seiichi haltingly asked, "So, can we have a few beers to celebrate?" hoping that Yoshio would get the joke.

Yoshio had been smiling, looking at Midori, who recently started dressing like him, even wearing his knit cap, but his expression underwent a sudden change. He spun in Seiichi's direction with a puppet-like movement and spoke with a completely blank face. "If you want to wind up like that pathetic father of yours, be my guest. Have that crazy drink every day. I won't stop you. But any idiot dumb enough to drink that stuff and even lose the tiniest amount of control over himself doesn't deserve to be here. Keep that in mind. So what do you say? You still want to drink that piss-colored liquid? Huh?"

Seiichi felt a fear deeper than anything he'd ever experienced in the face of Yoshio's reprimand and nearly wet his pants. For the first time in a while, Yoshio was close to a fit of convulsive anger. The four officers swallowed hard and stood stiffly. They followed Yoshio's sudden change with fearful looks.

Midori, in Yoshio's knit cap, glared at Seiichi as though any insult directed at Yoshio was also directed at him, wishing that he could have the same kind of anger fits. *I'd scream this shit-for-brains into the grave.*

Midori had seen Yoshio have a fit once and only once. He and Yoshio were in a coffee shop in Akabanebashi, and he'd suggested that Yoshio actually hated his parents for abusing him. It took five minutes for the fit to subside. He hadn't seen any fits since, though, perhaps because everything was going according to plan.

With Midori and the other officers watching warily, the spark of sanity finally returned to Yoshio's eyes. He had succeeded in reasserting control over himself before becoming completely engulfed in the black swarm of flying insects. He had perhaps acquired the ability to suppress his fits of anger through sheer force of will.

"Let's go to lunch," Yoshio said, as though nothing had happened. "Oh right, what were we talking about? You wanted a beer, right, Seiichi?" He turned his sharp gaze on Seiichi, who was weeping from fear.

"Please forgive me! Please, forgive me! I will never drink again! I don't ever want to become like my dad!"

Yoshio's voice took a gentle tone. "Seiichi, listen. People like your dad who turn to alcohol as an escape are mentally weak. You're your father's son. If you can't overcome that problem, then you can't be here. You haven't even completed the final rite of initiation so in a way this kind of thing is to be expected. But you know what? I want you to hurry up and get the killing over with, so you can stand here with Midori, Takeshi, and Kazuhiko with your head held high, a full member of the team."

"Thank you. I want my own victim as soon as possible. I'll kill anyone. I'll even kill my dad, if that's what you want."

Yoshio was getting sick of Seiichi, but he didn't let it show. "You really aren't very bright, are you?" he said. "Why would I want you to kill the guy who's in charge of the fucking warehouses? Did you do as I said? Did you make him feel happy and then beat him up, giving him a psychological shock?"

"Yes. I did exactly as you said. He's in total shock. He'll take sick leave and is lying in bed with his finger wrapped in bandage as we speak. He'll do anything I say now. If the company ever notices the missing inventory, his only option will be to make up some fake receipts. There's no way he could tell them that his own family stole it. Plus he's so scared of me physically now that he'll continue to hide the inventory numbers from the company as long as possible. The guy's an idiot. He's always going on about how he's been at that shitty company for over thirty years. He'd kill himself if he got fired."

"All right. Then it's cool. You've done a lifetime of work for me. You don't have to do anything else."

"Thank you very much."

"Seiichi."

"Yes, Yoshio?"

"I'll take you out to lunch, but I want you to eat all the dead animal flesh and drink all the piss beer you want. Just for today, you have my permission."

With this, he gestured to the other officers and they headed out onto Sakurada Street. Like some personal guard, Midori walked right next to Yoshio, followed by Kazuhiko and Takeshi. Seiichi brought up the rear with his tail between his legs, cursing himself for having messed up after accomplishing so much.

27—The Tragedy of S

Kazuma Hoshino met with Detective Dan of the Public Security Bureau about once every two weeks. They would meet at a different place every time. Today's meeting was at a pachinko parlor in Ikebukuro. Kazuma found the machine Dan had told him about on the phone. Someone had saved it by putting a pack of cigarettes in the ball tray. Dan was absorbed by the moving balls in the machine to the right. Without saying anything, he scooped up a fistful of his own balls and put them in Kazuma's tray, nodding at him to start playing. Kazuma hated pachinko and was no good at it. The balls were gone in an instant. Another fistful of the little metal balls was deposited in his tray. They looked like relatives, the kindly uncle sharing his winnings with a nephew.

"How's it been going?" Dan asked.

The place was filled with an earsplitting din from the machines and music. Kazuma hated places like this and wished Dan would just pick a coffee shop or something where they could meet every time for these updates. Dan always picked a different place and never asked Kazuma, which got him mad. There wasn't anything he could do about it, though, with Dan hanging the shoplifting charge over his head.

"So how have things been going?" Dan asked again.

"Uh, just normal, I guess."

"What are they up to?"

"I don't really have much contact with the officers, so I don't know, but Yoshio seems to be running around all the time super-busy."

"No names. I told you before."

Kazuma rolled his eyes in irritation. He was starting to hate this. He had signed on as a volunteer at *Society of Victims of Abuse for the Prevention of Abuse* in December. He went to the Akabanebashi office twice a week on weekdays after school and on Saturdays. All he did was odd jobs and cleaning. They told him to keep the place spotless because Yoshio was a clean freak. There were about fifteen other young people like Kazuma there. They worked in rotating shifts.

His first interview had been with some guy named Midori Sonoda.

"Why do you want to join our society?" he asked.

"I saw the website. I don't get along with my mom," Kazuma answered honestly. It was apparently the right answer, too, because Midori asked him in detail about his warped feelings for his mom, his hatred of her, and things like that. Before he knew it, he'd told Midori everything. It was strangely like that psychological evaluation he'd undergone once.

He passed the interview and was hired. *How can they "hire" me if they aren't going to be paying me?* he thought, irritated, but once he started going it grew on him. Kids his age were working with amazing discipline. His leader was a guy who had joined the non-profit right after finishing his last year of mandatory schooling. It was all kind of military, and he followed orders faithfully and efficiently.

"Anything changed recently?" Another fistful of little metal balls.

"Actually, yeah. Some cop called the other day."

Dan's expression shifted for an instant, and his thin lips twitched at the edges. "And then?"

"I just happened to answer the phone. The guy said he was with the Miyazaki Prefectural Police. Asked if Chairman Iizu—if the chairman was in. I didn't know, so I handed the phone to one of the officers. I was listening nearby, and the guy called the chairman's cell phone asking for instructions."

Dan wondered what was going on. Could it be a detective on another case in Miyazaki that was calling Iizuka's office? He would have to check it out.

"Did he come to the office?"

"Someone did come to the office about half an hour later. That might've been him."

"When was this? I want you to remember the exact date."

Kazuma's head started to hurt. The pachinko parlor was filled with smoke and he hated the smell. His throat hurt, too.

"Mr. D, listen. I want out."

Dan made Kazuma call him "Mr. D." Kazuma's tray was empty, so Mr. D added another fistful of balls.

"I need you to hang in there just a bit longer. All right? So, when did the detective come?"

"It was in January, maybe on the... I don't know! Sometime in January. Oh, it was that real cold day when it was sleeting in the morning. Then it started snowing in the afternoon."

There had been a day in January whose weather matched that description. Dan could look it up. "And what did he want?"

Kazuma was about to lose it. "How the fuck am I supposed to know?!"

Dan squinted and looked at the kid next to him who had his head in his arms, down against the machine. That was probably all he could take for the day.

"Take it easy. You're done for today. I'll see you in two weeks, okay? Actually, our talk was real interesting today, so I might have to arrange a meeting sometime next week." He pulled his wallet out of his jacket and handed Kazuma a crumpled 5,000-yen note. "Here. Treat your mom to a nice dinner with this."

Dan left the Ikebukuro pachinko parlor and immediately passed on his informant's information to Onodera, who sat deeply in his armchair, pondering what it could mean. He got the feeling it was only tangentially related to the current case.

"All right. I'll have a Public Security man at the Miyazaki Prefectural Police look into it. How's your informant doing, by the way?"

"He's a minor, so I'm being careful not to ride him too hard. He's emotionally unstable, though. I'm kind of worried about that."

"We're in the midst of a national crisis. A few eggs are going to get broken. There isn't anything we can do about it. The frontline officers in special investigations are picking people up for minor charges, and we're starting to hear complaints. We have to catch the attackers before it gets out of hand. Remember, you can't get too focused on one thing. You'll lose sight of the big picture. This non-profit is just one possibility in a thousand. But that doesn't mean 'one over a thousand.' It's 'a thousand over one.' Score one and score them all—that's how intelligence gathering works. Keep that in mind."

28—A Flash in the Dark

Mariko kept working, snapping pictures for *In Focus* week in, week out, but whenever she relaxed for a moment, Yoshio came to mind. When he took her to Ryozenan, which was really too classy a place for him with its subdued elegance, she saw his emotional scars and was touched by it. The young man, who for twenty years had fought his inner demons and put on a brave face of idealism to the world, opened up to her, and to her alone.

Mariko and Yoshio got together for dinner twice more after that. She picked the venue for their second date, taking him to a tofu restaurant in Ebisu since he was a vegetarian. She wanted to pay him back for the first time.

He made a strange impression on her when she watched him eat. It was as though he had no sense of taste. No matter what he ate, he chewed it mechanically and gulped it down like he was having a mouthful of sand. She felt like she was dining with a visitor from another plant, especially since the way he held himself and moved his body was rather inconsiderate for a dinner date.

He always lacked a certain natural grace as they talked as if, until meeting her, he'd never felt any of the emotions that arise as a matter of course from living life. She assumed that those aspects of his personality were symptoms of some kind of emotional dysfunction that came from having been abused at such a young age.

When she thought of it that way, she felt like she could accept his awkwardness with a smile.

Saturday, April 7, 2012. A phone call from Yoshio.

"Hi," Mariko said. "It's been a while. Still busy as ever?"

"Thanks for dinner the other day. I paid the first time, but you've paid ever since. Sorry!"

"Don't worry about it. You've got a lot of things you're dealing with. Just think of it as a small investment on my part. I'm expecting a high ROI!"

Yoshio laughed in good spirits. The "real Yoshio Iizuka" mask had become second nature. Giving occasional glimpses of the damaged, vulnerable abuse victim within had become routine. Like an actor for whom a scenarist had written a tailor-made script, Yoshio was playing himself in a fictional role in a way that blurred distinctions between reality and fiction.

"ROI, huh? In that case I recommend buying all the stock in Yoshio Iizuka you can while it's still dirt-cheap. My prediction is that the price is going to explode starting in 2013."

"Really? Thanks for the tip. But isn't this insider trading? I don't want any trouble with the SEC," Mariko laughed.

"Do you have some time tonight?"

"I don't have anything on my schedule today. That's why I'm organizing my old pictures today at home."

"Can I ask a favor?"

"Sure. What is it?"

"Remember talking about your Tokyo Tower photographs at that first interview?"

"Yeah. That seems like such a long time ago."

"I was wondering if you could let me take a look at them."

Mariko hesitated for a second. Even back then she'd wondered what it was that interested him about the photographs. There wasn't that much to think about, though. Those shots were a thing of the past for her now.

"All right. I'll bring the photographs. It'll give us something to talk about."

"Thanks. I've been wanting to see them for a while. By the way, it's my turn to pay, but I don't really know that many restaurants. Would Ryozenan be okay?"

"That would be wonderful. I love that place. The food was great."

"Fantastic. I'll make a reservation in my name. How does eight o'clock sound?"

Mariko agreed and hung up. She went back to the living room and lay back deep in the sofa. She closed her eyes and imagined Yoshio's face. He had become much more human to her than before. He was still just an awkward kid, although calling him a kid was kind of rude. He was twenty, after all. But the more often she saw him, the more he felt like a kid to her. Part of him refused to grow up, like some kind of Peter Pan. *No, he's not like some fairytale fantasy. He has this…pure darkness.*

Mariko felt funny cataloguing the impressions she had of him the way she organized her herbal teas. The twenty-year-old beau and the thirty-three-year-old matron. They probably looked like an odd couple to other people. She wasn't going to let it bother her, though.

She got to Ryozenan five minutes after the appointed time, and Yoshio was already there, waiting in the same private room they'd used before. It was just as peacefully elegant, enveloped in the soft light coming through the paper screens.

"Sorry I'm late! I rode the train part way and then took a taxi from Shinbashi, but it was really crowded."

"It's okay. I just got here, too." Yoshio had arrived fifteen minutes early, sipping water as he waited for her.

Mariko hadn't seen him in two weeks. In January they had gotten together for the first time since the interview, and today was going to be their fourth date. They were strange dates. They always met at a restaurant, where they drank water with their dinner and talked about various things before heading their separate ways.

Mariko liked to drink, but she knew Yoshio couldn't even stand the smell of it. He insisted every time after the first, but she decided she wouldn't drink on their dates.

"I didn't really have anything I wanted to talk to you about, but I wanted to get together with you because I'm going to start getting really busy sometime next month, and I might not be able to see you for a while."

Mariko's heart skipped a beat. "Oh, really? Lonely for me," she admitted honestly but, she hoped, casually.

"My non-profit has been up and running for six months now. We've started a counseling service for parents who abuse their children, and it's about time we took this to the next stage."

"All of that in only half a year! You're the darling of the media, too."

"Yeah, the denizens of TV-land seem to have taken quite a liking to me, but I'm not a TV personality or anything like that. I'm a social reformer. Plus I've already spilled my guts to you. You know a lot about me."

"It's better that way. It makes you more human. But now whenever I hear you described as a 'young idealist' it does sound kind of phony."

"Yeah, but at the end of the day, all I can do is live my life in the manner allowed by the way I came into the world."

Their gazes met and locked for an instant—hers innocent, his world-weary—but he looked away first. She felt her heart begin to race. She saw him as a man now. Underneath the attractive appearance, there was something that aroused in her something like maternal instinct.

"Yoshio."

"What?"

"Are we friends?"

Yoshio got a strange look on his face, which seemed somehow faded. "More than friends. You're the only woman I can reveal the darkness in my heart to."

The words moved her. Was it a confession of love? "You remember, at that first interview, I asked you about your dream."

"My dream?"

"Yeah, you don't remember? Didn't you say you were going to organize some kind of big festival or something?"

"Oh, that. Yeah, that's what I'm working on right now. And that's part of the reason I'm going to be super-busy for the next six months."

"That's so exciting! What kind of festival will it be?"

"Still a secret. I like giving people surprises. When we've hammered down a date, I'll give a press conference."

"Wow. Invite me, too!" Mariko said innocently.

Yoshio looked at her and thought, *Uh, you're not going to be invited to anything.* What was this woman to him, really? Why was he here? He felt like he was forgetting his original purpose for meeting this woman at the same restaurant back in January.

The season had changed since they were last here, and the many dishes brought in now mainly used spring vegetables. Mariko enjoyed the *tsukushi* and slightly bitter boiled *zenmai*. As always, Yoshio emptied each dish in his strange way, moving his jaw up and down mechanically, as though he were counting each chew, and swallowing with a gulp.

The woman who brought the food didn't ask them what they wanted to drink, perhaps remembering the previous time. She brought two glasses and a bottle of natural spring water, which Yoshio and Mariko drank while eating the simple dishes in silence. They seemed to run out of things to talk about in the second half of the dinner, and time passed with few words spoken.

"Oh, I brought the photographs, by the way."

"That's right. I asked you, then forgot about them. Sorry."

The gruesome images of Tokyo Tower being blown up had held a powerful attraction for Yoshio ever since that first interview. There was a narcissistic aspect to his interest.

Mariko pulled a thick sheaf of prints out of the protective felt case and placed them on the table before Yoshio. Mariko had brought *all* the photographs, her apprehension about the "signature of death" images a thing of the past. She wanted Yoshio to see them all.

"Ah, wonderful." Yoshio began looking at each picture. As she watched him, Mariko thought about how she was taken aback before the meal began when Yoshio said they wouldn't be able to meet for a while. She was overcome with affection for the young man sitting before her whom she would surely miss.

All of a sudden, Yoshio was screaming.

With his mouth open like a broken robot, he continued to emit a series of meaningless sounds. Mariko jumped up, dashed around the table to him, and held him from behind.

"Yoshio! Are you all right?" His body was shaking. Was it an epileptic fit? She gripped his body tightly as the convulsions grew in intensity. After a while it relaxed in her arms. He slumped over onto her. "Yoshio, what's going on? Are you okay?" she asked.

The photograph Yoshio had been holding fell to the *tatami* mat. It was an image of the baby hanging in mid-air, stretching its arms out into the void like a fetus floating in amniotic fluid.

"Thanks, Mariko. I'm fine now." Yoshio slowly pushed her away and stretched his back. He downed a glass of water that was on the table.

Mariko was suddenly embarrassed at having held him so tightly. "You almost gave me a heart attack. It was like you were having some kind of fit. I was worried you were going to bite your tongue off…"

"I'm sorry I surprised you like that. I've had these little fits ever since I was a kid. They don't happen that often. They pass if I just grit my teeth and bear them, though. There's no need for you to worry."

"Are you sure we shouldn't call a doctor?"

"Completely sure. Seriously, I'm perfectly okay now. But it looks like I got a couple of the pictures dirty…"

"Don't worry about that. I can make more prints."

"These are really amazing photographs. The people really look like they're floating in mid-air."

"Did those pictures bring on the fit?"

"No. There's no connection. I don't actually know what it is that brings them on."

Indeed, Yoshio looked perfectly okay. His face had regained

its color. Though that night was the first time Mariko registered serious affection for Yoshio, things didn't seem to go according to script after that. His unfortunate fit had robbed her feelings of momentum.

Dinner over, they went outside where the wet street indicated that a light rain had fallen during the meal. Above, the rain clouds were already gone, and a misty half-moon hung in the early summer night sky.

"Thanks for dinner. Next time it's my treat, okay? Goodnight," Mariko said, looking at Yoshio with a slightly sad look on her face before turning around and getting into a waiting cab. Yoshio watched closely as her feet in their deep purple high heels disappeared behind the door. A strange fear rose up from the pit of his stomach. He felt something he'd never felt in his entire life, a pain in his chest like he was being pierced with a needle.

Yoshio had no idea what the turmoil in his heart meant.

The multiple dinner dates Yoshio had with Mariko to murder her rested precariously on his playing the role of "Yoshio Iizuka, human being." The Will that controlled him found this pleasing. Having eliminated every last trace of humanity that Yoshio had perchance been born with, it was staging a demonic performance for a woman.

Yet the comfort of sensing control over a woman's fate had allowed for a small crack to appear in the Will's total dominion. In fact, until the previous day, Yoshio had considered a different woman for Seiichi's initiation, thanks perhaps to a hint of human sentiment hatching deep inside him. We might hazard that Yoshio's own soul, barely breathing in a corner of his mind under the Will's dominion, was trying to put off Mariko's killing.

Let Mariko Amo live—of course, this wasn't so much a wish as a slight palpitation in his unconscious that he himself did not notice.

Tonight, however, Yoshio did notice that he'd made a mistake.

When he saw the picture of the baby falling out of Tokyo Tower he experienced fear—through the emotions of the "human" Yoshio Iizuka, who was supposed to be nothing more than an act. The thespian putting on a compelling show had seen through his role for a moment and glimpsed the terror of his demonic behavior. Unable to bear the tremendous weight of his own evil, Yoshio had screamed out of fear at a reality that existed beyond his convoluted performance.

The Will wasted no time in making a decision: the woman was to be eliminated without delay. She posed an immediate threat to Yoshio. The demon's playfulness had reached its end.

Yoshio saw Mariko off. He stood watching the taxi until its tail lights disappeared. He felt like he'd seen, in the dark of a total solitude devoid of inhabitants, a brief flash. Burning distantly for but an instant, it faded.

29—The Demon Invites

Mallow—she hadn't tried this herb before. It had cute bluish purple petals. She pinched a few and dropped them into the steaming cup. The color dissolved, turning the tea lavender. The encyclopedia said you shouldn't add it directly to the pot because it would turn the inside red, reacting with even trace amounts of metal present in ceramic.

She breathed in the aroma. It was a bright smell, like sunlight. She had some honey ready to conduct a little experiment described in the book. In France they called it *tisane de l'aube,* "dawn tea," because of what was supposed to happen. Mariko wondered if it would work. She scooped some honey up with a spoon and let some drip into the cup. She stirred the tea.

"It's true!" The lavender liquid in the cup turned pink. "When honey or lemon is added to the tea, it takes on a pink color," the book said. "Poetically, the French call this *dawn*."

It was a Thursday like any other, but her schedule was empty. She decided to sip tea while sorting photographs that had accumulated over the past two years, deleting ones she no longer needed. She had been doing this whenever she found the time over the past few weeks.

For a photographer like Mariko, keeping her data organized was critical because it could become unmanageable very quickly. She didn't really have the chance to reuse old pictures, but she sometimes got calls towards the end of the year from directors at news programs that were doing specials recapping the big events of the year, asking if she had pictures of this or that event.

Just then her cell phone rang. She stood to get it, as she had left it on the dining table. The LCD screen said "Yoshio Iizuka," and Mariko's face brightened.

"Yoshio! How are you doing? Thanks for dinner the other night."

"Hi. Listen, there's something I need to talk to you about." There was tension in his voice.

"Has something happened?"

"It's complicated. Could we get together and talk about it?"

"Of course, but don't leave me totally in suspense. What's up?"

Yoshio didn't have anything to talk about with Mariko. He just wanted to get her to come to the office, and he hadn't come up with anything concrete to tell her. "It's about one of my officers," he improvised. "I'm kind of worried about him."

"Oh, okay. Who is it?"

"Did I introduce you to Midori Sonoda?"

Mariko recalled the beautiful young man who had brought her tea in the waiting room. "A good-looking kid?"

"That's him."

"What's going on with him?"

"I can give you the details when we meet…" Yoshio got an

urge to tell her something very close to the truth. He again sensed his power of life and death over the woman—like he could say anything. "Well, the truth is that I didn't tell you at the restaurant because I didn't want to worry you, but a detective with the Miyazaki Prefectural Police paid us a visit at the beginning of January, apparently in connection with the killing of the director of Jiiku Hospital. He was killed on the beach in the Nichinan Coast."

"The director of Jiiku Hospital—isn't that the doctor who saved your life?"

"It is. I didn't want to think about it because the whole thing was so sad."

"What did the detective want?"

"He was kind of vague, but I got the impression that he thought someone close to me was involved in the case."

"What? That's ridiculous... Wait. He was saying Midori had something to do with the killing?"

"Exactly. The police suspect that he might somehow be involved."

"Do they have any evidence?"

"I can't really say on the phone, but Midori is kind of unbalanced. The way he practically worships me, to begin with. I lost my hat the other day, and then I find out that he's been wearing it. It's creepy. He's even started to dress like me. When I first met him he had long hair, and he dyed it brown. Now he's started cutting his hair short. Like me." Everything he was telling Mariko was the truth; it made him laugh to think it. *If I tell him to kill Dr. Watanabe, he says yessir and gets to it,* he mused, just stopping himself from saying it out loud. "Could you come tomorrow around seven? I'd like to get your opinion on how I should handle this. We can grab a bite afterwards."

"Tomorrow's Friday, right? Sounds good. I haven't had any work lately, so I've got plenty of free time."

"You made a lot of money from the Tokyo Tower pictures,

didn't you?"

"Touché. But I still made less last year than the year before. Plus, I got put through the wringer for 'profiting off the misfortunes of others.'"

"Don't let the sheeple get you down. What do they know, anyway?"

"Thanks. So tomorrow at your office, then."

"I'll be waiting."

Mariko pondered what could have happened with Midori, and worried. Teenagers could do unpredictable things. *Yoshio must be a hundred times more worried than I am, though. I've got to be strong for him. I am, after all, his only friend.* With this she collected herself and sat down at her work desk. *So the kid in Yoshio's office was Midori.* She had definitely felt his resemblance to Yoshio. When she thought that, a little pulse ran through her mind, like when she was trying to recall some trifle that quickly slipped out of reach.

She suddenly felt uncomfortable. Some misfortune was coming her way, filling her with dread. She had to protect Yoshio no matter what, even if Midori was in some way involved with the crime. *It can't be easy putting idealist principles into practice, running a non-profit that brings together psychologically scarred kids and rehabilitating them.*

She went back to organizing the photographs.

30—Violation

"Seiichi, we've decided on a victim for you. It's going to happen tomorrow at seven in the evening, right here in the waiting room. You still can't handle anything too complicated, so I've put together a simple scenario for this killing. The prey is a beautiful young woman named Mariko Amo, so strangling her should be almost too easy for you with your…freakish strength. The instant she dies, I want you to have all your circuits open and receiving.

Okay? I want you to savor the moment. If you don't, you won't have passed the initiation, no matter how many people you kill." Yoshio gave Seiichi a rare grin as he spoke.

Seiichi had begun worrying over the past few months that Yoshio wasn't giving him his own victim because Yoshio didn't like him. *I got him what he wanted from my father through blackmail and force, so he can't fire me. But maybe he doesn't actually want to let me into his inner circle...*

This order to kill cleared up all his worries, though. Seiichi almost cried for joy when he found out that Yoshio hadn't abandoned him. His heart raced with excitement at the thought of being able to strangle a young woman to death. He would finally be completing the initiation Yoshio had given him. Finally, he would be a core member like the other officers.

One of the reasons Seiichi was so excited was that the prey allotted him was Mariko Amo, a good-looking woman who was still in her early thirties. He went over in his mind the instructions he had received from Yoshio the previous evening and his heart raced even faster.

Kazuhiko had killed a drunken salaryman, Takeshi a wrinkled old woman. To think that his initiation was going to be a lady, and attractive to boot! Seiichi still thought Yoshio was pretty cold-hearted, but to crush him and make him feel so pathetic and then give him this treat—Yoshio was a master. It made Seiichi want to pledge his undying loyalty to him.

Seiichi could not exactly be called bright, so he repeated Yoshio's instructions about what to do for the killing over and over to himself. The woman, Mariko Amo, would arrive at seven to see Yoshio. Seiichi was to tell her, "The chairman will be right back" and take her to the waiting room, where he would strangle her. It would be a walk in the park! It was probably after that that the real heavy lifting would come. He had a wood-chopping axe, a cleaver, and plastic sheets all ready to go.

He wondered what kind of attractive woman his victim was

going to be. Just imagining it made his heart race. He became agitated and couldn't calm down. He had inherited his father's timidity, and when the clock struck five a kind of cowardice began muddying his excitement. His resolve wilted at the thought of actually killing someone when he pictured himself going through with it. He was afraid his hands would lose their strength in the middle of strangling the woman. Nothing would be worse than if he failed to finish her off and she somehow escaped. That had to be avoided at all costs.

At six o'clock all the officers and volunteers vacated the office, leaving Seiichi alone. He was overcome by a mounting dread. His ragged nerves started to tire him out, so he went to a nearby convenience story to buy some beer. His nerves finally began to settle down after the second can. The bell rang at last. He looked at his watch: it was just past 6:45. Seiichi opened the front door with trepidation.

"Um, hi. I'm looking for Yoshio Iizuka. Is he in?"

Seiichi's heart pumped away in his chest. She was indeed very beautiful. He had heard she was thirty-three years old, but nobody would doubt her if she said she were younger. "Oh, uh, yeah. We've been waiting for you. The chairman will be right back. If you would please come this way, you can wait, uh, inside." Seiichi's voice shook and stuttered, and he was afraid she would guess his murderous intentions. He was practically panting.

"Oh, really? Thanks, I think I will."

When she stepped into the room, for some reason Seiichi recalled the time a fish had swum into a trap he had laid in the Yanase River in Ibaraki when he was a child. His father was next to him, laughing.

That asshole. Seiichi blacked out the image of his father looking at him and laughing affectionately. *The time has come to change my life.*

He used the full extent of his limited mental capacities to make sure he was following the scenario written out for him by

Yoshio. First, he was to take the woman Mariko Amo to the waiting room and then leave the room right away. "Go into the hallway and take a few deep breaths," he heard Yoshio's voice in his mind. He did as he was told, and his cringing fear evaporated.

She was as attractive as Yoshio had said she would be. It was almost a shame to kill her. Yoshio had said to strangle her to death, but that would be such a waste. Doing anything superfluous could be a fatal mistake, though.

Seiichi was getting so excited that his thoughts became a jumble. He returned to his desk, opened a drawer, and pulled out the length of narrow cord he had bought at Tokyu Hands, yanking it taut between his hands, confirming the strength. He put it in the back pocket of his jeans and tiptoed back to the waiting room. He had a paper cup filled with the barley tea they served guests.

He knocked on the waiting room door. Like the well-trained, well-mannered young man he had become, he bowed his head slightly as he entered the room and placed the tea on the side table. He bowed again, took a step back, and turned around. Here he would normally walk the three steps to the door and place his hand on the knob, but instead he quickly walked around behind the sofa. "Today I actually—" the woman began to speak. He cut her off by pulling the white cord out of his pocket and winding it around her neck from behind. He yanked the cord tight with all his strength, constricting her throat and pulling her clear off the sofa. Seiichi was already 5'9" even though he had only just graduated from ninth grade, so it was easy for him to hang the petite woman, like a human gallows. Her body twisted and flipped around like a fish as she kicked her legs wildly, only succeeding in causing the cord to dig further into her neck from her own body weight.

She swung her arms around trying to grab the man behind her, but her fingertips were already beginning to twitch. Her fingers were so splayed out that they looked like they would tear apart if they splayed any further. She was in the throes of death, striking out at thin air, trying to grasp anything she could.

Recalling Yoshio's words, Seiichi looked around at the hanging woman's face from behind. "I want you to fully absorb that moment of death," Yoshio had said.

Saliva was hanging in long strands from her mouth now, but she was still alive. Seiichi pulled even harder and raised his arms above his head like a gesture of victory, pulling the woman's body even higher. Eventually her arms and legs stopped their flailing and fell slack, lifeless.

"I did it!" Seiichi exulted. "My initiation!" He lowered the corpse onto the sofa and looked closely at the now lifeless face of the woman, contorted in a rictus of pain. She had been a living, breathing being until a moment ago, and now she was just lying there, the life gone out of her. Where did it go? The conglomeration of flesh and bones that had been "Mariko Amo" was now simply a physical object with no need for a name.

It was weird to think about. Was this strange feeling what you felt the moment you extinguished a life? He touched her face and wrists. They were still warm. But lifeless. His gaze dropped to the flesh under her blouse, twisted and untucked from all the flailing about.

What kind of relationship did Yoshio and this Amo lady have? Seiichi wondered. *Had they dated?* No. Seiichi couldn't imagine Yoshio getting romantically involved with a woman. Seiichi feared Yoshio but had followed his exact instructions, the strangling scenario had played out exactly as scripted, and nobody would yell at him if he added a little violation.

Seiichi still didn't understand that Yoshio was a perfectionist who tolerated absolutely no deviation from his orders. When he rationalized his fear of Yoshio out of the way, a searing desire ran through his body. He began tearing the clothes off the dead body.

31—A Blind Spot Called the Past

Inspector Yoshida slept at his desk, reclined deep in his chair, the smell of leftovers from the previous night's take-out still in the air. His suit jacket, dark gray with a few faintly glossy fibers mixed in, lay wrinkled on top of him, like a blanket.

The view from the window looked down onto the National Diet Building. The verdant trees visible beyond were the woods surrounding the Crown Prince's Palace. To the right, just barely visible, was part of the moat around the Imperial Palace. Daybreak was not far off, but a heavy layer of clouds covering the sky made it seem like night even though it was already 5:30 a.m.

Ever since August 27th, when the special investigation headquarters for the Tokyo Tower bombing had been set up in Atagoyama Police Station, Yoshida had spared no effort to solve the case as leader of the team canvassing local residences and businesses for information. He had returned to his desk at headquarters for the first time in a while the previous night and, in the large room reserved for members of Criminal Investigation Section One, spent the entire night on the daunting task of reading reports covering the past eight months.

Between 7 p.m. and 4 a.m. he went over all the reports with a fine-toothed comb to see if there wasn't something they had missed, some place one of the investigation teams had slipped up. Unfortunately, he slept right through to morning overcome with fatigue. One of his colleagues, miraculously managing to retain a bit of human kindness despite the stress of the circumstances, must have placed Yoshida's suit jacket over his shoulders.

For the first six months the public raged against the investigation headquarters, with one wag suggesting they change their official name to Tokyo Tower Bombing Attack Investigation and Navel-Gazing Headquarters.

The growing burden on the investigators who were under daily pressure, whether they were with Criminal Investigation or Public

Security, filled the hall during the joint meeting the previous night. The special investigation got a boost in December when information came in from a witness who had possibly seen one of the culprits in the crowd watching Tokyo Tower topple from the observation deck at Roppongi Hills. Four months later, that barely glimpsed suspect was disappearing into the mist before the detectives' eyes.

But the investigation went on, canvassing local residents, teasing out possible acquisition routes for the bomb-making materials, collecting and analyzing substances and objects from the site of the bombing. Every possible angle was followed—which was fine as long as they were busy. When the detectives gradually started having time on their hands, they all started getting a queasy feeling inside. Rust and mud would eventually bog down the engine of their minds.

≈

At that moment, another man was asleep in the Miyazaki Prefectural Police Headquarters. Shuji Fukada was slumped on his desk in Criminal Investigation Section One dreaming about Yusuke Watanabe. Yusuke was fishing on the Nichinan Coast, flashing Fukada a big smile as he told him something. Fukada couldn't make out what he was saying, though. Behind Yusuke in the distance, the wind off the sea blew through a thicket of palm trees. There was something on the ground at the foot of the trees. A pair of white Converse.

Fukada woke with a start. He looked around. The detectives and employees were at their desks busy at work. Some were on the phone. It was the same scene as always. Fukada had just woken but sat there for a moment, groggily wondering which was real, the place with the Converse, or here.

Then it occurred to him: if he jumped from the roof of the Prefectural Police building, then both would become equally unreal, and he would be freed from the burden of having to find an answer.

The row of cherry trees in front of the building were a vibrant green, the season for the pale pink blooms having passed. Southern Kyushu started getting warm in the middle of April, and people started to relax and take things a bit easier.

Fukada also appeared to be relaxing, since there was nothing left to do in connection with the killing of Yusuke Watanabe, but inside he was anything but relaxed. He was staring down death in the closed, lightless space of his mind. One reason, naturally, was the unavenged death of a close friend, but more than that, he was just tired. His psychological burden was not relieved by the reduction in his workload. He felt helpless and on the edge of a nervous breakdown.

Fukada pondered his dream after waking up at his desk, then got up unsteadily. He climbed the stairs to the roof.

The sky was cloudless and beautiful. He looked over the railing and saw the cherry trees lined up in front of the building in full bloom like a pale pink mist. He shook his head and looked down again. He realized that he'd seen a phantom of exuberantly blooming cherry trees as though his mind had been on pause for more than a month.

If I jump from here, I'll hit the curb in front of the main entrance. That would create one hell of an uproar in the department. The national media would descend on this quiet city like a swarm. "POLICE DETECTIVE JUMPS TO DEATH IN BROAD DAYLIGHT"... The thoughts played lazily in his head. Just then, the cell phone in his jacket pocket rang. *Who cares? It's too late anyway.* His mind was heavy but he looked at the LCD screen. It was from a young technician in the forensics lab. Something about the call caught Fukada's attention. He pressed the "talk" button and reluctantly put the phone to his ear.

"Detective Fukada! We've got a positive! Hello?"

"A what? A positive on what?"

"The hat you brought by a while back. You seemed to be under a lot of pressure recently, so we ran the DNA tests again."

"Wait, are you saying the results from the first test were wrong?"

"No. Two of the hairs in the cap were from someone else! We ran DNA tests on them, and they matched the hairs we collected at the beach on Nichinan Coast."

Isogai got a call from Detective Fukada of the Miyazaki Prefectural Police on Friday, April 27th, in the evening. He reminded Isogai that he had come to Tokyo in the winter and on Isogai's suggestion had visited the offices of Yoshio Iizuka's non-profit organization, where he had obtained a knit cap that turned out to contain hairs belonging to someone other than Iizuka. And as luck would have it, those hairs matched strands picked up at the scene of Yusuke Watanabe's killing.

Isogai concealed his profound shock and just sighed as he listened on the phone, speaking in his usual laidback tone. "So you're telling me that someone close to Yoshio Iizuka killed Yusuke Watanabe?"

"Without a doubt."

"Probably someone who works at his non-profit, then?"

"That's right."

"Detective Fukada, you said that Dr. Watanabe had saved Iizuka's life when he was a baby."

"He did. I don't know what kind of mixed-up personal conflict we're looking at here, but there's got to be something, some kind of hatred. My department isn't looking at Iizuka as a suspect, though."

"Right."

"The problem is, I got this piece of evidence illegally, so we can't act on it in any way. Which is why I was wondering if you guys in Tokyo maybe couldn't give us a hand somehow."

"All right. You'll have to submit an official request to the

Investigation Coordination Department at the Metropolitan Police from your Criminal Investigation Department so that we can link up with your Miyazaki case here in Tokyo. I'll get someone here to stake them out. They probably don't know we've got this evidence, so it won't occur to them that we're keeping such a close eye on them that we're actually staking them out. And if we get a chance, we'll see if we can't get another piece of evidence from someone close to Iizuka."

"Thank you very much," Fukada said, and hung up.

Isogai replaced the handset and took a deep breath. His palms were still sweaty, though, and he had trouble controlling the beating in his chest. Even before his brain kicked in, his detective's instincts were running ahead, and he felt as though something scary, something demonic were coming after him from the darkness in his mind.

The information that Fukada had brought him was that the killing of a doctor in Miyazaki Prefecture, which was totally unrelated to the case on the special investigation's plate, was in some way connected to the young man Yoshio Iizuka. This fact so unsettled Isogai that it almost made him feel dizzy. The case that Isogai had handled of the killing of the teenager in Atagoyama was "cold," simply waiting to be filed away, the investigation for which had long been dismantled, any further efforts a mere formality. Learning that the five-year-old murder case and the stabbing death of Yusuke Watanabe had some point of contact in Yoshio Iizuka, Isogai had a reaction he could neither understand nor suppress.

He felt that following the line pursued by Detective Fukada would result in the present and the past becoming connected like a Moebius strip, strangely twisted together, each side the obverse of itself. Not only that, but it was also possible that his subconscious had been preventing him from arriving at a new line of reasoning. He placed his hand against his forehead and felt the cold sweat.

Could these doubts have been Detective Fukada's own when he came to visit three months ago?

In response to the investigation request from Fukada, Isogai had the idea of putting Sergeant Maruyama, who was working in Area Six of the canvassing operation, on a stakeout of Yoshio Iizuka's non-profit and keeping it a secret from the station. It had nothing to do with the investigation of the Tokyo Tower bombing case, but he justified it as a merely temporary assignment to another case. If he tried to bring it up at an investigation meeting at this stage, he'd find it impossible to present a logical connection between the case and the Tokyo Tower bombing. *Investigations sometimes require a little finesse,* Isogai mumbled to himself.

"Maruyama, you said you had your eye on that Iizuka kid, didn't you?"

"What's that, sir?" Maruyama was caught off guard by the unexpected voice from behind.

"Don't 'what's that' me. I'm asking you if you hadn't an interest in Yoshio Iizuka."

"Yes, back then I did. But right now Area Six is focusing on video-game arcades and other places where young people congregate."

"Huh, didn't peg you for a quitter."

"Sir?" Maruyama scratched his head, having trouble figuring out what Isogai was getting at.

"Listen, I've got a favor to ask. I want you to stake out the office of the non-profit organization run by Yoshio Iizuka, which is technically Area Four's coverage. I want you to keep tabs on things over there for a while. The four people whose names are written on this piece of paper should be there, and I want you to get your hands on something that will allow us to get DNA samples from them. Got it?"

"Wait, you mean Iizuka's now a suspect in the Tokyo Tower bombing case?"

"I said no such thing. All I told you to do is to get your hands on something that they used, like a piece of gum, a Kleenex, a coffee cup from Starbucks, that kind of thing, from which we can collect a saliva sample, a sweat sample, or something. Call this a special assignment from me. Got it?"

"Yes, sir. I don't really understand why you want me to do this, but if it's an order, then I'll do it." Maruyama straightened his tie and saluted. "Can I ask one thing, though? Please let the guys in Area Four know that I'm going to be intruding. They're as territorial as lions over there."

"Actually, no can do. This is a top-secret mission." Isogai put a finger to his lips as he said this and squinted his eyes theatrically.

The stakeout of Yoshio Iizuka's office started on the thirtieth, which was Monday of the following week, when Maruyama was able to disengage from his canvassing of Area Six.

That was three days after Isogai's order.

Yoshio Iizuka and his partners were still unaware of the advance in Detective Fukada's investigation, so Isogai believed that three days wasn't too much of a wait. What he didn't know was that those three days wrought fateful changes.

32—Confession

Saturday, April 28, 2012. 11 a.m.

A heavy layer of clouds hovered above Tokyo all morning. The weather report said there could be thunderstorms that night.

Kazuma was scheduled to do volunteer work at the office of Yoshio's non-profit today. There was no school, so he left his house in Numabukuro with plenty of time to get to the office by noon. He took the Seibu Shinjuku line to Nakai, where he transferred to the Oedo line, heading for the office in Akabanebashi.

He had made a decision that day. He'd been coming to the

office more often in the past month, and he was gnawed by guilt seeing how other young people his age respected the chairman, Yoshio Iizuka, and worked their heads off. Plus, he was sick of being pushed around by Detective Dan. *I don't care if they put me in juvie. When I get out, I want to work with these people.* Kazuma himself was beginning to respect Yoshio Iizuka.

He opened the office door and exchanged greetings with everyone in the office. "Where's Midori today?" he asked, looking around the big room and not seeing Midori Sonoda anywhere. The officers had four desks facing the staff members' desks and the outside wall of the waiting room, and Midori's desk was the second one from the right.

"He was just here. He'll probably be back pretty soon," said one of the members that Kazuma knew well. After a short while, he heard the door of the waiting room open and a few people walking down the hall speaking and laughing among themselves. He heard Midori's voice among them. Midori had begun acting as a PR liaison, shielding the chairman from visitors. Kazuma's interview had been with Midori, so he was the first one Kazuma turned to whenever he needed to talk about something.

"Midori!" Kazuma called out as his mentor came back to the office room. He jogged over to him and whispered something. The pair immediately headed back to the waiting room, which was empty of visitors now.

"Shall I bring some hot coffee?" somebody asked before they disappeared into the room.

Midori looked back with a scowl and said sternly, "No. Everybody stay out for a while."

Midori listened to everything Kazuma had to say and was stunned to find out that they were under police surveillance. When the detective had come from Miyazaki at the beginning of the year, Midori thought it was all over, that they had figured out he'd killed the doctor. And the Tokyo police had planted a mole in their organization! Exactly how much did they know? Fear rose up in Midori's throat, giving him a strangling sensation.

"I just told him the regular things. That you guys gave a talk somewhere, that people from the child welfare center came for a meeting, that some lady reporter from a TV station was here..." Kazuma didn't mention that at the last meeting with Detective Dan he had buckled and told him that someone from the Miyazaki Prefectural Police had visited the office. "I'll understand if you fire me. But I never had anything against you. The police basically blackmailed me into doing this, and there was nothing else I could do. I always told them that Mr. Iizuka is a great person, so I don't think he'll have any problems. It's true, after all."

Kazuma felt great in a way, now that he'd been able to get the heavy load off his chest. Though he said he wouldn't mind if they fired him, he secretly hoped that his honesty would be noted and that they would let him stay on. As he looked at Midori, who sat on the sofa, his head in his hands, Kazuma wondered, *Why's he shaking like that? Is it that big a deal? The cops have obviously made some kind of mistake and are making one of their pointless investigations.* Trying to make a good impression, Kazuma asked, "So, what should I do, Midori?"

A year ago Midori was probably as naive as the boy, unable to imagine the gaping hell hole that yawned below the illusion of peace. But now things were different. He had learned to fear Yoshio. "Something very bad is going to happen," Midori said, and he couldn't control the trembling that was rising up from the soles of his feet.

Listening to Midori's report, Yoshio initially experienced a feeling of quiet humiliation.

Like a helpless child, the world had to receive the violence he meted out from beyond the reach of the law. That had been his own relationship to violence as an infant. He could not tolerate his desires being suddenly blocked by a party as incompetent as the police.

Yoshio felt the cold sweat that preceded the sparking of his anger into a raging conflagration. "Is that it?"

"Yes," Midori said with a quavering voice. He could sense that Yoshio was about to unleash *it*. He was scared. He sat on the sofa looking down, stealing the occasional glance.

"Wait outside..." Yoshio kicked Midori out of the room and managed to get the door locked. Sweat was flowing from his forehead and the whites of his eyes were beginning to show. A powerful convulsive fit rocked his body for the first time in a long time, a black wave of bile running riot through his mind.

Midori's report had changed the status of his genocidal plan to full alert in a single move. There was a spy in his organization!

The plan for genocide that used the human being named Yoshio Iizuka like a rag, like something disposable, faced a crisis. This was an obstacle that had to be removed at whatever cost. If the Demonic Will that controlled Yoshio could avert the plan's failure by delivering the human named Yoshio to the police, it would have tossed him through the Metropolitan Police's front door immediately.

Something strange was happening to Yoshio's face. The shadowy swirl of anger moving over his face became another face, creating an overlapping expression on top of the look of anguish below. The faint shadowy expression that floated above let out a soundless roar with a look of fury.

A flying black swarm filled with spite burrowed deep into Yoshio's brain and darted around his neural synapses. The pain was such that Yoshio thought he was about to die. He couldn't care less about his own life, but he would not tolerate dying here without taking a single soul with him. He bit down into his lower lip in an effort to avoid swallowing his tongue as he withstood the force of the wave after wave of convulsions that shook him.

His instincts knew perfectly well what to do. They delivered to Yoshio the assessment that the Miyazaki Prefectural Police was about to identify Yusuke Watanabe's killer and that the power of the law was about to reach himself, defying all odds. Yoshio's head felt like it was about to split in two as his emotions fractured between his instinct and his left brain, which was trying to reject the facts of the situation with all its acumen.

His instincts told him that there was still time to mitigate this crisis. But there was not a moment to lose. That, at least, was clear enough.

Amidst his tortuous headache, Yoshio finally succeeded in subjugating to his instincts all wishful thoughts rejecting the situation. He clearly heard the condescending voice of the black swarm.

I'm disappointed in you. I thought I had found someone with the talent needed to kill millions, but what? You knock over your little toy tower and that's it? Weren't you going to massacre the entire population of Tokyo?

Yoshio slumped back onto the sofa, waiting for the storm blowing violently through his mind to subside.

Finally stillness came. A gentle breeze rippled through the calm. The damaged soul of Yoshio Iizuka, now disdained by the demon, was raising up a voiceless cry. The only peace was death. The time for the final event had come.

Vigor began to fill him. The demon smiled and made it its own.

There was not a second to lose. Midori Sonoda had to be *excised.*

Yoshio locked himself into his room that night and told his staff that he was not to be disturbed under any circumstances. He needed time alone to concentrate all his mental resources to find the best way to deal with the new crisis. Like a chess player, he considered the scenarios that a single move would bring. If one was too risky, he would return the piece and try another route.

He sat with his head held upright and his eyes closed. He almost looked like he was accustomed to practicing yoga or Zen meditation. Yet, his spirit was focused on finding the surest way to carry out his project to kill as many people as possible.

He opened his eyes just after three in the morning. He ordered Midori to summon all the officers immediately. Naturally all four of the officers were awake, awaiting the signal from Yoshio.

3:15 a.m. Yoshio told the other officers to wait outside the room and Midori to sit next to him on the sofa. He put his arm around his shoulder.

"The time for your swan song has come."

"S-Swan song?"

"You will be the first kamikaze."

"Kamikaze?" Midori's brain refused to process the information it was receiving, and he looked imploringly at Yoshio. Angry that Midori had simply regurgitated his words like a parrot, twice at that, Yoshio responded with a cold, rejecting gaze. But Midori, on the verge of tears, simply kept begging with his eyes.

"At exactly 1 p.m. on May 1st, you will blow yourself up at the Shibuya pedestrian crosswalk. You have to take as many of the people there with you when you leave this world. You are the opening act in a horror show."

"I can't. Blow myself up? I can't." As if a bomb might go off right then and there if he looked away even for a second, Midori's eyes remained transfixed on Yoshio and big tears started to run down his cheeks.

Yoshio smiled with the gentlest look Midori had ever seen and put Midori's head against his chest. "Midori, it's your fate to do this. It's already been decided. You have to fulfill your duty. The bomb is ready. The blasting cap is set. All you have to do is push a button. At five seconds before one in the afternoon, you will start to cross the intersection, and at five seconds after, you will stop in the middle of it. You press the button and BOOM! Your job is done.

"I read a book on suicide bombers written by a jihadist once, and you know what? It doesn't hurt. It doesn't burn. Of course, I don't quite know how the writer could write about it like he had done it himself," Yoshio chuckled. "But you know what I think? Not only does it not hurt, I bet you experience a kind of euphoria when it happens. I will eventually blow myself up along with a huge number of people, so you have to be the top batter, the fireworks display that raises the curtain on the final event of terror. You see?"

Yoshio gently stroked Midori's head, which he'd cradled against his chest, and whispered to him as to a small child. Midori raised his tear-streaked face to Yoshio. "Then let me blow myself up at your event."

Yoshio stood up and gave Midori a severe look. "Look, are you in or not? If you can't do it, then don't. I'll just get the other officers to take care of you. In fact, I could just have them bury you in the concrete room."

An image of the basement storeroom in Minamisuna flashed through Midori's mind. The cement floor of the storeroom was bumpy from the twelve bodies buried under it. Like a distant memory, he remembered how he had enjoyed performing those cruel acts under orders from Yoshio, who had laughed to see him dripping in blood.

There was no comparing the sullen and withdrawn teenager rebelling against his parents that he had been and the young man he was now. He had no place to call home in this world. A stillness filled his emotions, and he regained his composure.

"Yoshio, these have been the happiest few months in my life," he said, wiping his tears with his sleeves. "I want to continue doing this with you."

"That's all well and good, but one of these days that detective, Fukada, is going to figure out it was you who killed Yusuke Watanabe. It'll be the big house for you. You can't possibly want to be arrested by those imbeciles and tried in accordance with their hypocritical logic?"

Midori shook his head with a somber look.

"Well, then. It's settled. Go visit your family tomorrow. It's been a while. Bid them your final farewell."

It wasn't to bid them farewell, however, that Yoshio wanted Midori to visit his family. Before the bomb named Midori Sonoda fell into the lives of Kaoru Sonoda, his wife, and his eldest son, before the family began its rapid descent into ruin with the news that "the young suicide bomber in the middle of the Shibuya pedestrian crosswalk today was the second son of an executive at a major corporation," Yoshio wanted them to see what their boy was like on the eve of his self-destruction.

Midori was to visit his family in order to make sure that they would worry themselves raw with regret later on, wondering why they hadn't been able to see in his manner or expression the previous night some sign of the tragedy that would befall the family the next day.

Midori's life was set to expire three days later. Midori no longer felt anything at the thought. He did as he was told and packed up his things early the next morning in the dormitory and headed for his house in Denen Chofu.

33—The Devil Howls

Monday, April 30, 2012. Maruyama immediately noticed the change. He had been staking out Yoshio Iizuka's non-profit since early that morning, and the volunteer staff who ordinarily started arriving at the Akabanebashi office around eight to begin cleaning up didn't show up. Not a single person. Eight thirty and then nine o'clock came and went, but the shutter in front of the main entrance stayed firmly closed.

Maruyama got a bad feeling. He had parked the car on the street a ways from the office and was observing through the rear window. He got out of the car and passed in front of the office, pretending to be a pedestrian.

Something was definitely wrong. The window visible from the narrow alley between the buildings was pitch black, and there was no sign of anyone inside. Nobody was coming to work.

They're on to us! Maruyama thought. He returned to the car and called the station on the radio, asking for instructions from Isogai, who immediately contacted the real estate company that managed the Akabanebashi office and rushed to the office himself. When the representative from Tono Real Estate Company arrived, he first checked Isogai's badge then opened the shutter and the front door.

"What the..." Isogai and Maruyama both cried out. The fixtures in the office were all still in place, but the desks and shelves were totally empty. The move was already complete. Of course this meant there was no need to continue surreptitious surveillance of the location. Isogai got the real estate company rep to show him the second floor above the office, which had been rented out as living quarters for the officers.

Same thing. All the furniture in apartments 302 and 303 remained, but not a single piece of clothing or a single personal article was left behind.

Back at the special investigation headquarters, Isogai sat in his chair, lost in thought. He asked himself over and over, *Didn't I sense something when Detective Fukada came from Miyazaki?*

The Converse and the survival knife, separated from the present by six long years. Miyazaki Prefecture and Atagoyama. A newborn's life saved by Yusuke Watanabe. The handsome young man seen by witnesses at Roppongi Hills. And yet, he couldn't connect the pieces of this jigsaw puzzle into the image of Yoshio Iizuka.

He was held back from doing so by the pity he'd felt for Yoshio Iizuka at the Tsurumaki Garden Orphanage in Akabanebashi six years ago, by the fighting spirit he'd seen in Iizuka, summed up by the worn but well-washed Converse high tops, and more than anything else by a well-intentioned desire to laud the youth for his good deeds. But what if that image was just a clever manipulation of human psychology by a demon? Isogai felt himself slowly slipping into the quicksand of inscrutable feelings...

A few minutes later, the incredible happened.

≈

The crosswalk light was red. He stood there, waiting. A movie preview was being shown on the huge display screen on the side of the building before him. Some Hollywood film playing at a theater here in Shibuya. *I wanted to see that,* Midori thought absently.

As he left the house that morning, his brother had turned to him and said, "You're looking content, for a change."

Midori had looked straight at his brother Akira for a moment and thought to himself, *You poor bastard... Once what I do is all over the TV, life will become hell for this family. How content will* you *be then?* Although he'd thought that, the strongest feeling was "You poor bastard," as though it were all someone else's problem, not his own.

Five seconds before one. The signal turned green and Midori started walking. Another kid started walking at the same time, and Midori noticed his shoes: Converse low tops, faded black canvas. He had probably bought them used. A single pink line ran the length of the outsole.

Midori was wearing white Converse All-Stars. The exact same ones Yoshio wore. Midori took a look at the kid. He seemed a bit younger than Midori and had a passive air about him. *He probably doesn't get along with his parents, either,* Midori thought. He kept up with the kid as far as the center of the X-shaped crosswalk, then stopped. The kid kept walking, and then, for no particular reason, looked back.

Midori gripped the detonator, his finger on the button, and looked up at the sky. The jumbotron on the side of the Tsutaya Building was playing the same movie trailer from a moment ago. That image was the last thing in Midori's sight in his sixteen brief years of life.

"Yoshio," he said softly.

He pressed the button. A couple of seconds later, the belt filled with homemade explosives detonated with a blinding flash and a tremendous roar.

≈

"A bomb went off at exactly 1 p.m. today in the middle of the Shibuya pedestrian crosswalk, injuring many people in the vicinity. Eyewitnesses report seeing a youth stop in the middle of the crosswalk, followed by a loud explosion from where he was, after which there was no trace of him. Nearby pedestrians were knocked over by the blast. Emergency crews are on the scene attending to the injured, who are being taken to local hospitals. Police from the Shibuya Sakuragaoka Station are investigating the crime scene. Once again, a bomb went off at exactly..."

"What on earth have they done?" Isogai said to himself as he watched images of the Shibuya pedestrian crosswalk on the small television set. The day had finally come when suicide bombers blew themselves up in the middle of Tokyo. Isogai felt a cold dread in the pit of his stomach. Jihadists came to mind first, but what with the Tokyo Tower bombing last year and now this, he had the uneasy feeling that something terrible, something evil was beginning to take root in Japan.

That night, every newspaper ran headlines like "SUICIDE BOMBING IN SHIBUYA" accompanied by large and disturbing photographs of the black scarring on the asphalt at the pedestrian crosswalk from the explosion. Readers could easily make out where the forensics team had scraped charred human remains off the ground.

Media outlets had differing takes on the incident, but it was clear from eyewitness accounts of the terrorist attack that the suicide bomber appeared to be a middle school student. The fact that a mere boy had blown himself up made the already frightening situation all the more serious was something all the newspapers seemed to agree on.

The forensics team spent that day and night at the pedestrian crosswalk collecting the various organs and parts of the bomber's body, 568 small pieces in all, which were then transferred to Metropolitan Police Headquarters.

Testifying to the power of the blast were the small bits of flesh adhered to the glass windows of the Tsutaya Building, which the bomber had been facing as he stood in the middle of the intersection. The police were working as quickly as possible to identify the bomber from the remains of the clothes he was wearing, and his shoes, which remained fairly intact, but were having trouble because so little was left of his body.

The answer they were looking for, however, was delivered the very next day to the Metropolitan Police.

On Tuesday, May 1st, 11:35 a.m., the day after an unidentified individual had blown himself up in the middle of the Shibuya pedestrian crosswalk near the statue of Hachiko the dog, the press club located in a corner of the ninth floor of Metropolitan Police Headquarters in Sakuradamon, Tokyo, received an envelope postmarked the previous day at the Akabanebashi Post Office.

Television, radio, and newspaper media outlets had spent a frantic night reporting on the "Shibuya crosswalk suicide bombing" and reacted with a kind of stunned numbness to the letter, which had been sent to each of them, all the copies apparently printed out of the same computer. The following was the horrifying content of the letter.

Statement

To Whom It May Concern:

On August 26th of last year, a bombing attack was carried out against Tokyo Tower. Just before that, on August 15th, the director of Jiiku Hospital in Miyazaki Prefecture was stabbed to death. On October 16th, a temp worker was stabbed to death under the Ikebukuro guardrail. On December 17th, an elderly lady was stabbed to death in a park west of Shibuya Station. This year, too, the body of a woman who had been strangled and decapitated was found in the Meguro River. Judging from your reporting of these incidents, the police have been investigating them as isolated criminal acts, unrelated to one another.

Why is it, however, that the police are unable to conjecture that these crimes, which they have had no success at all in solving, are the work of a single demon? This, more than anything, is proof of police incompetence. They are blind to evils too large to fit in their narrow field of vision.

This police force nevertheless has a detective in the Public Security Bureau pursuing the demon without knowing it. The man groomed a fifteen-year-old boy as an informant and placed him in the demon's lair. It is fair, I believe, to commend this detective's courage, which perhaps borders on foolhardiness, but grieving for the victim should also be his lot.

In the interests of social justice (ha!), I will reveal the detective's name. He had instructed the informant to call him "D," but my investigation has revealed that he is Kunio Dan, thirty-five years of age. The poor kid he used as an informant is now in his final resting place, together with twelve others, buried in the cement floor of a underground room which was used over a period of one year as the demon's workshop.

The demon has interpreted this act of espionage on the part of the

Public Security Bureau as a declaration of war and has accordingly begun preparations for the Final Event. Yesterday's suicide bombing show was the cannon shot announcing to the Japanese people that the curtain has been raised. We will be bringing you suicide shows by more of the demon's underlings every other month, culminating in the fatal achievement of the demon himself, who will take with him untold thousands of sacrificial victims. Stay tuned for X-Day of the Festival of Death, which will make 2012 go down in history as a year of terror for humanity.

The demon's only wish is to extinguish and massacre the seed of Adam.

And to the esteemed representatives of the fourth estate, to whom we owe so much, we graciously request that you not let the scoop of the new millennium pass you by.

Cordially,
Yoshio Iizuka
Chairman, Society of Victims of Abuse for the Prevention of Abuse
A Non-Profit Organization

Outside the window, Sakurada Street was filled with men in suits, government bureaucrats and secretaries all headed to lunch. The press club on the ninth floor of the Metropolitan Police Headquarters was filled with a sense of dread that made the scene outside look like an idyllic dream. A stunned silence reigned among the reporters who had finished reading the statement. They were in a state of confusion after having been forced to look at something that was, in fact, too large to fit in their field of vision.

The same thoughts ran through their minds. *Yoshio Iizuka—the guy who runs that non-profit?* The statement was clear and concise and left no room for doubt that all those crimes had been the work of the same "demon." *Kunio Dan of Public Security?* That was the hardest thing to figure out... Suddenly, their brains, which had been shut down from the sheer surprise of it all, rushed toward an understanding.

"Oh my God!!"

As they all raised their voices at once and started moving, the Metropolitan Police press club fell into a state of pandemonium so frenetic that the panic the suicide bombing had thrown them into paled by comparison. Some were rushing out of the room with the statement in hand, some were on their cell phones calling their newsrooms, while others were sitting on the floor typing on their laptops...

A few of the reporters in the room had met Yoshio Iizuka face to face, and a number had even had him on their shows, conversing with him in a public setting. TV news shows, magazines, newspapers—they all had described Yoshio Iizuka as a likable and good-looking young man, a fresh young idealist out to reform society. He had been the media's darling and a ratings boon.

That Yoshio Iizuka was the "demon"?

Mass media swarmed to police headquarters like a zombie horde. The Superintendent General, whose job it was to bear the brunt of questioning, was naturally unable to deal with the rapidly evolving situation. The best he could do was to assure that "We are looking into the matter right now" to conceal the state of confusion the special investigation headquarters had been thrown into. Frustrated, the media outlets began doing their own background research, each eager to beat the rest to the scoop, and found out that the non-profit in question had ceased operations all of a sudden on April 30th and that Yoshio Iizuka had disappeared without a trace. The reports that came out of this were a mixture of speculation and assumptions that grew in feverish intensity as time passed.

Finally the police began calling Yoshio Iizuka a "material witness," so the press took that and ran with it, deciding that he was the mastermind behind a criminal spree of unprecedented scale. The release of this piece of news on May 6th would spark a media circus in Japan and around the world.

The nice young man everyone was familiar with had suddenly turned back and thrown off his mask of fresh-faced good looks. How cruel and base was the face that was revealed? Was he really the person behind those evil acts, as the statement had said? Were there any other related incidents? And what was that about twelve people buried in some basement? What was the real face of the non-profit organization that he had started as a force for social change? Were the young people who worked with Yoshio Iizuka all victims he had brainwashed? Who was the perpetrator of the suicide bombing in Shibuya? How much more horror and fear would Tokyo be subjected to? Would the "Final Event" mentioned in the statement really take place?

Who was Yoshio Iizuka?

34—Torrent

All the detectives at the special investigation headquarters felt as though they had been wading in a murky but gently flowing stream one minute only to be swallowed by a furious torrent of water the next, thanks to the flood unleashed by the statement.

Attempts to confirm the authenticity of the statement had made absolutely no progress at Atagoyama Police Station that night.

The first thing that had to be done was to make sure the content of the statement accorded with reality, which was why the investigation needed to treat Yoshio Iizuka as a material witness and not a suspect. The detectives could not ignore the possibility that the whole thing was a trap designed to frame Iizuka. The copy of the statement in their possession had tested negative for fingerprints.

The idea that a handsome young idealist supposedly working for the betterment of society was in fact working towards much more nefarious ends, using his non-profit organization as a cover for his activities, could not be denied as a plausible line of investigation despite the lurid aspect of such a scenario, the kind pictorial weeklies and sports dailies loved so much. It had been a blind spot for the police, a bold maneuver that probably allowed greater protection than hiding away. The special investigation headquarters had been totally caught off guard by the unexpected turn of events.

At Sakuragaoka Police Station in Shibuya, investigators had succeeded in extracting a blood sample from one of the 568 pieces of human body that had been blown in every direction by the bomb. They performed a DNA test on the blood, but the results did not match any criminal record in the Metropolitan Police database.

At the same time, investigators began a search of Yoshio Iizuka's office space as soon as they got a warrant. This time they found many samples of flecks and hair on the desks, toilets, and coffee room whose DNA matched that collected from the hair at the beach in Nichinan City in Miyazaki. They were still unable to identify whose DNA it was, however.

But not for long: the DNA samples matched that of the suicide bomber being investigated by Sakuragaoka Police Station, which had a few of its forensics team detectives visiting the families and guardians of the four officers of *Society of Victims of Abuse for the Prevention of Abuse*—Midori Sonoda, Kazuhiko Yuasa, Takeshi Abe, and Seiichi Imamura—in order to get background information.

They quickly established that the suicide bomber's DNA was that of Midori Sonoda, the second son of Kaoru Sonoda, an executive at a large corporation who lived in a large house in the wealthy Denen Chofu district. An investigator at Sakuragaoka Station passed the information on to Isogai, adding that he "felt bad for Kaoru Sonoda, standing there in the doorway, stunned, while his wife fell to her knees beside him."

Isogai immediately notified Detective Fukada at the Miyazaki Prefectural Police of the forensics results. Fukada let out a sigh on the other end. Driven to the brink of suicide in his desperate search for the murderer, he had finally found his man only to learn that he'd ended his own life—by blowing himself up in the middle of a noonday crowd.

Isogai heard what sounded like the faint sounds of someone crying on the other end of the line and realized that he himself was in the midst of a mortal struggle.

Yoshio Iizuka's statement, which had been sent out to press clubs all over the country, had shaken the Metropolitan Police Headquarters to its very core. An envelope with the same statement had been delivered to its public relations office.

The statement explicitly named Assistant Inspector Kunio Dan. That was the first shock. Public Security Bureau Chief Iwagami was pushed into a corner by the relentless demands of the media and lost all trace of his cool demeanor as an elite bureaucrat. The Public Security Bureau press conference the next day, initially planned as a routine affair in the small press club conference room in the Metropolitan Police Headquarters, was attended by more reporters and photographers than could fit in. Iwagami was pelted with questions about the "underage spy operation" scandal. His cheeks looked drawn under the camera flashes, and his eyes were bloodshot. All he could do was hang his head, unable to find the words to reply.

"We haven't confirmed the authenticity of the statement yet. Yes, there is someone by the name of Kunio Dan with the force, but he has categorically denied any involvement whatsoever in any kind of spy operation."

"Seriously? You can deny all you want, but there's a single mother who saw the news about the statement and filed a missing person report on her son, whom she thinks is involved in this somehow."

When Iwagami had confronted Onodera about the spy operation allegations the day before the press conference, the superintendent had turned pale.

"The Public Security Bureau did use Kunio Dan as a covert investigator, but I had not heard anything about an underage informant," he lied to Iwagami.

"Where is he now?" Iwagami asked.

"The press surrounded his house, so we got him out of there. I had to plead with the labor association to let us put him in the Police Hospital, where we have him hidden. I'll go to the hospital and ask him about it, but if he was using an underage informant, then that was his own decision. I never approved anything like that," Onodera tried desperately to cover himself.

"There should be a special psych ward room with bars—the one we installed for the pilot who crashed his JAL plane on purpose. Put Dan in there." Iwagami looked up at the ceiling and thought, *Where did it start going wrong?*

The tremor running through the Police Department would eventually turn into an earthquake that would see Iwagami and other top brass at the Public Security Bureau lose their jobs.

35—Underground Storeroom

Isogai entered the special investigation headquarters and made straight for Yoshida's desk. "We got a search warrant for Yoshio Iizuka's apartment."

"Just what I was waiting for. In an hour, we'll send forensics in first. Public Security Mobile Unit's bomb squad will go in with them. The squad leader boasted that if the place was used to make explosives, he'd be able to tell what kind just by sniffing the air."

"They may be Public Security, but some of them are true artists, that's for sure. But they don't need to get all gung-ho. All we really need is to find some sodium chlorate."

"Take it easy on them, Isogai. Public Security is having a tough time right now. The top brass are under fire. Everyone else is in a state of confusion. As long as they do their job, we're all on the same team."

"It's a shame, though, because we were just starting to put together a picture of the people behind this."

"Right. Now they've gotten away thanks to Public Security trying to play this on their own. Makes you grind your teeth."

"You can say that again. After you brought up the possibility that someone had done this out of personal amusement, the investigation was heading toward the course it's on now."

"Either way, we now know who it is, so that aspect of the case is taken care of."

"If we had kept up the meticulous work, we probably would've nabbed him before long."

"He was right in our grasp. But that's over with. The endgame starts now."

"If we turn up any evidence of sodium chlorate in his apartment, we'll have no problem getting an arrest warrant."

"Right. We couldn't get any fingerprints off of the envelope or the paper the statement was printed on. The media is making a huge fuss based on some assumptions, which they have no evidence for, really. Keep in mind that we don't have any solid proof against this guy. Just because we got a note claiming, 'I'm the guy you're looking for,' that doesn't mean a court is going to say 'Oh yeah?' and throw him in prison. Respecting civil rights during an investigation is no cake walk."

May 6, 2012, 4:10 p.m.

A row of vehicles was parked in front of Yoshio Iizuka's apartment building in Minamisuna, Koto Ward: two vans, one belonging to the crime scene team and the other to the mobile unit's bomb squad, two patrol cars from Atagoyama Station, and a sedan belonging to Criminal Investigation Section One Chief

Kunugida. An assistant on the crime scene team had arrived earlier and placed yellow police tape around the apartment complex.

Younger officers from Atagoyama Station and officers sent over from Joto Police Station's Community Safety Department were handling the crowd of curious onlookers that had gathered. Chief Kunugida had on a red armband that said "C.I.1." Someone from the crime scene unit handed him a pair of rubber gloves and shoe covers as he ducked under the yellow tape. Yoshida followed.

Maruyama and Isogai arrived in another patrol car. Isogai pulled gloves and shoe covers out of his pocket and got ready as he ducked under the yellow tape.

"Detective Isogai, I'm coming in too," Maruyama called.

"You wait here," Isogai said. "Too many people will get in the way of the crime scene team. Actually, the apartment manager is over there, so why don't you go and find out what you can about that 'underground storeroom' from him? I'm just going to have a quick look in here and then I'll go with you."

Maruyama grumbled to himself but followed Isogai's instructions. Maruyama was still a greenhorn without much experience in investigations and had never seen the crime scene team at work.

The apartment, which Iizuka had lived in for two years, had a wooden-floored kitchenette and two rooms with *tatami* mat floors, one about a hundred square feet and the other about eighty square feet. The company managing the apartment complex said they had not had anyone in to clean it because they were going to tear down the building, but a sense of cleanliness and order could still be felt in the empty room.

The crime scene team wore blue hats, blue uniforms, white gloves, and armbands, and the leader with close-cropped white hair under his hat was giving rapid-fire instructions to his men. The members in charge of fingerprints were using brushes to apply a fine dusting of aluminum powder to the edges of the sink, faucet handles, and other spots. They added lycopodium powder on top of the aluminum powder and transferred any fingerprints which appeared onto a special adhesive tape which was then attached to a black board. They were carrying this out with the skill of experienced craftsmen, following their intuition, sensing small changes in humidity and heat.

The crime scene team would take the collected fingerprints back to the station to try to identify who else had been in the apartment other than Yoshio Iizuka and what, if any, relationship those people had to him. They were hoping to find evidence that Midori Sonoda, who had blown himself up in the suicide bombing, and the others listed in the non-profit's articles of incorporation, had used the apartment for secret meetings that could not be held in the office. And if they found fingerprints belonging to a certain Kazuma Hoshino, the boy whose mother in Numabukuro, in Nakano Ward, had filed a missing person's report for, they would be able to establish the fact that Iizuka had been involved in yet another case.

The bomb specialist, an assistant inspector with the mobile unit, was close in age to the leader of the crime scene squad but still had thick black hair. He stood in front of the doorway, arms akimbo and nostrils flared. "Nope," he said, "nothing that smells like explosives in here."

When the force veteran declared his pessimism before even collecting trace substances to check for chemical reactions, Kunugida protested, "There has to be something. The consensus at the investigation meeting was that he must have made weed-killer bombs at home. If we can prove that, then getting an arrest warrant will be a definite possibility. Don't just use your nose, bring it back to forensics."

The specialist glanced at him contemptuously. *No wonder, careerist balloon-heads never get anything right,* he said only to himself as he started collecting trace substances. *If I can't smell it, there'll be no reaction.*

Although Kunugida had been promoted to Chief of Criminal Investigation Section One the previous year from Chief of Forensics—a standard path of advancement for the elite of the elite at Metropolitan Police—he did not have much experience investigating actual crime scenes.

"You'll never make a good crime scene investigator if you've got a pedigree," Isogai said to himself, and headed out to meet up with Maruyama.

There was still no physical evidence that proved Yoshio Iizuka was behind Midori Sonoda's suicide bombing. All they had was someone claiming to be Iizuka hinting at his complicity. Whether it was a letter or a confession made after arrest by the suspect himself, words alone weren't enough to bring charges. The ever-cautious prosecutor's office was always reluctant to move forward without some kind of physical evidence, like a weapon, that would back up the words. At the very least they would want something like a statement revealing a fact known only to the suspect, leading investigators to where a body was buried, for example. Without that, the prosecutors wouldn't budge.

Isogai explained all this to the still-inexperienced Maruyama, who was liable to believe what he heard on TV, to spur him on to talk to neighbors who might offer some clue that would lead the investigation to a decisive piece of evidence.

"But why is the prosecutor's office so stubborn?" Maruyama asked naively.

"They have to be. What do you think happens when a prosecutor loses a case due to lack of evidence? Sayonara, hopes of any future advancement."

This wasn't something in a movie, a book, or a TV show, but the reality of Japan's "precision justice system." At this point, Isogai thought they were more likely to find some revealing clue in the statement rather than through the forensic investigation of Iizuka's now-vacant apartment.

The statement mentioned "the cement floor of an underground room which was used over a period of one year as the demon's workshop," but the representative of the real estate company that managed Yoshio Iizuka's room on the building owner's behalf said he knew nothing about a cellar. Was the cellar near the apartment, here in Minamisuna? Or was it a secret hideout somewhere else? Could the bombs have been made there, and not at the apartment?

Isogai saw Maruyama talking to an elderly woman on the embankment of the Arakawa River. She had apparently been walking her dog. Maruyama was smiling as they talked. Isogai thought approvingly, *Being able to engage strangers in conversation like that is a useful skill for canvassing local residents.*

Isogai heard someone call out and saw Maruyama running towards him.

"Sorry, I just heard something interesting."

"Interesting? How so?"

"The lady I was just talking to, it turns out she lives in the Minamisuna Mitsuwa Nursing Home, and they don't let people keep dogs there, so she's in some kind of pitched battle with the director."

"What's so interesting about that?"

"Well, another resident is fighting her, a mean old guy who really hates dogs, and it turns out that the dog-hater is none other than the owner of the apartment building Yoshio Iizuka lived in."

"Iizuka's apartment?"

"Yeah, apparently he owns lots of land in this area. He's outlived everyone in his family, and all he cares about is money. A real curmudgeon, apparently," Maruyama laughed.

Isogai watched Maruyama from behind the thick lenses of his black-framed glasses.

"Isn't that an amazing coincidence? So I asked if the old curmudgeon owned a cellar or something like that."

"And?"

"And he does, apparently. The old lady called him an old geezer and said that he owns all this real estate he won't be able to take with him to the grave—old buildings, warehouses, things like that."

"She said the cellar was around here?"

"Well, I don't know if it'll be the 'demon's workshop,' but I'll check it out."

"Where is it?"

"Apparently there's a supermarket north of here in Higashisuna that shut down when a huge shopping center went up, taking all its customers. It's been shuttered since the beginning of last year. The building itself is forty years old, so he can't find any tenants. Apparently everyone's waiting patiently for the old guy to kick the bucket." Maruyama laughed again.

"And the supermarket has a cellar?"

"Well, I don't know if it qualifies as a cellar per se, but it has an underground storeroom where they kept their inventory."

The Atagoyama Station crime scene squad successfully collected many different fingerprints from the apartment where Iizuka had lived just weeks before, but no trace of any chemicals used in making the bombs, like sodium chlorate, sulfur, or charcoal, could be detected. The bomb squad leader had told Kunugida as much—nothing worth taking to the forensics lab.

Meanwhile, the bankrupt supermarket's underground storeroom, which they'd looked into with only faint hope, produced an embarrassment of riches that they also took back to the station. It was like a museum of physical evidence proving Yoshio Iizuka was indeed a demonic criminal mastermind and verifying for the first time the authenticity of the statement. The major find had actual judicial value because it represented a credible revelation of hitherto unknown information.

After finishing with the apartment room, the forensics squad had headed to the location to follow up on Detective Isogai's report. The building stood alone and bleak on one corner of the block facing Kasaibashi Street, about a fifteen-minute walk north of Iizuka's Minamisuna apartment along the Arakawa River. The first floor of the old faded five-story building was occupied by the shuttered, spent-looking supermarket, left behind by the times in stark contrast to the huge shopping center whose rear side loomed over it.

The slapdash way the windows had been covered with newspaper from the inside in order to keep prying eyes out of the vacant space only served to heighten the dilapidated feel of the place. The floors above were run-down apartments, and on the left side of the building, separate from the main staircase for the people who lived in the apartments, was a small entrance to stairs leading to the underground storeroom.

When a young real estate agent went down the dark staircase first and opened the door, he recoiled. "What's that smell?!"

A pungent odor filled the staircase as soon as the door into the underground room was opened, and all the detectives instinctively covered their noses and mouths.

The real estate agent fumbled for the light switch and turned on the fluorescent lights. Chief Kunugida, Inspector Yoshida, Detective Isogai, Sergeant Maruyama, and the forensics team and mobile unit bomb squad that hadn't been dismissed, despite finishing at the apartment, immediately saw the strange contraption installed on the concrete wall in front of them. It was a square frame made out of the kind of steel pipes and joints found on construction sites. Behind it, on the wall, were dull red stains that looked like they had been washed down. There was a leather belt at each corner of the frame.

It was crystal clear to all of them what the room had been used for. The pungent odor that filled it caused images to flash through the men's brains, coloring their thoughts with a dark dread.

They climbed the angled floor that sloped up from the door, noticing how low the ceiling was. No, it wasn't the ceiling that was low; it was the floor that was high. Isogai remembered what the statement said: "...in his final resting place, together with twelve others, buried in the cement floor of a underground storeroom."

With a nimble motion the forensics squad leader fell to the floor and aimed his flashlight at it. He crawled across it very slowly holding his white-gloved hand just above the surface, illuminating narrow gaps with the flashlight, which he held level to the floor. He found human hairs "growing" out of the cement in several places. There was a coin-sized hole in the floor in one place where a bubble had apparently formed in the cement. He pointed the light at it and saw a chalky patch of human skin covered in short hairs inside the hole.

"How's it look, squad leader? Are there bodies under the floor?"

"Without a doubt. I bet we're going to find quite a few. This is a job for archaeologists down here, though, not the foren-sics squad. We're going to have to break up the cement carefully to avoid damaging the bodies as we take them out."

"And if the statement's right, we're going to have twelve of them to deal with," said Yoshida.

"But the Hoshino kid's in here too, isn't he?" corrected Isogai.

"This is going to take all night," the squad leader said. "We need backup from headquarters and other stations. We're going to need hammers and pickaxes. And body bags. Get a coroner out here, too."

Maruyama had been trying to control his nausea, but the squad leader's words were too much for his imagination, and he ran out of the room and up the stairs.

"Assistant Inspector, we need to test for explosives, too," Kunugida said, his voice muffled by the handkerchief over his mouth. "That's got priority for the special investigation."

The mobile squad's leader stood in front of metal pipes that had been used to execute people, his arms crossed and legs apart. "Don't worry about it, Chief, there's no doubt on that front. This smell isn't just bodies rotting under cement. The whole room reeks of bombs being made on a daily basis."

May was nearing its end. Since the release of "the Demon's Statement," as the media christened it, the Tokyo Tower bombing special investigation headquarters had been spinning and swirling, and now, as it turned into the appendage of a huge national investigation drawing on the full force of the police network, it was sucked into the very vortex.

The murders listed in the statement had been treated as independent cases, handled by the local police stations, but now a unified investigation with full information sharing was being carried out, bringing together Miyazaki Prefectural Police Headquarters, Ikebukuro Kishimojin Police Department, Shinjuku Kabukicho Police Department, Shibuya Sakuragaoka Police Department, Meguro Himonya Police Department, and Minato Ward Atagoyama Police Department. Prefectural police departments all over the country were also providing the special investigation headquarters with information. It was the largest single dragnet ever implemented in the history of the Metropolitan Police.

CHAPTER 4

36—TEARS

Yoshio awoke from a deep sleep, his first in a long time. Outside the large window of the room he used as a bedroom he saw a clear summer sky. He was at an orphanage in Higashi Kurume City called Tensei Garden, which had gone bankrupt before the new year and shut down. It was a relatively large facility that he had visited for a talk on the future of child welfare when he was still running his non-profit. The main building had been built on a section of what had at one time been a leper colony. Behind it was a wooded area, and beyond a beautiful view of a large forest park. The facility itself was hidden from view.

Yoshio had developed a close relationship with Kaoru Kurita, the sixty-eight-year-old director of the orphanage. The land under it belonged to his charitable organization, and Yoshio signed a lease contract for one year when he heard that Kurita was going to shut the orphanage down.

Kurita, whose wife had died before him, lived alone in his home in Tokorozawa. Yoshio had the full trust of the hale old man.

Kurita had smiled and shaken Yoshio's hand as he said, "Listen, kid, you're so young you're almost too young. Don't worry about failure. You just keep at it. I'll do what I can for you while I still have all my marbles. But don't ever give up. There aren't enough people in the world who are really doing what it takes to make life better for these kids."

Kurita was fond of an old Chinese saying: *garyo tensei,* or "paint the dragon and dot the eyes." It meant "to add the finishing touches," and he had borrowed part of it to name the orphanage he had made into a success in just one generation.

He had died very recently. The night before Yoshio had written the statement that would be made public the next day, he'd buried the old man in the wooded area visible from the kitchen's north window.

The main building that stood next to the annex Yoshio was staying in was a large wooden two-story affair with an outer courtyard. It was completely still now. For about a month, however, its classrooms had been filled with the continuous whimpering of the non-profit staff, although none of it could be heard outside. They had lived there for about a month after Yoshio had shut down the non-profit.

He finally released them the previous day, letting them go home. "Home" of course was a relative term, since most of the kids came from dysfunctional families. The kids went back to the orphanages they had been living in, to the alcoholic single mothers who had been raising them, to the homes they had wrecked through domestic violence.

The only ones living in the main building now were the three remaining officers, Kazuhiko, Takeshi, and Seiichi, who had spent the last month taking care of the other staff, shielding them from prying eyes. But now that was done, they spent their days idle, awaiting the inevitable.

Kazuhiko and Takeshi, who had been abused as small children by their mothers and lived through hell, had become top-level members, selfless and completely dedicated to their jobs, after being reformed by Yoshio. Seiichi had earned his place by successfully acquiring the methyl isothiocyanate but wasn't really capable of much else, and would soon be making the ultimate sacrifice as part of Yoshio's plan.

Yoshio dressed and got ready, looking as neat and clean as always, and sat down at the desk in his office next door to look through newspapers and magazines, which he had his officers covertly go into town to buy on a regular basis. At the beginning he had enjoyed reading the stories about himself but quickly tired of the inane, insipid articles and specials that the mass media put out. It would not be too long now before the articles got a lot more interesting again, once the officers started making their impact on society, as it were.

Yoshio took one of the magazines from the stack. It was *In Focus,* the pictorial weekly that had interviewed him. The magazine had sent him a copy of each weekly issue ever since the interview, and Yoshio had flipped through them, reading only those articles that caught his attention, tossing each copy into the trash once he was done. A top-heavy model graced the cover of the latest issue, as always, with the words "Tokyo: Random Murder Wonderland" in large lettering underneath. Subheaders listed ten murders, including the stabbing of a salaryman in Ikebukuro, the violent death of an old woman in Shinjuku, and the strangulation and decapitation of a woman recovered from Meguro River.

Yoshio opened up the magazine and started flipping through the inside pages, satisfied to see that the murders he had arranged were getting coverage. Starting on the top page opposite the pictorial of the model, the special report featured a map of Tokyo indicating where each indiscriminate act of murder had taken place and little illustrations luridly depicting the crime scenes.

The article about the old lady whose neck had been slashed with a large knife in a park near Shinjuku Station had an illustration showing a little Maltese worried about its master and sniffing around her body. That job, Yoshio had scripted for Takeshi. He remembered watching through binoculars from a distance: an old lady was sitting on a bench knitting or something; as Takeshi walked past her, he sliced open her neck with a butcher knife; an ugly little dog was wagging its tail and contemplating at the blood drip-ping thickly from the lady's neck. Yoshio decided to let the animal live. Dogs didn't talk.

He read the short descriptions accompanying the special report. The writer described the randomness of the acts, which had occurred over the past year or so, and also the apparent inconsistency of motive. He mentioned the three murders Yoshio had orchestrated and concluded that if they were indeed the handiwork of "Yoshio Iizuka, Unparalleled Criminal Mastermind," as asserted in "the Demon's Statement," then the seeming randomness of the acts did indeed display a chilling brutality.

The various killings, which had been treated as unrelated events, were now with the release of the Demon's Statement known to be the doing of Yoshio Iizuka or at least somehow connected to him, and that meant the media had to come up with a catchy phrase to refer to them as a whole. What they came up with was "a series of crimes committed by Yoshio Iizuka, *Unparalleled Criminal Mastermind*."

Yoshio was impressed with the layout of the pages, which ably paired the hostile tone of the report with illustrations that were designed to rile up readers' feelings. *These people know what they're doing. I hope they keep up this inflammatory coverage for the events I'm about to put in motion. Make the sheeple tremble!*

He turned the page and flinched.

Body of Woman Found in Meguro River: Strangled, Raped, and Decapitated

...who was strangled and abused before being decapitated is a chilling example of the savagery which continues to perplex investigators. The assailant strangled the victim from behind with some kind of cord or rope, killing her, then sexually abused the victim. As though that were not brutal enough, the murderer then decapitated the body, adding to the bizarreness of the act. If this is indeed another example of a crime perpetrated by Yoshio Iizuka, as stated in the

Demon's Statement, then the sheer perversion clearly sets it apart from the other three...

Yoshio stared intently at the photograph next to the title, his face blank. The photograph was by an amateur and showed the lower half of a naked body partially protruding from a surfboard case on the bare concrete floor of a riverbed about five meters below ground level. Yoshio had ordered Seiichi to put Mariko Amo's body in a surfboard bag and dump the body in Meguro River late at night. Removing her head after strangling her would pose no challenge for Seiichi's freakish strength. Since the victim had interviewed him, Yoshio had feared that their relationship would become known to the police and lead them directly to him. He needed a way to buy time until the body was identified.

Seiichi had reported to Yoshio that he had strangled Mariko, cut off her head on the blue sheet he'd laid out on the floor of the office, and dumped the headless corpse in Meguro River. He hadn't mentioned anything about sexually abusing the woman, though. Yoshio had only found that out from the article.

He felt anger welling up in him towards Seiichi. His orders were not to be disobeyed, either by doing more or by doing less. It was an inviolable rule, something Yoshio had to make the officers understand down to the marrow. The absoluteness implicit in his orders had to define the precision of the Final Event like the gears in a clock.

What punishment does that dirty stupid alcoholic deserve? Yoshio pondered. He considered several brutal options. *Wait a second. Seiichi already got the chemicals I needed for the Final Event from his dad's company, so what need do I have of either him or his dad? It would be a waste to make that idiot the opening act for the Final Event. I'm going to have to apply a little re-education to the bastard, put him in his place. Intellectual lightweights like him are the most susceptible to mind control.*

Flames of hatred flickered in the depths of his eyes, and he noticed something dripping onto the magazine he was holding.

The drops, falling one by one, dampened the headline, "Strangled, Raped, and Decapitated," turning the paper gray. Yoshio was taken aback and touched his cheek with his right hand. The salty liquid was coming from his eyes! They were tears, the first he had ever shed in his life. He had no idea what they meant; the large meaningless tears continued to flow, and the page absorbed them, slowly turning to mush.

37—Reformed

A blinding light illuminated a single spot in the corner of a dark room. At one of those old wooden desks they used to have in grammar school classrooms, Seiichi was nodding off, his head down. Kazuhiko grabbed him by the hair and pulled it up. Takeshi shined the light on Seiichi's face; a long string of saliva hung down from his face to the desktop. His eyes were half-closed, but he couldn't get to sleep. He moaned painfully.

Kazuhiko's and Takeshi's faces also betrayed signs of fatigue. They had been at this for three days and three nights as part of Seiichi's renewed brainwashing. Working in shifts had not alleviated the exhaustion. The two officers had forced Seiichi to stay awake for more than seventy hours now.

"Come on, Seiichi. Be a good boy and say it again," Takeshi commanded, forcing open Seiichi's eyes to let in the light. Tears, which the same eyes had shed so much of, returned.

"Hey, look at that. I thought your tears had dried up," Takeshi said.

Kazuhiko, holding Seiichi's head up by the hair, looked around at Seiichi's face and let out a rasping laugh.

"You wanna cry? Huh, Seiichi?" Takeshi asked. "Go ahead. I'll let you, as long as you repeat the mission you need to carry out, one more time." Seiichi's tears had dampened his fingers, and he wiped them on his jeans. "Go ahead and say it."

"I...I am to...kill...both of them. Please, I'm begging you...let me...sleep." Seiichi's face contorted into a mask of suffering as he tried, his head unclear, to speak clearly.

Takeshi looked at Kazuhiko, who stood behind Seiichi, and said, "Think that's enough?"

"Hold on. The music box stopped." Picking up the box that sat on the table, Kazuhiko wound the key. The melody started—the same melody they'd been playing over and over during the brainwashing session. The spring was weakening, and the pitch wobbled, giving the melody an eerie lilt.

One day, I came upon a bear, deep in a forest...

The music box played the melody of a traditional Japanese children's song whose words instantly came to mind. It was a cheery song, but Kazuhiko and Takeshi now knew how terrifying it could sound under the right circumstances. Of course the one experiencing the full brunt of that terror was Seiichi, who had been made to listen to the same melody hundreds of times. Kazuhiko and Takeshi needed to use ear plugs every once in a while to maintain their own mental balance. Takeshi had asked Yoshio why this particular song was used for brainwashing, and the answer had been chillingly convincing: "Children need nursery songs, don't they?"

"Kazuhiko, switch with me. I'm seriously about to collapse. I've got to get some sleep."

"No problem. I'll take over for an hour, but we switch after that. I'm about to fall over too."

"All right, good night. Wake me when it's time. I won't be able to get myself up." Takeshi staggered into the adjacent classroom, where they had laid out a mattress.

≈

At the same moment, the seventeen youths who had worked at Yoshio Iizuka's non-profit were the topic of discussion at a regular meeting of the special investigation headquarters at Atagoyama Station. Yoshida gave a progress report on the interviews being conducted with them.

"There's a blank of about a month between the time Iizuka's non-profit was dissolved and the time these kids returned to their homes. We're interviewing them to see if we can find out what happened during that period, but so far they haven't been able to tell us anything. They say that they just don't remember, and somehow I get the feeling they aren't lying."

Kunugida of Criminal Investigation Section One sat back with his arms crossed and his chin buried deep in his chest, adding a dark note to the mood.

"But the young men I've talked to," Maruyama said, "all testify to having become new people since they started working at Iizuka's non-profit. One of the kids was extremely violent at home when he was in seventh grade. Nobody in his family could handle him, and his father had to call the police a few times. The situation must've been pretty bad if they were calling the cops on their own son. But now he's completely reformed and is working hard at a part-time job. The father is just a regular salaryman, and let me tell you, he's so happy he could cry. 'My son has come back a new person!' Those were his words."

Many of the other detectives interviewing the seventeen youths told similar stories. One of the veterans said, "You try to interview the mothers of some of these kids, and the women are just barely functional. It's no surprise the kids get so screwed up in a lot of these home situations. And many of the fathers spend all their time at work, leaving everything in their wives' hands."

"Some of these kids were taking care of their alcoholic mothers, stuff like doing the paperwork to get them admitted to a hospital," another detective said.

Kunugida turned to Isogai. "How's it going with your

interviews?"

"They're about the same. They worked the front office of the organization, so there's no doubt in my mind they weren't involved in any of the dirty stuff. My suspicion is that the back-door operations were handled under orders from Iizuka by the three officers we haven't found yet: Abe, Yuasa, and Imamura."

"It would be pretty ironic," Yoshida said, shaking his head, "if it turns out to be true that these teenage kids who'd had their lives and dreams destroyed at home were reformed by a monster."

"Well, either way, we've still got a lot of gaps to fill in. Continue the daily surveillance of the kids who were in direct contact with Iizuka. That's all," Kunugida concluded, breaking up the meeting.

38—Killing Power

The non-stop media coverage of crimes perpetrated by "Yoshio Iizuka, Unparalleled Criminal Mastermind" had the effect of desensitizing the Japanese populace to the point where small things stopped surprising anyone. Even in that desensitized state, the country received the Ibaraki Prefectural Police's announcement of a multiple murder-suicide with a shudder—less an expression of fear at something that had already happened than apprehension at what lay ticking away like a time-bomb in the future.

In the immediate aftermath of Midori's suicide bombing, the various police departments had begun interviewing family members of the officers who'd worked at Iizuka's non-profit. Seiichi Imamura's family home was in Tsukuba City, Ibaraki Prefecture, and the Tsukuba Police Department, which was handling Seiichi Imamura's family, sent two detectives down to the house that Masao Imamura had bought in a new development near a chicken farm on the southern edge of Tsukuba University Science City.

Masao's wife Yasue opened the door to the detectives, who later reported exchanging a glance between themselves because they both instantly sensed something. Yasue was as pale as a ghost and gaunt, her eyes sunken, her cheeks so drawn they were in shadow. The concerned detectives asked if she was okay. She told them that her husband had been injured and fallen ill, that he was now bedridden, and that she was just tired from taking care of him. The story sounded plausible enough. The detectives' task was to get information about Seiichi, however, and not the family itself, so they asked a few prepared questions about their son's recent behavior and got a few personal items of his that would allow them to perform DNA tests.

Two months later, on Sunday, July 22nd, a call was placed by one of the Imamuras' neighbors to the emergency services number regarding "an unpleasant smell." The patrol officer on duty at the police box near Tsukuba University hurried to the house on his bicycle and found the entire family dead in the bedroom, stabbed to death with a butcher knife. The patrol officer reported that the gate was half-open and the front door was unlocked. He sent out a signal and, in response, the Tsukuba Police Department and the Ibaraki Prefectural Police arrived on the scene promptly. They investigated, and that night issued a statement about the multiple murder-suicide committed by Seiichi Imamura, son of Masao Imamura.

The housewife next door had seen Seiichi unexpectedly return home a few days before. "He was a nice kid when he was in seventh grade. He played basketball. He'd always say hi if he saw me on the street. I was fumigating my roses in the garden when I saw him. He just appeared out of the blue. I called to him, but he walked right past me, like he hadn't heard anything, and went inside his house."

Seiichi grabbed a butcher knife from the kitchen and went into his father's room, where he was lying ill in bed, and stabbed him multiple times. His mother heard the commotion and screams and came to the bedroom, where Seiichi stabbed her once in the chest. He then turned the knife on himself. He slit his own throat.

Nobody was really terrorized by the incident, though the tentacles of society did ripple at the news that Seiichi Imamura had been a "former officer in Yoshio Iizuka's now-defunct non-profit organization."

It was a few days afterwards that the truly astonishing piece of information came to light. Large quantities of an extremely toxic chemical had been stolen from one of the warehouses belonging to Nippon Chemical Industries, which had employed Seiichi Imamura's father, Masao Imamura. Masao Imamura had been in charge of storage and was suspected of having known about the theft and concealing it from his employers. The Ibaraki Prefectural Police, which handled the investigation, following up the multiple murder-suicide, was convinced that Seiichi Imamura was responsible for the theft and that Yoshio Iizuka, his former boss, now possessed the chemicals.

Nippon Chemical Industries was shaken at the enormity of what had happened and held a press conference, where the president of the company, Shinobu Hiromoto, described in pedantic detail the supposedly foolproof security system the company had in place—but admitted, in the end, that while the system worked against intruders, it contained loopholes open to exploitation by agents working from the inside, and apologized to the entire country for this failure. The company announced that the stolen chemical was methyl isothiocyanate (C_2H_3NS), occasionally used in some agricultural pesticides, but mainly a substance needed in industrial disinfectants. The highly flammable liquid was clear with a yellowish cast and extremely toxic. Inhaling large amounts would result in instant death, while exposure to even trace amounts caused irritation of the trachea and lungs, pneumonia, glottal spasms, and pulmonary edema.

Twenty drums containing fifty-four liters of the chemical each were stolen, which according to the company was a quantity sufficient to kill tens of thousands of people in a densely populated area depending on how the chemical was dispersed.

August 2012.

The population of Tokyo now knew, thanks to the media, that a monster was walking in their midst like he was in charge, in possession not just of bombs but also large quantities of a deadly poison. The many news reports boosted the terror caused by the release of the Demon's Statement early in the month of May and underlined the reality of the Final Event which it foretold.

The time, place, and nature of the impending tragedy were matters of speculation and rumor, exciting an already terrified nation's imagination to ever greater heights of fear. In addition to existing landmarks that were under guard, the Metropolitan Police Department ordered the Second Riot Police Unit to protect the Kanamachi Water Purification Plant, and the Fourth Riot Police Unit, which was stationed in Tachikawa, to protect Tama Lake. Riot Police personnel were also dispatched in great numbers to look out for suspicious items in subway stations and additional crowded landmarks.

Immediately after the Nippon Chemical Industries press conference, Kusanagi of the forensics lab brought with him a technician from the neighboring First Chemical Lab to inform the special investigation headquarters of the chilling fact that, according to the technician, the poison gas which inflicted more than 2,500 deaths and caused more than 20,000 people to fall ill during the Union Carbide chemical disaster—the world's worst—in Bhopal, India, in 1984, was none other than methyl isothiocyanate. The immediate cause of the accident was that "water had entered" the tanks holding the methyl isothiocyanate. A wave of dread washed over the detectives. *Water got into the tanks? That's it?*

Methyl isothiocyanate's low boiling-point, at 102.4°F, meant that any heat produced through contact with water resulted in the liquid evaporating, instantly generating a cloud of deadly poison gas. Moreover, since methyl isothiocyanate gas was denser than air, it turned into a ground-hugging fog, killing everyone on contact.

The Bhopal disaster had created an ongoing legal situation that remained unresolved. Some reports indicated that the poisoned soil remained unusable. The detectives could imagine the sensational headlines that would be concocted if the media ever got hold of this information, bound as they were by no moral guidelines. The country was already on the verge of panic thanks to bombs that might or might not be planted in crowded landmarks; this new terror was of a different magnitude altogether.

The Superintendent General had had the urge over the previous few months to call for a cessation to all activity in Tokyo in order to conduct a top-to-bottom search for possible bombs planted in all large buildings. Now, it was no longer just buildings that had to be protected. This direct threat to the country's lifelines could occur anywhere, at any time, and produce deaths in numbers that would make the sarin gas attack of 1995 pale in comparison.

Of course, the swarming, pulsing megalopolis that was Tokyo could never be brought to a standstill. The special investigation set up to solve the Tokyo Tower bombing had no choice but to frantically search for the monster, Yoshio Iizuka, who had vanished.

39—Flower of Fire

Wednesday, September 9, 2012. A cold drizzle had fallen on Tokyo since early morning, but by now Shinjuku was filled with commuters, students, and others, the colorful flowers of overlapping umbrellas abloom.

Kazuhiko had caught the Seibu Line train that morning in Higashi Kurume and changed to the Oedo Line to get to Shinjuku Station. By 8:45 a.m. he had exited the station by the south exit. He had an umbrella in his right hand as he entered the side road to the left of Koshu Avenue. He walked with a firm step along the narrow street crowded on both sides by gaudy multi-use buildings.

His right shoulder was slumped down as he hunched his back a bit to compensate for the thing strapped to his abdomen. He timed his arrival in front of the Shinjuku Alta department store to merge with the stream of people flowing towards the third district.He had ditched the umbrella along the way and let the raindrops roll down his face freely.

His face looked normal—eyebrows, nose, two eyes, a mouth—but besides that, it lacked all expression.

If expressions reflected inner states, then Kazuhiko's mind was empty, free of any emotion whatsoever. Although his eyes hinted at a sort of determination, he did not give any impression of excitement or eager anticipation. Like a well-trained jihadist, his only conviction was to obey Yoshio's commands as he walked forward, one step at a time.

At exactly 9 a.m. he passed in front of the Kinokuniya bookstore together with a crowd of umbrellas that was dripping water on his shoulders. At that exact moment and without any hesitation, Kazuhiko pressed the button on the detonator he was holding in the pocket of his thin, cream-colored raincoat.

≈

The second suicide bombing had finally happened. The blast of wind which carried the shredded pieces of Kazuhiko's flesh pulverized the ground-floor windows of the bookstore facing Shinjuku Avenue and caused serious damage to the small restaurants and stalls lining the corridor leading in from the street. The majority of the deaths and injuries were caused not by the power of the blast but rather by the shards of glass from the bookstore windows.

Approximately four months had passed since the first suicide bombing. The country had gradually started to forget the Demon's

Statement, which had promised to deliver such attacks every other month. The timing of this blast was calculated to destroy any anguished hope the country had that such a horrible incident would not be repeated. Yoshio had diligently delivered on his promise.

Though the attack had been announced beforehand, who could possibly imagine, on a drizzly Wednesday morning, that the young man trotting along in a crowd of jostling and colorful umbrellas would suddenly blow himself up? The suicide attack made the population of Japan, and of Tokyo in particular, realize that it was an unwilling participant in a deadly game of roulette presided over by a monster.

The media had breathed a sigh of relief at the recent paucity of "Yoshio Iizuka, Unparalleled Criminal Mastermind" stories, but at the same time was, by force of habit, starving for more. Having nearly overdosed on electrifying stories over the previous year, the media now jumped like crazed addicts at this drug: suicide bombings carried out by teenagers.

Today at 9 a.m. a suicide bombing was carried out on the street in front of Kinokuniya Bookstore in Shinjuku. Ten people died and as of this moment fifty-eight people are listed as wounded, some seriously. This attack is thought to be the second suicide bombing orchestrated by Yoshio Iizuka, who is currently sought throughout the nation as the perpetrator of a series of terrible crimes including the destruction of Tokyo Tower and the suicide bombing at the Shibuya pedestrian crossing on May 1st of this year. The Tokyo Metropolitan Police are investigating. After some months of calm, residents of Tokyo were beginning to breathe a sigh of relief, but will surely be in for more sleepless nights after this attack.

The extra editions of the newspapers carried huge headlines: *Second Suicide Bombing! Countdown to Death Fest?*

The Shinjuku Kabukicho Police collected the blasted bits of flesh at the scene of the bombing and ran DNA tests on them, comparing the results to the DNA samples they had for Kazuhiko Yuasa and Takeshi Abe, the two remaining officers in Yoshio Iizuka's non-profit, and announced at the press conference that night that the perpetrator of the suicide bombing in Shinjuku was sixteen-year-old Kazuhiko Yuasa. The police decided to use his name despite the fact that he was a minor, since the media would make his identity public anyway when they inevitably found it out in spite of the Metropolitan Police Department's best efforts to suppress it.

The Shinjuku Kabukicho Police sent all the information they had on the suicide bombing to the overseeing Metropolitan Police Headquarters and set up its own special investigation headquarters dedicated to pursuing yet another crime by "Yoshio Iizuka, Unparalleled Criminal Mastermind."

"We ask the public's understanding and forgiveness for the anguish caused by the fact that for over a year we have been unable to apprehend the orchestrator of these many horrific acts, which we regret deeply. The suicide bombing two days ago is proof that the person behind these attacks has ended his period of retreat and is once again active, which could in fact be the chance we have been waiting for to apprehend him. We promise to catch this monster before year's end and are mobilizing all our resources to attain that goal..."

The following day Superintendent General Kamoshita collapsed in his office from the sheer stress of the situation and was rushed to the police hospital. Contrary to the promise made by the desperate top cop at the press conference, the police department was seriously demoralized. Cracks were running through its structure, reminiscent of the time in 1995 when the Commissioner General of the National Police Agency was nearly assassinated by a serving police officer who was also a member of the Veda Truth cult. Junichiro Iwagami, deputy chairman of the special investigation for the Tokyo Tower bombing, had resigned after being demoted from head of Public Security earlier in the year for his responsibility in the death of Kazuma Hoshino, in what Yoshio Iizuka had denounced in the Demon's Statement as the use of a minor for the purpose of espionage. Superintendent Akira Onodera had continued to assert that it had been an unauthorized operation by a junior officer, but in the end he too was removed from the active ranks of the Bureau. Despite the best efforts of the media, the whereabouts of the Public Security Bureau detective who had handled the operation, Kunio Dan, remained shrouded in mystery.

The "paper bomb" Yoshio Iizuka had tossed into the Tokyo Metropolitan Police had delivered a debilitating blow to the heart of the organization.

40—Faster

Pictures of Yoshio Iizuka and Takeshi Abe were displayed on posters on the 5,112 bulletin boards in front of police boxes, sub-stations, and stations facing busy streets, under the words "Responsible for the Worst Bombings in Recent History." The posters exhorted citizens to provide any information they may have and warned residents of Tokyo to avoid leaving the house on November 11, 2012.

The special investigation headquarters had come up with a hypothesis through analysis of the two suicide bombings. Midori Sonoda had blown himself up on April 30, 2012, at one in the afternoon. Kazuhiko Yuasa's suicide bombing had been at 9 a.m. on September 9th. The investigators were betting on the next attack being on November 11th, either at eleven in the morning or eleven at night. The fact that the statement had announced one attack every other month but had been followed by approximately four months of silence led the detectives to suspect that something had gone wrong with Iizuka's plans.

Detective Isogai's hypothesis was that Yoshio had discovered the presence of a mole in his organization, planted there by the Public Security Bureau, and had panicked, realizing that the police investigation was closing in on him. He had therefore decided to move the plan forward, and the first step was Midori Sonoda's suicide bombing. By nature, Yoshio Iizuka required precision and was almost compulsively obsessed with numbers. Although he set the time and date for his first human bomb to April 30th at 1 p.m., he had originally—according to this hypothesis—intended for it to happen on May 5th. The danger was too great as the net of the investigation closed in and he'd had no time to lose.

If his plan had gone as intended, then the next bombing after Midori Sonoda's would have occurred on July 7th, at either seven in the morning or seven at night, whichever was more suitable. The one after that would likewise be on September 9th at nine o'clock, and the next one on November 11th at eleven o'clock. There were four officers in the organization that Iizuka had put together: Midori Sonoda, Kazuhiko Yuasa, Takeshi Abe, and Seiichi Imamura. The last one had been appointed this year. Assuming the "opening acts" leading up to the Final Event, or the Festival of Death, were originally to be put on by these four young men, the bombings would take place in May, July, September, and then November.

The perfectionist monster, one of the cruelest pleasure seekers in the history of mankind, was no doubt satisfied with this little number game, but something happened that forced him to change his plans. Perhaps something threw a monkey wrench in them. What that something was perplexed Isogai as well as Yoshida, who agreed with Isogai's hypothesis. The only thing that seemed out of character for Iizuka in terms of his orchestrations of crimes was the murder-suicide in the Imamura family. As a matter of fact, the Ibaraki Prefecture Police had gathered fairly convincing evidence by interviewing neighbors that Seiichi Imamura must have been subjected to brainwashing by Iizuka, killing his parents and then himself as though in a sleepwalking state according to a scenario scripted by Iizuka.

If it had indeed been Imamura who had gotten hold of the large quantities of the chemical, he must have done something that incurred Iizuka's wrath in a spectacular way to merit being forced to die so horribly. If whatever he did was somehow related to the change in Iizuka's original schedule, it was reasonable to assume that Imamura's mistake had angered Iizuka enough to get him yanked from the "prestigious" playbill of the suicide shows opening for the final Festival of Death.

But only Yoshio Iizuka knew the answer to this riddle. Either way, Iizuka was now starting over, having made changes and adjustments to his plan, which meant that they couldn't be sure what the pacing of his new scheme would be. But if 9 a.m. on September 9th was an acceleration towards the Festival of Death, and if 2012 was to be the cursed year of terror as Iizuka promised, then the massacre had to be carried out before the end of the year, and that left November 11th at 11 a.m. as the only remaining option for Takeshi Abe to blow himself up. What about Iizuka himself? He probably intended to carry out his crime before the end of the year, judging from the statement, which promised to make 2012 go down in history as a year of terror, so the likeliest scenario was...

"December 12th, at either noon or midnight. Mr. Yoshida, X-Day for Iizuka's Final Event has to be December 12th, at either noon or midnight! That has to be correct if Takeshi Abe's suicide attack does come on the eleventh of this month at 11 a.m..."

"Isogai! The eleventh is tomorrow!"

≈

Sunday, November 11, 2012. 10:52 a.m.

Takeshi Abe exited the south entrance of Ikebukuro Station and began walking towards Sunshine 60. It was a warm late-autumn Sunday and the street was full of young couples thanks to the movie theaters facing the street. It was Yoshio's twenty-first birthday today. Takeshi wasn't a Christian, but he made a cross in front of his chest and whispered, "Happy birthday."

He wondered if he would be meeting up with Yoshio in a month and a day. Were Kazuhiko and Midori waiting for him? Did a place like that even exist? Takeshi walked on, his thoughts betraying his sentimental nature.

Glancing at the G-Shock watch with gold lettering Yoshio had given him, he saw that it was 10:58. He had to be in front of the movie theater in two minutes. He walked a bit faster. Yoshio always insisted on the utmost punctuality. Of course, Takeshi wasn't being observed and Yoshio couldn't know if he wasn't doing as he was told. That was precisely why Yoshio had locked Takeshi's mind so he couldn't deviate from the orders.

The movie theater came into view. He was ten steps away. Now nine steps. Eight. Seven, six...five, four...three, two...one.

A middle-aged man, maybe the manager, in a shabby gray suit, stepped out of the movie theater. Takeshi thought of his father, the father he hated, and whispered to him, "Sorry, old man."

He pressed the button on the detonator he was gripping in his left hand.

41—Melody

Wednesday, December 12, 2012.

Superintendent General Kenji Kamoshita was discharged from the police hospital temporarily and was giving all the orders. The First through Ninth Riot Police Units were deployed to Roppongi Hills and other landmarks: Tokyo Sky Tree, which was the new radio tower, Tokyo Dome, Nippon Budokan, Ajinomoto Stadium, and other major concert venues, and twenty-seven potential bombing targets on the existing watch list including Tokyo City Hall, the Diet Building, and the Imperial Palace. A state of heightened alert was already in place.

Large numbers of riot police had been sent to guard other potential targets ever since the theft of toxic chemicals from Nippon Chemical Industries, such as the Kanamachi Water Purification Plant, Lake Tama, and the subway system. Police checkpoints were set up along all entrances and exits to major arteries inside Tokyo as well as the expressways, where metal detectors were used to inspect vehicles for bombs. Officers were on the alert for suspicious behavior.

Surveillance cameras recorded everything whenever a vehicle passed tollbooths on the expressways. The vehicle license number recording devices that were part of the N-System would come in handy if the attackers were using the national routes or toll roads. Once a suspicious vehicle was identified on one of the N-System cameras, the computer system at Tokyo Metropolitan Police Headquarters would locate another camera that had caught it too and punch out the path and direction of the vehicle.

As soon as the location of the next attack was established, all that needed to be done was for teams from the First through Ninth Riot Police Units in the Tokyo Metropolitan Police Guard Department to deploy to their pre-assigned standby points. The elite corps among the Riot Police were waiting, itching to hit those locations. As soon as they knew when and where it was going down, they would completely cordon off the surrounding area, prevent all above- and below-ground trains from stopping at any nearby station, close off entrances and exits, and set up roadblocks on all roads leading to Point X.

In the days before, half-wishing they could just declare martial law as had been permitted under the earlier Meiji Constitution, the Chief of Public Relations at Tokyo Metropolitan Police had called to residents of Tokyo via the media to avoid leaving the house on the twelfth. For the Japanese populace, the knowledge that "a massacre might happen somewhere" didn't always translate into "it could happen in my own neighborhood."

Just after 4 p.m. that day, the cell phones of seventeen youths living in Tokyo and surrounding areas rang one after another. One teenager living in Ichikawa City, Chiba Prefecture, stopped what he was doing at his convenience store job and pulled the phone out of his pocket. He had been working hard over the past few months and had demonstrated such skill in his interaction with customers that the manager had complimented him on it. The only people who knew of his past involvement with the non-profit organization run by Yoshio Iizuka were his parents and detectives at Atagoyama Station. The young man knew that detectives had been keeping constant track of him for three months after he had been released by Yoshio Iizuka. The watchers, however, were nowhere in sight these days

Leaving cell phones on during working hours was against the rules except during breaks, but he had allowed himself to disregard the rule this one day. He pressed the "talk" button. There were no customers at the counter, but the other part-timer working that day, a Chinese woman, gave him a reproachful look from the next register over.

The young man heard the melody. An achingly familiar childhood melody. A crazed expression came over his face as though his blood were boiling. No singing accompanied the melody, but the gentle lyric came to mind.

One day, I came upon a bear, deep in the forest...

The pitch of the familiar nursery song warbled up and down, giving it an air of misfortune and evil. The young man's eyes suddenly became vacant as though veiled in a white film. He walked out from behind the register counter and headed slowly to the door. "Hey, where are you going? It's not time for your break," the other part-timer called to him from behind, but he didn't hear anything.

Another young man who was in an orphanage in Akishima City answered his cell phone at the same time and heard the same melody. A young man in Machida City was in the lobby of a hospital where he was taking care of his mother and heard the melody on his way to the pharmacy.

All of the seventeen youths who had volunteered at Yoshio Iizuka's non-profit heard the same melody coming from their cell phones at around the same time that day and started doing the same thing: walking as though in their sleep.

A young man who was at home in Koenji reading while scratching at the eczema around his neck dropped his book, opened the closet in his room, and pulled out a plastic clothing box from the very back of the closet. He opened the box, revealing a neatly folded blue down jacket on top. He tried to lift it with one hand but wasn't strong enough. He grabbed it with both hands and slid it down. He took off the Adidas jacket he had on and put the down jacket on over his sweater. The incredible weight of the jacket was too great to attribute to low-quality down. The fabric around his shoulders strained under the load from below.

The young man got up slowly and left the room.

42—Killing Fields

The seventeen youths all made their way from where they lived to a prearranged destination. They were dressed very casually, looking like they were on their way to their girlfriends' houses. The only thing they had in common were their cheap down jackets of various colors. Some of them went through Ikebukuro to the Tokyo Metro Yurakucho Line where they boarded the 6:14 train for Shinkiba.

It was around this time that all the train cars seemed to start filling with young people, all around the same age and apparently heading in the same direction. The platform at Toyosu Station for the 6:46 train for Shinbashi was overflowing with young people. The salarymen and secretaries on their way home from work looked around with worried expressions, wondering what was going on. Even the station workers patrolling the platforms were taken aback at the size of the crowd. This was the type of crowd you saw at train stations near Tokyo Dome or Ajinomoto Stadium when there was a concert. They wondered if Shinbashi Station on the Yurikamome Line was experiencing the same thing.

The crowd of youths arrived at Ichibamae Station at exactly 6:49. Ichibamae Station normally saw almost no traffic because there was nothing there, not even a wholesale fish market, but today all the young people packed into the full train cars got out and ran down the stairs trying to suppress their growing excitement.

The seventeen youths brainwashed by Yoshio were also among the crowd which spilled out of the modest station as though pushed.

Once out, they gasped at the sight. A pure-white air dome of enormous proportions rose majestically in the distance. When Yoshio had brought them here on reconnaissance before dissolving his non-profit, the expanse of leveled ground had been a completely empty lot. It was now dominated by a hemispherical air dome that looked like it had risen out of the earth itself and into the winter night sky.

What surprised the youths, however, was not the giant air dome, which was easily fifteen stories tall, but the sheer numbers that swamped a space that was ordinarily nothing more than a 450-hectare wind-blown patch of land by the bay, lying in the middle of Tokyo like an abandoned lot.

The sun had gone down completely, leaving only a stain of dark red in the black sky above Tokyo Bay to the west. Ginza and Shinbashi stood silhouetted behind the air dome, with the skyscrapers of Shiodome, Ariake, and Odaiba further behind and around, all floating in the night air. The place was like a round ditch dug out of the center of Tokyo.

The plans for the *White Christmas in Toyosu* event to be hosted by the city of Tokyo were finalized in January 2012, and the venue was to be here, at Toyosu 6-chome, also known as the Shin-Toyosu Artificial Island. The land was originally intended as a new home for the renowned Tsukiji Fish Market but was abandoned due to soil and groundwater pollution. The previous owner, Toto Gas, had manufactured coal gas here from 1956 to 1976. The refining process involved using an arsenic compound as a catalyst that generated benzene and cyanide compounds as byproducts.

After the city of Tokyo half-forced Toto Gas to sell it the land, suspicions of pollution came to light. In 2008, a study was initiated of the soil and groundwater of blocks five, six and seven. The results showed high concentrations of pollutants. The city of Tokyo spent 58.4 billion yen in taxpayer money on a project to replace the polluted soil.

With the failure of the previous governor's plans to move Tsukiji Fish Market, as well as the plan to build an Olympic Village there for the 2016 Olympics, the grand project of creating a vibrant waterfront district in Shin-Toyosu stalled. In response to vociferous criticism about wasting taxpayer money, the new governor, Kozo Aragaki, joined forces with Sonimage, a major record company, to launch a bold makeover campaign for the area in the form of a so-called "off-season festival" with lots of concerts, environmental symposiums, and other events.

Governor Aragaki would attend the ceremony on Christmas Day, the last day of the festival, during which a press conference would be held about a new vision for 2013 for the waterfront area in Toyosu, so mired in controversy over the past few years.

The opening concert to be held in the air dome on the first day was an invitation-only event and boasted a lineup of major artists, including Misa, a popular singer adored by teenagers and young adults. Having a star-studded concert on the first day was a type of enticement by the governor, a way to draw attention to the last day's press conference. Yoshio had gotten wind of the still unannounced details of the plan that spring from a city government employee and had begun his preparations.

New vision, huh? he had thought. *I'll swipe that future right out from under your noses by massacring thousands of people.* The demon's only lament was that this perfect occasion for a slaughter would have to be the last.

Well before the city's PR department and Sonimage released information about the event to the general populace, the Tokyo Metropolitan Police Disaster Preparedness Office had asked the city of Tokyo to postpone the festival due to the vulnerability of a large crowd congregating in such a large space without even normal levels of security when "Yoshio Iizuka, Unparalleled Criminal Mastermind" had not yet been caught.

Governor Aragaki had responded by saying, "The invitational concert will only hold around three thousand people, and we can make it even smaller as long we can attract media attention on the last day, for the press conference, which is where we'll be announcing our future vision for the Toyosu waterfront development." And the governor was being sincere.

But the number of people who now gathered on the old Toto Gas area was enormous—the crowd completely filled the 12.9 hectares of block five. There were easily more than ten thousand people there. The crowd had grown so large it was spilling into the adjacent block seven. And nobody had any idea why this was happening—nobody, except for the internet hackers Yoshio had hired...

A message which had been placed on Misa's fan club website as well as every possible bulletin board, social networking site, and blog had passed from friend to friend like a vast chain mail, soon reaching the entire country. Young people had emailed each other a particular image on their cell phones, and now they were here, gathered in Shin-Toyosu, young men and women full of excitement and expectations.

The message written and distributed by the hackers was simple:

Governor Aragaki is going to have a big surprise for everyone on December 12th, the first day of the Festival: Misa's concert is going to be free and open to the public!! The venue is huge, so everyone will fit!

Send this message to everyone you know! A special live performance by Misa—free of charge! ↓↓Don't forget to bring this image↓↓

The chance to see a live performance by a superstar like Misa in Harumi Wharf, smack in the middle of Tokyo, in a huge open space jutting into Tokyo Bay, was too good to pass up. The message filled many young people who had never visited Tokyo, much less Toyosu, with excitement. They had shimmering visions of a bright white stage floating in the inky darkness of night.

And they came. Devoted teenage Misa fans, youths who longed for the excitement of a rave, simple curiosity seekers: they all congregated in block five of Shin-Toyosu 6-chome, filling it in the blink of an eye.

A long fence surrounded the air dome, starting just outside Ichibamae Station where everyone entered the grounds from the station, and along Route 484. The fence was adorned with colorful posters displaying logos and symbols of a futuristic vision and anti-pollution messages. The works had been commissioned by the city on the theme of "Toyosu in the New Century."

One part of the fence was a gate divided into four sections over which brightly lit arches glittered. Ticket-takers separated the concert-goers into those who had received the invitational tickets, who would enter the air dome, and those without them, who would sit outside on the butt-freezing ground on a first-come, first-served basis. The security plan, which was supposed to be simple, allowed only three thousand ticket-holders through and guided them into the enclosed area. That plan was in tatters, however. The situation was about to turn into a riot.

A group of young men with mohawks were crowded around the gates, so angry they had forgotten the biting cold. "Listen, you assholes, they told us we could get in if we showed you this image on our cell phones! So let us in or we're going to destroy this place!" The image they were showing was an email attachment that read *WHITE X'MAS IN TOYOSU* below a grinning Jolly Roger flashing a victory sign.

The gate attendants, provided by Densen Technica, which had subcontracted event planning and production for the festival, were responding slowly and with confusion to a situation they had not heard anything about. The scene was getting worse by the minute.

A large, deeply tanned middle-aged man in a black suit and goatee was yelling into a bullhorn. "The skull-and-crossbones image you are presenting at the gate was not sent out by the City of Tokyo. Displaying that image will not grant you access to the concert arena. Please leave the area in a rapid and orderly manner. I repeat..."

"Fuck you, asshole! I came all the way from Tokushima to see this thing and I'm not..."

"I came from Gunma! I woke up at six in the morning to..."

"I came from Saitama!"

"That's not that far."

"Yeah, but the Yurikamome train was full, so I fucking walked here from fucking Shinbashi!"

Everyone in the crowd started in on it.

"If you won't let us in the dome, at least let us inside the gate!"

"I'm sorry, but the area inside the gate is already packed."

"Who's in charge here? Get the manager!"

The crowd in front of the gates started chanting "Manager! Manager!" and was starting to get out of control, but was also having fun. There were easily more than ten thousand youths all gathered on the sprawling field by now, and just that was cause for excitement. It was a new experience. Plus, a vast darkness, capable of accommodating all of them with room to spare, spread out limitlessly beyond the unending sea of people, and beyond that, the enclosing embrace of Tokyo.

"Hey! How long are you going to make us fucking wait here? Get the governor out here, now! He's got some explaining and apologizing to do!"

Now the crowd started chanting "Governor! Governor! Governor!" People were rubbing their backs against strangers next to them to keep warm, couples were hugging, and the whole group was yelling and screaming at the Man.

43—Mr. M.

Meanwhile on Tokorozawa Avenue, a truck was driving very carefully into Tokyo, scrupulously observing the speed limit. It was the one that had been used when the late Midori, Takeshi, and Kazuhiko had stolen methyl isothiocyanate from Seiichi's father's company. The twenty drums carrying a total of approximately one ton of the toxic chemical were still loaded on the truck under tarpaulin. The only change was that weed-killer bombs were now mounted on the drums, connected with wires allowing detonation at any moment.

Yoshio, boldly undisguised, was driving the truck from Tensei Garden Orphanage in Higashi Kurume City to his destination. He expected he might get stopped at a police roadblock. But if it happened, it happened. He was completely unaware, however, of the fact that a few cars behind him in the traffic an innocuous passenger car was tailing him.

Just after 8:40 p.m., a phone in Atagoyama Station rang. Maruyama answered.

"I have information on Yoshio Iizuka," the male voice said, without identifying himself. Maruyama immediately transferred the call to Isogai, who was in the special investigation headquarters. The direct number was listed on the Tokyo Metropolitan Police webpage asking for cooperation with the investigation, and prank calls had not stopped for three months after the Tokyo Tower bombing. Jokers claiming responsibility were common, but ever since the statement had been released, nobody was in the mood for jokes and prank calls had stopped.

Isogai picked up the phone with a faint sense of hope, mixed with apprehension at the possibility of more pranks due to the lack of progress on the teenage suicide bombings in Shibuya, Shinjuku, and Ikebukuro. All the investigators in the room watched with bated breath. Maruyama switched to speakerphone so everyone could hear and focused his attention on the voice coming through.

"Yes, may I help you?" Isogai answered in an intentionally relaxed voice and listened.

After a pause a voice so hoarse it made the listeners want to clear their throats emanated from the phone. The investigators moved closer and swallowed hard. The voice sounded at least fifty years old, and educated: "I'm sorry, I didn't catch your name."

"I'm Detective Isogai and I'm with the special investigation headquarters. If you have information you would like to provide, I'll be more than happy to take it."

Another pause. Like something being weighed. Isogai glanced at the phone to make sure that like all calls placed directly to the headquarters it was being digitally recorded.

"Oh, Detective Isogai? A sergeant in Criminal Investigation at Atagoyama Police Station, right?"

"Do you know me?"

"We've never met, but a friend told me about you once."

"You mean we have a common acquaintance?"

"Listen, detective. Iizuka's on the move. Today is X-Day."

Isogai was startled by this. He needed to authenticate the source. "I'm really sorry, but could you provide more detail?"

"Iizuka got going just an hour ago. He's on Tokorozawa Avenue headed for the city center right now. I don't know what his target is."

"What?!" Yoshida said in a loud voice, standing near the phone.

The man on the phone paused to swallow, and then went on. "He's in a black two-ton truck with a covering over the bed. It has Katsushika plates, number 990X. I have no doubt that the truck is carrying the methyl isothiocyanate that was all over the news."

A shockwave ran through the room. Kunugida immediately placed a call to the Communication and Command Center and ordered a security alert for the area Iizuka was headed for. Yoshida called all the investigators in the room over and began discussing potential targets. They had no time to worry about who the mystery caller might be. Verifying the information he had provided took priority.

"We had also guessed that today would be the day, but we had no idea what he might be targeting."

"I don't know, either."

"But why do you know what Iizuka is up to?"

"We've been watching him."

"Why didn't you tell us earlier?"

"We couldn't confirm our observations, but as soon as the suicide bombings happened, it all became clear."

"You mean you saw the kids blow themselves up?"

"They may have been Iizuka's underlings, but these were teenagers who blew themselves up. I just can't understand how people that young..."

Isogai's imagination glimpsed what the man seemed to have observed. "Do you have any idea what Iizuka's planning to do, or where he's going to do it?"

"No. All I know is he's been preparing for a long time and intends to commit a horrendous massacre. And it's getting closer by the minute."

There was a finality to the words that made it sound like the man was about to hang up. Isogai hurriedly said, "Hello? Please don't hang up. I have one question."

"Go ahead."

"If you had let us know about Iizuka earlier, we could've arrested him before he arranged this thing. Why didn't you call us earlier?"

"Listen, Detective Isogai. I believe I have a duty as an upstanding citizen of Tokyo to stop Iizuka from committing some kind of atrocity. But I also wanted to know exactly what evil vision the criminal of the decade had in mind."

"Are you with the media? What's your name?"

"I can't tell you. Just call me 'Mr. M.' Another thing, detective..."

"What?"

"I'm doing the right thing by calling you. If I hadn't made this call, Iizuka would have been free to kill as many people as he wanted. And in tomorrow's newspaper it would be police that had lost to this demon, as he calls himself, and been on the receiving end of a media assault."

"Are you saying I should thank you?"

"No. I'm just thinking aloud about the profound significance of what I have done today."

There was a short pause, then: "Win. That's all I ask. Beat this guy."

With that, Mr. M hung up.

If Mr. M's information were correct, it wouldn't take long to find the truck Iizuka was driving. Kunugida had already contacted the leader of the riot police unit that could deploy quickest to Hibiya Street and had a helicopter in the air searching for Iizuka's truck. They had no idea where he was headed, though.

There were no landmarks in the vicinity which had been considered candidates for heightened security. Isogai couldn't imagine that a terrorist whose object was to kill as many people as possible would attack the Imperial Palace. Would he set off bombs in a hotel or department store, or maybe in the Ginza shopping district? No matter where he released the toxic chemicals he was transporting, the damage would be severe and widespread. But considering what Iizuka had said and done already, Isogai couldn't picture him being satisfied with killing "merely" hundreds or even thousands.

"Mr. Yoshida, you think it might be..."

"What?"

"Isn't there some kind of event going on in Toyosu tonight?"

"Toyosu? Where in Toyosu?"

"Inspector Yoshida, are we talking about the huge artificial island in Shin-Toyosu?" asked Maruyama. "Governor Aragaki is going to be having a press conference there to announce his plans for a new waterfront development. Today is the first day of the events, but the press conference with the governor isn't going to be until Christmas. Today they're just having a music concert to drum up interest. Misa's going to be performing, so lots of people have been talking about it."

Kunugida turned to one of the young investigators. "Contact someone on-site immediately."

"But it's not supposed to be that big of an event. Misa's concerts are always popular, but this one is invitation-only. I'm sure everyone who scored one nabbed it within two minutes of the concert being announced," Maruyama explained, himself a fan of the popular singer.

Just then a call came in from the Communication and Command Center. The detective that answered yelled, "They've located a white truck! It's on Harumi Street!"

"Isogai, you're right! It must be heading to the Shin-Toyosu event."

"Someone check to see if the crowd is the size predicted for tonight's concert," Kunugida said, and one of the detectives immediately got on the phone. At the same time, Kunugida ordered the riot police unit on standby closest to the site to set up a checkpoint in front of Kachidoki Bridge and block off the road leading to Toyosu.

"What horror is he planning?" Isogai asked, exasperated. He inhaled and let out a sigh.

The detective who was checking on the crowd size spoke up. "Chief Kunugida, the capacity for tonight's concert is three thousand. They've enclosed an area on the old Toto Gas lot with a temporary fence. But it looks like they've already got more than ten thousand people there right now."

"What?! Why are there so many people there when the venue capacity is only three thousand?" Yoshida's voice was close to a scream.

"Are any units on crowd control there?"

"Yes, but they apparently don't have as many men as other landmarks. The governor's going to be at a press conference there on the 25th, so we were planning on sending men from the Sixth Unit from Shinagawa that day."

"Okay," said Kunugida. "I've let the Communication and Command Center know that the plan is to stop Iizuka before Kachidoki Bridge. Everyone, we're heading to the event site now! From here we'll have to cross from the Rainbow Bridge side so we'll miss the Kachidoki roadblock. Get on your radios and monitor the unit's progress in blocking him off."

With this, he took his men and headed for Shin-Toyosu.

Yoshida called the young detectives still in the room. "Okay, listen up! This guy has been laughing in our faces for over a year now. Our mission tonight is to stop him. We're all together on this: officers going to Shin-Toyosu, officers awaiting further orders here, even all the police officers around the country who are watching over us. We're a single team, and we're going to get this guy!"

"Yes, sir!" The room thundered with the force of their assent.

"Isogai, you and I are going, too," Yoshida said.

"Yes, sir. It is my duty."

44—Countdown

Despite the inordinate confusion outside, the concert had started on time. The thumping beat of dance music filtered out of the air dome. The opening acts had already finished.

Those who had managed to squeeze into the enclosed area were moving their bodies where they were, dancing like crazy. They had been waiting what seemed an eternity for the concert to start, frigid from the damp sea air. The huge crowd that had gathered outside the fence had given up trying to get in and were moving their bodies to the music audible from inside the huge chalk-white dome. Since the lights set up at the four corners of the enclosed area were all pointing in, making the dome stand out against the night sky, the area outside the fence was enveloped in darkness.

Countless pale lights like fireflies spread out over the huge lot which was shrouded in ever blacker darkness further out. They looked like thousands of penlights bidding farewell as if this were Misa's last concert, but they were in fact cell phone screens. Everyone in the crowd was holding theirs up, the screen displaying *WHITE X'MAS IN TOYOSU* and a grinning Jolly Roger, which they had been told they could show to get into the concert.

The night sky was pitch black. It looked like a canopy of low clouds had formed; the searchlights twirling around and pointed at the sky lit up the hanging, heavy cloud cover. The sound from the concert was transmitted to the layer of clouds and flowed far away from the Shin-Toyosu artificial island.

Seventeen youths had blended into the crowd surrounding the circular air dome, spaced evenly apart, awaiting the moment they would carry out the simple action that had been ingrained into their brains, over and over. They were all wearing thick down jackets. Donned in the way they had been trained to in Higashi Kurume, the jackets hung with a solid weight from their shoulders and backs. They weren't all that warm.

The young men had been supplied with cheap jackets containing artificial down. They were heavy not because of the down's poor quality but because each contained ten one-kilo bombs sewn into the pockets in the lining all around where the down was supposed to be. Yoshio had selected jackets in which the inner and outer linings were sewn together in large patches forming pockets in between containing the down. He had removed the down from ten pockets and replaced them with elliptical aluminum pipes filled with explosives, which were then connected by wires. The switch to the detonator that connected to the wires through the left pocket was designed to allow activation with a single movement of the thumb.

If they put their hands in their pockets as if they were trying to stay warm, they could hold the detonator loosely by the ergonomically designed grip and gently press the detonator button. There would be a gap of 1.5 seconds before the triggering assembly ignited the explosive inside the pipes. To avoid accidental detonation, a safety cap covered the switch and had to be flipped up with the thumb. The suicide squad had been brainwashed with the same method used on Seiichi Imamura and would without the slightest hesitation flip up the cap and press the button below, at midnight, December 12th. A flip of the thumb, a press of the button.

That was all there was to it.

At 8:55, a general deployment order had gone out from Superintendent General Kamoshita through the Tokyo Metropolitan Police Communication and Command Center over General System One, the radio bandwidth with the widest coverage, which could be monitored by all officers. All members of the Sixth Riot Police Unit, which had been standing by in Shina-gawa for deployment to Shin-Toyosu on the 25th, when the governor would be giving his press conference, were sent in early, arriving at 9:37.

The backup units arrived just behind them, making a total of nine hundred and fifty men deployed to Shin-Toyosu. Five armored vehicles and five large police vans were parked in a row along Route 484 near Ichibamae Station, and two armored vehicles, four personnel transports, and a commander's sedan were parked side by side in block seven facing the air dome.

Seiji Kayama, the head of the Sixth Unit, was stunned when he saw that the situation on the ground was nothing like what he had anticipated. He would have to rearrange his men, who were supposed to be positioned around the festival grounds. He had not expected such a large crowd to be surrounding the concert venue that was Yoshio's target; the dome's maximum capacity was just three thousand people.

The troops were lined up in perfect order in two lines facing each other, one in block five, which included the air dome, and one on the other side of Route 484. "Atten-*shun*!" Chief Kayama called out.

"At ease. You're going to have to be on your toes today, men," he began, displaying what seemed like a warm personality for a riot police chief. "The terrorist is a bomber with no thought for his own life. Fear him. I want you men to keep your wits about you as you follow the orders of the site commander."

A few minutes later the howling of overlapping sirens could be heard. The rotating red lights of several vehicles came down Route 484 from Harumi Street. From the opposite direction, too, patrol cars and unmarked cars with lights swiveling on the roofs arrived from Metropolitan Police HQ and Atagoyama Station. Thanks to a command issued by the Communication and Command Center, all traffic on Shin-Toyosu was now completely blocked off and shut in. The intersection on Harumi Street west of Kachidoki Bridge was blocked off by a riot police truck. Entry from the other side was blocked off at the Ariake Tennis Club. The intersection in front of Toyosu Station, where Harumi Street crosses Route 484, which passes through Shin-Toyosu, was also blocked, and riot police units were deployed to three sides of Shin-Toyosu 6-chome, thereby totally cutting the artificial island off from the rest of Tokyo. The eastern end of the island was "blocked off" by Tokyo Bay.

Kunugida, in a suit with a red armband, hopped out of his unmarked car. Yoshida, Isogai, Maruyama, and other members of the special investigation team followed him. "What is going on here?!" Kunugida yelled. He was flabbergasted at the sight of the crowd milling around outside the fence enclosing the air dome. It wasn't just Kunugida who stared, dumbfounded; the other detectives were overwhelmed by the size of the crowd, too.

Kunugida introduced himself to Chief Kayama as they joined up with the riot police. "I'm Kunugida, Chief of Criminal Investigation Section One."

"Kayama at your service. These are the members of the death-defying Sixth Unit. They are completely at your command tonight. The special assault teams are standing by."

"Thank you. What on earth is going on? This was supposed to be a much smaller event."

"Same here. I wasn't expecting this."

Maruyama, who had been speaking with some of the young people milling around outside the gates, came running up. "Apparently some message saying that Governor Aragaki declared free entry for the concert today went viral on the internet. I just got a copy. The story was that you just had to show this image to get in." Maruyama pulled up the image on the screen of his cell phone and showed it to everyone: the grinning Jolly Roger above the festival name.

"Isogai, call the Communication and Command Center and

have the high-tech crime unit investigate what's been happening on the internet since last night," Yoshida ordered.

"Yes, sir."

"Chief Kayama," Kunugida said. "I'm going to be overseeing this whole thing, but Yoshida here is going to be your go-to man. He's got way more experience as a detective than a forensics nerd like me."

"You know they say modesty will buy you a bullet," Yoshida mumbled.

Kunugida continued, "I'm going to need to borrow a few of your men to set up the front-line command post here for the general staff. That's everyone including the chairman of the special investigation headquarters on down."

Kayama immediately shouted an order and had twenty men follow Kunugida to set up the command post for the top brass that would arrive soon by helicopter to the rooftop heliport at Bayside Police Station. The front-line command post would be set up in the seventh-floor hall at the station due to the circumstances of the potential crime scene.

Kayama went on. "Since taking over, the Sixth Unit has shut off access in all directions so the crowd shouldn't grow any more than it already has. The problem is we can't let them get out of here, either. If we do, we risk letting the bad guys slip out."

"Our main concern right now is whether there are any bombs planted," Yoshida said.

"That and toxic gas," said Kayama. "He must not under any circumstances be allowed to bring any of that into this area."

"The units at Kachidoki Bridge ought to take care of that."

Yoshida felt ill with anxiety. He couldn't escape the feeling that Iizuka was indeed going to show up. The twenty members of the hazmat team had already been deployed and were in position in full alert status. A year after having their fingers burned by the sarin gas attack that occurred on March 20, 1995 in the Kasumigaseki subway station, the Tokyo Metropolitan Police had set up hazmat teams in all riot police emergency rescue squads.

But if somebody were to set off a bomb containing methyl isothiocyanate in the middle of this huge crowd, dispersing the lethal poison, the number of deaths would be staggering. The teams in their hazmat suits would be helpless to stop it. The scale of the tragedy would far outstrip that of the 1995 subway attack, the first poison gas terror attack targeting civilians in peacetime. It would be a massacre in the full sense of the word.

Yoshida turned to Isogai. "We were totally focused on landmarks while the bad guys were quietly planning a major massacre in an empty lot."

"The high-tech crimes unit called, saying that the internet is overflowing with messages and posts saying people could get into the concert for free, with no limit on attendance," Isogai said. He looked around. A giant transformer loomed up like a black cylinder in block six, which lay across the air dome and the road. Beyond, in the distance, the high-rise apartment buildings of Toyosu, Kachidoki, and Tsukudashima were visible. To the north were the Ginza and Shiodome landmarks. In the direction of Rainbow Bridge, which they had crossed in unmarked cars, Tokyo Tower had once been visible. Realizing anew that it was missing, Isogai was overcome with an indescribable sense of terror.

A perp capable of horrific deeds was planning an unprecedented massacre on this huge artificial island, now cut off of the transit system, a graveyard in thrall to a demon.

9:48 p.m.

Maruyama came running towards them from the direction of the dome, out of breath. "I can't do it by myself. Can you help me try to convince them?" From the car on the way to the scene, Isogai had called the organizers of tonight's Misa concert to no avail.

"Mr. Yoshida," he said now, "the first thing we have to do is con-vince the organizers to call the concert off."

"All right, Isogai, get on it. I'll get the lay of the land from the Sixth Unit's trucks. Contact me on the investigation's radio frequency if you get any new information."

Yoshida looked around, trying to get a handle on what was going on. TV news trucks had started arriving on the scene, having figured out that something big was going on, and were engaging the officers in the riot police contingent in arguments about freedom of the press. Eventually the PR officer in charge of media liaisons got some of the helmeted men to create a cordoned-off press area next to the Seventh Unit on the other side of Route 484 and corralled all the live feed trucks, newspaper reporters, and photographers into it.

Several helicopters thundered in the air above the scene: three of them police choppers there to establish a no-fly zone above the scene; the others, from TV stations and newspapers, hovering outside the no-fly zone. Certain that something huge was going to happen, video and still cameras were all pointed at the chalky white air dome. TV reporters from the various local stations, still kicking themselves for having missed the toppling of Tokyo Tower, were dead-set on capturing whatever was going to happen here. The new radio tower would broadcast its digital waves around the globe.

Some of the riot police officers were screaming into bull-horns. "Everyone outside the air dome is to follow orders and evacuate the area, moving in an orderly fashion to the area behind the transformer in block six."

The youths who were dancing to the music streaming out of the air dome even though they couldn't get in had started to notice something going on in the area opposite them and were getting suspicious. One person wondered aloud, "I know Misa's a huge star and everything, but do they really need riot police and police cars to provide security?"

"They're telling us to evacuate? Fuck that shit! I traveled a long way to be here. I'm going to dance even if I can't get into the concert. Evacuate this, assholes! It's cold enough as it is out here!"

"Who the fuck do they think they are? There aren't even any toilets outside the fence. I had to go take a leak way over there away from everybody."

"Mr. Yoshida, Isogai here. I talked to the organizers and they said they can't call off the concert if we're not sure there's a bomb. Misa just got on stage, so stopping it now might cause the audience to riot, which could result in deaths. I'll keep pressing them, but it's going to take a bit more time. Over."

"This guy had the skill to destroy Tokyo Tower like it was the easiest thing in the world. I'm sure we'll stop him at the Kachidoki checkpoint, but if he does get in, then what? Plus, bombs might already be planted here. Either way, convince them that they have to stop that concert and evacuate everyone stat! We'll look for bombs afterwards. Better safe than sorry. If we don't find anything, then we don't find anything, but at least no one will have gotten hurt. The losses from the concert can be paid back somehow, insurance money or tax breaks or something. That doesn't matter—what matters is saving lives!"

"Roger that. I'll keep at it."

Isogai continued the negotiations with Masataka Munekiyo, the chairman of Sonimage. The pounding beat of the dance music by Misa, Sonimage's golden-egg-laying goose, was playing so loudly that Isogai felt his insides shaking.

"If you don't stop the concert, everyone here might die. You know what happened to Tokyo Tower, don't you? The guy we're dealing with here is very dangerous!"

"You're saying someone, you don't know who, called saying, what, a bomb was going to go off here? What if it's a prank? Who's going to take responsibility then?"

Munekiyo was a businessman in his early forties. Before him stood a detective intent on getting him to stop the concert, a look of desperation in his little eyes behind black-framed glasses.

The chairman of Sonimage wasn't prepared to oblige.

Although Misa was in Sonimage's stable of artists, it had not been easy arranging her performance at this concert, something the new governor of Tokyo himself had requested. The city had already paid a huge fee, too.

"I'm going to say it again, Mr. Chairman. HQ at Atagoyama Police Station received an anonymous tip from a man claiming that he had been observing Yoshio Iizuka and had seen him go into action today. Iizuka is on his way here. There is no doubt that his target is here, Shin-Toyosu. We're dealing with someone who might have already planted bombs here!"

Isogai shook his head as if to say they were running out of time. Maruyama stood behind him, quietly putting his hands together, praying that the executive would consent, and soon.

"What's the guy demanding?" Munekiyo frowned and looked at Isogai.

"There are no demands. All he wants to do is kill as many people as possible. And himself."

Munekiyo looked up and groaned, then turned to his young female assistant. "Hey! Get the stage manager over here!"

The assistant dashed behind the stage, heading for the sound booth where the manager was stationed.

About four and a half minutes later, a tall, rough-looking man appeared, his hair down to his shoulders.

Munekiyo addressed him. "Kusuo, they're saying there's a bomb."

"Huh?" The music from the stage was so loud it was hard to hear. "A balm?" He had heard the sounds but couldn't comprehend the meaning.

"The guy who knocked down Tokyo Tower has apparently planted a *bomb* here. Stop the concert and get everyone out of the air dome in an orderly fashion. I don't want anyone getting hurt."

The stage manager stared slack-jawed at Munekiyo. He knew the boss had a penchant for making this kind of joke sometimes, but the chairman was pale and the picture of seriousness. Kusuo just stood there, dumbfounded.

Munekiyo was a man who acted quickly once he'd made a decision. He took the headset himself and communicated the situation to the entire staff. He concluded, "I don't want anyone getting hurt, so focus! The air dome's exits are narrow revolving doors. Rushing will cause accidents. I don't know where any bombs might be, but you guys watch out for yourselves, too. The audience comes first, though! Just think of this as improv. Perform like your lives depend on it! All right? Get to it!" Munekiyo then picked up his cell phone and called someone.

"Hi, this is Munekiyo from Sonimage..."

Someone was soon hopping mad on the other end.

"But human life comes first."

The person on the other end was none other than Governor Kozo Aragaki, with whom the chairman was acquainted.

"Forget it. No! I've made the decision to stop it, and that's it!" Munekiyo said and hung up, mumbling, "The fuck do I care about the press conference?"

Watching Munekiyo, Isogai wondered, *Where in his small body is all that energy? I don't know much about folks in show biz but this guy's composure in the face of a bomb threat is impressive. I wouldn't mind if my son worked in this guy's outfit...*

9:52 p.m.

Yoshio's truck had pulled off of Ome Avenue onto Harumi Street at the Hibiya intersection and came to a stop a ways before the Kachidoki Bridge roadblock. He had noticed that something was amiss and pulled onto the left shoulder. Riot police trucks were blocking the road off in front of the bridge, and quite a few officers in full gear were standing before the trucks. Two lights illuminated the road in front of the roadblock.

Yoshio's mind was clear and cold as ice. The edges of his mouth twisted up into a cynical smile, and he eased down on the accelerator to approach the roadblock. He saw the police trucks ahead; they were parked perpendicular to the road, totally shutting off Harumi Street. The incredibly bright lights on either side of the road lit up the center of the road like a stage. Yoshio stopped the truck just before that.

The dozen or so riot police were lined up in front of the trucks, pistols in hand. One of them lifted up a bullhorn and spoke. His voice was tense and shaking. "Are you Yoshio Iizuka?"

Yoshio maintained a placid silence.

"I repeat: are you Yoshio Iizuka? If you are, then give yourself up immediately."

Yoshio liked the vapidity of "if you are." He smiled and honked three times: *Yes. I. Am.*

The police reacted to the sound by turning their weapons on Yoshio. He opened the window and put his left hand out and way up, displaying the detonator. They all looked at it. He beckoned to a young policeman who was near him. The officer hesitated at being singled out and looked around a few times before gingerly approaching the driver's side window. Yoshio lowered it and said, "If you don't open up the roadblock, lots of people are going to die. Pass that on to someone in a position of authority, it doesn't matter who."

The young policeman was unsure what to do and went off to communicate the ultimatum to a man who looked like the squad leader. Again Yoshio heard the voice on the bullhorn.

"Your threats are futile! You're surrounded! Give yourself up now!"

Yoshio shook his head, disappointed, and got out of the truck, leaving it idling. The line of officers tensed: was this a chance to terminate him? But they couldn't do anything hasty. They saw the thing he was holding in his left hand, his thumb held up.

Yoshio raised up his left hand. "If I press this button, the toxic chemicals loaded on the truck will explode, taking all of you with it. The gas will spread out through all of Ginza, killing tens of thousands of people."

"We don't negotiate with terrorists! Surrender yourself immediately!"

"Well, shit," Yoshio muttered to himself. "If I blow this up now the whole plan'll go down the drain." He pulled his cell phone out of his right pocket. It rang, calling. Someone picked up.

It was one of the seventeen suicide bombers, the least remarkable of them all, a short kid. Nondescript, with no real problems in his family but psychologically wounded, he had worked diligently in Yoshio's organization as if to make up for something. Yoshio made a split-second decision that the boy was ideal for the task at hand. It would be better to avoid getting too extravagant just yet.

He was positioned on the edge of the crowd, awaiting midnight at the northern side of the line connecting the air dome with the Nichei Television building in Shiodome.

Seeing that the call was from Yoshio, he twitched, as though a current had run through his body. He answered the phone with trepidation.

One day, I came upon a bear, deep in the forest...

Yoshio chanted the spell, releasing the boy's mind from the command to press the detonation button at exactly midnight. This did not, however, release the boy's mind from its hypnotic state.

"It's not the appointed hour yet, but go ahead and blow yourself up, all right?"

"Yes, sir." The young man put his hand in the pocket of his down jacket, initiating the series of actions that had been drilled in through brainwashing.

A flip of the thumb, a press of the button.

There was a click, followed exactly one point five seconds later by a sky-splitting roar as flames shot out and up from the center of his body, sending thousands of pieces of flesh flying over the darkened field. At the very moment of the blast, his mind was released from hypnosis, and he returned to himself: Kenichi Sato.

He thought of his problem-free, peaceful family as he disappeared from this world.

All the young people in a ten-meter radius around him were blown down by the blast and covered in his charred remains. Those outside the blast radius, where there was no damage, began screaming and calling for help.

Let us call him by name as a gesture of mourning: Kenichi Sato wasn't in the densest part of the crowd so there were no instant deaths other than his own. The injured, however, who lay bleeding on the ground, were in need of immediate first aid. The police EMS team finally arrived after about ten minutes and began tending to the victims while a crowd looked on.

Thus the first suicide bombing of the night had occurred on the north side of block five, Shin-Toyosu. A clearing about ten meters in radius was created around the blast center. It was not a very large movement for the rest of the vast crowd.

It was as though the gathering had become some enormous living creature writhing in the darkness of night. A small part of its body had been stung—the crowd continued to cover the empty grounds. People far away from the blast remained where they were, not knowing whether it had been some kind of explosion or perhaps a cannon salute as part of the festival.

Many riot police officers continued screaming into their bullhorns: "Everyone outside the air dome is to follow our instructions and evacuate to safety in block six behind the transformer."

They were receiving transmissions on their radios at the same time: "Block six here. Area is completely full. We cannot take any more people. Keep everyone where they are and set up security positions in the crowd for officers to head to in order to provide security there."

"Roger!" they replied. But many of the officers could not but hesitate. "Provide security in the crowd? How are we supposed to do that?"

Yoshio hung up and got back in the driver's seat. He watched the officers in silence. Eventually a squad leader received instructions, and there was a flurry of activity around the commander's car, which was parked on the shoulder.

"Iizuka! What did you just do?" the voice from the bullhorn demanded to know.

Yoshio sighed and waved the same young guy from before over.

"Tell your boss that if you make me wait any longer, I'm going to detonate the human bombs I've deployed in the crowd and that people are going to die."

The officer selected to transmit the message opened his eyes wide at this and ran over to the commander's car. About five minutes later, the security vans blocking Harumi Street moved apart just enough to allow a single truck through. Saluting the officers with his right hand, Yoshio drove through the opening and crossed Kachidoki Bridge. Once on the other side, however, his way was again obstructed by armored trucks. Four large police trucks were parked across the center of the road in two rows, blocking the way forward. He also saw a smaller truck parked in front of them in the middle of the road. Although his field of vision was obscured by the many vehicles, Yoshio could see an armored truck with a body made out of thick steel plates idling in the very front. The riot police vehicles were all lined up in rows facing away from Yoshio's truck and not at it.

Yoshio rolled down the window and shouted, "What the fuck! Do you want more hostages to die?"

When Yoshio's truck approached, however, the vehicles blocking Harumi Street split into two lines, creating an opening in between. Yoshio slowed down and proceeded down the middle of the road. The police trucks that had split left and right began moving now, keeping a tight formation around Yoshio, with the smaller truck driving ahead, as though guiding him, and the armored one bringing up the rear. Yoshio was completely surrounded by police vehicles, which were escorting him in the direction of Shin-Toyosu 6-chome.

He eventually passed a huge transformer and a dreamlike landscape came into view, a bright white air dome rising up into the night sky. Yoshio drove past the front of it and into a crowd that was still dumbfounded by the blast. The police vehicles in formation around him also stopped in the middle of the crowd about a hundred meters from the air dome. Yoshio exited the truck and was surrounded on all sides by officers. There was no shoot-to-kill order; nobody knew what kind of destruction the object he held in his left hand would cause.

Yoshio raised his head high and walked slowly toward the air dome. The officers walked sideways along with him, their guns drawn. Other officers pushed people back using yellow police tape but were unable to make space against the huge crowd, which seemed to be sprouting up from the ground itself.

10:07 p.m.

The music stopped. The crowd groaned. Clouds of dry ice smoke rolled around the stage, concealing Misa, clad in a hot pink miniskirt, from the knees down. She herself didn't know what was going on and just stood there startled by the sudden absence of music. The five dancers behind her also froze, perplexed. The jumbotrons in the wings transmitted the awkwardly still scene on the stage as the audience seated in the back watched.

The sound of the explosion outside the dome had been inaudible to the audience inside thanks to the loud music pumping away. Or rather, a barely perceptible boom had been heard but had only seemed like some effect on the part of the festival.

Misa sensed there'd been a disaster—the sound system had broken down, stopping the show. The "disaster" was a lot worse than she imagined, however.

The audience on the huge dance floor in front of the stage was composed almost exclusively of teenagers, but there were about one hundred metal folding chairs in a partition to one edge of the tent that were occupied by people who seemed distinctly out of place, looking like the audience's parents. In reality they were residents of the nearby apartment complexes in Shin-Toyosu and leaders of the local council who had been invited by Densen Technica to preempt any complaints about noise pollution.

Some in the audience suspected the sudden sound stoppage was an innovative part of the show. They realized that something had unexpectedly gone wrong when Kusuo, the stage manager, walked out onto the stage, his headset on. A split second later, the audience turned on the organizers with a roar. Objects were hurled at the stage.

"You're going to pay for stopping the music! Right at the best part of Misa's show, you assholes!"

"Restart the concert!"

"Die!"

The stage manager took Misa's microphone and started making an announcement. "Um, I'm sorry to interrupt this way, but if you're a fan of Misa, then I hope you'll listen to what I have to say."

"Fuck you!"

The insults kept flying, but Kusuo had a flash of inspiration. He walked over to Misa and whispered something in her ear. Clearly shocked, Misa staggered a few steps away from him and glanced around the arena. She looked like she was on the verge of tears.

Kusuo grabbed her by the arm and yanked her back, screaming, "Your fans' lives are at stake! You're a star, so act like one!"

Misa winced as though from an electric shock, then nodded tearfully. She turned to her fans. "Listen, everyone. I have something really important to tell you. You have to stay calm, okay? Don't like start running around or anything, 'cause it's really important, okay? Right now, somewhere in this arena, there's a bomb."

Everyone in the audience started screaming.

The dancers took off. The hubbub of the crowd turned into a swell as the crowd's panic swirled and grew.

Misa screamed, "Please! Everyone calm down! I'm scared, too!"

With this, the panic that had been ready to blow the roof off the air dome cooled in an instant. The audience was suddenly quiet as if a bucket of water had been thrown in its face.

I'm scared, too!—that single statement had made saints of her fans.

Strangely, all of a sudden dying wasn't so terrifying anymore. *My Misa's scared! I'm going to save her!*

"I'm going to make sure everyone's safe, but you have to do exactly as I say." Misa said that much and then broke down from the fear. Her knees buckled and she squatted down on the stage.

And then something strange happened. Her fans, standing out in the audience, suddenly raised up their hands with their fingers crossed, making the sign they always used when cheering during her concerts.

Kusuo was impressed—and kind of frightened—by Misa's star power. Did the young woman really have the ability to replace a crowd's fear of death with a stronger emotion?

He wasn't the only one awed by the scene. Yoshio was standing at the entrance to the air dome, watching. "What a nice little show," he muttered.

He was surrounded on all sides by riot police and special attack team forces, as if by bodyguards. Though the men were waiting for the right time to shoot him, they could only follow his every move, not being sure what the detonator in his left hand was designed to blow up or when and how it would be triggered.

When riot police tried to take possession of the truck Yoshio had gotten out of, four young men appeared out of nowhere and took up positions around it, guarding the contents under the tarp. Like Yoshio, they had pulled detonators out of their left pockets and released the cap, ready to press the button underneath. The officers were unsettled by the vacant, ominous atmosphere surrounding the young men. They just stared each other down.

If the truck's cargo were detonated right now, most of the people on the artificial island would probably die. Everyone would suffer some kind of effect from the toxic gas. The soil that billions of yen had been spent cleaning would once again be polluted; the memory of an abhorrent massacre would be ingrained forever.

10:14 p.m.

Misa saw a man coming up out of the audience towards her: a young man with a beautiful face.

Misa watched him, still dazed. *One of my fans is here to save me. But how's that going to help? What's going to happen—am I going to die here? I'm successful, I'm worshipped by adoring fans, and I'm going to die here? No way! What kind of fan tries to get on stage with me right now? Creep!*

Yoshio climbed up onto the stage, scooped up the mic that was on the floor next to where Misa had collapsed and was sitting, and addressed the panicked hall. "Hey, everyone! Listen up!"

The crowd making for the revolving doors as they were being requested looked back towards the stage, surprised by the words.

"If you try to go past the turnstiles, you'll die. I'm going to blow them up."

Once again screams went up.

People rushed away from the turnstiles, tripping over each other.

Yoshio glowed in the blinding spotlight, on his first-ever concert stage. He smiled. *A once-in-a-lifetime experience. Literally.*

The SAT squads that had entered the dome behind Yoshio lined up against the walls all around the hall and trained their sights directly on Yoshio up on stage. The telescopic sights of the Remington rifles that the crack team of dozens of elite police were equipped with were trained directly on various parts of Yoshio's body, just above the heads of the people in the audience. As the snipers were trained to do, some were aiming at his temples, some were aiming at his heart, and some were ready to blow his legs off in order to render him immobile. It was as though the cold gazes of the SAT team members, all directly on a single figure on the stage, formed a visible pattern of white lines that crackled with tension.

After consulting with Criminal Investigation Department Chief Ogata, Kunugida recommended to Deputy Superintendent General Kokura that the SAT team enter the dome. The order from the special headquarters chairman came immediately. The lives of the hostages were the number one priority, of course, but that didn't mean there wasn't a chance to shoot Yoshio dead.

"The twelfth day of the twelfth month of 2012: it's got a nice ring, doesn't it? I think all of you are pretty lucky to be here today," Yoshio spoke to the three-thousand-strong audience, mic in hand. It was like some kind of religious gathering: the holy man addressing the masses.

"Some of you might know me. Until about six months ago I ran a little non-profit outfit called *Society of Victims of Abuse for the Prevention of Abuse*. When I was just a few days old, I was dropped off into this thing called the Stork's Mailbox—a trash can for unwanted babies, if you will. I started the non-profit because I wanted to turn that horrible experience into something positive for society. But that's done with now. Yep, today it all comes to an end.

"Oh, by the way, I just wanted to express my gratitude to the members of the SAT team in back. Spending so much tax money on little old me! Thanks, guys, and glad you could all make it! But one thing, though: be careful where you aim."

Yoshio tapped his abdomen with the mic. He then took off his jacket, and with his right hand started unbuttoning his washed-out white collarless shirt. Again with his right hand, he dexterously slipped the shirt off his body and tossed it into the crowd, like a rock star. He never let go of the object he was holding in his left hand, even when passing that arm through the sleeve.

The crowd in the first few rows, where the view was clear, let out a scream. The members of the SAT team reflexively released the tension in their trigger fingers and lowered their muzzles. Yoshio's bared upper body was wound around with innumerable bands of explosive material packed tightly in what looked like slim aluminum cans. The beam from the spotlight illuminated the skin above them, making his scars shine like glossy pink latex.

"The truth is, I'm here because I intend to go to heaven with all of you. Of course I might be headed to hell instead, but it looks like we've got quite a few bad apples among you who will probably be joining me for the ride."

Surprisingly, the crowd laughed. Despite their fear, the young men and women were captivated by Yoshio's bold speech.

It was a strange sight to behold. Some in the crowd even thought the guy on the stage, talking to them so matter-of-factly, was cool—despite the fact that he had taken them hostage and intended to kill them.

"Oh, and you elite SAT team guys, keep this in mind: I don't know how much of our tax money goes into training you guys, but I have no doubt you could lay me out with a single shot. I came here today to die, so I could tell you to fire away, but unfortunately we can't quite let that happen. You guys probably already suspect this, but I've got human bombs all over the place in here. If you guys try to mess with my show, I'll have all of them blow themselves up at the same time. I mean, if you guys really want to, then you could all shoot at the same time at a signal from me—a little improvisation, if you will—and we'll all go out with a bang, our own twenty-one gun salute."

10:37 p.m.

Isogai listened to Yoshio talking on stage and walked around backstage to a position behind him. He peeked around a curtain, his gun in hand. Only Isogai and Maruyama had come into the dome for the negotiations with Sonimage. Maruyama didn't have a lot of crime-scene experience. He stood behind Isogai and pulled his gun—which he had never used—out of his shoulder holster, imitating Isogai.

So that's Yoshio, Isogai thought, *the kid I interrogated six years ago.* He watched the young man with the slight build standing on the stage, mic in hand, and felt a sense of dread, but also a strange connection.

Isogai dialed Yoshida's cell phone. Cell phones were more convenient than radios in situations like this. "Mr. Yoshida, I see him. There's no doubt about it. It's Yoshio Iizuka."

"What? We already know that!"

Yoshida was right, of course. But somewhere deep inside, Isogai retained his judgment that Yoshio Iizuka was decent. That young man he had met during the investigation into the murder of Atsushi Sakamoto. The penniless fifteen year old with the worn-out but spotless Converse. Even after Isogai had learned that the mastermind behind all of it was Iizuka, the memory of the young man's innocent face, which had been burned into his memory, never went away and prevented him from accepting the truth.

"It was Yoshio Iizuka." Isogai said it aloud once more to himself.

"Isogai, what's the matter?" Yoshida asked through the phone. "You all right?"

"Yeah, I'm fine. Sorry about that. I just got dizzy for a second. But to think that the biggest mistake I ever made is coming to this…"

"Isogai, listen. We don't have time to reflect on our past sins right now."

"He's the one. There's no doubt, he's the one who killed Atsushi Sakamoto."

"Atsushi Sakamoto?" Yoshida knew about the Atsushi

Sakamoto murder case that Isogai had been in charge of at Atagoyama. Was Isogai saying that the root of this unprecedented crime lay in that case from six years before?

A strange feeling came over Yoshida. Who was this Yoshio Iizuka? The man behind the audacious destruction and murder was barely twenty years old? What dark stuff inside him motivated him to kill? Where did it come from?

"Mr. Yoshida, Iizuka is alone on the stage, but the blast just now suggests that he has other human bombs planted in the crowd all over the hall, so we can't make any rash moves."

Yoshida listened to Isogai with a pained look on his face.

"Did anyone die in the blast?"

"I can't tell from here," Yoshida answered. "The EMS team is on the scene. There must be others with bombs interspersed among the crowd out here too. What a messy situation."

The special investigation had been badly burned by Iizuka time and again since August 26th of the previous year. The investigators had worked tirelessly despite being the targets of harsh criticism and abuse in the media and from the victims' families. The culprit himself was in their sights now.

But if Iizuka was ready to blow himself up, then the situation was very precarious. No one knew when the truck loaded down with explosives would blow up in the middle of the crowd outside. The scariest situation the police had to deal with: a criminal who was willing to die.

"Isogai, can you hear me?"

"Loud and clear."

"Does Iizuka have some kind of detonator switch in his hand?"

"I can't tell from here. He's got his left hand in his jacket. He could be holding it there. He's got the mic in his right hand as he's giving his speech."

"His speech?"

"That's right. He's talking to the audience, which he's taken hostage. He's telling them that his huge team will all blow themselves up, taking everyone here with them."

"It could be a bluff. He could just have one or two of his bomb-boys in the crowd. In fact, he could be the one with the biggest bomb."

"I'd say that's true. His entire body is covered with bombs."

Yoshida fell silent, at a loss for words.

10:53 p.m.

The plan—and it had been a beautiful plan—was for his Final Event to start right as the Misa concert was at its climax and the crowd was going wild. He would come onto the stage and emcee one more show, a show of annihilation and murder. But thanks to the idiotic police, his life's final plan was ruined. The crybaby wouldn't continue her show to the end, and now his own performance had descended into a completely unprofessional mess.

Yoshio wanted to unveil his recipe for massacre to everyone in the hall and squeeze screams of terror out of them, like a lemon. He had planned on plunging them in psychological terror and making them do a countdown with him as he watched the tears run down their faces. That plan was spoiled. *It was going to be perfect! Who ratted to the police?*

He didn't feel any anger, strangely enough. All he felt was a dark lethargy, like his body was rotting alive. The only thing that was left was a listless emptiness now. All that was left was to get it over with—blow himself up and kill everyone in the area. No beauty, no aesthetics, nothing.

The Demonic Will lamented humanity's lack of perfection. It had ridden the human named Yoshio and worked him like a rag in order to make the regrettably final chapter of the genocidal show a success. But even that hadn't worked out.

"Do any of you find any interest at all in this world?"

The crowd was silent.

"Oh, right. You're all here for this concert, so obviously you like this Misa person. Or whatever her name is. But what is it that you like about her? You know I was just thinking what a baby she is, but—lo and behold, she really has wet herself!"

Yoshio let out a raucous laugh that echoed ghoulishly around the curved ceiling of the dome. The singer had been humiliated with a maximal insult but felt no embarrassment. She felt nothing. Her mind was completely focused on waiting for the maniac to look away so she could get backstage and run away—even if she had to drag her body, half-paralyzed with fear.

11:19 p.m.

Deputy Superintendent General Kokura, Criminal Investigation Department Chief Ogata, and other members of the general staff were at the frontline command center set up on the seventh floor of the Bayside Police Station, where they watched the progress of events at Shin-Toyosu on ten TV monitors which had been set up an hour earlier so they could take in all of the vast crime scene. Kunugida had radioed the chief of the General Administration Department and had him deploy relay vehicles equipped with cutting-edge parabolic antennas belonging to the mobile communication squad of the Tokyo Metropolitan Police Data Communications Department.

Ten camera operators in the mobile communication squad had made their way into the crowd. They entered the air dome that Yoshio had taken over and continuously broadcast his showdown with the SAT team to all the monitors. The figure of someone standing in the center of the stage was displayed on the jumbotrons at stage left and right, making Yoshio visible to everyone in the audience.

It probably wouldn't be difficult to shoot him—not even to target the muscle tissue of his left wrist if it were visible. But the concert venue was filled with other human bombs. The brass at the front-line command center had no choice but to grind their teeth and watch as the deadlock inside went on.

The Bayside HQ was hashing out a plan to counter the possibility of toxic gas being released, but no concrete strategy was emerging. The poison control team could handle the sources of the gas, but that would only be cleaning up after the massacre.

All they could do now was pray.

Kunugida turned to Ogata. "Either way, if methyl isothiocyanate is released, we need to stop the toxic particles from spreading, and to do that the Specialized Vehicle Squad's high-pressure hose trucks must be ordered into place right away. Water won't do. They have to be carrying extinguishing foam. We don't have time."

"Okay, relay the order through the Communication and Command Center."

The order was dispatched right away, but they were informed that it would take time to fill the trucks with the extinguishing foam. Preparing for the worst, Kunugida had the Communication and Command Center order the Shinagawa, Fukagawa, Kanemachi, Joto, and Kameido fire stations to deploy their special firefighter teams.

"Expect to deal with: poison gas; removal of victims. Please deploy your special teams. We could be looking at casualties in the tens of thousands. Everyone here on Shin-Toyosu could die."

Of course, any situation where the special teams would play a major role had to be avoided at all costs. But they had to prepare for the worst.

11:22 p.m.

Isogai's cell phone rang as he was watching Yoshio from stage left. It was Yoshida.

"I personally have no idea what makes this Iizuka character tick, but maybe you could try talking to him, you know, as an acquaintance. We don't have time to get an actual negotiator in there. Talk to him. Give him the old 'what would your poor old mother think?' line. We received the go-ahead on this from the top."

"Mr. Yoshida, this is no time for jokes. The kid was orphaned when he was a few days old. He ain't got no poor old mother."

"Whatever, the point is to get him talking, try to shake him. I know he's not going to surrender just like that, but you might find some kind of opening. We're deadlocked as it is anyway. It's worth a shot."

"All right. If you've got a bullhorn, send it over."

"I'm taking it myself."

"Okay. Maruyama, go get me a bomb shield."

Maruyama, who had been standing rigid, watching the events unfold with a dry mouth, dashed, glad to have something to do.

≈

The voice resounded around the hall.

"Yoshio. If I might interrupt you for a second..."

It was Isogai. The bomb shield was set up on the other side of the stage, and he was next to it, talking through the bullhorn. Maruyama was squatting behind the shield.

Yoshio shielded his eyes from the spotlights with his hand and squinted in the direction of the voice. A middle-aged man in a rumpled gray suit was looking at him. *Who is this joker? He's a detective? With that frumpy look?*

"We met, you and me, about six years ago. My name's Isogai. I'm a detective. You probably don't remember me."

Yoshio searched back through his memory. *Detective Isogai? Six years ago would be when I killed that kid, Atsushi Sakamoto. Ah, I do remember. The guy from Atagoyama Police Station. What's the detective who was in charge of that case six years ago doing here now?*

"I remember you," he said. "You came to the Tsurumaki Garden Orphanage where I was living at the time, didn't you?"

"That's right. Glad you remember me."

"You failed to solve that case. What are you doing here?"

Isogai was finally able to ask the question that had been haunting him ever since Yoshio revealed his true self with his written statement. "Well, as a matter of fact, I'd like to ask you something. You're the one who killed Atsushi Sakamoto, aren't you?"

Yoshio was taken aback for a second and then laughed out loud. *Who would've thought I'd be discussing a six-year-old murder here?* He didn't give a damn now if the cops found out about all his past misdeeds, but it was kind of absurd to be playing courtroom drama up on a stage with some hick detective over his first murder.

Atsushi Sakamoto. He remembered all too clearly how he stuck the survival knife in his back—the kid's empty gaze as Yoshio watched the life trickle out of him. Thinking back, that was the boundary line he'd crossed on his way to the world of mass murder. He was just an innocent kid back then.

Was making Yoshio Iizuka recall his "first time" part of Detective Isogai's psychological tactic? Perhaps he merely wanted to find the last piece in the puzzle of a murder case he had failed to solve, like any detective. Regardless, making someone on the point of massacring thousands of innocents think back to his first murder was not at all a bad move for a negotiator.

"You said your name was Isogai, right? Well, Detective Isogai, you're going to die here tonight just like the rest of us, and you probably want to die knowing the truth. Yes, I killed Atsushi Sakamoto. It's too bad, isn't it? You came out to the orphanage, too. I guess I was just a grade or two above you."

Yoshio felt disgusted. This wasn't supposed to be a corny soap opera. The concert was supposed to climax, then segue directly into its second act, a massacre. Countdown to genocide, beautiful genocide. But that whole plan was shot to hell.

Yoshio couldn't take it any longer.

11:34 p.m.

Twenty-six minutes until midnight. Yoshio was tempted to tell all his bombers to get it over with already and bring the curtain down on the fiasco of his ruined performance.

"Iizuka, what you did was unforgivable. You're getting the chair, no doubt about it. But you can't take all these people with you. If you have even the tiniest shred of human feeling left in you, then I beg you to give yourself up. Take me as your hostage, if that's what you want. Let's go somewhere else and talk there."

The dome was filled with the same raucous laughter. Chills ran down the backs of everyone in the audience. None of them had ever heard such grotesque malice in a voice.

Ugly, Yoshio thought. *Too hideous for words. I can't take it anymore.*

Nine more minutes of patience. And then it will be all over.

The Will that controlled Yoshio watched the pathetic performance indifferently. It had resigned itself to the imperfection of human creatures. No matter how hard it tried to immerse them in perfect evil, something always got in the way, something it couldn't understand.

The limited lifetime of the one known as Yoshio Iizuka would soon be over, though. He would be snuffed out and disappear from this world in less than nine minutes. Yoshio Iizuka's life would have lasted twenty-one years, thirty days, nineteen hours, and twenty-six minutes, from the moment he was delivered to the Stork's Mailbox at 4:34 a.m. on November 11, 1991, until midnight, December 12, 2012, when he would blow himself up. He would become utter nothingness, cease to exist in the world.

All the pain ends here. Yoshio's mind, controlled by the Will, thought for just an instant. Fate moved forward inexorably, minute by minute, towards the finale.

Just then, Yoshio heard a different voice: someone was calling his name. It wasn't a yell, but it penetrated his mind. It was raw and close and touched his soul.

Yoshio had lived his life alone in a vast darkness for twenty-one years. No one's voice had resonated in the icy cell of his mind. But now an unsure voice, like a mother calling for a lost child, penetrated his dark world like a slim ray of light. For Yoshio, who had never known another person in any real way, it was the biggest shock of his life.

The woman walked out from behind Isogai's bomb shield and held her hands together before her, as in prayer. Yoshio squinted to get a better look.

It was Mariko Amo.

But she was killed! What's she doing here?!

Yoshio's mind swirled with a confusion of thoughts, but he thought quickly. The conclusion he immediately reached from the undeniable fact of the woman's presence was that that imbecile Seiichi Imamura had screwed up.

He had successfully acquired a new massacre weapon by getting involved with that idiot, but idiots were idiots, and even after death the idiot was screwing up his plan, coming back with dirty idiot hands, the kind that abused a corpse after snuffing the life out of it.

The Demonic Will that had driven Yoshio's life was beside itself with anger. It was on the point of losing control.

11:56:38 p.m.

Yoshio looked at his watch. Remaining even a moment longer in the world of humans had become intolerable. He lifted the detonator he had been gripping in his left hand up to the level of his face. Isogai, Maruyama, the SAT teams, and the entire audience knew exactly what the gesture signified.

Once he pressed the button on the device he held in his hand, an unspeakable tragedy would befall the air dome in the blink of an eye, and havoc would ensue over the entire Shin-Toyosu artificial island.

Everyone held their breath; it was all they could do. Only one person—Mariko Amo—screamed with all her might. It was less a voice than a prayer pulsating through the air.

The meaning to which the voice gave form was: *No.* A single prayer: *Don't.* Inside her mind the scream echoed: *It isn't too late to atone.*

Yoshio heard her cry with his very soul. He looked at her. Never before had Yoshio Iizuka cast a gaze so human, accepting and acknowledging the existence of another.

But the Will turned it down right away. It turned down the human Yoshio Iizuka, and turned down Mariko.

It rejected her prayer to put a stop to it.

11:58:42 p.m.

Yoshio pressed the detonator button.

A tremendous ball of fire rose and was sucked towards the back of the stage, the blast reducing its environs to pieces. The youths in the back watched as the jumbotrons to either side of the stage disintegrated, sending down showers of broken pieces.

The steel pipes supporting the stage were destroyed along with the floorboards, and the stage buckled in the middle. The lights, the speakers, and the PA equipment hanging at the back were blown to pieces and tore a gaping hole in the fabric as they made their exit. The warm air inside the dome rushed out.

The suicide bombers outside heard the thundering explosion inside the air dome and froze. *What was that? I wasn't told about anything going off in there first!*

Not long after, an amplified voice thundered through the vast darkness.

The heat of the blast didn't deter Isogai from making a quick decision when he realized that Iizuka had blown himself up. He called Yoshida and told him to make sure all the other young people knew that Yoshio Iizuka had died. Otherwise, a catastrophe would ensue.

"Yoshio Iizuka is dead! He has blown himself up!"

Like a muezzin's call to prayer from the mosque, the voice had no direction: it wandered through the darkness before disappearing.

The sixteen youths heard the call in confusion. It was a sound devoid of sense at first. Yet, it did not take long for the words' profound significance to worm into their brains.

The youths were instantly faced with a fearful choice. They were to press their detonator buttons at exactly midnight—not before, not after.

"Not a second before, not a second after! Now's the time!" The command that had been ground into their heads hundreds of times by Takeshi and Kazuhiko echoed in their minds. It had been made unconditional by the brainwashing.

Yet, for their absolute leader, Yoshio Iizuka, to blow himself up first was completely unexpected. The youths who had been subjected to flawless brainwashing at the abandoned orphanage in Higashi Kurume had pledged to blow themselves up at exactly midnight, together with Yoshio Iizuka, the object of their worship—that was the whole point of it. It had been pressed into their minds over the period of a month. They had been re-educated to believe that there was no other fate for them, so the fact that Yoshio had blown himself up one minute and eighteen seconds too soon was something beyond their comprehension. The control exercised over their minds by the brainwashing wrinkled at that moment.

Faced with a completely unforeseen situation, they were in a state of terrible confusion when the time came.

Midnight

They flicked the safety caps off, as they had been trained to do. Their uncertainty, however, interfered with the next motion. 12:00:01 came slowly, and went. By the time two seconds had passed, that command—"not a second before, not a second after"—worked to inhibit them.

They all stood frozen in place, unable to press the detonator button, until inordinate fear overtook them.

When some of the human bombs crumpled to the ground, their teeth were chattering.

12:00:08 a.m.

The riot police got the order to take control of the four youths protecting the truck loaded with methyl isothiocyanate. They stood impassively, stunned by the fact that Yoshio had blown himself up. An officer flicked the detonator device out of the hand of one of the youths who held it vacantly. Soon, all four were dragged away. Other officers took control of the truck and radioed that the situation was under control.

Two armored police vehicles drove up next to the south fence along the road. A few officers attached wire ropes to the top of the posts and pulled the fence over. They formed a wall to guide the crowd that came rushing out to safety.

45—Sincere Thanks

6:41 a.m.

Three police helicopters circled above Shin-Toyosu, the dry sound of the propellers filling the air. Media helicopters, prevented from flying into the restricted airspace, hovered in the distance, relaying a live feed of the events to living rooms all over Japan. Seen from above, the air dome looked like a tremendous deflated balloon spread out on the ground. Now that there was no hemisphere filled with a nightmare, the vast barrenness of the undeveloped land stood out.

The area around the stage inside the dome where Yoshio had blown himself up had the highest concentration of victims as shards from the jumbotrons rained down all around and mangled pieces of lighting and sound equipment were sent flying.

By the time police rescue squads, special teams from the fire department, the Sixth Unit and others present pulled injured survivors out from under the plastic sheet of the collapsed air dome, it was past four in the morning.

Many of the audience towards the front had been exposed to the blast of the explosion and suffered abrasions and severe burns even where they hadn't been showered with debris. In all, several hundred people had been injured inside the air dome. It was a major disaster; the silver lining was that none had been discovered dead.

At around 3 a.m., the police and fire department rescue squads that were busy giving first aid to survivors and transporting them to Tokyo hospitals were approached by youths almost mute with fear seeking to be taken in. Since they showed signs of severe psychological trauma, the rescue personnel helped them off with their jackets as they guided them into the ambulances. Noticing the jackets' unusual weight, they inspected them, found that they were filled with explosives, and promptly radioed the riot police chief.

Every jacket tested positive for explosives and was collected and placed in an open area. Bomb squad personnel dressed in thick blast-proof outfits and sturdy gloves removed the explosives from the cut-open jackets and carefully carried them into the disposal vehicle that had been parked nearby.

The bombs were placed in a silo-like structure mounted on the rear of the vehicle. This silo was then covered, and liquid nitrogen injected in through an attached tank, instantaneously freezing the bombs.

Yoshio had made the bombs by placing explosives into specially made aluminum pipes about half an inch thick. Ten of these were distributed around the down filling of each jacket for about ten kilograms of explosive per jacket: sobering killing power.

After evacuating other personnel, a bomb squad had K-9s from Criminal Investigation Section Two sniff the area, and another squad with metal detectors conducted a section-by-section sweep for any remaining explosive materials. None were found that hadn't been strapped to the human bombs who'd surrendered after their minds had been released from their locked states.

When all the work was completed on the cold field, now empty of the tens of thousands who had populated it until recently, the cloudy winter sky above Tokyo was beginning to brighten.

A criminal case of unprecedented proportions that had lasted one year and four months from August 26, 2011 and seen the involvement of one hundred thousand investigators thus came to a close.

6:46 a.m.

From the low thick clouds something white began to flutter down at last. That morning Tokyo recorded the lowest temperature so far of the winter. Appearing like flower petals blown in on a distant wind, the snow soon began falling in earnest, covering the city in a blanket of white.

The plastic sheet that had been the dome gone, *White Christmas in Toyosu*'s destroyed stage and burnt remains lay exposed, and on these too the snow fell, turning the field white in a short time. Despite the deteriorating weather a lone helicopter remained in the air.

The Metropolitan Police public relations chief surveyed the snowscape, which extended far into Tokyo Bay over the reclaimed land and elsewhere seemed to dye Tokyo a pure white—an almost purifying white.

The chief verified with his own eyes that there was nothing more to be done and radioed his report to Superintendent General Kamoshita.

About two minutes later, an address was broadcast from the police Communication and Command Center on the open channel that all police personnel in Japan could hear:

"December 13, 2012, 6:54 a.m. After one year and four months of intense investigation, a criminal case of unprecedented scale has come to an end. The perpetrator blew himself up, but thanks to the brave officers on the scene, the more than three thousand hostages that were trapped and tens of thousands of others in the vicinity were saved without a single fatality. Thank you all for your hard work over these many months. We would also like to extend our thanks to all the civilians who cooperated with us and to officers throughout the country who lent their support to the Tokyo Metropolitan Police."

epilogue

The heating had made the room too warm. She opened the windows to let in some fresh air. The winter night rushing in felt good against her cheeks. The canal on the other side of the street reflected light from the small Christmas tree that had been set up again this year in the yard of one of the warehouses. The reflection waved brightly on the dark surface like sparks of life.

Mariko knew that at the Harbor Plaza Hotel, recently built on the Tennozu Isle waterfront beyond the large warehouses that rose up before her apartment, an extravagant thirty-foot-high Christmas tree was glimmering.

The Rainbow Bridge was lit up in the seven colors of its namesake. Driving her Cherokee over it a few hours earlier, she'd felt for the first time that she was recovering from the aftereffects.

The heavy snow that fell the morning after the fateful night was almost entirely gone now except for a few dirty patches on the north side of the canal that sunlight didn't reach even during the day.

She bathed and changed into loose silk pajamas she had recently bought. She paused to consider which herb to use today. Wormwood would have "a relaxing effect on a worn-out body," while sweet violet would restore "your faith in people." Mariko sighed heavily and dropped a pinch of sweet violet into the teacup filled with boiling water.

I need something for my soul first, she thought. The past year and a half had been like a storm. She had never suffered so much or worked so hard, wearing down both mind and body. *I feel like an army photographer back from the front!*

Fate—did it arise because individual lives intertwined in countless combinations to make time and space crisscross in some way? A coincidence that would slip past unnoticed if it only occurred once created an attractive force when it recurred, drawing total strangers together into the center of a whirlpool.

Even for Mariko, who tended to approach things in a right-brain way, generally relying on her instincts and feelings for guidance, the events of the past year and a half seemed in retrospect to be governed by some causality of fate. Where had the inauspicious threads of her and Yoshio Iizuka's fates first woven together?

What a strange thing fate is, she thought to herself, and took a sip of the tea which would restore her faith in people. *Yoshio played with my heart and hurt me deeply. But the same could be said about what I did to myself.*

Her recent big scoop was her first gigantic success—and the last, she hoped, if she needed to go through anything of the sort again. She had put her life literally on the line to get it, regardless of her own will, enchanted by fate's fearsome gaze.

Life had a slightly bitter taste.

Friday, April 13, 2012, 7:00 p.m. Yoshio had asked Mariko to come to his Akabanebashi office because he wanted her advice on something.

On the phone the day before, Yoshio had told Mariko that one of his officers, Midori Sonoda, was suspected of involvement in the stabbing murder of a doctor in Miyazaki Prefecture. She had worried and empathized with Yoshio and intended to do whatever she could to help him.

The minute she hung up, however, something stirred inside her, somewhere deep, something she couldn't name. It was like having something on the tip of your tongue, or trying to remember where you misplaced something. It was an aching sensation in her memory.

Eventually a single blurred image began to assert itself from underneath the rubble of her past memories. A shard of a memory, something she had seen sometime, somewhere, and had soon forgotten about. Midori Sonoda, Miyazaki Prefecture, Yoshio Iizuka... The three signs went round and round in Mariko's head.

If Yoshio hadn't mentioned Midori, whom Mariko had seen just once before in the office, the mechanism of her memory would undoubtedly never have been activated. Two shards of a broken mirror: Yoshio reflected in one, Midori in the other. When she fit the pieces together an indistinct form rose up for the first time like a specter.

Struck by a sudden flash, Mariko jumped up and ran to her work desk. She started looking for the pictures she had taken of that actress on the plane back from Miyazaki.

The set of photographs was filed under "Miyazaki: Romantic Post-Divorce Escape" and she found it right away. She clicked on the folder to open it up and scrolled to the last pictures. The data she was looking for followed the ones for the actress and her boyfriend.

"Here they are!" she cried, breathlessly.

The inchoate fear that welled up was enough to make her start sobbing, her upper body sprawled over her desk.

She had snuck up to shoot pics of the actress without the flight attendants noticing. As she returned to her economy-class seat, she had covered the lens with her hand and taken a series of shots in rapid succession. It was the habit of a professional photographer, something she did reflexively.

In the blackness she found what she'd barely remembered. She usually covered the whole lens with her hand but had left a slight gap without meaning to. Captured in the 1/250th-of-a-second sliver of light that had made its way into the camera: *them.*

More than one-third of the square frame was in darkness, covered by Mariko's hand, but in the remaining small space the faces of Yoshio and Midori were clearly visible, like ghosts. Two beautiful faces, like twins, but expressionless, looking straight forward.

They must have been sitting somewhere behind Mariko on the plane. A single opening of the shutter, not intended to capture anything but darkness, had happened to capture their faces.

When, back from Miyazaki, Mariko had been going through the pictures of the actress on her computer at home, her eyes had stopped on this picture for just an instant. *What's this?* she'd thought. The young men in the pictures had a striking appearance. *Nice-looking guys...*

And that had been it. Except for a slight impression burned into her mind, the moment had been tossed into the dustbin of her memory together with all the other unneeded data.

Yet, that unneeded data was now slapping Mariko in the face with the shocking fact that the day after August 15, 2011, which was when the doctor was murdered, Yoshio Iizuka and Midori Sonoda were on JAL flight 1890 with Mariko, returning to Tokyo from Miyazaki.

"The police suspect Midori might've had something to do with a murder case." Yoshio's voice on the phone came back to her, and a chill ran up her spine, colder than ice. A terrifying suspicion thundered in her mind: *Yoshio had something to do with the murder too!*

Still, Mariko couldn't figure out what Yoshio's intention had been in calling her. *Is he just lying to me,* she wondered, *or does he want to see me so he can tell me the truth?* The fear she'd felt upon first finding the picture was already being nudged over by her genuine affection for him. She began to reason. *Maybe he's just an innocent bystander who somehow got implicated in a murder case. He's probably trying to hide Midori, who's the one who committed the murder, to help him somehow. That's what he does, after all. He's an idealist who helps troubled kids, rehabilitates them. Right? It's not impossible.*

Friday, the appointed day: torn between her suspicions of Yoshio and her desire to believe him, Mariko headed to his office. Her gut instinct was telling her not to go, but her stubborn heart, which wanted someone to love, overruled it.

She passed through the turnstile at Akabanebashi and walked down the street with the public health office on it. The building housing Yoshio's office came into view. She looked at her watch: 6:42. She was early. She stood on the street in front of the office and took a few deep breaths to calm her beating heart. *Why am I so scared?* she wondered. *If I trust him—if I love him—then I should open the door.*

Just then a woman passed in front of her towards Yoshio's office. She was younger than Mariko, and beautiful, with an intelligent air about her. The woman hesitated for a moment, then rang the bell.

A tall young man came to the door and let her in. "We've been expecting you," Mariko heard him say.

Mariko found out about the murder the next day on the morning news. A naked decapitated body stuffed into a surfboard bag had been discovered at the concrete bottom of Meguro River by a secretary on her way to work, who reported it to the police. The news said that the Meguro Himonya police were working on identifying the body as quickly as possible. The victim had been strangled, after which the murderer had raped the corpse before decapitating it and dumping it in Meguro River, not too far from Yoshio's office. The time of death was estimated to be between 7 and 9 p.m. on Friday, April 13: the time Mariko was supposed to be meeting Yoshio.

A wave of fear washed over Mariko when she heard the news

report. Though the truth of the matter was elusive, her suspicions of Yoshio doubled and redoubled. The scariest thought was that the murder victim on the news might be the woman who had entered Yoshio's office at 6:45 that evening, before Mariko. Now the premonition that some evil contraption had an axe aimed at her neck was almost too powerful to bear.

That evening, Mariko had done an about-face in front of Yoshio's office and gone right home. When she analyzed her behavior, she felt relief at having dodged a bullet, but also a little humiliated.

A smart-looking woman younger than herself had been invited to Yoshio's office at the same hour, and Mariko felt somewhat jealous—perhaps "inadequate" was a better word. She'd ignored the loud danger signals from her gut and stood there as though to prove her love no matter what. Yet the precarious balance had been tipped by that smallest feeling of jealousy, and she had run home feeling pathetic.

≈

It took a long time to identify the headless body.

The person Mariko had seen in front of Yoshio's office that evening was Yukiko Hatakeyama, lifestyle reporter for *Morning Daily.*

Yoshio garnered attention for the first time thanks to her interview with him, and she felt proud as she watched him enter the media spotlight and become famous. Yoshio invited her out to dinner after that and they became friendly, though for Yoshio she was nothing more than a candidate for Seiichi's initiation, like Mariko.

Yukiko had graduated from a top-ranked university and landed a job at a major newspaper. Talented, she'd been put in charge of a feature in the lifestyle section in no time. But she was helpless in the clutches of a demon. With her, Yoshio had donned the mask of messiah that he used to fool the world—the opposite of the mask he'd worn for Mariko. Alas, Yukiko quickly became a devout worshipper of Yoshio.

She had in fact been designated for Seiichi's initiation at one point. Yoshio had told her to come to his office at 7 p.m. on Friday, April 13th but changed the plan, or rather reverted to the original plan, right after his last dinner with Mariko. Just for an instant, a picture of a child falling through the sky had overwhelmed him with unbearable fear at the enormity of what he'd done.

The Demon, intoxicated by its own performance of a human, was swift to decide that the victim would not be Yukiko Hatakeyama. It had to be Mariko Amo.

Strangle that woman Mariko Amo. Tear off her head for good measure.

The truly pitiful one, however, was Yukiko.

Around noon on April 12th, Yoshio called her cell phone. "You are no longer of use to me. We won't be meeting again," he said, abruptly canceling the date.

Yukiko didn't understand what he meant by "no longer of use." If he was dumping her, then it was intolerable: she couldn't bear to lose the object of worship that had stolen her soul.

Yoshio had set his phone to reject her calls; when she called his office, she was brushed off with a cold "he's not in right now." She despaired. The thirteenth, the day after being told she was "no longer of use," Yukiko took time off and waited outside Yoshio's office for him to show up. Mariko had seen her that evening.

She waited until 6:45 p.m. but could wait no longer. She put her hand on the door knob and turned it. It wasn't locked, and the door opened. She closed it shut and rang the bell.

≈

Mariko was staking out Yoshio's office from early in the morning the day after he announced to his staff the closing of *Society of Victims of Abuse for the Prevention of Abuse*. It was a Sunday. A white van pulled up in front, and three young men got in the back, accompanied by Yoshio.

Mariko did not know their faces, but she believed they were Takeshi Abe, Kazuhiko Yuasa, and Seiichi Imamura, the officers in Yoshio's non-profit. Mariko snapped the shutter. She hopped in her Cherokee, which was parked in a lot not too far away, and discovered that Yoshio's new hideout was an abandoned orphanage in Higashi Kurume. She began observing their activities, going back and forth between Higashi Kurume and her apartment in Higashi Shinagawa.

Soon after that, the Demon's Statement shocked the whole world. Mariko initially had some trouble believing that it was Yoshio who had authored the statement. Even after she found out that the young man who had blown himself up was Midori Sonoda, she foolishly continued to make excuses to herself. Midori Sonoda was a bad kid—he murdered that doctor in Miyazaki, so how surprising was it for him to blow himself up? Yoshio had tried to get him to turn himself in but had failed to save the young man, no doubt.

Little by little, as she continued her surveillance, her surviving affection for Yoshio bent as if by sheer force and transformed into fear. The intensity of her fear bespoke the depth, which she'd failed fully to register, of the love it replaced.

She could not but see that Yoshio's activities as he hid and regrouped in the abandoned orphanage backed up the statement's threat to carry out a massacre.

And one day, tailing Kazuhiko Yuasa from the orphanage, she witnessed his suicide bombing in Shinjuku. From that moment on she felt a tremendous pressure that was too great for her to bear.

What she'd wanted was to figure out the mystery of the murdered doctor in Miyazaki so she could wipe away her suspicions of Yoshio. What she realized was that she'd wandered into the garden of evil of an unprecedented crime spree. She stopped her surveillance and shut herself in her apartment.

The thought of having dined with a diabolical criminal four times frightened Mariko enough that she began having the same dream over and over again. She was in a restaurant, but her hands and feet were bound, and she couldn't move. Yoshio appeared, wearing the expression of a lonely little boy, and tried to feed her with a spoon. She clamped her mouth shut, but he laughed and pinched her nose, preventing her from breathing. When she opened her mouth he shoved the food down her throat.

Mariko was completely undone after she started having the dream. Given the massacre Yoshio was planning, this was no longer a question of a photographer getting a scoop. She was at a loss, however, about what to do with her information. The first face that came to mind was the kindly one of Detective Isogai.

She dialed his number on her cell phone. As she listened to the tone, waiting for him to pick up, a contrary urge so powerful that it seemed capable of crushing her very being clutched at her heart.

"Isogai here."

She hung up the moment he answered.

Isogai checked the call history in his phone and saw that it had been Mariko. He called her right back, but Mariko just sat watching the blinking LCD screen with fear in her eyes, waiting for the ringing to stop.

Then she called Kohei Sendo. She met with him early the next day.

Monday, October 22nd, 8:00 a.m. The editorial office of *In Focus* in the main Koshunsha building was completely empty except for Sendo, whose puffy face gave him a toad-like appearance. He was not a morning person.

Mariko was at a loss. Giving Sendo information she should be giving the police was not right. An evil glimmer shone in Sendo's eyes once he'd heard her story.

"I don't know what to do."

"What are you talking about? This is a once-in-a-lifetime scoop. You won't get another chance like this, as a journalist." Sendo used all his powers of persuasion as editor-in-chief of *In Focus* to convince Mariko to complete the project.

"I can't, I just can't. First Midori Sonoda, now Kazuhiko Yuasa..." Tears streamed down Mariko's cheeks. Through her surveillance, Yuasa had become a person to her. "Now that he's blown himself up, I'm sure the Abe kid's turn is next. Lots of people are going to die."

"Mariko, listen. I've learned this Iizuka character is—I had my eyes on him, remember—the criminal of the decade, and I want to catch a glimpse of his demonic final vision. Just the vision of what he's trying to do. And anyway, you're the one who brought this up! You called me, not the cops, because you want a scoop."

At this, Mariko had to acknowledge that her ambition as a journalist had reared its head—as when Tokyo Tower teetered. She couldn't stop wanting it even if it meant putting herself in harm's way. "But if we know where he is and don't tell the cops, we're going to be prosecuted. I know you've got lots of 'trophies' like that, but give a thought to this innocent damsel. Who'll want to marry me?"

"'A person unaware that he or she is committing a crime shall not be penalized in accordance with the severity of the offense.' Ever hear that?"

"No. What is it?"

"Article 38 of the criminal code. What it means is that we don't know what Iizuka intends to do. Not only that, but I don't know for sure that Iizuka has even killed anyone. He's such a devil that he probably has his underlings do the dirty work. Either way, all we're doing is watching a guy who's hypothesized to be a demon, so we can't be held culpable for anything. I'm an expert when it comes to police interest in my job."

"You're being sophistic. Public opinion might not be so generous."

"We're invisible. How's the public going to find out how we got the scoop?"

"But what if thousands of people are killed because of us?"

Unmoved by logic, begging, or financial inducements, Mariko declared that she would call a detective she knew at Atagoyama Station. Sendo looked so frightening when she said that, it was enough to set a demon fleeing.

At a loss in the face of her stubbornness, he hewed to the compromise. "All right, fine. I'll help you get the bad guy. But not now. Iizuka isn't on to us, so right now he's like a bird in a cage. A caged demon! We can tell the police anytime we want, so why don't we wait until he's about to do something? You can't have a problem with that. Chin up, and keep watching them. Take lots of pictures of what he's up to. You're not doing this for me, are you? If you take all those pictures, you're bound to get a Pulitzer."

Mariko shook her head in amazement.

But Sendo had a point. Plus, she did feel a dark urge to observe the hell out of this devil who'd tried to kill her. It would be the final accounting for a severe romance that life had deemed her lot.

"Okay," she said. "But call Detective Isogai at Atagoyama Station right away and tell him that we intend to contribute to the police investigation."

Thus did Mariko succumb to the temptation of Kohei Sendo, demon of capitalism.

Sendo did call Isogai and report that he had the criminal under watch. He did not do so until December 12th, almost two months after his promise to Mariko. It was the very day they found out it was going down.

Call the cops so soon, Mariko? They'll just get to us first. Don't be so naive.

An advance copy of *In Focus* lay spread out on Mariko's table. Sendo had sent it over by courier. It was the last, special edition of 2012, to be delivered two weeks after December 12th, the day of the "Shin-Toyosu Multiple Suicide Bombing Attempt."

"From the Tokyo Tower Bombing to the Shin-Toyosu Multiple Suicide Bombing Attempt: The Whole Story"—this was splashed across the cover so large that it could be mistaken for the title of the magazine. The special double issue with a print run of one million copies delved into every aspect of a crime spree unprecedented in Japanese history. It would go on to win the Koshunsha "President's Award" for Kohei Sendo.

The waist-up photo on the cover was of Yoshio Iizuka.

It was one that Mariko had taken. It captured the look on his face as he stood on stage shortly after noticing her. While "demon" and "human" had flashed in his soul like a slot machine, the 1/640th shutter speed had caught a "human" instant.

He looked like a tween who was undergoing puberty, confused and on the verge of tears, imploring the viewer.

Mariko had expected Sendo to go to the mat over the selection of the cover shot, but he didn't say a word. Ordinarily the sort of man who kept feeding the slot machine until "demon" came up, he just nodded at Mariko's choice and sent the photo in with the final proofs he'd forced the printers to wait on, thereby completing all editorial tasks for the special double issue.

Mariko had wanted to love and be loved, deeply. She had wanted to get to know a troubled young man. Perhaps that meant she had begun to love Yoshio.

But that love was nothing more than bait in a terrifying trap. When she thought back on Yoshio, she still fell into a terrible confusion. He had worn a mask that deceived her into thinking he was opening up to her. All just a cruel, calculated act—he'd gotten close to her in order to kill her.

It was as though she'd starred in a movie whose scenes now

had inverse meanings. When she thought she was performing in a romance, it was actually a thriller, even a horror, movie. What a dumb actress!

But was everything about Yoshio really an act?

Mariko thought about Yoshio's expression of confusion when he saw her last. Perhaps a sliver of humanity remained in his heart, which had been taken over by a demon.

She thought she'd glimpsed an expression akin to joy, for just an instant, amid the surprise of seeing, right before him, a woman he believed he'd had killed.

She thought she'd seen him kick the stage floor and jump backwards in the instant before blowing himself up, as if not to harm Mariko.

It was true that Detective Isogai and the other young officer had used the bomb shield and mat to protect her, but considering the situation, it was close to miraculous that Mariko had survived without a scratch.

There was no way now to find out what had been in Yoshio's mind.

The demon I loved is dead.

Mariko swallowed what was left of the herb tea in the bone china teacup, got up from her chair, and went to the window. The light from the Christmas tree was no longer reflected in the canal. *Why don't they leave it on all night? Because of the recession?*

Oh, that boat... On the canal where she gazed, there appeared a cargo boat she'd seen many times. The black corrugated roof of the wheelhouse was adorned with lights that twinkled in the darkness.

How nice! Christmas has come to the old guy manning the rudder, too. She snapped the shutter of her mind's eye.

She turned towards Tokyo Bay; the faint smell of salt wafted her way. Sensing the sea at night instilled a deep loneliness.

It wasn't a bad feeling. She felt that something had changed inside her. She had grown a lot tougher as a journalist, for one thing.

Maybe I'll move into an apartment on the waterfront next year, with a view of Tokyo Bay and Rainbow Bridge, she mused.

After all, she'd be getting quite a hefty paycheck from that demon of an editor-in-chief in the new year.